More Praise for
The Martian

"A perfect novel in almost every way."

—Crimespree *magazine*

"Almost literally an un-put-downable book. I recommend it to anyone who loves the manned space program or who loves science or who loves a brilliantly written novel of unrelenting suspense and intelligence."

—*Dan Simmons*, New York Times *bestselling author of* Drood *and* Hyperion

"*Robinson Crusoe* on Mars, twenty-first-century style. Set aside a chunk of free time when you start this one. You're going to need it because you won't want to put it down."

—*Steve Berry*, New York Times *bestselling author of* The King's Deception

"An exciting, insightful science-based tale [that] kept me turning the pages to see what ingenious solution our hero would concoct to survive yet another impossible dilemma."

—*Terry Brooks*, New York Times *bestselling author of*
The Sword of Shannara

"A great read with inspiring attention to technical detail and surprising emotional depth. Loved it!"

—*Daniel H. Wilson*, New York Times *bestselling author of* Robopocalypse

"An excellent first novel . . . Weir laces the technical details with enough keen wit to satisfy hard science-fiction fan and general reader alike [and] keeps the story escalating to a riveting conclusion."

—Publishers Weekly *(starred review)*

"Gripping . . . Shapes up like Defoe's *Robinson Crusoe* as written by someone brighter."

—*Larry Niven*, Hugo and Nebula Award–winning author of the Ringworld
series and Lucifer's Hammer

"Weir combines the heart-stopping with the humorous in this brilliant debut novel. . . . The perfect mix of action and space adventure."

—Library Journal *(starred review)*

"The tension simply never lets up, from the first page to the last, and at no point does the believability falter for even a second. You can't shake the feeling that this could all really happen."

—*Patrick Lee*, New York Times *bestselling author of* The Runner

"Riveting . . . A tightly constructed and completely believable story of a man's ingenuity and strength in the face of seemingly insurmountable odds."

—Booklist

"A page-turning thriller . . . This survival tale with a high-tech twist will pull you right in."

—Suspense *magazine*

"Sharp, funny, and thrilling, with just the right amount of geekery . . . Weir displays a virtuosic ability to write about highly technical situations without leaving readers far behind. The result is a story that is as plausible as it is compelling."

—Kirkus Reviews

THE MARTIAN

THE MARTIAN

A NOVEL

ANDY WEIR

B\D\W\Y
Broadway Books
New York

Copyright © 2011, 2014 by Andy Weir
Reader's Guide and Author Q&A copyright © 2014 by Random House LLC

All rights reserved.
Published in the United States by Broadway Books, an imprint of the Crown Publishing Group, a division of Random House LLC, a Penguin Random House Company, New York.
www.crownpublishing.com

BROADWAY BOOKS and its logo, B \ D \ W \ Y, are trademarks of Random House LLC.

"Extra Libris" and the accompanying colophon are trademarks of Random House LLC.

Originally self-published as an ebook in 2011 and subsequently published in hardcover in a different form in the United States by Crown Publishers, an imprint of the Crown Publishing Group, a division of Random House LLC, New York, in 2014.

"How Science Made Me a Writer" first appeared in a slightly different form on Salon.com in February 2014.

Library of Congress Cataloging-in-Publication Data is available upon request.

ISBN 978-0-553-41802-6
eBook ISBN 978-0-8041-3903-8

Printed in the United States of America

Book design by Elizabeth Rendfleisch
Map by Fred Haynes
Photograph by Antonio M. Rosario/Stockbyte/Getty Images
Cover design by Eric White
Cover photography: NASA (astronaut)

10 9 8 7

First Paperback Edition

For Mom,
who calls me "Pickle,"
and Dad,
who calls me "Dude."

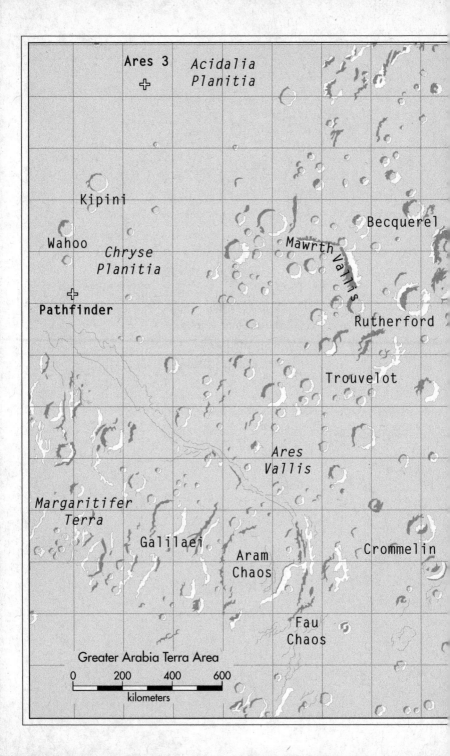

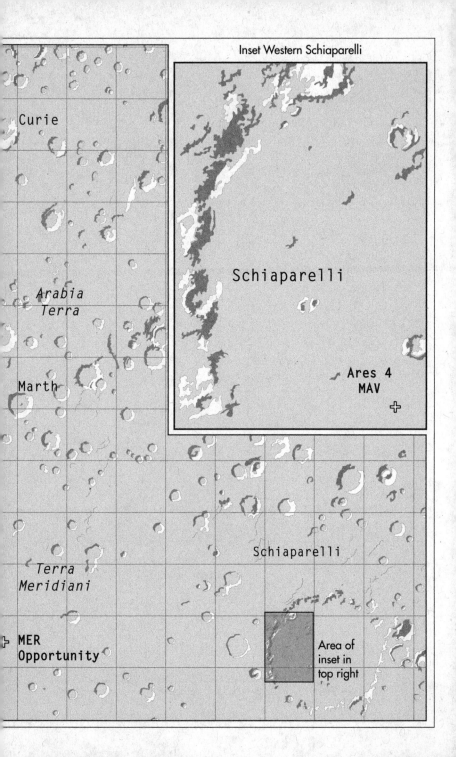

THE MARTIAN

LOG ENTRY: SOL 6

I'm pretty much fucked.

That's my considered opinion.

Fucked.

Six days into what should be the greatest month of my life, and it's turned into a nightmare.

I don't even know who'll read this. I guess someone will find it eventually. Maybe a hundred years from now.

For the record . . . I didn't die on Sol 6. Certainly the rest of the crew thought I did, and I can't blame them. Maybe there'll be a day of national mourning for me, and my Wikipedia page will say, "Mark Watney is the only human being to have died on Mars."

And it'll be right, probably. 'Cause I'll surely die here. Just not on Sol 6 when everyone thinks I did.

Let's see . . . where do I begin?

The Ares Program. Mankind reaching out to Mars to send people to another planet for the very first time and expand the horizons of humanity blah, blah, blah. The Ares 1 crew did their thing and came back heroes. They got the parades and fame and love of the world.

Ares 2 did the same thing, in a different location on Mars. They got a firm handshake and a hot cup of coffee when they got home.

Ares 3. Well, that was my mission. Okay, not *mine* per se. Commander Lewis was in charge. I was just one of her crew. Actually, I was the very lowest ranked member of the crew. I would only be "in command" of the mission if I were the only remaining person.

What do you know? I'm in command.

I wonder if this log will be recovered before the rest of the crew die of old age. I presume they got back to Earth all right. Guys, if you're reading this: It wasn't your fault. You did what you had to do. In your position I would have done the same thing. I don't blame you, and I'm glad you survived.

I guess I should explain how Mars missions work, for any layman who may be reading this. We got to Earth orbit the normal way, through an ordinary ship to *Hermes*. All the Ares missions use *Hermes* to get to and from Mars. It's really big and cost a lot so NASA built only one.

Once we got to *Hermes*, four additional unmanned missions brought us fuel and supplies while we prepared for our trip. Once everything was a go, we set out for Mars. But not very fast. Gone are the days of heavy chemical fuel burns and trans-Mars injection orbits.

Hermes is powered by ion engines. They throw argon out the back of the ship really fast to get a tiny amount of acceleration. The thing is, it doesn't take much reactant mass, so a little argon (and a nuclear reactor to power things) let us accelerate constantly the whole way there. You'd be amazed at how fast you can get going with a tiny acceleration over a long time.

I could regale you with tales of how we had great fun on the trip, but I won't. I don't feel like reliving it right now. Suffice it to say we got to Mars 124 days later without strangling each other.

From there, we took the MDV (Mars descent vehicle) to the

surface. The MDV is basically a big can with some light thrusters and parachutes attached. Its sole purpose is to get six humans from Mars orbit to the surface without killing any of them.

And now we come to the real trick of Mars exploration: having all of our shit there in advance.

A total of fourteen unmanned missions deposited everything we would need for surface operations. They tried their best to land all the supply vessels in the same general area, and did a reasonably good job. Supplies aren't nearly so fragile as humans and can hit the ground really hard. But they tend to bounce around a lot.

Naturally, they didn't send us to Mars until they'd confirmed that all the supplies had made it to the surface and their containers weren't breached. Start to finish, including supply missions, a Mars mission takes about three years. In fact, there were Ares 3 supplies en route to Mars while the Ares 2 crew were on their way home.

The most important piece of the advance supplies, of course, was the MAV. The Mars ascent vehicle. That was how we would get back to *Hermes* after surface operations were complete. The MAV was soft-landed (as opposed to the balloon bounce-fest the other supplies had). Of course, it was in constant communication with Houston, and if there had been any problems with it, we would have passed by Mars and gone home without ever landing.

The MAV is pretty cool. Turns out, through a neat set of chemical reactions with the Martian atmosphere, for every kilogram of hydrogen you bring to Mars, you can make thirteen kilograms of fuel. It's a slow process, though. It takes twenty-four months to fill the tank. That's why they sent it long before we got here.

You can imagine how disappointed I was when I discovered the MAV was gone.

It was a ridiculous sequence of events that led to me almost dying, and an even more ridiculous sequence that led to me surviving.

The mission is designed to handle sandstorm gusts up to 150

kph. So Houston got understandably nervous when we got whacked with 175 kph winds. We all got in our flight space suits and huddled in the middle of the Hab, just in case it lost pressure. But the Hab wasn't the problem.

The MAV is a spaceship. It has a lot of delicate parts. It can put up with storms to a certain extent, but it can't just get sandblasted forever. After an hour and a half of sustained wind, NASA gave the order to abort. Nobody wanted to stop a monthlong mission after only six days, but if the MAV took any more punishment, we'd all have gotten stranded down there.

We had to go out in the storm to get from the Hab to the MAV. That was going to be risky, but what choice did we have?

Everyone made it but me.

Our main communications dish, which relayed signals from the Hab to *Hermes*, acted like a parachute, getting torn from its foundation and carried with the torrent. Along the way, it crashed through the reception antenna array. Then one of those long thin antennae slammed into me end-first. It tore through my suit like a bullet through butter, and I felt the worst pain of my life as it ripped open my side. I vaguely remember having the wind knocked out of me (pulled out of me, really) and my ears popping painfully as the pressure of my suit escaped.

The last thing I remember was seeing Johanssen hopelessly reaching out toward me.

I awoke to the oxygen alarm in my suit. A steady, obnoxious beeping that eventually roused me from a deep and profound desire to just fucking die.

The storm had abated; I was facedown, almost totally buried in sand. As I groggily came to, I wondered why I wasn't more dead.

The antenna had enough force to punch through the suit and my side, but it had been stopped by my pelvis. So there was only one hole in the suit (and a hole in me, of course).

I had been knocked back quite a ways and rolled down a steep hill. Somehow I landed facedown, which forced the antenna to a strongly oblique angle that put a lot of torque on the hole in the suit. It made a weak seal.

Then, the copious blood from my wound trickled down toward the hole. As the blood reached the site of the breach, the water in it quickly evaporated from the airflow and low pressure, leaving a gunky residue behind. More blood came in behind it and was also reduced to gunk. Eventually, it sealed the gaps around the hole and reduced the leak to something the suit could counteract.

The suit did its job admirably. Sensing the drop in pressure, it constantly flooded itself with air from my nitrogen tank to equalize. Once the leak became manageable, it only had to trickle new air in slowly to relieve the air lost.

After a while, the CO_2 (carbon dioxide) absorbers in the suit were expended. That's really the limiting factor to life support. Not the amount of oxygen you bring with you, but the amount of CO_2 you can remove. In the Hab, I have the oxygenator, a large piece of equipment that breaks apart CO_2 to give the oxygen back. But the space suits have to be portable, so they use a simple chemical absorption process with expendable filters. I'd been asleep long enough that my filters were useless.

The suit saw this problem and moved into an emergency mode the engineers call "bloodletting." Having no way to separate out the CO_2, the suit deliberately vented air to the Martian atmosphere, then backfilled with nitrogen. Between the breach and the bloodletting, it quickly ran out of nitrogen. All it had left was my oxygen tank.

So it did the only thing it could to keep me alive. It started backfilling with pure oxygen. I now risked dying from oxygen toxicity, as the excessively high amount of oxygen threatened to burn up my nervous system, lungs, and eyes. An ironic death for someone with a leaky space suit: too much oxygen.

Every step of the way would have had beeping alarms, alerts, and warnings. But it was the high-oxygen warning that woke me.

The sheer volume of training for a space mission is astounding. I'd spent a week back on Earth practicing emergency space suit drills. I knew what to do.

Carefully reaching to the side of my helmet, I got the breach kit. It's nothing more than a funnel with a valve at the small end and an unbelievably sticky resin on the wide end. The idea is you have the valve open and stick the wide end over a hole. The air can escape through the valve, so it doesn't interfere with the resin making a good seal. Then you close the valve, and you've sealed the breach.

The tricky part was getting the antenna out of the way. I pulled it out as fast as I could, wincing as the sudden pressure drop dizzied me and made the wound in my side scream in agony.

I got the breach kit over the hole and sealed it. It held. The suit backfilled the missing air with yet more oxygen. Checking my arm readouts, I saw the suit was now at 85 percent oxygen. For reference, Earth's atmosphere is about 21 percent. I'd be okay, so long as I didn't spend too much time like that.

I stumbled up the hill back toward the Hab. As I crested the rise, I saw something that made me very happy and something that made me very sad: The Hab was intact (yay!) and the MAV was gone (boo!).

Right that moment I knew I was screwed. But I didn't want to just die out on the surface. I limped back to the Hab and fumbled my way into an airlock. As soon as it equalized, I threw off my helmet.

Once inside the Hab, I doffed the suit and got my first good look at the injury. It would need stitches. Fortunately, all of us had been trained in basic medical procedures, and the Hab had excellent medical supplies. A quick shot of local anesthetic, irrigate the wound, nine stitches, and I was done. I'd be taking antibiotics for a couple of weeks, but other than that I'd be fine.

I knew it was hopeless, but I tried firing up the communications array. No signal, of course. The primary satellite dish had broken off, remember? And it took the reception antennae with it. The Hab had secondary and tertiary communications systems, but they were both just for talking to the MAV, which would use its much more powerful systems to relay to *Hermes*. Thing is, that only works if the MAV is still around.

I had no way to talk to *Hermes*. In time, I could locate the dish out on the surface, but it would take weeks for me to rig up any repairs, and that would be too late. In an abort, *Hermes* would leave orbit within twenty-four hours. The orbital dynamics made the trip safer and shorter the earlier you left, so why wait?

Checking out my suit, I saw the antenna had plowed through my bio-monitor computer. When on an EVA, all the crew's suits are networked so we can see each other's status. The rest of the crew would have seen the pressure in my suit drop to nearly zero, followed immediately by my bio-signs going flat. Add to that watching me tumble down a hill with a spear through me in the middle of a sandstorm . . . yeah. They thought I was dead. How could they not?

They may have even had a brief discussion about recovering my body, but regulations are clear. In the event a crewman dies on Mars, he stays on Mars. Leaving his body behind reduces weight for the MAV on the trip back. That means more disposable fuel and a larger margin of error for the return thrust. No point in giving that up for sentimentality.

So that's the situation. I'm stranded on Mars. I have no way to communicate with *Hermes* or Earth. Everyone thinks I'm dead. I'm in a Hab designed to last thirty-one days.

If the oxygenator breaks down, I'll suffocate. If the water reclaimer breaks down, I'll die of thirst. If the Hab breaches, I'll just kind of explode. If none of those things happen, I'll eventually run out of food and starve to death.

So yeah. I'm fucked.

CHAPTER 2

LOG ENTRY: SOL 7

Okay, I've had a good night's sleep, and things don't seem as hopeless as they did yesterday.

Today I took stock of supplies and did a quick EVA to check up on the external equipment. Here's my situation:

The surface mission was supposed to be thirty-one days. For redundancy, the supply probes had enough food to last the whole crew fifty-six days. That way if one or two probes had problems, we'd still have enough food to complete the mission.

We were six days in when all hell broke loose, so that leaves enough food to feed six people for fifty days. I'm just one guy, so it'll last me three hundred days. And that's if I don't ration it. So I've got a fair bit of time.

I'm pretty flush on EVA suits, too. Each crew member had two space suits: a flight spacesuit to wear during descent and ascent, and the much bulkier and more robust EVA suit to wear when doing surface operations. My flight spacesuit has a hole in it, and of course the crew was wearing the other five when they returned to *Hermes*. But all six EVA suits are still here and in perfect condition.

The Hab stood up to the storm without any problems. Outside, things aren't so rosy. I can't find the satellite dish. It probably got blown kilometers away.

The MAV is gone, of course. My crewmates took it up to *Hermes*. Though the bottom half (the landing stage) is still here. No reason to take that back up when weight is the enemy. It includes the landing gear, the fuel plant, and anything else NASA figured it wouldn't need for the trip back up to orbit.

The MDV is on its side and there's a breach in the hull. Looks like the storm ripped the cowling off the reserve chute (which we didn't have to use on landing). Once the chute was exposed, it dragged the MDV all over the place, smashing it against every rock in the area. Not that the MDV would be much use to me. Its thrusters can't even lift its own weight. But it might have been valuable for parts. Might still be.

Both rovers are half-buried in sand, but they're in good shape otherwise. Their pressure seals are intact. Makes sense. Operating procedure when a storm hits is to stop motion and wait for the storm to pass. They're made to stand up to punishment. I'll be able to dig them out with a day or so of work.

I've lost communication with the weather stations, placed a kilometer away from the Hab in four directions. They might be in perfect working order for all I know. The Hab's communications are so weak right now it probably can't even reach a kilometer.

The solar cell array was covered in sand, rendering it useless (hint: solar cells need sunlight to make electricity). But once I swept the cells off, they returned to full efficiency. Whatever I end up doing, I'll have plenty of power for it. Two hundred square meters of solar cells, with hydrogen fuel cells to store plenty of reserve. All I need to do is sweep them off every few days.

Things indoors are great, thanks to the Hab's sturdy design.

I ran a full diagnostic on the oxygenator. Twice. It's perfect. If anything goes wrong with it, there's a short-term spare I can use. But it's solely for emergency use while repairing the main one. The spare doesn't actually pull CO_2 apart and recapture the oxygen. It just absorbs the CO_2 the same way the space suits do. It's intended to last five days before it saturates the filters, which means thirty days for me (just one person breathing, instead of six). So there's some insurance there.

The water reclaimer is working fine, too. The bad news is there's no backup. If it stops working, I'll be drinking reserve water while I rig up a primitive distillery to boil piss. Also, I'll lose half a liter of water per day to breathing until the humidity in the Hab reaches its maximum and water starts condensing on every surface. Then I'll be licking the walls. Yay. Anyway, for now, no problems with the water reclaimer.

So yeah. Food, water, shelter all taken care of. I'm going to start rationing food right now. Meals are pretty minimal already, but I think I can eat a three-fourths portion per meal and still be all right. That should turn my three hundred days of food into four hundred. Foraging around the medical area, I found the main bottle of vitamins. There's enough multivitamins there to last years. So I won't have any nutritional problems (though I'll still starve to death when I'm out of food, no matter how many vitamins I take).

The medical area has morphine for emergencies. And there's enough there for a lethal dose. I'm not going to slowly starve to death, I'll tell you that. If I get to that point, I'll take an easier way out.

Everyone on the mission had two specialties. I'm a botanist and mechanical engineer; basically, the mission's fix-it man who played with plants. The mechanical engineering might save my life if something breaks.

I've been thinking about how to survive this. It's not completely hopeless. There'll be humans back on Mars in about four years when Ares 4 arrives (assuming they didn't cancel the program in the wake of my "death").

Ares 4 will be landing at the Schiaparelli crater, which is about 3200 kilometers away from my location here in Acidalia Planitia.

No way for me to get there on my own. But if I could communicate, I might be able to get a rescue. Not sure how they'd manage that with the resources on hand, but NASA has a lot of smart people.

So that's my mission now. Find a way to communicate with Earth. If I can't manage that, find a way to communicate with *Hermes* when it returns in four years with the Ares 4 crew.

Of course, I don't have any plan for surviving four years on one year of food. But one thing at a time here. For now, I'm well fed and have a purpose: Fix the damn radio.

LOG ENTRY: SOL 10

Well, I've done three EVAs and haven't found any hint of the communications dish.

I dug out one of the rovers and had a good drive around, but after days of wandering, I think it's time to give up. The storm probably blew the dish far away and then erased any drag-marks or scuffs that might have led to a trail. Probably buried it, too.

I spent most of today out at what's left of the communications array. It's really a sorry sight. I may as well yell toward Earth for all the good that damned thing will do me.

I could throw together a rudimentary dish out of metal I find around the base, but this isn't some walkie-talkie I'm working with here. Communicating from Mars to Earth is a pretty big deal, and requires extremely specialized equipment. I won't be able to whip something up with tinfoil and gum.

I need to ration my EVAs as well as food. The CO_2 filters are not cleanable. Once they're saturated, they're done. The mission accounted for a four-hour EVA per crew member per day. Fortunately, CO_2 filters are light and small, so NASA had the luxury of sending more than we needed. All told, I have about 1500 hours' worth of CO_2 filters. After that, any EVAs I do will have to be managed with bloodletting the air.

Fifteen hundred hours may sound like a lot, but I'm faced with spending at least four years here if I'm going to have any hope of rescue, with a minimum of several hours per week dedicated to sweeping off the solar array. Anyway. No needless EVAs.

In other news, I'm starting to come up with an idea for food. My botany background may come in useful after all.

Why bring a botanist to Mars? After all, it's famous for not having anything growing there. Well, the idea was to figure out how well things grow in Martian gravity, and see what, if anything, we can do with Martian soil. The short answer is: quite a lot . . . almost. Martian soil has the basic building blocks needed for plant growth, but there's a lot of stuff going on in Earth soil that Mars soil doesn't have, even when it's placed in an Earth atmosphere and given plenty of water. Bacterial activity, certain nutrients provided by animal life, etc. None of that is happening on Mars. One of my tasks for the mission was to see how plants grow here, in various combinations of Earth and Mars soil and atmosphere.

That's why I have a small amount of Earth soil and a bunch of plant seeds with me.

I can't get too excited, however. It's about the amount of soil you'd put in a window box, and the only seeds I have are a few species of grass and ferns. They're the most rugged and easily grown plants on Earth, so NASA picked them as the test subjects.

So I have two problems: not enough dirt, and nothing edible to plant in it.

But I'm a botanist, damn it. I should be able to find a way to make this happen. If I don't, I'll be a really hungry botanist in about a year.

LOG ENTRY: SOL 11

I wonder how the Cubs are doing.

LOG ENTRY: SOL 14

I got my undergrad degree at the University of Chicago. Half the people who studied botany were hippies who thought they could return to some natural world system. Somehow feeding seven billion people through pure gathering. They spent most of their time working out better ways to grow pot. I didn't like them. I've always been in it for the science, not for any New World Order bullshit.

When they made compost heaps and tried to conserve every little ounce of living matter, I laughed at them. "Look at the silly hippies! Look at their pathetic attempts to simulate a complex global ecosystem in their backyard."

Of course, now I'm doing exactly that. I'm saving every scrap of biomatter I can find. Every time I finish a meal, the leftovers go to the compost bucket. As for other biological material . . .

The Hab has sophisticated toilets. Shit is usually vaccum-dried, then accumulated in sealed bags to be discarded on the surface.

Not anymore!

In fact, I even did an EVA to recover the previous bags of shit from before the crew left. Being completely desiccated, this particular shit didn't have bacteria in it anymore, but it still had complex proteins and would serve as useful manure. Adding it to water and active bacteria would quickly get it inundated, replacing any population killed by the Toilet of Doom.

I found a big container and put a bit of water in it, then added the dried shit. Since then, I've added my own shit to it as well. The worse it smells, the better things are going. That's the bacteria at work!

Once I get some Martian soil in here, I can mix in the shit and spread it out. Then I can sprinkle the Earth soil on top. You might not think that would be an important step, but it is. There are dozens of species of bacteria living in Earth soil, and they're critical to plant growth. They'll spread out and breed like . . . well, like a bacterial infection.

People have been using human waste as fertilizer for centuries. It's even got a pleasant name: "night soil." Normally, it's not an ideal way to grow crops, because it spreads disease: Human waste has pathogens in it that, you guessed it, infect humans. But it's not a problem for me. The only pathogens in this waste are the ones I already have.

Within a week, the Martian soil will be ready for plants to germinate in. But I won't plant yet. I'll bring in more lifeless soil from outside and spread some of the live soil over it. It'll "infect" the new soil and I'll have double what I started with. After another week, I'll double it again. And so on. Of course, all the while, I'll be adding all new manure to the effort.

My asshole is doing as much to keep me alive as my brain.

This isn't a new concept I just came up with. People have speculated on how to make crop soil out of Martian dirt for decades. I'll just be putting it to the test for the first time.

I searched through the food supplies and found all sorts of things that I can plant. Peas, for instance. Plenty of beans, too. I also found several potatoes. If *any* of them can still germinate after their ordeal, that'll be great. With a nearly infinite supply of vitamins, all I need are calories of any kind to survive.

The total floor space of the Hab is about 92 square meters. I plan to dedicate all of it to this endeavor. I don't mind walking on dirt. It'll be a lot of work, but I'm going to need to cover the entire floor to a depth of 10 centimeters. That means I'll have to transport 9.2 cubic meters of Martian soil into the Hab. I can get maybe one-tenth of a cubic meter in through the airlock at a time, and it'll be backbreaking work to collect it. But in the end, if everything goes to plan, I'll have 92 square meters of crop-able soil.

Hell yeah I'm a botanist! Fear my botany powers!

LOG ENTRY: SOL 15

Ugh! This is backbreaking work!

I spent twelve hours today on EVAs to bring dirt into the Hab. I only managed to cover a small corner of the base, maybe five square meters. At this rate it'll take me weeks to get all the soil in. But hey, time is one thing I've got.

The first few EVAs were pretty inefficient; me filling small containers and bringing them in through the airlock. Then I got wise and just put one big container in the airlock itself and filled that with small containers till it was full. That sped things up a lot because the airlock takes about ten minutes to get through.

I ache all over. And the shovels I have are made for taking samples, not heavy digging. My back is killing me. I foraged in the medical supplies and found some Vicodin. I took it about ten minutes ago. Should be kicking in soon.

Anyway, it's nice to see progress. Time to start getting the bacteria to work on these minerals. After lunch. No three-fourths ration today. I've earned a full meal.

LOG ENTRY: SOL 16

One complication I hadn't thought of: water.

Turns out being on the surface of Mars for a few million years eliminates all the water in the soil. My master's degree in botany makes me pretty sure plants need wet dirt to grow in. Not to mention the bacteria that has to live in the dirt first.

Fortunately, I have water. But not as much as I want. To be viable, soil needs 40 liters of water per cubic meter. My overall plan calls for 9.2 cubic meters of soil. So I'll eventually need 368 liters of water to feed it.

The Hab has an excellent water reclaimer. Best technology available on Earth. So NASA figured, "Why send a lot of water up there? Just send enough for an emergency." Humans need three liters of water per day to be comfortable. They gave us 50 liters each, making 300 liters total in the Hab.

I'm willing to dedicate all but an emergency 50 liters to the cause. That means I can feed 62.5 square meters at a depth of 10 centimeters. About two-thirds of the Hab's floor. It'll have to do. That's the long-term plan. For today, my goal was five square meters.

I wadded up blankets and uniforms from my departed crewmates to serve as one edge of a planter box with the curved walls of the Hab being the rest of the perimeter. It was as close to five square meters as I could manage. I filled it with sand to a depth of 10 centimeters. Then I sacrificed 20 liters of precious water to the dirt gods.

Then things got disgusting. I dumped my big container o' shit onto the soil and nearly puked from the smell. I mixed this soil and shit together with a shovel, and spread it out evenly again. Then I sprinkled the Earth soil on top. Get to work, bacteria. I'm counting on you. That smell's going to stick around for a while, too. It's not like I can open a window. Still, you get used to it.

In other news, today is Thanksgiving. My family will be gathering in Chicago for the usual feast at my parents' house. My guess is it won't be much fun, what with me having died ten days ago. Hell, they probably just got done with my funeral.

I wonder if they'll ever find out what really happened. I've been so busy staying alive I never thought of what this must be like for my parents. Right now, they're suffering the worst pain anyone can endure. I'd give anything just to let them know I'm still alive.

I'll just have to survive to make up for it.

Wow. Things really came along.

I got all the sand in and ready to go. Two-thirds of the base is now dirt. And today I executed my first dirt-doubling. It's been a week, and the former Martian soil is rich and lovely. Two more doublings and I'll have covered the whole field.

All that work was great for my morale. It gave me something to do. But after things settled down a bit, and I had dinner while listening to Johanssen's Beatles music collection, I got depressed again.

Doing the math, this won't keep me from starving.

My best bet for making calories is potatoes. They grow prolifically and have a reasonable caloric content (770 calories per kilogram). I'm pretty sure the ones I have will germinate. Problem is I can't grow enough of them. In 62 square meters, I could grow maybe 150 kilograms of potatoes in 400 days (the time I have before running out of food). That's a grand total of 115,500 calories, a sustainable average of 288 calories per day. With my height and weight, if I'm willing to starve a little, I need 1500 calories per day.

Not even close.

So I can't just live off the land forever. But I can extend my life. The potatoes will last me 76 days.

Potatoes grow continually, so in those 76 days, I can grow another 22,000 calories of potatoes, which will tide me over for another 15 days. After that, it's kind of pointless to continue the trend. All told it buys me about 90 days.

So now I'll start starving to death on Sol 490 instead of Sol 400. It's progress, but any hope of survival rests on me surviving until Sol 1412, when Ares 4 will land.

There's about a thousand days of food I don't have. And I don't have a plan for how to get it.

Shit.

CHAPTER 3

<u>LOG ENTRY: SOL 25</u>

Remember those old math questions you had in algebra class? Where water is entering a container at a certain rate and leaving at a different rate and you need to figure out when it'll be empty? Well, that concept is critical to the "Mark Watney doesn't die" project I'm working on.

I need to create calories. And I need enough to last the 1387 sols until Ares 4 arrives. If I don't get rescued by Ares 4, I'm dead anyway. A sol is 39 minutes longer than a day, so it works out to be 1425 days. That's my target: 1425 days of food.

I have plenty of multivitamins; over double what I need. And there's five times the minimum protein in each food pack, so careful rationing of portions takes care of my protein needs for at least four years. My general nutrition is taken care of. I just need calories.

I need 1500 calories every day. I have 400 days of food to start off with. So how many calories do I need to generate per day along the entire time period to stay alive for around 1425 days?

I'll spare you the math. The answer is about 1100. I need to create 1100 calories per day with my farming efforts to survive until Ares 4 gets here. Actually, a little more than that, because it's Sol 25 right now and I haven't actually planted anything yet.

With my 62 square meters of farmland, I'll be able to create about 288 calories per day. So I need almost four times my current plan's production to survive.

That means I need more surface area for farming, and more water to hydrate the soil. So let's take the problems one at a time.

How much farmland can I really make?

There are 92 square meters in the Hab. Let's say I could make use of all of it.

Also, there are five unused bunks. Let's say I put soil in on them, too. They're 2 square meters each, giving me 10 more square meters. So we're up to 102.

The Hab has three lab tables, each about 2 square meters. I want to keep one for my own use, leaving two for the cause. That's another 4 square meters, bringing the total to 106.

I have two Martian rovers. They have pressure seals, allowing the occupants to drive without space suits during long periods traversing the surface. They're too cramped to plant crops in, and I want to be able to drive them around anyway. But both rovers have an emergency pop-tent.

There are a lot of problems with using pop-tents as farmland, but they have 10 square meters of floor space each. Presuming I can overcome the problems, they net me another 20 square meters, bringing my farmland up to 126.

One hundred and twenty-six square meters of farmable land. That's something to work with. I still don't have the water to moisten all that soil, but like I said, one thing at a time.

The next thing to consider is how efficient I can be in growing potatoes. I based my crop yield estimates on the potato industry back on Earth. But potato farmers aren't in a desperate race for survival like I am. Can I get a better yield?

For starters, I can give attention to each individual plant. I can trim them and keep them healthy and not interfering with each other. Also, as their flowering bodies breach the surface, I can replant them deeper, then plant younger plants above them. For normal potato farmers, it's not worth doing because they're working with literally millions of potato plants.

Also, this sort of farming annihilates the soil. Any farmer doing it would turn their land into a dust bowl within twelve years. It's not sustainable. But who cares? I just need to survive for four years.

I estimate I can get 50 percent higher yield by using these tactics. And with the 126 square meters of farmland (just over double the 62 square meters I now have) it works out to be over 850 calories per day.

That's real progress. I'd still be in danger of starvation, but it gets me in the range of survival. I might be able to make it by nearly starving but not quite dying. I could reduce my caloric use by minimizing manual labor. I could set the temperature of the Hab higher than normal, meaning my body would expend less energy keeping its temperature. I could cut off an arm and eat it, gaining me valuable calories and reducing my overall caloric need.

No, not really.

So let's say I could clear up that much farmland. Seems reasonable. Where do I get the water? To go from 62 to 126 square meters of farmland at 10 centimeters deep, I'll need 6.4 more cubic meters of soil (more shoveling, whee!) and that'll need over 250 liters of water.

The 50 liters I have is for me to drink if the water reclaimer breaks. So I'm 250 liters short of my 250-liter goal.

Bleh. I'm going to bed.

LOG ENTRY: SOL 26

It was a backbreaking yet productive day.

I was sick of thinking, so instead of trying to figure out where I'll get 250 liters of water, I did some manual labor. I need to get a whole assload more soil into the Hab, even if it is dry and useless right now.

I got a cubic meter in before getting exhausted.

Then, a minor dust storm dropped by for an hour and covered the solar collectors with crap. So I had to suit up *again* and do *another* EVA. I was in a pissy mood the whole time. Sweeping off a huge field of solar cells is boring and physically demanding. But once the job was done, I came back to my Little Hab on the Prairie.

It was about time for another dirt-doubling, so I figured I might as well get it over with. It took an hour. One more doubling and the usable soil will all be good to go.

Also, I figured it was time to start up a seed crop. I'd doubled the soil enough that I could afford to leave a little corner of it alone. I had twelve potatoes to work with.

I am one lucky son of a bitch they aren't freeze-dried or mulched. Why did NASA send twelve whole potatoes, refrigerated but not frozen? And why send them along with us as in-pressure cargo rather than in a crate with the rest of the Hab supplies? Because Thanksgiving was going to happen while we were doing surface operations, and NASA's shrinks thought it would be good for us to make a meal together. Not just to eat it, but to actually prepare it. There's probably some logic to that, but who cares?

I cut each potato into four pieces, making sure each piece had at least two eyes. The eyes are where they sprout from. I let them sit for a few hours to harden a bit, then planted them, well spaced apart, in the corner. Godspeed, little taters. My life depends on you.

Normally, it takes at least 90 days to yield full-sized potatoes. But I can't wait that long. I'll need to cut up all the potatoes from this crop to seed the rest of the field.

By setting the Hab temperature to a balmy 25.5°C, I can make the plants grow faster. Also, the internal lights will provide plenty of "sunlight," and I'll make sure they get lots of water (once I figure out where to get water). There will be no foul weather, or any parasites to hassle them, or any weeds to compete with for soil or nutrients. With all this going for them, they should yield healthy, sproutable tubers within forty days.

I figured that was enough being Farmer Mark for one day.

A full meal for dinner. I'd earned it. Plus, I'd burned a ton of calories, and I wanted them back.

I rifled through Commander Lewis's stuff until I found her personal data-stick. Everyone got to bring whatever digital entertainment they wanted, and I was tired of listening to Johanssen's Beatles albums for now. Time to see what Lewis had.

Crappy TV shows. That's what she had. Countless entire runs of TV shows from forever ago.

Well. Beggars can't be choosers. *Three's Company* it is.

LOG ENTRY: SOL 29

Over the last few days, I got in all the dirt that I'll need. I prepped the tables and bunks for holding the weight of soil, and even put the dirt in place. There's still no water to make it viable, but I have some ideas. Really bad ideas, but they're ideas.

Today's big accomplishment was setting up the pop-tents.

The problem with the rovers' pop-tents is they weren't designed for frequent use.

The idea was you'd throw out a pop-tent, get in, and wait for rescue. The airlock is nothing more than valves and two doors. Equalize the airlock with your side of it, get in, equalize with the other side, get out. This means you lose a lot of air with each use. And I'll need to get in there at least once a day. The total volume of each pop-tent is pretty low, so I can't afford to lose air from it.

I spent *hours* trying to figure out how to attach a pop-tent airlock to a Hab airlock. I have three airlocks in the Hab. I'd be willing to dedicate two to pop-tents. That would have been awesome.

The frustrating part is pop-tent airlocks *can* attach to other airlocks! You might have injured people in there, or not enough space suits. You need to be able to get people out without exposing them to the Martian atmosphere.

But the pop-tents were designed for your crewmates to come rescue you in a rover. The airlocks on the Hab are much larger and completely different from the airlocks on the rovers. When you think about it, there's really no reason to attach a pop-tent to the Hab.

Unless you're stranded on Mars, everyone thinks you're dead, and you're in a desperate fight against time and the elements to stay alive. But, you know, other than that edge case, there's no reason.

So I finally decided I'd just take the hit. I'll be losing some air every time I enter or exit a pop-tent. The good news is each pop-tent has an air feed valve on the outside. Remember, these are emergency shelters. The occupants might need air, and you can provide it from a rover by hooking up an air line. It's nothing more than a tube that equalizes the rover's air with the pop-tent's.

The Hab and the rovers use the same valve and tubing standards, so I was able to attach the pop-tents directly to the Hab. That'll automatically replenish the air I lose with my entries and exits (what we NASA folk call ingress and egress).

NASA was not screwing around with these emergency tents. The moment I pushed the panic button in the rover, there was an ear-popping whoosh as the pop-tent fired out, attached to the rover airlock. It took about two seconds.

I closed the airlock from the rover side and ended up with a nice, isolated pop-tent. Setting up the equalizer hose was trivial (for once I'm using equipment the way it was designed to be used). Then, after a few trips through the airlock (with the air-loss automatically equalized by the Hab) I got the dirt in.

I repeated the process for the other tent. Everything went really easily.

Sigh . . . water.

In high school, I played a lot of Dungeons and Dragons. (You may not have guessed this botanist/mechanical engineer was a bit of nerd in high school, but indeed I was.) In the game I played a cleric. One of the magic spells I could cast was "Create Water." I always thought it was a really stupid spell, and I never used it. Boy, what I wouldn't give to be able to do that in real life right now.

Anyway. That's a problem for tomorrow.

For tonight, I have to get back to *Three's Company*. I stopped last night in the middle of the episode where Mr. Roper saw something and took it out of context.

LOG ENTRY: SOL 30

I have an idiotically dangerous plan for getting the water I need. And boy, do I mean *dangerous*. But I don't have much choice. I'm out of ideas and I'm due for another dirt-doubling in a few days. When I do the final doubling, I'll be doubling on to all that new soil I've brought in. If I don't wet it first, it'll just die.

There isn't a lot of water here on Mars. There's ice at the poles, but they're too far away. If I want water, I'll have to make it from scratch. Fortunately, I know the recipe: Take hydrogen. Add oxygen. Burn.

Let's take them one at a time. I'll start with oxygen.

I have a fair bit of O_2 reserves, but not enough to make 250 liters of water. Two high-pressure tanks at one end of the Hab are my entire supply (plus the air in the Hab of course). They each contain 25 liters of liquid O_2. The Hab would use them only in an emergency; it has the oxygenator to balance the atmosphere. The reason the O_2 tanks are here is to feed the space suits and rovers.

Anyway, the reserve oxygen would only be enough to make 100 ʼters of water (50 liters of O_2 makes 100 liters of molecules that only ⟶e one O each). That would mean no EVAs for me, and no emer- ⟶ reserves. And it would make less than half the water I need. ⟶the question.

But oxygen's easier to find on Mars than you might think. The atmosphere is 95 percent CO_2. And I happen to have a machine whose sole purpose is liberating oxygen from CO_2. Yay, oxygenator!

One problem: The atmosphere is very thin—less than 1 percent of the pressure on Earth. So it's hard to collect. Getting air from outside to inside is nearly impossible. The whole purpose of the Hab is to keep that sort of thing from happening. The tiny amount of Martian atmosphere that enters when I use an airlock is laughable.

That's where the MAV fuel plant comes in.

My crewmates took away the MAV weeks ago. But the bottom half of it stayed behind. NASA isn't in the habit of putting unnecessary mass into orbit. The landing gear, ingress ramp, and fuel plant are still here. Remember how the MAV made its own fuel with help from the Martian atmosphere? Step one of that is to collect CO_2 and store it in a high-pressure vessel. Once I get the fuel plant hooked up to the Hab's power, it'll give me half a liter of liquid CO_2 per hour, indefinitely. After ten sols it'll have made 125 liters of CO_2, which will make 125 liters of O_2 after I feed it through the oxygenator.

That's enough to make 250 liters of water. So I have a plan for oxygen.

The hydrogen will be a little trickier.

I considered raiding the hydrogen fuel cells, but I need those batteries to maintain power at night. If I don't have that, it'll get too cold. I could bundle up, but the cold would kill my crops. And each fuel cell has only a small amount of H_2 anyway. It's just not worth sacrificing so much usefulness for so little gain. The one thing I have going for me is that energy is not a problem. I don't want to give that up.

So I'll have to go a different route.

I often talk about the MAV. But now I want to talk about the MDV.

During the most terrifying twenty-three minutes of my life, four of my crewmates and I tried not to shit ourselves while Martinez piloted the MDV down to the surface. It was kind of like being in a tumble-dryer.

First, we descended from *Hermes*, and decelerated our orbital velocity so we could start falling properly. Everything was smooth until we hit the atmosphere. If you think turbulence is rough in a jetliner going 720 kph, just imagine what it's like at 28,000 kph.

Several staged sets of chutes deployed automatically to slow our descent, then Martinez manually piloted us to the ground, using the thrusters to slow descent and control our lateral motion. He'd trained for this for years, and he did his job extraordinarily well. He exceeded all plausible expectations of landings, putting us just nine meters from the target. The guy just plain owned that landing.

Thanks, Martinez! You may have saved my life!

Not because of the perfect landing, but because he left so much fuel behind. Hundreds of liters of unused hydrazine. Each molecule of hydrazine has four hydrogen atoms in it. So each liter of hydrazine has enough hydrogen for *two* liters of water.

I did a little EVA today to check. The MDV has 292 liters of juice left in the tanks. Enough to make almost 600 liters of water! Way more than I need!

There's just one catch: Liberating hydrogen from hydrazine is . . . well . . . it's how rockets work. It's really, really hot. And dangerous. If I do it in an oxygen atmosphere, the hot and newly liberated hydrogen will explode. There'll be a lot of H_2O at the end, but I'll be too dead to appreciate it.

At its root, hydrazine is pretty simple. The Germans used it as far back as World War II for rocket-assisted fighter fuel (and occasionally blew themselves up with it).

All you have to do is run it over a catalyst (which I can extract from the MDV engine) and it will turn into nitrogen and hydrogen. I'll spare you the chemistry, but the end result is that five molecules of hydrazine becomes five molecules of harmless N_2 and ten molecules of lovely H_2. During this process, it goes through an intermediate step of being ammonia. Chemistry, being the sloppy bitch it is, ensures there'll be some ammonia that doesn't react with the hydrazine, so it'll just stay ammonia. You like the smell of ammonia? Well, it'll be prevalent in my increasingly hellish existence.

The chemistry is on my side. The question now is how do I actually make this reaction happen slowly, and how do I collect the hydrogen? The answer is: I don't know.

I suppose I'll think of something. Or die.

Anyway, much more important: I simply can't abide the replacement of Chrissy with Cindy. *Three's Company* may never be the same after this fiasco. Time will tell.

CHAPTER 4

LOG ENTRY: SOL 32

So I ran into a bunch of problems with my water plan.

My idea is to make 600 liters of water (limited by the hydrogen I can get from the hydrazine). That means I'll need 300 liters of liquid O_2.

I can create the O_2 easily enough. It takes twenty hours for the MAV fuel plant to fill its 10-liter tank with CO_2. The oxygenator can turn it into O_2, then the atmospheric regulator will see the O_2 content in the Hab is high, and pull it out of the air, storing it in the main O_2 tanks. They'll fill up, so I'll have to transfer O_2 over to the rovers' tanks and even the space suit tanks as necessary.

But I can't create it very quickly. At half a liter of CO_2 per hour, it will take twenty-five days to make the oxygen I need. That's longer than I'd like.

Also, there's the problem of storing the hydrogen. The air tanks of the Hab, the rovers, and all the space suits add up to exactly 374 liters of storage. To hold all the materials for water, I would need a whopping 900 liters of storage.

I considered using one of the rovers as a "tank." It would certainly be big enough, but it just isn't designed to hold in that much pressure. It's made to hold (you guessed it) one atmosphere. I need vessels that can hold fifty times that much. I'm sure a rover would burst.

The best way to store the ingredients of water is to make them be water. So what's what I'll have to do.

The concept is simple, but the execution will be incredibly dangerous.

Every twenty hours, I'll have 10 liters of CO_2 thanks to the MAV fuel plant. I'll vent it into the Hab via the highly scientific method of detaching the tank from the MAV landing struts, bringing it into the Hab, then opening the valve until it's empty.

The oxygenator will turn it into oxygen in its own time.

Then, I'll release hydrazine, *very slowly*, over the iridium catalyst, to turn it into N_2 and H_2. I'll direct the hydrogen to a small area and burn it.

As you can see, this plan provides many opportunities for me to die in a fiery explosion.

Firstly, hydrazine is some serious death. If I make any mistakes, there'll be nothing left but the "Mark Watney Memorial Crater" where the Hab once stood.

Presuming I don't fuck up with the hydrazine, there's still the matter of burning hydrogen. I'm going to be setting a fire. In the Hab. On purpose.

If you asked every engineer at NASA what the worst scenario for the Hab was, they'd all answer "fire." If you asked them what the result would be, they'd answer "death by fire."

But if I can pull it off, I'll be making water continuously, with no need to store hydrogen or oxygen. It'll be mixed into the atmosphere as humidity, but the water reclaimer will pull it out.

I don't even have to perfectly match the hydrazine end of it with the fuel plant CO_2 part. There's plenty of oxygen in the Hab, and plenty more in reserve. I just need to make sure not to make so much water I run myself out of O_2.

I hooked up the MAV fuel plant to the Hab's power supply. Fortunately they both use the same voltage. It's chugging away, collecting CO_2 for me.

Half-ration for dinner. All I accomplished today was thinking up a plan that'll kill me, and that doesn't take much energy.

I'm going to finish off the last of *Three's Company* tonight. Frankly, I like Mr. Furley more than the Ropers.

LOG ENTRY: SOL 33

This may be my last entry.

I've known since Sol 6 there was a good chance I'd die here. But I figured it would be when I ran out of food. I didn't think it would be this early.

I'm about to fire up the hydrazine.

Our mission was designed knowing that anything might need maintenance, so I have plenty of tools. Even in a space suit, I was able to pry the access panels off the MDV and get at the six hydrazine tanks. I set them in the shadow of a rover to keep them from heating up too much. There's more shade and a cooler temperature near the Hab, but fuck that. If they're going to blow up, they can blow up a rover, not my house.

Then I pried out the reaction chamber. It took some work and I cracked the damn thing in half, but I got it out. Lucky for me I don't need a proper fuel reaction. In fact, I really, super-duper don't want a proper fuel reaction.

I brought the reaction chamber in. I briefly considered only bringing one tank of hydrazine in at a time to reduce risk. But some back-of-the-napkin math told me even one tank was enough to blow the whole Hab up. So I brought them all in. Why not?

The tanks have manual vent valves. I'm not 100 percent sure what they're for. Certainly we were never expected to use them. I think they're there to release pressure during the many quality checks done during construction and before fueling. Whatever the reason, I have valves to work with. All it takes is a wrench.

I liberated a spare water hose from the water reclaimer. With some thread torn out of a uniform (sorry, Johanssen), I attached it to the valve output. Hydrazine is a liquid, so all I have to do is lead it to the reaction chamber (more of a "reaction bowl" now).

Meanwhile, the MAV fuel plant is still working. I've already brought in one tank of CO_2, vented it, and returned it for refilling.

So there are no more excuses. It's time to start making water.

If you find the charred remains of the Hab, it means I did something wrong. I'm copying this log over to both rovers, so it's more likely it'll survive.

Here goes nothin'.

LOG ENTRY: SOL 33 (2)

Well, I didn't die.

First thing I did was put on the inner lining of my EVA suit. Not the bulky suit itself, just the inner clothing I wear under it, including the gloves and booties. Then I got an oxygen mask from the medical supplies and some lab goggles from Vogel's chem kit. Almost all of my body was protected and I was breathing canned air.

Why? Because hydrazine is *very* toxic. If I breathe too much of it, I'll get major lung problems. If I get it on my skin, I'll have chemical burns for the rest of my life. I wasn't taking any chances.

I turned the valve until a trickle of hydrazine came out. I let one drop fall into the iridium bowl.

It undramatically sizzled and disappeared.

But hey, that's what I wanted. I just freed up hydrogen and nitrogen. Yay!

One thing I have in abundance here are bags. They're not much different from kitchen trash bags, though I'm sure they cost $50,000 because of NASA.

In addition to being our commander, Lewis was also the geologist. She was going to collect rock and soil samples from all over the operational area (10-kilometer radius). Weight limits restricted how much she could actually bring back to Earth, so she was going to collect first, then sort out the most interesting 50 kilograms to take home. The bags were to store and tag the samples. Some are smaller than a Ziploc, while others are as big as a Hefty lawn and leaf bag.

Also, I have duct tape. Ordinary duct tape, like you buy at a hardware store. Turns out even NASA can't improve on duct tape.

I cut up a few Hefty-sized bags and taped them together to make a sort of tent. Really it was more of a supersized bag. I was able to cover the whole table where my hydrazine mad scientist setup was. I put a few knickknacks on the table to keep the plastic out of the iridium bowl. Thankfully, the bags are clear, so I can still see what's going on.

Next, I sacrificed a space suit to the cause. I needed an air hose. I have a surplus of space suits, after all. A total of six; one for each crew member. So I don't mind murdering one of them.

I cut a hole in the top of the plastic and duct-taped the hose in place. Nice seal, I think.

With some more string from Johannsen's clothing, I hung the other end of the hose from the top of the Hab's dome by two angled threads (to keep them well clear of the hose opening). Now I had a little chimney. The hose was about one centimeter wide. Hopefully a good aperture.

The hydrogen will be hot after the reaction, and it'll want to go up. So I'll let it go up the chimney, then burn it as it comes out.

Then I had to invent fire.

NASA put a lot of effort into making sure nothing here can burn. Everything is made of metal or flame-retardant plastic and the uniforms are synthetic. I needed something that could hold a flame, some kind of pilot light. I don't have the skills to keep enough H_2 flowing to feed a flame without killing myself. Too narrow a margin there.

After a search of everyone's personal items (hey, if they wanted privacy, they shouldn't have abandoned me on Mars with their stuff) I found my answer.

Martinez is a devout Catholic. I knew that. What I didn't know was he brought along a small wooden cross. I'm sure NASA gave him shit about it, but I also know Martinez is one stubborn son of a bitch.

I chipped his sacred religious item into long splinters using a pair of pliers and a screwdriver. I figure if there's a God, He won't mind, considering the situation I'm in.

If ruining the only religious icon I have leaves me vulnerable to Martian vampires, I'll have to risk it.

There were plenty of wires and batteries around to make a spark. But you can't just ignite wood with a small electric spark. So I collected ribbons of bark from local palm trees, then got a couple of sticks and rubbed them together to create enough friction to . . .

No not really. I vented pure oxygen at the stick and gave it a spark. It lit up like a match.

With my mini-torch in hand, I started a slow hydrazine flow. It sizzled on the iridium and disappeared. Soon I had short bursts of flame sputtering from the chimney.

The main thing I had to watch was the temperature. Hydrazine breaking down is extremely exothermic. So I did it a bit at a time, constantly watching the readout of a thermocouple I'd attached to the iridium chamber.

Point is, the process worked!

Each hydrazine tank holds a little over 50 liters, which would be enough to make 100 liters of water. I'm limited by my oxygen production, but I'm all excited now, so I'm willing to use half my reserves. Long story short, I'll stop when the tank is half-empty, and I'll have 50 liters of water at the end!

Well, that took a really long time. I've been at it all night with the hydrazine. But I got the job done.

I could have finished faster, but I figured caution's best when setting fire to rocket fuel in an enclosed space.

Boy is this place a tropical jungle now, I'll tell ya.

It's almost 30°C in here, and humid as all hell. I just dumped a ton of heat and 50 liters of water into the air.

During this process, the poor Hab had to be the mother of a messy toddler. It's been replacing the oxygen I've used, and the water reclaimer is trying to get the humidity down to sane levels. Nothing to be done about the heat. There's actually no air-conditioning in the Hab. Mars is cold. Getting rid of excess heat isn't something we expected to deal with.

I've now grown accustomed to hearing the alarms blare at all times. The fire alarm has finally stopped, now that there's no more fire. The low oxygen alarm should stop soon. The high humidity alarm will take a little longer. The water reclaimer has its work cut out for it today.

For a moment, there was yet another alarm. The water reclaimer's main tank was full. Booyah! That's the kind of problem I want to have!

Remember the space suit I vandalized yesterday? I hung it on its rack and carried buckets of water to it from the reclaimer. It can hold an atmosphere of air in. It should be able to handle a few buckets of water.

Man I'm tired. Been up all night, and it's time to sleep. But I'll drift off to dreamland in the best mood I've been in since Sol 6.

Things are finally going my way. In fact, they're going great! I have a chance to live after all!

I am fucked, and I'm gonna die!

Okay, calm down. I'm sure I can get around this.

I'm writing this log to you, dear future Mars archaeologist, from Rover 2. You may wonder why I'm not in the Hab right now. Because I fled in terror, that's why! And I'm not sure what the hell to do next.

I guess I should explain what happened. If this is my last entry, you'll at least know why.

Over the past few days, I've been happily making water. It's been going swimmingly. (See what I did there? "Swimmingly"?)

I even beefed up the MAV fuel plant compressor. It was very technical (I increased the voltage to the pump). So I'm making water even faster now.

After my initial burst of 50 liters, I decided to settle down and just make it at the rate I get O_2. I'm not willing to go below a 25-liter reserve. So when I dip too low, I stop dicking with hydrazine until I get the O_2 back up to well above 25 liters.

Important note: When I say I made 50 liters of water, that's an assumption. I didn't *reclaim* 50 liters of water. The additional soil I'd filled the Hab with was extremely dry and greedily sucked up a lot of the humidity. That's where I want the water to go anyway, so I'm not worried, and I wasn't surprised when the reclaimer didn't get anywhere near 50 liters.

I get 10 liters of CO_2 every fifteen hours now that I souped up the pump. I've done this process four times. My math tells me that, including my initial 50-liter burst, I should have added 130 liters of water to the system.

Well my math was a damn liar!

I'd gained 70 liters in the water reclaimer and the space-suit-turned-water-tank. There's plenty of condensation on the walls and domed roof, and the soil is certainly absorbing its fair share. But that doesn't account for 60 liters of missing water. Something was wrong.

That's when I noticed the other O_2 tank.

The Hab has two reserve O_2 tanks. One on each side of the structure, for safety reasons. The Hab can decide which one to use whenever it wants. Turns out it's been topping off the atmosphere from Tank 1. But when I add O_2 to the system (via the oxygenator), the Hab evenly distributes the gain between the two tanks. Tank 2 has been slowly gaining oxygen.

That's not a problem. The Hab is just doing its job. But it does mean I've been gaining O_2 over time. Which means I'm not consuming it as fast as I thought.

At first, I thought "Yay! More oxygen! Now I can make water faster!" But then a more disturbing thought occurred to me.

Follow my logic: I'm gaining O_2. But the amount I'm bringing in from outside is constant. So the only way to "gain" it is to be using less than I thought. But I've been doing the hydrazine reaction with the assumption that I was using all of it.

The only possible explanation is that I haven't been burning all the released hydrogen.

It's obvious now, in retrospect. But it never occurred to me that some of the hydrogen just wouldn't burn. It got past the flame, and went on its merry way. Damn it, Jim, I'm a botanist, not a chemist!

Chemistry is messy, so there's unburned hydrogen in the air. All around me. Mixed in with the oxygen. Just . . . hanging out. Waiting for a spark so it can *blow the Hab up!*

Once I figured this out and composed myself, I got a Ziploc-sized sample bag and waved it around a bit, then sealed it.

Then, a quick EVA to a rover, where we keep the atmospheric analyzers. Nitrogen: 22 percent. Oxygen: 9 percent. Hydrogen: 64 percent.

I've been hiding here in the rover ever since.

It's Hydrogenville in the Hab.

I'm very lucky it hasn't blown. Even a small static discharge would have led to my own private *Hindenburg*.

So, I'm here in Rover 2. I can stay for a day or two, tops, before the CO_2 filters from the rover and my space suit fill up. I have that long to figure out how to deal with this.

The Hab is now a bomb.

CHAPTER 5

LOG ENTRY: SOL 38

I'm still cowering in the rover, but I've had time to think. And I know how to deal with the hydrogen.

I thought about the atmospheric regulator. It pays attention to what's in the air and balances it. That's how the excess O_2 I've been importing ends up in the tanks. Problem is, it's just not built to pull hydrogen out of the air.

The regulator uses freeze-separation to sort out the gasses. When it decides there's too much oxygen, it starts collecting air in a tank and cooling it to 90 kelvin. That makes the oxygen turn to liquid, but leaves the nitrogen (condensation point: 77K) still gaseous. Then it stores the O_2.

But I can't get it to do that for hydrogen, because hydrogen needs to be below 21K to turn liquid. And the regulator just can't get temperatures that low. Dead end.

Here's the solution:

Hydrogen is dangerous because it can blow up. But it can only blow up if there's oxygen around. Hydrogen without oxygen is harmless. And the regulator is all about pulling oxygen out of the air.

There are four different safety interlocks that prevent the regulator from letting the Hab's oxygen content get too low. But they're designed to work against technical faults, not deliberate sabotage (bwa ha ha!).

Long story short, I can trick the regulator into pulling all the oxygen out of the Hab. Then I can wear a space suit (so I can breathe) and do whatever I want without fear of blowing up.

I'll use an O_2 tank to spray short bursts of oxygen at the hydrogen, and make a spark with a couple of wires and a battery. It'll set the hydrogen on fire, but only until the small bit of oxygen is used up.

I'll just do that over and over, in controlled bursts, until I've burned off all the hydrogen.

One tiny flaw with that plan: It'll kill my dirt.

The dirt is only viable soil because of the bacteria growing in it. If I get rid of all the oxygen, the bacteria will die. I don't have 100 billion little space suits handy.

It's half a solution anyway.

Time to take a break from thinking.

Commander Lewis was the last one to use this rover. She was scheduled to use it again on Sol 7, but she went home instead. Her personal travel kit's still in the back. Rifling through it, I found a protein bar and a personal USB, probably full of music to listen to on the drive.

Time to chow down and see what the good commander brought along for music.

LOG ENTRY SOL 38 (2)

Disco. God damn it, Lewis.

I think I've got it.

Soil bacteria are used to winters. They get less active, and require less oxygen to survive. I can lower the Hab temperature to 1°C, and they'll nearly hibernate. This sort of thing happens on Earth all the time. They can survive a couple of days this way. If you're wondering how bacteria on Earth survive longer periods of cold, the answer is they don't. Bacteria from further underground where it is warmer breed upward to replace the dead ones.

They'll still need some oxygen, but not much. I think a 1 percent content will do the trick. That leaves a little in the air for the bacteria to breathe, but not enough to maintain a fire. So the hydrogen won't blow up.

But that leads to yet another problem. The potato plants won't like the plan.

They don't mind the lack of oxygen, but the cold will kill them. So I'll have to pot them (bag them, actually) and move them to a rover. They haven't even sprouted yet, so it's not like they need light.

It was surprisingly annoying to find a way to make the heat stay on when the rover's unoccupied. But I figured it out. After all, I've got nothing but time in here.

So that's the plan. First, bag the potato plants and bring them to the rover (make sure it keeps the damn heater on). Then drop the Hab temperature to 1°C. Then reduce the O_2 content to 1 percent. Then burn off the hydrogen with a battery, some wires, and a tank of O_2.

Yeah. This all sounds like a great idea with no chance of catastrophic failure.

That was sarcasm, by the way.

Well, off I go.

Things weren't 100 percent successful.

They say no plan survives first contact with implementation. I'd have to agree. Here's what happened:

I summoned up the courage to return to the Hab. Once I got there, I felt a little more confident. Everything was how I'd left it. (What did I expect? Martians looting my stuff?)

It would take a while to let the Hab cool, so I started that right away by turning the temperature down to 1°C.

I bagged the potato plants, and got a chance to check up on them while I was at it. They're rooting nicely and about to sprout. One thing I hadn't accounted for was how to bring them from the Hab to the rovers.

The answer was pretty easy. I put all of them in Martinez's space suit. Then I dragged it out with me to the rover I'd set up as a temporary nursery.

Making sure to jimmy the heater to stay on, I headed back to the Hab.

By the time I got back, it was already chilly. Down to 5°C already. Shivering and watching my breath condense in front of me, I threw on extra layers of clothes. Fortunately I'm not a very big man. Martinez's clothes fit over mine, and Vogel's fit over Martinez's. These shitty clothes were designed to be worn in a temperature-controlled environment. Even with three layers, I was still cold. I climbed into my bunk and under the covers for more warmth.

Once the temperature got to 1°C, I waited another hour, just to make sure the bacteria in the dirt got the memo that it was time to take it slow.

The next problem I ran into was the regulator. Despite my swaggering confidence, I wasn't able to outwit it. It *really* does not want to pull too much O_2 out of the air. The lowest I could get it to was 15 percent. After that, it flatly refused to go lower, and nothing I did mattered. I had all these plans about getting in and reprogramming it. But the safety protocols turned out to be in ROMs.

I can't blame it. Its whole purpose is to *prevent* the atmosphere from becoming lethal. Nobody at NASA thought, "Hey, let's allow a fatal lack of oxygen that will make everyone drop dead!"

So I had to use a more primitive plan.

The regulator uses a different set of vents for air sampling than it does for main air separation. The air that gets freeze-separated comes in through a single large vent on the main unit. But it samples the air from nine small vents that pipe back to the main unit. That way it gets a good average of the Hab, and one localized imbalance won't throw it off.

I taped up eight of the intakes, leaving only one of them active. Then I taped the mouth of a Hefty-sized bag over the neck-hole of a spacesuit (Johanssen's this time). In the back of the bag, I poked a small hole and taped it over the remaining intake.

Then I inflated the bag with pure O_2 from the suit's tanks. "Holy shit!" the regulator thought, "I better pull O_2 out right away!"

Worked great!

I decided not to wear a space suit after all. The atmospheric pressure was going to be fine. All I needed was oxygen. So I grabbed an O_2 canister and breather mask from the medical bay. That way, I had a hell of a lot more freedom of motion. It even had a rubber band to keep it on my face!

Though I did need a space suit to monitor the actual Hab oxygen level, now that the Hab's main computer was convinced it was 100 percent O_2. Let's see . . . Martinez's space suit was in the rover. Johanssen's was outwitting the regulator. Lewis's was serving as a water tank. I didn't want to mess with mine (hey, it's custom-fitted!). That left me two space suits to work with.

I grabbed Vogel's suit and activated the internal air sensors while leaving the helmet off. Once the oxygen dropped to 12 percent, I put the breather mask on. I watched it fall further and further. When it reached 1 percent, I cut power to the regulator.

I may not be able to reprogram the regulator, but I can turn the bastard off completely.

The Hab has emergency flashlights in many locations in case of critical power failure. I tore the LED bulbs out of one and left the two frayed power wires very close together. Now, when I turned it on, I got a small spark.

Taking a canister of O_2 from Vogel's suit, I attached a strap to both ends and slung it over my shoulder. Then I attached an air line to the tank and crimped it with my thumb. I turned on a very slow trickle of O_2; small enough that it couldn't overpower the crimp.

Standing on the table with a sparker in one hand and my oxygen line in the other, I reached up and gave it a try.

And holy hell, it worked! Blowing the O_2 over the sparker, I flicked the switch on the flashlight and a wonderful jet of flame fired out of the tube. The fire alarm went off, of course. But I'd heard it so much lately, I barely noticed it anymore.

Then I did it again. And again. Short bursts. Nothing flashy. I was happy to take my time.

I was elated! This was the best plan ever! Not only was I clearing out the hydrogen, I was making more water!

Everything went great right up to the explosion.

One minute I was happily burning hydrogen; the next I was on the other side of the Hab, and a lot of stuff was knocked over. I stumbled to my feet and saw the Hab in disarray.

My first thought was: "My ears hurt like hell!"

Then I thought, "I'm dizzy," and fell to my knees. Then I fell prone. I was *that* dizzy. I groped my head with both hands, looking for a head wound I desperately hoped would not be there. Nothing seemed to be amiss.

But feeling all over my head and face revealed the true problem. My oxygen mask had been ripped off in the blast. I was breathing nearly pure nitrogen.

The floor was covered in junk from all over the Hab. No hope of finding the medical O_2 tank. No hope of finding anything in this mess before I passed out.

Then I saw Lewis's suit hanging right where it belonged. It hadn't moved in the blast. It was heavy to start with and had 70 liters of water in it.

I rushed over, quickly cranked on the O_2, and stuck my head into the neck hole (I'd removed the helmet long ago, for easy access to the water). I breathed a bit until the dizziness faded, then took a deep breath and held it.

Still holding my breath, I glanced over to the space suit and Hefty bag I'd used to outsmart the regulator. The bad news is I'd never removed them. The good news is the explosion removed them. Eight of the nine intakes for the regulator were still bagged, but this one would at least tell the truth.

Stumbling over to the regulator, I turned it back on.

After a two-second boot process (it was made to start up fast for obvious reasons), it immediately identified the problem.

The shrill low-oxygen alarm blared throughout the Hab as the regulator dumped pure oxygen into the atmosphere as fast as it safely could. *Separating* oxygen from the atmosphere is difficult and time-consuming, but *adding* it is as simple as opening a valve.

I clambered over debris back to Lewis's space suit and put my head back in for more good air. Within three minutes, the regulator had brought the Hab oxygen back up to par.

I noticed for the first time how burned my clothing was. It was a good time to be wearing three layers of clothes. Mostly the damage was on my sleeves. The outer layer was gone. The middle layer was singed and burned clean through in places. The inner layer, my own uniform, was in reasonably good shape. Looks like I lucked out again.

Also, glancing at the Hab's main computer, I saw the temperature had gone up to 15°C. Something very hot and very explodey had happened, and I wasn't sure what. Or how.

And that's where I am now. Wondering what the hell happened.

After all that work and getting blown up, I'm exhausted. Tomorrow I'll have to do a million equipment checks and try to figure out what exploded, but for now I just want to sleep.

I'm in the rover again tonight. Even with the hydrogen gone, I'm reluctant to hang out in a Hab that has a history of exploding for no reason. Plus, I can't be sure there isn't a leak.

This time, I brought a proper meal, and something to listen to that isn't disco.

LOG ENTRY: SOL 41

I spent the day running full diagnostics on every system in the Hab. It was incredibly boring, but my survival depends on these machines, so it had to be done. I can't just assume an explosion did no long-term damage.

I did the most critical tests first. Number one was the integrity of the Hab canvas. I felt pretty confident it was in good shape, because I'd spent a few hours asleep in the rover before returning to the Hab, and the pressure was still good. The computer reported no change in pressure over that time, other than a minor fluctuation based on temperature.

Then I checked the oxygenator. If that stops working and I can't fix it, I'm a dead man. No problems.

Then the atmospheric regulator. Again, no problem.

Heating unit, primary battery array, O_2 and N_2 storage tanks, water reclaimer, all three airlocks, lighting systems, main computer . . . on and on I went, feeling better and better as each system proved to be in perfect working order.

Got to hand it to NASA. They don't screw around when making this stuff.

Then came the critical part . . . checking the dirt. I took a few samples from all over the Hab (remember, it's all dirt flooring now) and made slides.

With shaking hands, I put a slide into the microscope and brought the image up on-screen. There they were! Healthy, active bacteria doing their thing! Looks like I won't be starving to death on Sol 400 after all. I plopped down in a chair and let my breathing return to normal.

Then I set about cleaning up the mess. And I had a lot of time to think about what had happened.

So what happened? Well, I have a theory.

According to the main computer, during the blast, the internal pressure spiked to 1.4 atmospheres, and the temperature rose to 15°C in under a second. But the pressure quickly subsided back to 1 atm. This would make sense if the atmospheric regulator were on, but I'd cut power to it.

The temperature remained at 15°C for some time afterward, so any heat expansion should still have been present. But the pressure dropped down again, so where did that extra pressure go? Raising the temperature and keeping the same number of atoms inside should permanently raise the pressure. But it didn't.

I quickly realized the answer. The hydrogen (the only available thing to burn) combined with oxygen (hence combustion) and became water. Water is a thousand times as dense as a gas. So the heat added to the pressure, and the transformation of hydrogen and oxygen into water brought it back down again.

The million dollar question is, where the hell did the oxygen come from? The whole plan was to limit oxygen and keep an explosion from happening. And it was working for quite a while before blowing up.

I think I have my answer. And it comes down to me brain-farting. Remember when I decided not to wear a space suit? That decision almost killed me.

The medical O_2 tank mixes pure oxygen with surrounding air, then feeds it to you through a mask. The mask stays on your face with a little rubber band that goes around the back of your neck. Not an airtight seal.

I know what you're thinking. The mask leaked oxygen. But no. I was breathing the oxygen. When I was inhaling, I made a nearly airtight seal with the mask by sucking it to my face.

The problem was *exhaling*. Do you know how much oxygen you absorb out of the air when you take a normal breath? I don't know either, but it's not 100 percent. Every time I exhaled, I added more oxygen to the system.

It just didn't occur to me. But it should have. If your lungs grabbed up all the oxygen, mouth-to-mouth resuscitation wouldn't work. I'm such a dumb-ass for not thinking of it! And my dumb-assery almost got me killed!

I'm really going to have to be more careful.

It's a good thing I burned off most of the hydrogen before the explosion. Otherwise that would have been the end. As it is, the explosion wasn't strong enough to pop the Hab. Though it was strong enough to almost blast my eardrums in.

This all started with me noticing a 60-liter shortfall in water production. Between deliberate burn-off and a bit of unexpected explosion, I'm back on track. The water reclaimer did its job last night and pulled 50 liters of the newly created water out of the air. It's storing it in Lewis's spacesuit, which I'll call "The Cistern" from now on, because it sounds cooler. The other 10 liters of water was directly absorbed by the dry soil.

Lots of physical labor today. I've earned a full meal. And to celebrate my first night back in the Hab, I'll kick back and watch some shitty twentieth-century TV courtesy of Commander Lewis.

The Dukes of Hazzard, eh? Let's give it a whirl.

LOG ENTRY: SOL 42

I slept in late today. I deserved it. After four nights of awful sleep in the rover, my bunk felt like the softest, most profoundly beautiful feather bed ever made.

Eventually, I dragged my ass out of bed and finished some post-explosion cleanup.

I moved the potato plants back in today. And just in time, too. They're sprouting. They look healthy and happy. This isn't chemistry, medicine, bacteriology, nutrition analysis, explosion dynamics, or any other shit I've been doing lately. This is *botany*. I'm sure I can at least grow some plants without screwing up.

Right?

You know what really sucks? I've only made 130 liters of water. I have another 470 liters to go. You'd think after almost killing myself *twice*, I'd be able to stop screwing around with hydrazine. But nope. I'll be reducing hydrazine and burning hydrogen in the Hab, every ten hours, for another ten days. I'll do a better job of it from now on. Instead of counting on a clean reaction, I'll do frequent "hydrogen cleanings" with a small flame. It'll burn off gradually instead of building up to kill-Mark levels.

I'll have a lot of dead time. Ten hours for each tank of CO_2 to finish filling. It only takes twenty minutes to reduce the hydrazine and burn the hydrogen. I'll spend the rest of the time watching TV.

And seriously . . . It's clear that General Lee can outrun a police cruiser. Why doesn't Rosco just go to the Duke farm and arrest them when they're *not* in the car?

CHAPTER 6

VENKAT KAPOOR returned to his office, dropped his briefcase on the floor, and collapsed into his leather chair. He took a moment to look out the windows. His office in Building 1 afforded him a commanding view of the large park in the center of the Johnson Space Center complex. Beyond that, dozens of scattered buildings dominated the view all the way to Mud Lake in the distance.

Glancing at his computer screen, he noted forty-seven unread e-mails urgently demanding his attention. They could wait. Today had been a sad day. Today was the memorial service for Mark Watney.

The President had given a speech, praising Watney's bravery and sacrifice, and the quick actions of Commander Lewis in getting everyone else to safety. Commander Lewis and the surviving crew, via long-range communication from *Hermes*, gave eulogies for their departed comrade from deep space. They had another ten months of travel yet to endure.

The administrator had given a speech as well, reminding everyone that space flight is incredibly dangerous, and that we will not back down in the face of adversity.

They'd asked Venkat if he was willing to make a speech. He'd declined. What was the point? Watney was dead. Nice words from the director of Mars operations wouldn't bring him back.

"You okay, Venk?" came a familiar voice from the doorway.

Venkat swiveled around. "Guess so," he said.

Teddy Sanders swept a rogue thread off his otherwise immaculate blazer. "You could have given a speech."

"I didn't want to. You know that."

"Yeah, I know. I didn't want to, either. But I'm the administrator of NASA. It's kind of expected. You sure you're okay?"

"Yeah, I'll be fine."

"Good," Teddy said, adjusting his cuff links. "Let's get back to work, then."

"Sure." Venkat shrugged. "Let's start with you authorizing my satellite time."

Teddy leaned against the wall with a sigh. "This again."

"Yes," Venkat said. "This again. What is the problem?"

"Okay, run me through it. What, exactly, are you after?"

Venkat leaned forward. "Ares 3 was a failure, but we can salvage something from it. We're funded for five Ares missions. I think we can get Congress to fund a sixth."

"I don't know, Venk . . ."

"It's simple, Teddy." Venkat pressed on. "They evac'd after six sols. There's almost an entire mission's worth of supplies up there. It would only cost a fraction of a normal mission. It normally takes fourteen presupply probes to prep a site. We might be able to send what's missing in three. Maybe two."

"Venk, the site got hit by a 175 kph sandstorm. It'll be in really bad shape."

"That's why I want imagery," Venkat said. "I just need a couple of shots of the site. We could learn a lot."

"Like what? You think we'd send people to Mars without being sure everything was in perfect working order?"

"Everything doesn't have to be perfect," Venkat said quickly. "Whatever's broken, we'd send replacements for."

"How will we know from imagery what's broken?"

"It's just a first step. They evac'd because the wind was a threat to the MAV, but the Hab can withstand a lot more punishment. It might still be in one piece.

"And it'll be really obvious. If it popped, it'd completely blow out and collapse. If it's still standing, then everything inside will be fine. And the rovers are solid. They can take any sandstorm Mars has to offer. Just let me take a look, Teddy, that's all I want."

Teddy paced to the windows and stared out at the vast expanse of buildings. "You're not the only guy who wants satellite time, you know. We have Ares 4 supply missions coming up. We need to concentrate on Schiaparelli crater."

"I don't get it, Teddy. What's the problem here?" Venkat asked. "I'm talking about securing us another mission. We have twelve satellites in orbit around Mars; I'm sure you can spare one or two for a couple of hours. I can give you the windows for each one when they'll be at the right angle for Ares 3 shots—"

"It's not about satellite time, Venk," Teddy interrupted.

Venkat froze. "Then . . . but . . . what . . ."

Teddy turned to face him. "We're a public domain organization. There's no such thing as secret or secure information here."

"So?"

"Any imagery we take goes directly to the public."

"Again, so?"

"Mark Watney's body will be within twenty meters of the Hab. Maybe partially buried in sand, but still very visible, and with a comm antenna sticking out of his chest. Any images we take will show that."

Venkat stared. Then glared. "*This* is why you denied my imagery requests for two months?"

"Venk, come on—"

"Really, Teddy?" he said. "You're afraid of a PR problem?"

"The media's obsession with Watney's death is finally starting to taper off," Teddy said evenly. "It's been bad press after bad press for two months. Today's memorial gives people closure, and the media can move on to some other story. The last thing we want is to dredge everything back up."

"So what do we do, then? He's not going to decompose. He'll be there forever."

"Not forever," Teddy said. "Within a year, he'll be covered in sand from normal weather activity."

"A year?" Venkat said, rising to his feet. "That's ludicrous. We can't wait a year for this."

"Why not? Ares 4 won't even launch for another five years. Plenty of time."

Venkat took a deep breath and thought for a moment.

"Okay, consider this: Sympathy for Watney's family is really high. Ares 6 could bring the body back. We don't say that's the *purpose* of the mission, but we make it clear that would be part of it. If we framed it that way, we'd get more support in Congress. But not if we wait a year. In a year, people won't care anymore."

Teddy rubbed his chin. "Hmm . . ."

. . .

MINDY PARK stared at the ceiling. She had little else to do. The three a.m. shift was pretty dull. Only a constant stream of coffee kept her awake.

Monitoring the status of satellites around Mars had sounded like an exciting proposition when she took the transfer. But the satellites tended to take care of themselves. Her job turned out to be sending e-mails as imagery became available.

"Master's degree in mechanical engineering," she muttered. "And I'm working in an all-night photo booth."

She sipped her coffee.

A flicker on her screen announced that another set of images was ready for dispatch. She checked the name on the work order. Venkat Kapoor.

She posted the data directly to internal servers and composed an e-mail to Dr. Kapoor. As she entered the latitude and longitude of the image, she recognized the numbers.

"31.2°N, 28.5°W . . . Acidalia Planitia . . . Ares 3?"

Out of curiosity, she brought up the first of the seventeen images.

As she'd suspected, it was the Ares 3 site. She'd heard they were going to image it. Slightly ashamed of herself, she scoured the image for any sign of Mark Watney's dead body. After a minute of fruitless searching, she was simultaneously relieved and disappointed.

She moved on to perusing the rest of the image. The Hab was intact; Dr. Kapoor would be happy to see that.

She brought the coffee mug to her lips, then froze.

"Um . . . ," she mumbled to herself. "Uhhh . . ."

She brought up the NASA intranet and navigated through the site to the specifics of the Ares missions. After some quick research, she picked up her phone.

"Hey, this is Mindy Park at SatCon. I need the mission logs for Ares 3, where can I get 'em? . . . Uh huh . . . uh-huh . . . Okay . . . Thanks."

After some more time on the intranet, she leaned back in her seat. She no longer needed the coffee to keep awake.

Picking up the phone again, she said, "Hello, Security? This is Mindy Park in SatCon. I need the emergency contact number for Dr. Venkat Kapoor. . . . Yes it's an emergency."

. . .

MINDY FIDGETED in her seat as Venkat trudged in. To have the director of Mars operations visiting SatCon was unusual. Seeing him in jeans and a T-shirt was even more unusual.

"You Mindy Park?" he asked with the scowl of a man operating on two hours of sleep.

"Yes," she quavered. "Sorry to drag you in."

"I'm assuming you had a good reason. So?"

"Um," she said, looking down. "Um, it's. Well. The imagery you ordered. Um. Come here and look."

He pulled another chair to her station and seated himself. "Is this about Watney's body? Is that why you're shook up?"

"Um, no," she said. "Um. Well . . . uh." She winced at her own awkwardness and pointed to the screen.

Venkat inspected the image. "Looks like the Hab's in one piece. That's good news. Solar array looks good. The rovers are okay, too. Main dish isn't around. No surprise there. What's the big emergency?"

"Um," she said, touching her finger to the screen. "That."

Venkat leaned in and looked closer. Just below the Hab, beside the rovers, two white circles sat in the sand. "Hmm. Looks like Hab canvas. Maybe the Hab didn't do well after all? I guess pieces got torn off and—"

"Um," she interrupted. "They look like rover pop-tents."

Venkat looked again. "Hmm. Probably right."

"How'd they get set up?" Mindy asked.

Venkat shrugged. "Commander Lewis probably ordered them deployed during the evac. Not a bad idea. Have the emergency shelters ready in case the MAV didn't work and the Hab breached."

"Yeah, um," Mindy said, opening a document on her computer, "this is the entire mission log for Sols 1 through 6. From MDV touchdown to MAV emergency liftoff."

"Okay, and?"

"I read through it. Several times. They never threw out the pop-tents." Her voice cracked at the last word.

"Well, uh . . . ," Venkat said, furrowing his brow. "They obviously did, but it didn't make it into the log."

"They activated two emergency pop-tents and never told anyone?"

"Hmm. That doesn't make a lot of sense, no. Maybe the storm messed with the rovers and the tents autodeployed."

"So after autodeploying, they detached themselves from the rovers and lined up next to each other twenty meters away?"

Venkat looked back to the image. "Well obviously they activated somehow."

"Why are the solar cells clean?" Mindy said, fighting back tears. "There was a huge sandstorm. Why isn't there sand all over them?"

"A good wind could have done it?" Venkat said, unsure.

"Did I mention I never found Watney's body?" she said, sniffling.

Venkat's eyes widened as he stared at the picture. "Oh . . . ," he said quietly. "Oh God . . ."

Mindy put her hands over her face and sobbed quietly.

• • •

"Fuck!" Annie Montrose said. "You have got to be fucking kidding me!"

Teddy glared across his immaculate mahogany desk at his director of media relations. "Not helping, Annie."

He turned to his director of Mars operations. "How sure are we of this?"

"Nearly a hundred percent," Venkat said.

"Fuck!" Annie said.

Teddy moved a folder on his desk slightly to the right so it would line up with his mouse pad. "It is what it is. We have to deal with it."

"Do you have any idea the *magnitude* of shit storm this is gonna be?" she retorted. "You don't have to face those damn reporters every day. I do!"

"One thing at a time," Teddy said. "Venk, what makes you sure he's alive?"

"For starters, no body," Venkat explained. "Also, the pop-tents are set up. And the solar cells are clean. You can thank Mindy Park in SatCon for noticing all that, by the way.

"But," Venkat continued, "his body could have been buried in the Sol 6 storm. The pop-tents might have autodeployed and wind could have blown them around. A 30 kph windstorm some time later would have been strong enough to clean the solar cells but not strong enough to carry sand. It's not likely, but it's possible.

"So I spent the last few hours checking everything I could. Commander Lewis had two outings in Rover 2. The second was on Sol 5. According to the logs, after returning, she plugged it into the Hab for recharging. It wasn't used again, and thirteen hours later they evac'd."

He slid a picture across the desk to Teddy.

"That's one of the images from last night. As you can see, Rover 2 is facing *away* from the Hab. The charging port is in the nose, and the cable isn't long enough to reach."

Teddy absently rotated the picture to be parallel with the edges of his desk. "She must have parked it facing the Hab or she wouldn't have been able to plug it in," he said. "It's been moved since Sol 5."

"Yeah," Venkat said, sliding another picture to Teddy. "But here's the real evidence. In the lower right of the image you can see the MDV. It's been taken apart. I'm pretty sure they wouldn't have done that without telling us.

"And the clincher is on the right of the image," Venkat pointed. "The landing struts of the MAV. Looks like the fuel plant has been completely removed, with considerable damage to the struts in the process. There's just no way that could have happened before lift-off. It would have endangered the MAV way too much for Lewis to allow it."

"Hey," Annie said. "Why not talk to Lewis? Let's go to CAP-COM and ask her directly."

Rather than answer, Venkat looked to Teddy knowingly.

"Because," Teddy said, "if Watney really is alive, we don't want the Ares 3 crew to know."

"What!?" Annie said. "How can you not tell them?"

"They have another ten months on their trip home," Teddy explained. "Space travel is dangerous. They need to be alert and undistracted. They're sad that they lost a crewmate, but they'd be devastated if they found out they'd abandoned him alive."

Annie looked to Venkat. "You're on board with this?"

"It's a no-brainer," Venkat said. "Let 'em deal with that emotional trauma when they're not flying a spaceship around."

"This'll be the most talked-about event since Apollo 11," Annie said. "How will you keep it from them?"

Teddy shrugged. "Easy. We control all communication with them."

"Fuck," Annie said, opening her laptop. "When do you want to go public?"

"What's your take?" he asked.

"Mmm," Annie said. "We can hold the pics for twenty-four hours before we're required to release them. We'll need to send out a statement along with them. We don't want people working it out on their own. We'd look like assholes."

"Okay," Teddy agreed, "put together a statement."

"That'll be fun," she grumbled.

"Where do we go from here?" Teddy asked Venkat.

"Step one is communication," Venkat said. "From the pics, it's clear the comm array is ruined. We need another way to talk. Once we can talk, we can assess and make plans."

"All right," Teddy said. "Get on it. Take anyone you want from any department. Use as much overtime as you want. Find a way to talk to him. That's your only job right now."

"Got it."

"Annie, make sure nobody gets wind of this till we announce."

"Right," Annie said. "Who else knows?"

"Just the three of us and Mindy Park in SatCon," Venkat said.

"I'll have a word with her," Annie said.

Teddy stood and opened his cell phone. "I'm going to Chicago. I'll be back tomorrow."

"Why?" Annie asked.

"That's where Watney's parents live," Teddy said. "I owe them a personal explanation before it breaks on the news."

"They'll be happy to hear their son's alive," Annie said.

"Yes, he's alive," Teddy said. "But if my math is right, he's doomed to starve to death before we can possibly help him. I'm not looking forward to the conversation."

"Fuck," Annie said, thoughtfully.

· · ·

"NOTHING? Nothing at all?" Venkat groaned. "Are you kidding me? You had twenty experts working for twelve hours on this. We have a multibillion-dollar communications network. You can't figure out *any* way to talk to him?"

The two men in Venkat's office fidgeted in their chairs.

"He's got no radio," said Chuck.

"Actually," said Morris, "he's got a radio, but he doesn't have a dish."

"Thing is," Chuck continued, "without the dish, a signal would have to be really strong—"

"Like, melting-the-pigeons strong," Morris supplied.

"—for him to get it," Chuck finished.

"We considered Martian satellites," Morris said. "They're way closer. But the math doesn't work out. Even SuperSurveyor 3, which has the strongest transmitter, would need to be fourteen times more powerful—"

"Seventeen times," Chuck said.

"Fourteen times," Morris asserted.

"No, it's seventeen. You forgot the amperage minimum for the heaters to keep the—"

"Guys," Venkat interrupted, "I get the idea."

"Sorry."

"Sorry."

"Sorry if I'm grumpy," Venkat said. "I got like two hours sleep last night."

"No problem," Morris said.

"Totally understandable," Chuck said.

"Okay," Venkat said. "Explain to me how a single windstorm removed our ability to talk to Ares 3."

"Failure of imagination," Chuck said.

"Totally didn't see it coming," Morris agreed.

"How many backup communications systems does an Ares mission have?" Venkat asked.

"Four," Chuck said.

"Three," Morris said.

"No, it's four," Chuck corrected.

"He said *backup* systems," Morris insisted. "That means not including the primary system."

"Oh right. Three."

"So four systems total, then," Venkat said. "Explain how we lost all four."

"Well," Chuck said, "The primary ran through the big satellite dish. It blew away in the storm. The rest of the backups were in the MAV."

"Yup," Morris agreed. "The MAV is, like, a communicating *machine*. It can talk to Earth, *Hermes*, even satellites around Mars if it has to. And it has three independent systems to make sure nothing short of a meteor strike can stop communication."

"Problem is," Chuck said, "Commander Lewis and the rest of them took the MAV when they left."

"So four independent communications systems became one. And that one broke," Morris finished.

Venkat pinched the bridge of his nose. "How could we overlook this?"

Chuck shrugged. "Never occurred to us. We never thought someone would be on Mars *without* an MAV."

"I mean, come on!" Morris said. "What are the odds?"

Chuck turned to him. "One in three, based on empirical data. That's pretty bad if you think about it."

...

THIS WAS going to be rough and Annie knew it. Not only did she have to deliver the biggest mea culpa in NASA's history, every second of it would be remembered forever. Every movement of her arms, intonation of her voice, and expression on her face would be seen by millions of people over and over again. Not just in the immediate press cycle, but for decades to come. Every documentary made about Watney's situation would have this clip.

She was confident that none of that concern showed on her face as she took to the podium.

"Thank you all for coming on such short notice," she said to the assembled reporters. "We have an important announcement to make. If you could all take your seats."

"What this about, Annie?" Bryan Hess from NBC asked. "Something happen with *Hermes*?"

"Please take your seats," Annie repeated.

The reporters milled about and argued over seats for a brief time, then finally settled down.

"This is a short but very important announcement," Annie said. "I won't be taking any questions at this time, but we will have a full press conference with Q&A in about an hour. We have recently reviewed satellite imagery from Mars and have confirmed that astronaut Mark Watney is, currently, still alive."

After one full second of utter silence, the room exploded with noise.

...

A WEEK after the stunning announcement, it was still the top story on every news network in the world.

"I'm getting sick of daily press conferences," Venkat whispered to Annie.

"I'm getting sick of hourly press conferences," Annie whispered back.

The two stood with countless other NASA managers and executives bunched up on the small stage in the press room. They faced a pit of hungry reporters, all desperate for any scrap of new information.

"Sorry I'm late," Teddy said, entering from the side door. He pulled some flash cards from his pocket, squared them in his hands, then cleared his throat.

"In the nine days since announcing Mark Watney's survival, we've received a massive show of support from all sectors. We're using this shamelessly every way we can."

A small chuckle cascaded through the room.

"Yesterday, at our request, the entire SETI network focused on Mars. Just in case Watney was sending a weak radio signal. Turns out he wasn't, but it shows the level of commitment everyone has toward helping us.

"The public is engaged, and we will do our best to keep everyone informed. I've recently learned CNN will be dedicating a half-hour segment every weekday to reporting on just this issue. We will assign several members of our media relations team to that program, so the public can get the latest information as fast as possible.

"We have adjusted the orbits of three satellites to get more view time on the Ares 3 site and hope to catch an image of Mark outside soon. If we can see him outside, we will be able to draw conclusions on his physical health based on stance and activities.

"The questions are many: How long can he last? How much food does he have? Can Ares 4 rescue him? How will we talk to him? The answers to these questions are not what we want to hear.

"I can't promise we'll succeed in rescuing him, but I can promise this: The entire focus of NASA will be to bring Mark Watney home. This will be our overriding and singular obsession until he is either back on Earth or confirmed dead on Mars."

...

"NICE SPEECH," Venkat said as he entered Teddy's office.

"Meant every word of it," Teddy said.

"Oh, I know."

"What can I do for you, Venk?"

"I've got an idea. Well, JPL has an idea. I'm the messenger."

"I like ideas," Teddy said, gesturing to a seat.

Venkat sat down.

"We can rescue him with Ares 4. It's very risky. We ran the idea by the Ares 4 crew. Not only are they willing to do it, but now they're really pushing hard for it."

"Naturally," Teddy said. "Astronauts are inherently insane. And really noble. What's the idea?"

"Well," Venkat began, "it's in the rough stages, but JPL thinks the MDV can be misused to save him."

"Ares 4 hasn't even launched yet. Why misuse an MDV? Why not make something better?"

"We don't have time to make a custom craft. Actually, he can't even survive till Ares 4 gets there, but that's a different problem."

"So tell me about the MDV."

"JPL strips it down, loses some weight, and adds some fuel tanks. Ares 4's crew lands at the Ares 3 site, very efficiently. Then, with a full burn, and I mean a *full* burn, they can lift off again. It can't get back to orbit, but it can go to the Ares 4 site on a lateral trajectory that's, well, really scary. Then they have an MAV."

"How are they losing weight?" Teddy asked. "Don't they already have it as light as it can be?"

"By removing safety and emergency equipment."

"Wonderful," Teddy said. "So we'd be risking the lives of six more people."

"Yup," Venkat said. "It would be safer to leave the Ares 4 crew in *Hermes* and only send the pilot down with the MDV. But that would mean giving up the mission, and they'd rather risk death."

"They're astronauts," Teddy said.

"They're astronauts," Venkat confirmed.

"Well. That's a ludicrous idea and I'll never okay it."

"We'll work on it some more," Venkat said. "Try to make it safer."

"Do that. Any idea how to keep him alive for four years?"

"Nope."

"Work on that, too."

"Will do," Venkat said.

Teddy swiveled his chair and looked out the window to the sky beyond. Night was edging in. "What must it be like?" he pondered. "He's stuck out there. He thinks he's totally alone and that we all gave up on him. What kind of effect does that have on a man's psychology?"

He turned back to Venkat. "I wonder what he's thinking right now."

LOG ENTRY: SOL 61

How come Aquaman can control whales? They're mammals! Makes no sense.

CHAPTER 7

LOG ENTRY: SOL 63

I finished making water some time ago. I'm no longer in danger of blowing myself up. The potatoes are growing nicely. Nothing has conspired to kill me in weeks. And seventies TV keeps me disturbingly more entertained than it should. Things are stable here on Mars.

It's time to start thinking long-term.

Even if I find a way to tell NASA I'm alive, there's no guarantee they'll be able to save me. I need to be proactive. I need to figure out how to get to Ares 4.

Won't be easy.

Ares 4 will be landing at the Schiaparelli crater, 3200 kilometers away. In fact, their MAV is already there. I know because I watched Martinez land it.

It takes eighteen months for the MAV to make its fuel, so it's the first thing NASA sends along. Sending it forty-eight months early gives it plenty of extra time in case fuel reactions go slower than expected. But much more importantly, it means a precision soft landing can be done remotely by a pilot in orbit. Direct remote operation from Houston isn't an option; they're anywhere from four to twenty light-minutes away.

Ares 4's MAV spent eleven months getting to Mars. It left before us and got here around the same time we did. As expected, Martinez landed it beautifully. It was one of the last things we did before piling into our MDV and heading to the surface. Ahh, the good old days, when I had a crew with me.

I'm lucky. Thirty-two hundred km isn't that bad. It could have been up to 10,000 km away. And because I'm on the flattest part of Mars, the first 650 kilometers is nice, smooth terrain (Yay Acidalia Planitia!) but the rest of it is nasty, rugged, crater-pocked hell.

Obviously, I'll have to use a rover. And guess what? They weren't designed for massive overland journeys.

This is going to be a research effort, with a bunch of experimentation. I'll have to become my own little NASA, figuring out how to explore far from the Hab. The good news is I have lots of time to figure it out. Almost four years.

Some stuff is obvious. I'll need to use a rover. It'll take a long time, so I'll need to bring supplies. I'll need to recharge en route, and rovers don't have solar cells, so I'll need to steal some from the Hab's solar farm. During the trip I'll need to breathe, eat, and drink.

Lucky for me, the tech specs for everything are right here in the computer.

I'll need to trick out a rover. Basically it'll have to be a mobile Hab. I'll pick Rover 2 as my target. We have a certain bond, after I spent two days in it during the Great Hydrogen Scare of Sol 37.

There's too much shit to think about all at once. So for now, I'll just think about power.

Our mission had a 10-kilometer operational radius. Knowing we wouldn't take straight-line paths, NASA designed the rovers to go 35 kilometers on a full charge. That presumes flat, reasonable terrain. Each rover has a 9000-watt-hour battery.

Step one is to loot Rover 1's battery and install it in Rover 2. Ta-daa! I just doubled my full-charge range.

There's just one complication. Heating.

Part of the battery power goes to heating the rover. Mars is really cold. Normally, we were expected to do all EVAs in under five hours. But I'll be living in it twenty-four and a half hours a day. According to the specs, the heating equipment soaks up 400 watts. Keeping it on would eat up 9800 watt hours per day. Over half my power supply, every day!

But I do have a free source of heat: me. A couple million years of evolution gave me "warm-blooded" technology. I can just turn off the heater and wear layers. The rover has good insulation, too. It'll have to be enough; I need every bit of power.

According to my boring math, moving the rover eats 200 watt hours of juice to go 1 kilometer, so using the full 18,000 watt hours for motion (minus a negligible amount for computer, life support, etc.) gets me 90 kilometers of travel. Now we're talkin'.

I'll never *actually* get 90 kilometers on a single charge. I'll have hills to deal with, and rough terrain, sand, etc. But it's a good ball-park. It tells me that it would take *at least* 35 days of travel to get to Ares 4. It'll probably be more like 50. But that's plausible, at least.

At the rover's blazing 25 kph top speed, it'll take me three and a half hours before I run the battery down. I can drive in twilight, and save the sunny part of the day for charging. This time of year I get about thirteen hours of light. How many solar cells will I have to pilfer from the Hab's farm?

Thanks to the fine taxpayers of America, I have over 100 square meters of the most expensive solar paneling ever made. It has an astounding 10.2 percent efficiency, which is good because Mars doesn't get as much sunlight as Earth. Only 500 to 700 watts per square meter (compared to the 1400 Earth gets).

Long story short: I need to bring twenty-eight square meters of solar cell. That's fourteen panels.

I can put two stacks of seven on the roof. They'll stick out over the edges, but as long as they're secure, I'm happy. Every day, after driving, I'll spread them out then . . . wait all day. Man it'll be dull.

Well it's a start. Tomorrow's mission: transfer Rover 1's battery to Rover 2.

LOG ENTRY: SOL 64

Sometimes things are easy, and sometimes they're not. Getting the battery out of Rover 1 was easy. I removed two clamps on the undercarriage and it dropped right out. The cabling was easy to detach, too, just a couple of complicated plugs.

Attaching it to Rover 2, however, is another story. There's nowhere to put it!

The thing is *huge*. I was barely able to drag it. And that's in Mars gravity.

It's just too big. There's no room in the undercarriage for a second one. There's no room on the roof, either. That's where the solar cells will go. There's no room inside the cabin, and it wouldn't fit through the airlock anyway.

But fear not, I found a solution.

For emergencies completely unrelated to this one, NASA provided six square meters of extra Hab canvas and some really impressive resin. The same kind of resin, in fact, that saved my life on Sol 6 (the patch kit I used on the hole in my suit).

In the event of a Hab breach, everyone would run to the airlocks. Procedure was to let the Hab pop rather than die trying to prevent it. Then, we'd suit up and assess the damage. Once we found the breach, we'd seal it with the spare canvas and resin. Then reinflate and we're good as new.

The six square meters of spare canvas was a convenient one by six meters. I cut 10-centimeter-wide strips, then used them to make a sort of harness.

I used the resin and straps to make two 10-meter circumference loops. Then I put a big patch of canvas on each end. I now had poor man's saddlebags for my rover.

This is getting more and more *Wagon Train* every day.

The resin sets almost instantly. But it gets stronger if you wait an hour. So I did. Then I suited up and headed out to the rover.

I dragged the battery to the side of the rover and looped one end of the harness around it. Then I threw the other end over the roof. On the other side, I filled it with rocks. When the two weights were roughly equal, I was able to pull the rocks down and bring the battery up.

Yay!

I unplugged Rover 2's battery and plugged in Rover 1's. Then I went through the airlock to the rover and checked all systems. Everything was a-okay.

I drove the rover around a bit to make sure the harness was secure. I found a few largish rocks to drive over, just to shake things up. The harness held. Hell yeah.

For a short time, I wondered how to splice the second battery's leads into the main power supply. My conclusion was "Fuck it."

There's no need to have a continuous power supply. When Battery 1 runs out, I can get out, unplug Battery 1, and plug in Battery 2. Why not? It's a ten-minute EVA, once per day. I'd have to swap batteries again when I'm recharging them, but again, so what?

I spent the rest of the day sweeping off the solar cell farm. Soon, I shall be looting it.

LOG ENTRY: SOL 65

The solar cells were a lot easier to manage than the battery.

They're thin, light, and just lying around on the ground. And I had one additional bonus: I was the one who set them up in the first place.

Well, okay. It wasn't just me. Vogel and I worked together on it. And boy did we drill on it. We spent almost an entire *week* drilling on the solar array alone. Then we drilled more whenever they figured we had spare time. The array was mission-critical. If we broke the cells or rendered them useless, the Hab wouldn't be able to make power, and the mission would end.

You might wonder what the rest of the crew was doing while we assembled the array. They were setting up the Hab. Remember, everything in my glorious kingdom came here in boxes. We had to set it up on Sols 1 and 2.

Each solar cell is on a lightweight lattice that holds it at a 14-degree angle. I'll admit I don't know why it's a 14-degree angle. Something about maximizing solar energy. Anyway, removing the cells was simple, and the Hab can spare them. With the reduced load of only supporting one human instead of six, a 14 percent energy production loss is irrelevant.

Then it was time to stack them on the rover.

I considered removing the rock sample container. It's nothing more than a large canvas bag attached to the roof. Way too small to hold the solar cells. But after some thought I left it there, figuring it would provide a good cushion.

The cells stacked well (they were made to, for transport to Mars), and the two stacks sat nicely on the roof. They hung over the left and right edges, but I won't be going through any tunnels, so I don't care.

With some more abuse of the emergency Hab material, I made straps and tied the cells down. The rover has external handles near the front and back. They're there to help us load rocks on the roof. They made perfect anchor points for the straps.

I stood back and admired my work. Hey, I earned it. It wasn't even noon and I was done.

I came back to the Hab, had some lunch, and worked on my crops for the rest of the sol. It's been thirty-nine sols since I planted the potatoes (which is about forty Earth days), and it was time to reap and resow.

They grew even better than I had expected. Mars has no insects, parasites, or blights to deal with, and the Hab maintains perfect growing temperature and moisture at all times.

They were small compared to the taters you'd usually eat, but that's fine. All I wanted was enough to support growing new plants.

I dug them up, being careful to leave their plants alive. Then I cut them up into small pieces with one eye each and reseeded them into new dirt. If they keep growing this well, I'll be able to last a good long time here.

After all that physical labor, I deserved a break. I rifled through Johanssen's computer today and found an endless supply of digital books. Looks like she's a big fan of Agatha Christie. The Beatles, Christie . . . I guess she's an Anglophile or something.

I remember liking Hercule Poirot TV specials back when I was a kid. I'll start with *The Mysterious Affair at Styles*. Looks like that's the first one.

LOG ENTRY: SOL 66

The time has come (ominous musical crescendo) for some missions!

NASA gets to name their missions after gods and stuff, so why can't I? Henceforth, rover experimental missions will be "Sirius" missions. Get it? Dogs? Well if you don't, fuck you.

Sirius 1 will be tomorrow.

The mission: Start with fully charged batteries and solar cells on the roof, drive until I run out of power, and see how far I get.

I won't be an idiot. I'm not driving directly away from the Hab. I'll drive a half-kilometer stretch, back and forth. I'll be within a short walk of home at all times.

Tonight, I'll charge up both batteries so I can be ready for a little test drive tomorrow. I estimate three and a half hours of driving, so I'll need to bring fresh CO_2 filters. And, with the heater off, I'll wear three layers of clothes.

LOG ENTRY: SOL 67

Sirius 1 is complete!

More accurately, Sirius 1 was aborted after one hour. I guess you could call it a "failure," but I prefer the term "learning experience."

Things started out fine. I drove to a nice flat spot a kilometer from the Hab, then started going back and forth over a 500-meter stretch.

I quickly realized this would be a crappy test. After a few laps, I had compressed the soil enough to have a solid path. Nice, hard ground, which makes for abnormally high energy efficiency. Nothing like it would be on a long trip.

So I shook it up a bit. I drove around randomly, making sure to stay within a kilometer of the Hab. A much more realistic test.

After an hour, things started to get cold. And I mean *really cold*.

The rover's always cold when you first get in it. When you haven't disabled the heater, it warms up right away. I expected it to be cold, but Jesus Christ!

I was fine for a while. My own body heat plus three layers of clothing kept me warm, and the rover's insulation is top-notch. The heat that escaped my body just warmed up the interior. But there's no such thing as perfect insulation, and eventually the heat left to the great outdoors, while I got colder and colder.

Within an hour, I was chattering and numb. Enough was enough. There's no way I could do a long trip like this.

Turning the heater on, I drove straight back to the Hab.

Once I got home, I sulked for a while. All my brilliant plans foiled by thermodynamics. Damn you, Entropy!

I'm in a bind. The damn heater will eat half my battery power every day. I could turn it down, I guess. Be a little cold but not freezing to death. Even then I'd still lose at least a quarter.

This will require some thought. I have to ask myself . . . What would Hercule Poirot do? I'll have to put my "little gray cells" to work on the problem.

LOG ENTRY: SOL 68

Well, shit.

I came up with a solution, but . . . remember when I burned rocket fuel in the Hab? This'll be more dangerous.

I'm going to use the RTG.

The RTG (radioisotope thermoelectric generator) is a big box of plutonium. But not the kind used in nuclear bombs. No, no. This plutonium is *way* more dangerous!

Plutonium-238 is an incredibly unstable isotope. It's so radio-active that it will get red hot all by itself. As you can imagine, a material that can *literally fry an egg* with radiation is kind of dangerous.

The RTG houses the plutonium, catches the radiation in the form of heat, and turns it into electricity. It's not a reactor. The radiation can't be increased or decreased. It's a purely natural process happening at the atomic level.

As long ago as the 1960s, NASA began using RTGs to power unmanned probes. They have lots of advantages over solar power. They're not affected by storms; they work day or night; they're entirely internal, so you don't need delicate solar cells all over your probe.

But they never used large RTGs on manned missions until the Ares Program.

Why not? It should be pretty damned obvious why not! They didn't want to put astronauts next to a glowing hot ball of radio-active death!

I'm exaggerating a little. The plutonium is inside a bunch of pellets, each one sealed and insulated to prevent radiation leakage, even if the outer container is breached. So for the Ares Program, they took the risk.

An Ares mission is all about the MAV. It's the single most important component. It's one of the few systems that can't be replaced or worked around. It's the *only* component that causes a complete mission scrub if it's not working.

Solar cells are great in the short term, and they're good for the long term if you have humans around to clean them. But the MAV sits alone for years quietly making fuel, then just kind of hangs out until its crew arrives. Even doing nothing, it needs power, so NASA can monitor it remotely and run self-checks.

The prospect of scrubbing a mission because a solar cell got dirty was unacceptable. They needed a more reliable source of power. So the MAV comes equipped with an RTG. It has 2.6 kilograms of plutonium-238, which makes almost 1500 watts of heat. It can turn that into 100 watts of electricity. The MAV runs on that until the crew arrive.

One hundred watts isn't enough to keep the heater going, but I don't care about the electrical output. I want the heat. A 1500-watt heater is so warm I'll have to tear insulation out of the rover to keep it from getting too hot.

As soon as the rovers were unstowed and activated, Commander Lewis had the joy of disposing of the RTG. She detached it from the MAV, drove four kilometers away, and buried it. However safe it may be, it's still a radioactive core and NASA didn't want it too close to their astronauts.

The mission parameters don't give a specific location to dump the RTG. Just "at least four kilometers away." So I'll have to find it.

I have two things working for me. First, I was assembling solar panels with Vogel when Commander Lewis drove off, and I saw she headed due south. Also, she planted a three-meter pole with a bright green flag over where she buried it. Green shows up extremely well against the Martian terrain. It's made to ward us off, in case we get lost on a rover EVA later on.

So my plan is: Head south four kilometers, then search around till I see the green flag.

Having rendered Rover 1 unusable, I'll have to use my mutant rover for the trip. I can make a useful test mission of it. I'll see how well the battery harness holds up to a real journey, and how well the solar cells do strapped to the roof.

I'll call it Sirius 2.

LOG ENTRY: SOL 69

I'm no stranger to Mars. I've been here a long time. But I've never been out of sight of the Hab before today. You wouldn't think that would make a difference, but it does.

As I made my way toward the RTG's burial site, it hit me: Mars is a barren wasteland and I am *completely* alone here. I already knew that, of course. But there's a difference between knowing it and really experiencing it. All around me there was nothing but dust, rocks, and endless empty desert in all directions. The planet's famous red color is from iron oxide coating everything. So it's not just a desert. It's a desert so old it's literally rusting.

The Hab is my only hint of civilization, and seeing it disappear made me way more uncomfortable than I like to admit.

I put those thoughts behind me by concentrating on what was in front of me. I found the RTG right where it was supposed to be, four kilometers due south of the Hab.

It wasn't hard to find. Commander Lewis had buried it atop a small hill. She probably wanted to make sure everyone could see the flag, and it worked great! Except instead of avoiding it, I bee-lined to it and dug it up. Not exactly what she was going for.

It was a large cylinder with heat-sinks all around it. I could feel the warmth it gave off even through my suit's gloves. That's really disconcerting. Especially when you know the root cause of the heat is radiation.

No point in putting it on the roof; my plan was to have it in the cabin anyway. So I brought it in with me, turned off the heater, then drove back to the Hab.

In the ten minutes it took to get home, even with the heater off, the interior of the rover became an uncomfortably hot 37°C. The RTG would definitely be able to keep me warm.

The trip also proved that my rigging worked. The solar cells and extra battery stayed beautifully in place while traversing eight kilometers of random terrain.

I declare Sirius 2 to be a successful mission!

I spent the rest of the day vandalizing the interior of the rover. The pressure compartment is made of carbon composite. Just inside that is insulation, which is covered by hard plastic. I used a sophisticated method to remove sections of plastic (hammer), then carefully removed the solid foam insulation (hammer again).

After tearing out some insulation, I suited up and took the RTG outside. Soon, the rover cooled down again, and I brought it back in. I watched as the temperature rose slowly. Nowhere near as fast as it had on my trip back from the burial site.

I cautiously removed more insulation (hammer) and checked again. After a few more cycles of this, I had enough insulation torn out that the RTG could barely keep up with it. In fact, it was a losing battle. Over time, heat will slowly leach out. That's fine. I can turn on the heater for short bursts when necessary.

I brought the insulation pieces with me back into the Hab. Using advanced construction techniques (duct tape), I reassembled some of them into a square. I figure if things ever get really cold, I can tape that to a bare patch in the rover, and the RTG will be winning the "heat fight."

Tomorrow, Sirius 3 (which is just Sirius 1 again, but without freezing).

Today, I write to you from the rover. I'm halfway through Sirius 3 and things are going well.

I set out at first light and drove laps around the Hab, trying to stay on untouched ground. The first battery lasted just under two hours. After a quick EVA to switch the cables, I got back to driving. When all was said and done, I had driven 81 kilometers in 3 hours and 27 minutes.

That's *very* good! Mind you, the land around the Hab is really flat, as is all of Acidalia Planitia. I have no idea what my efficiency would be on the nastier land en route to Ares 4.

The second battery still had a little juice left, but I can't just run it down all the way before I stop; remember, I need life support while recharging. The CO_2 gets absorbed through a chemical process, but if the fan that pushes it isn't working, I'll choke. The oxygen pump is also kind of important.

After my drive, I set up the solar cells. It was hard work; last time I had Vogel's help. They aren't heavy, but they're awkward. After setting up half of them, I figured out I could drag them rather than carry them, and that sped things up.

Now I'm just waiting for the batteries to recharge. I'm bored, so I'm updating the log. I have all the Poirot books in my computer. That'll help. It's going to take twelve hours to recharge, after all.

What's that, you say? Twelve hours is wrong? I said thirteen hours earlier? Well, my friend, let me set you straight.

The RTG is a *generator*. It's a paltry amount of power, compared to what the rover consumes, but it's not nothing. It's one hundred watts. It'll cut an hour off my total recharge time. Why not use it?

I wonder what NASA would think about me fucking with the RTG like this. They'd probably hide under their desks and cuddle with their slide rules for comfort.

As predicted, it took twelve hours to charge the batteries to full. I came straight home as soon as they were done.

Time to make plans for Sirius 4. And I think it'll be a multiday field trip.

Looks like power and battery recharging are solved. Food's not a problem; there's plenty of space to store things. Water's even easier than food. I need two liters per day to be comfortable.

When I do my trip to Ares 4 for real, I'll need to bring the oxygenator. But it's big and I don't want to screw with it right now. So I'll rely on O_2 and CO_2 filters for Sirius 4.

CO_2 isn't a problem. I started this grand adventure with 1500 hours of CO_2 filters, plus another 720 for emergency use. All systems use standard filters (Apollo 13 taught us important lessons). Since then, I've used 131 hours of filter on various EVAs. I have 2089 left. Eighty-seven days' worth. Plenty.

Oxygen's a little trickier. The rover was designed to support three people for two days, plus some reserve for safety. So its O_2 tanks can hold enough to last me seven days. Not enough.

Mars has almost no atmospheric pressure. The inside of the rover has one atmosphere. So the oxygen tanks are on the inside (less pressure differential to deal with). Why does that matter? It means I can bring along other oxygen tanks, and equalize them with the rover's tanks without having to do an EVA.

So today, I detached one of the Hab's two 25-liter liquid oxygen tanks and brought it into the rover. According to NASA, a human needs 588 liters of oxygen per day to live. Compressed liquid O_2 is about 1000 times as dense as gaseous O_2 in a comfortable atmosphere. Long story short: With the Hab tank, I have enough O_2 to last 49 days. That'll be plenty.

Sirius 4 will be a twenty-day trip.

That may seem a bit long, but I have a specific goal in mind.

Besides, my trip to Ares 4 will be at least forty days. This is a good scale model.

While I'm away, the Hab can take care of itself, but the potatoes are an issue. I'll saturate the ground with most of the water I have. Then, I'll deactivate the atmospheric regulator, so it doesn't pull water out of the air. It'll be humid as hell, and water will condense on every surface. That'll keep the potatoes well watered while I'm away.

A bigger problem is CO_2. The potatoes need to breathe. I know what you're thinking. "Mark, old chap! *You* produce carbon dioxide! It's all part of the majestic circle of nature!"

The problem is: Where will I put it? Sure, I exhale CO_2 with every breath, but I don't have any way to store it. I could turn off the oxygenator and atmospheric regulator and just fill the Hab with my breath over time. But CO_2 is deadly to me. I need to release a bunch at once and run away.

Remember the MAV fuel plant? It collects CO_2 from the Martian atmosphere. A 10-liter tank of compressed liquid CO_2, vented into the Hab, will be enough CO_2 to do the trick. That'll take less than a day to create.

So that's everything. Once I vent the CO_2 into the Hab, I'll turn off the atmospheric regulator and oxygenator, dump a ton of water on the crops, and head out.

Sirius 4. A huge step forward in my rover research. And I can start tomorrow.

CHAPTER 8

"HELLO, AND thank you for joining us," Cathy Warner said to the camera. "Today on CNN's *Mark Watney Report*: Several EVAs over the past few days . . . what do they mean? What progress has NASA made on a rescue option? And how will this affect the Ares 4 preparations?

"Joining us today is Dr. Venkat Kapoor, director of Mars operations for NASA. Dr. Kapoor, thank you for coming."

"A pleasure to be here, Cathy," Venkat said.

"Dr. Kapoor," Cathy said, "Mark Watney is the most-watched man in the solar system, wouldn't you say?"

Venkat nodded. "Certainly the most watched by NASA. We have all twelve of our Martian satellites taking pictures whenever his site's in view. The European Space Agency has both of theirs doing the same."

"All told, how often do you get these images?"

"Every few minutes. Sometimes there's a gap, based on the satellite orbits. But it's enough that we can track all his EVA activities."

"Tell us about these latest EVAs."

"Well," Venkat said, "it looks like he's preparing Rover 2 for a long trip. On Sol 64, he took the battery from the other rover and attached it with a homemade sling. The next day, he detached fourteen solar cells and stacked them on the rover's roof."

"And then he took a little drive, didn't he?" Cathy prompted.

"Yes he did. Sort of aimlessly for an hour, then back to the Hab. He was probably testing it. Next time we saw him was two days later, when he drove four kilometers away, then back. Another incremental test, we think. Then, over the past couple of days, he's been stocking it up with supplies."

"Hmm," Cathy said, "most analysts think Mark's only hope of rescue is to get to the Ares 4 site. Do you think he's come to the same conclusion?"

"Probably," Venkat said. "He doesn't know we're watching. From his point of view, Ares 4 is his only hope."

"Do you think he's planning to go soon? He seems to be getting ready for a trip."

"I hope not," Venkat said. "There's nothing at the site other than the MAV. None of the other presupplies. It would be a very long, very dangerous trip, and he'd be leaving the safety of the Hab behind."

"Why would he risk it?"

"Communication," Venkat said. "Once he reaches the MAV, he could contact us."

"So that would be a good thing, wouldn't it?"

"Communication would be a *great* thing. But traversing thirty-two hundred kilometers to Ares 4 is incredibly dangerous. We'd rather he stayed put. If we could talk to him, we'd certainly tell him that."

"He can't stay put forever, right? Eventually he'll need to get to the MAV."

"Not necessarily," Venkat said. "JPL is experimenting with modifications to the MDV so it can make a brief overland flight after landing."

"I'd heard that idea was rejected as being too dangerous," Cathy said.

"Their first proposal was, yes. Since then, they've been working on safer ways to do it."

"With only three and a half years before Ares 4's scheduled launch, is there enough time to make and test modifications to the MDV?"

"I can't answer that for sure. But remember, we made a lunar lander from scratch in seven years."

"Excellent point." Cathy smiled. "So what are his odds right now?"

"No idea," Venkat said. "But we're going to do everything we can to bring him home alive."

■ ■ ■

MINDY GLANCED nervously around the conference room. She'd never felt so thoroughly outranked in her life. Dr. Venkat Kapoor, who was four levels of management above her, sat to her left.

Next to him was Bruce Ng, the director of JPL. He'd flown all the way to Houston from Pasadena just for this meeting. Never one to let precious time go to waste, he typed furiously on his laptop. The dark bags under his eyes made Mindy wonder just how over-worked he truly was.

Mitch Henderson, the flight director for Ares 3, swiveled back and forth in his chair, a wireless earpiece in his ear. It fed him a real-time stream of all the comm chatter from Mission Control. He wasn't on shift, but he was kept apprised at all times.

Annie Montrose entered the conference room, texting as she walked. Never taking her eyes off her phone, she deftly navigated around the edge of the room, avoiding people and chairs, and sat in her usual spot. Mindy felt a pang of envy as she watched the director of media relations. She was everything Mindy wanted to be. Confident, high-ranking, beautiful, and universally respected within NASA.

"How'd I do today?" Venkat asked.

"Eeeh," Annie said, putting her phone away. "You shouldn't say things like 'bring him home alive.' It reminds people he might die."

"Think they're going to forget that?"

"You asked my opinion. Don't like it? Go fuck yourself."

"You're such a delicate flower, Annie. How'd you end up NASA's director of media relations?"

"Beats the fuck out of me," Annie said.

"Guys," Bruce said, "I need to catch a flight back to LA in three hours. Is Teddy coming or what?"

"Quit bitching, Bruce," Annie said. "None of us want to be here."

Mitch turned the volume down on his earpiece and faced Mindy. "Who are you, again?"

"Um," Mindy said, "I'm Mindy Park. I work in SatCon."

"You a director or something?"

"No, I just work in SatCon. I'm a nobody."

Venkat looked to Mitch. "I put her in charge of tracking Watney. She gets us the imagery."

"Huh," said Mitch. "Not the director of SatCon?"

"Bob's got more to deal with than just Mars. Mindy's handling all the Martian satellites, and keeps them pointed at Mark."

"Why Mindy?" Mitch asked.

"She noticed he was alive in the first place."

"She gets a promotion 'cause she was in the hot seat when the imagery came through?"

"No," Venkat frowned, "she gets a promotion 'cause she figured out he was alive. Stop being a jerk, Mitch. You're making her feel bad."

Mitch raised his eyebrows. "Didn't think of that. Sorry, Mindy."

Mindy looked at the table and managed to say, "'kay."

Teddy entered the room. "Sorry I'm late." He took his seat and pulled several folders from his briefcase. Stacking them neatly, he opened the top one and squared the pages within. "Let's get started. Venkat, what's Watney's status?"

"Alive and well," Venkat said. "No change from my e-mail earlier today."

"What about the RTG? Does the public know about that yet?" Teddy asked.

Annie leaned forward. "So far, so good," she said. "The images are public, but we have no obligation to tell them our analysis. Nobody has figured it out yet."

"Why did he dig it up?"

"Heat, I think," Venkat said. "He wants to make the rover do long trips. It uses a lot of energy keeping warm. The RTG can heat up the interior without soaking battery power. It's a good idea, really."

"How dangerous is it?" Teddy asked.

"As long as the container's intact, no danger at all. Even if it cracks open, he'll be okay if the pellets inside don't break. But if the pellets break, too, he's a dead man."

"Let's hope that doesn't happen," Teddy said. "JPL, how are the MDV plans coming along?"

"We came up with a plan a long time ago," Bruce said. "You rejected it."

"Bruce," Teddy cautioned.

Bruce sighed. "The MDV wasn't made for liftoff and lateral flight. Packing more fuel in doesn't help. We'd need a bigger engine and don't have time to invent one. So we need to lighten the MDV. We have an idea for that.

"The MDV can be its normal weight on primary descent. If we made the heat shield and outer hull detachable, they could ditch a lot of weight after landing at Ares 3, and have a lighter ship for the traverse to Ares 4. We're running the numbers now."

"Keep me posted," Teddy said. He turned to Mindy. "Miss Park, welcome to the big leagues."

"Sir," Mindy said. She tried to ignore the lump in her throat.

"What's the biggest gap in coverage we have on Watney right now?"

"Um," Mindy said. "Once every forty-one hours, we'll have a seventeen-minute gap. The orbits work out that way."

"You had an immediate answer," Teddy said. "Good. I like it when people are organized."

"Thank you, sir."

"I want that gap down to four minutes," Teddy said. "I'm giving you total authority over satellite trajectories and orbital adjustments. Make it happen."

"Yes, sir," Mindy said, with no idea how to do it.

Teddy looked to Mitch. "Mitch, your e-mail said you had something urgent?"

"Yeah," Mitch said. "How long are we gonna keep this from the Ares 3 crew? They all think Watney's dead. It's a huge drain on morale."

Teddy looked to Venkat.

"Mitch," Venkat said. "We discussed this—"

"No, *you* discussed it," Mitch interrupted. "They think they lost a crewmate. They're devastated."

"And when they find out they *abandoned* a crewmate?" Venkat asked. "Will they feel better then?"

Mitch poked the table with his finger. "They deserve to know. You think Commander Lewis can't handle the truth?"

"It's a matter of morale," Venkat said. "They can concentrate on getting home—"

"I make that call," Mitch said. "I'm the one who decides what's best for the crew. And I say we bring them up to speed."

After a few moments of silence, all eyes turned to Teddy.

He thought for a moment. "Sorry, Mitch, I'm with Venkat on this one," he said. "But as soon as we come up with a plan for rescue, we can tell *Hermes*. There needs to be some hope, or there's no point in telling them."

"Bullshit," Mitch grumbled, crossing his arms. "Total bullshit."

"I know you're upset," Teddy said calmly, "We'll make it right. Just as soon as we have some idea how to save Watney."

Teddy let a few seconds of quiet pass before moving on.

"Okay, JPL's on the rescue option," he said with a nod toward Bruce. "But it would be part of Ares 4. How does he stay alive till then? Venkat?"

Venkat opened a folder and glanced at the paperwork inside. "I had every team check and double-check the longevity of their systems. We're pretty sure the Hab can keep working for four years. Especially with a human occupant fixing problems as they arise. But there's no way around the food issue. He'll start starving in a year. We *have* to send him supplies. Simple as that."

"What about an Ares 4 presupply?" said Teddy. "Land it at Ares 3 instead."

"That's what we're thinking, yeah," Venkat confirmed. "Problem is, the original plan was to launch presupplies a year from now. They're not ready yet.

"It takes eight months to get a probe to Mars in the best of times. The positions of Earth and Mars right now . . . it's not the best of times. We figure we can get there in nine months. Presuming he's rationing his food, he's got enough to last three hundred and fifty more days. That means we need to build a presupply in *three months*. JPL hasn't even started yet."

"That'll be tight," Bruce said. "Making a presupply is a six-month process. We're set up to pipeline a bunch of them at once, not to make one in a hurry."

"Sorry, Bruce," Teddy said. "I know we're asking a lot, but you have to find a way."

"We'll find a way," Bruce said. "But the OT alone will be a nightmare."

"Get started. I'll find you the money."

"There's also the booster," Venkat said. "The only way to get a probe to Mars with the planets in their current positions is to spend a butt-load of fuel. We only have one booster capable of doing that. The Delta IX that's on the pad right now for the EagleEye 3 Saturn probe. We'll have to steal that. I talked to ULA, and they just can't make another booster in time."

"The EagleEye 3 team will be pissed, but okay," said Teddy. "We can delay their mission if JPL gets the payload done in time."

Bruce rubbed his eyes. "We'll do our best."

"He'll starve to death if you don't," Teddy said.

...

VENKAT SIPPED his coffee and frowned at his computer. A month ago it would have been unthinkable to drink coffee at nine p.m. Now it was necessary fuel. Shift schedules, fund allocations, project juggling, out-and-out looting of other projects . . . he'd never pulled so many stunts in his life.

"*NASA's a large organization,*" he typed. "*It doesn't deal with sudden change well. The only reason we're getting away with it is the desperate circumstances. Everyone's pulling together to save Mark Watney, with no interdepartmental squabbling. I can't tell you how rare that is. Even then, this is going to cost tens of millions, maybe hundreds of millions of dollars. The MDV modifications alone are an entire project that's being staffed up. Hopefully, the public interest will make your job easier. We appreciate your continued support, Congressman, and hope you can sway the committee toward granting us the emergency funding we need.*"

He was interrupted by a knock at his door. Looking up, he saw Mindy. She wore sweats and a T-shirt, her hair in a sloppy ponytail. Fashion tended to suffer when work hours ran long.

"Sorry to bother you," Mindy said.

"No bother," Venkat said. "I could use a break. What's up?"

"He's on the move," she said.

Venkat slouched in his chair. "Any chance it's a test drive?"

She shook her head. "He drove straightaway from the Hab for almost two hours, did a short EVA, then drove for another two. We think the EVA was to change batteries."

Venkat sighed heavily. "Maybe it's just a longer test? An overnight trip kind of thing?"

"He's seventy-six kilometers from the Hab," Mindy said. "For an overnight test, wouldn't he stay within walking distance?"

"Yes, he would," Venkat said. "Damn it. We've had teams run every conceivable scenario. There's just no way he can make it to Ares 4 with that setup. We never saw him load up the oxygenator or water reclaimer. He can't possibly have enough basics to live long enough."

"I don't think he's going to Ares 4," Mindy said. "If he is, he's taking a weird path."

"Oh?" said Venkat.

"He went south-southwest. Schiaparelli crater is southeast."

"Okay, maybe there's hope," Venkat said. "What's he doing right now?"

"Recharging. He's got all the solar cells set up," Mindy said. "Last time he did that, it took twelve hours. I was going to sneak home for some sleep if that's okay."

"Sure, sounds good. We'll see what he does tomorrow. Maybe he'll go back to the Hab."

"Maybe," Mindy said, unconvinced.

· · ·

"WELCOME BACK," Cathy said to the camera. "We're chatting with Marcus Washington, from the US Postal Service. So, Mr. Washington, I understand the Ares 3 mission caused a postal service first. Can you explain that to our viewers?"

"Uh yeah," said Marcus. "Everyone thought Mark Watney was

dead for over two months. In that time, the postal service issued a run of commemorative stamps honoring his memory. Twenty thousand were printed and sent to post offices around the country."

"And then it turned out he was alive," Cathy said.

"Yeah," said Marcus. "We don't print stamps of living people. So we stopped the run immediately and recalled the stamps, but thousands were already sold."

"Has this ever happened before?" Cathy asked.

"No. Not once in the history of the postal service."

"I bet they're worth a pretty penny now."

Marcus chuckled. "Maybe. But like I said, thousands were sold. They'll be rare, but not super-rare."

Cathy chuckled then addressed the camera. "We've been speaking with Marcus Washington of the United States Postal Service. If you've got a Mark Watney commemorative stamp, you might want to hold on to it. Thanks for dropping by, Mr. Washington."

"Thanks for having me," Marcus said.

"Our next guest is Dr. Irene Shields, flight psychologist for the Ares missions. Dr. Shields, welcome to the program."

"Thank you," Irene said, adjusting her microphone clip.

"Do you know Mark Watney personally?"

"Of course," Irene said. "I did monthly psych evaluations on each member of the crew."

"What can you tell us about him? His personality, his mind-set?"

"Well," Irene said, "he's very intelligent. All of them are, of course. But he's particularly resourceful and a good problem-solver."

"That may save his life," Cathy interjected.

"It may indeed," Irene agreed. "Also, he's a good-natured man. Usually cheerful, with a great sense of humor. He's quick with a joke. In the months leading up to launch, the crew was put through a grueling training schedule. They all showed signs of stress and moodiness. Mark was no exception, but the *way* he showed it was to crack more jokes and get everyone laughing."

"He sounds like a great guy," Cathy said.

"He really is," Irene said. "He was chosen for the mission in part because of his personality. An Ares crew has to spend thirteen months together. Social compatibility is key. Mark not only fits well in any social group, he's a catalyst to make the group work better. It was a *terrible* blow to the crew when he 'died.'"

"And they still think he's dead, right? The Ares 3 crew?"

"Yes, they do, unfortunately," Irene confirmed. "The higher-ups decided to keep it from them, at least for now. I'm sure it wasn't an easy decision."

Cathy paused for a moment, then said, "All right. You know I have to ask: What's going through his head right now? How does a man like Mark Watney respond to a situation like this? Stranded, alone, no idea we're trying to help?"

"There's no way to be sure," Irene said. "The biggest threat is giving up hope. If he decides there's no chance to survive, he'll stop trying."

"Then we're okay for now, right?" Cathy said. "He seems to be working hard. He's prepping the rover for a long trip and testing it. He plans to be there when Ares 4 lands."

"That's one interpretation, yes," Irene said.

"Is there another?"

Irene carefully formed her answer before speaking. "When facing death, people want to be heard. They don't want to die alone. He might just want the MAV radio so he can talk to another soul before he dies.

"If he's lost hope, he won't care about survival. His only concern will be making it to the radio. After that, he'll probably take an easier way out than starvation. The medical supplies of an Ares mission have enough morphine to be lethal."

After several seconds of complete silence in the studio, Cathy turned to the camera. "We'll be right back."

. . .

"Heya, Venk." Bruce's voice came from the speakerphone on Venkat's desk.

"Bruce, hi," said Venkat, typing on his computer. "Thanks for clearing up some time. I wanted to talk about the presupply."

"Sure thing. What's on your mind?"

"Let's say we soft-land it perfectly. How will Mark know it happened? And how will he know where to look?"

"We've been thinking about that," said Bruce. "We've got some ideas."

"I'm all ears," Venkat said, saving his document and closing his laptop.

"We'll be sending him a comm system anyway, right? We could have it turn on after landing. It'll broadcast on the rover and EVA suit frequencies. It'll have to be a strong signal, too.

"The rovers were only designed to communicate with the Hab and each other; the signal origin was presumed to be within twenty kilometers. The receivers just aren't very sensitive. The EVA suits are even worse. But as long as we have a strong signal we should be good. Once we land the presupply, we'll get its exact location from satellites, then broadcast that to Mark so he can go get it."

"But he's probably not listening," said Venkat. "Why would he be?"

"We have a plan for that. We're going to make a bunch of bright green ribbons. Light enough to flutter around when dropped, even in Mars's atmosphere. Each ribbon will have 'MARK: TURN ON YOUR COMM' printed on it. We're working on a release mechanism now. During the landing sequence, of course. Ideally, about a thousand meters above the surface."

"I like it," Venkat said. "All he needs to do is notice one. And he's sure to check out a bright green ribbon if he sees one outside."

"Venk," said Bruce. "If he takes the 'Watneymobile' to Ares 4, this'll all be for nothing. I mean, we can land it at Ares 4 if that happens, but . . ."

"But he'll be without a Hab. Yeah," Venkat said. "One thing at a time. Let me know when you come up with a release mechanism for those ribbons."

"Will do."

After terminating the call, Venkat opened his laptop to get back to work. There was an e-mail from Mindy Park waiting for him. *"Watney's on the move again."*

* * *

"STILL GOING in a straight line," Mindy said, pointing to her monitor.

"I see," Venkat said. "He's sure as hell not going to Ares 4. Unless he's going around some natural obstacle."

"There's nothing for him to go around," Mindy said. "It's Acidalia Planitia."

"Are those the solar cells?" Venkat asked, pointing to the screen.

"Yeah," Mindy said. "He did the usual two-hour drive, EVA, two-hour drive. He's one hundred and fifty-six kilometers from the Hab now."

They both peered at the screen.

"Wait . . . ," Venkat said. "Wait, no way . . ."

"What?" Mindy asked.

Venkat grabbed a pad of Post-its and a pen. "Give me his location, and the location of the Hab."

Mindy checked her screen. "He's currently at . . . 28.9 degrees north, 29.6 degrees west." With a few keystrokes, she brought up another file. "The Hab's at 31.2 degrees north, 28.5 degrees west. What do you see?"

Venkat finished taking down the numbers. "Come with me," he said, quickly walking out.

"Um," Mindy stammered, following after. "Where are we going?"

"SatCon break room," Venkat said. "You guys still have that map of Mars on the wall?"

"Sure," Mindy said. "But it's just a poster from the gift shop. I've got high-quality digital maps on my computer—"

"Nope. I can't draw on those," he said. Then, rounding the corner to the break room, he pointed to the Mars map on the wall. "I can draw on that."

The break room was empty save for a computer technician sipping a cup of coffee. He looked up in alarm as Venkat and Mindy stormed in.

"Good, it has latitude and longitude lines," Venkat said. Looking at his Post-it, then sliding his finger along the map, he drew an X. "That's the Hab," he said.

"Hey," the technician said. "Are you drawing on our poster?"

"I'll buy you a new one," Venkat said without looking back. Then, he drew another X. "That's his current location. Get me a ruler."

Mindy looked left and right. Seeing no ruler, she grabbed the technician's notebook.

"Hey!" the technician protested.

Using the notebook as a straight-edge, Venkat drew a line from the Hab to Mark's location and beyond. Then took a step back.

"Yup! That's where he's going!" Venkat said excitedly.

"Oh!" Mindy said.

The line passed through the exact center of a bright yellow dot printed on the map.

"*Pathfinder*!" Mindy said. "He's going to *Pathfinder*!"

"Yup!" Venkat said. "Now we're getting somewhere. It's like eight hundred kilometers from him. He can get there and back with supplies on hand."

"And bring *Pathfinder* and Sojourner rover back with him," Mindy added.

Venkat pulled out his cell phone. "We lost contact with *Pathfinder* in 1997. If he can get it online again, we can communicate. It might just need the solar cells cleaned. Even if it's got a bigger problem, he's an engineer!" Dialing, he added, "Fixing things is his job!"

Smiling for what felt like the first time in weeks, he held the phone to his ear and awaited a response. "Bruce? It's Venkat. Everything just changed. Watney's headed for *Pathfinder*. Yeah! I know, right!? Dig up everyone who was on that project and get them to JPL now. I'll catch the next flight."

Hanging up, he grinned at the map. "Mark, you sneaky, clever, son of a bitch!"

CHAPTER 9

LOG ENTRY: SOL 79

It's the evening of my eighth day on the road. Sirius 4 has been a success so far.

I've fallen into a routine. Every morning I wake up at dawn. First thing I do is check oxygen and CO_2 levels. Then I eat a breakfast pack and drink a cup of water. After that, I brush my teeth, using as little water as possible, and shave with an electric razor.

The rover has no toilet. We were expected to use our suits' reclamation systems for that. But they aren't designed to hold twenty days' worth of output.

My morning piss goes in a resealable plastic box. When I open it, the rover reeks like a truck-stop men's room. I could take it outside and let it boil off. But I worked hard to make that water, and the last thing I'm going to do is waste it. I'll feed it to the water reclaimer when I get back.

Even more precious is my manure. It's critical to the potato farm, and I'm the only source on Mars. Fortunately, when you spend a lot of time in space, you learn how to shit in a bag. And if you think things are bad after opening the piss box, imagine the smell after I drop anchor.

After I'm done with that lovely routine, I go outside and collect the solar cells. Why didn't I do it the previous night? Because trying to dismantle and stack solar cells in *total darkness* isn't fun. I learned that the hard way.

After securing the cells, I come back in, turn on some shitty seventies music, and start driving. I putter along at 25 kph, the rover's top speed. It's comfortable inside. I wear hastily made cutoffs and a thin shirt while the RTG bakes the interior. When it gets too hot I detach the insulation duct-taped to the hull. When it gets too cold, I tape it back up.

I can go almost two hours before the first battery runs out. I do a quick EVA to swap cables, then I'm back at the wheel for the second half of the day's drive.

The terrain is very flat. The undercarriage of the rover is taller than any of the rocks around here, and the hills are gently sloping affairs, smoothed by eons of sandstorms.

When the other battery runs out, it's time for another EVA. I pull the solar cells off the roof and lay them on the ground. For the first few sols, I lined them up in a row. Now I plop them wherever, trying to keep them close to the rover out of sheer laziness.

Then comes the incredibly dull part of my day. I sit around for twelve hours with nothing to do. And I'm getting sick of this rover. The inside's the size of a van. That may seem like plenty of room, but try being trapped in a van for eight days. I look forward to tending my potato farm in the wide open space of the Hab.

I'm nostalgic for the Hab. How fucked up is that?

I have shitty seventies TV to watch, and a bunch of Poirot novels to read. But mostly I spend my time thinking about getting to Ares 4. I'll have to do it someday. How the hell am I going to survive a 3200-kilometer trip in this thing? It'll probably take fifty days. I'll need the water reclaimer and the oxygenator, maybe some of the Hab's main batteries, then a bunch more solar cells to charge everything. . . . Where will I put it all? These thoughts pester me throughout the long, boring days.

Eventually, it gets dark and I get tired. I lie among the food packs, water tanks, extra O_2 tank, piles of CO_2 filters, box of pee, bags of shit, and personal items. I have a bunch of crew jumpsuits to serve as bedding, along with my blanket and pillow. Basically, I sleep in a pile of junk every night.

Speaking of sleep . . . G'night.

LOG ENTRY: SOL 80

By my reckoning, I'm about 100 kilometers from *Pathfinder*. Technically it's "Carl Sagan Memorial Station." But with all due respect to Carl, I can call it whatever the hell I want. I'm the King of Mars.

As I mentioned, it's been a long, boring drive. And I'm still on the outward leg. But hey, I'm an astronaut. Long-ass trips are my business.

Navigation is tricky.

The Hab's nav beacon only reaches 40 kilometers, so it's useless to me out here. I knew that'd be an issue when I was planning this little road trip, so I came up with a brilliant plan that didn't work.

The computer has detailed maps, so I figured I could navigate by landmarks. I was wrong. Turns out you can't navigate by landmarks if you can't find any god damned landmarks.

Our landing site is at the delta of a long-gone river. NASA chose it because if there are any microscopic fossils to be had, it's a good place to look. Also, the water would have dragged rock and soil samples from thousands of kilometers away. With some digging, we could get a broad geological history.

That's great for science, but it means the Hab's in a *featureless wasteland*.

I considered making a compass. The rover has plenty of electricity, and the med kit has a needle. Only one problem: Mars doesn't have a magnetic field.

So I navigate by Phobos. It whips around Mars so fast it actually rises and sets twice a day, running west to east. It isn't the most accurate system, but it works.

Things got easier on Sol 75. I reached a valley with a rise to the west. It had flat ground for easy driving, and I just needed to follow the edge of the hills. I named it "Lewis Valley" after our fearless leader. She'd love it there, geology nerd that she is.

Three sols later, Lewis Valley opened into a wide plain. So, again, I was left without references and relied on Phobos to guide me. There's probably symbolism there. Phobos is the god of fear, and I'm letting it be my guide. Not a good sign.

But today, my luck finally changed. After two sols wandering the desert, I found something to navigate by. It was a five-kilometer crater, so small it didn't even have a listed name. But it was on the maps, so to me it was the Lighthouse of Alexandria. Once I had it in sight, I knew exactly where I was.

I'm camped near it now, as a matter of fact.

I'm finally through the blank areas of the map. Tomorrow, I'll have the Lighthouse to navigate by, and Hamelin crater later on. I'm in good shape.

Now on to my next task: sitting around with nothing to do for twelve hours.

I better get started!

LOG ENTRY: SOL 81

Almost made it to *Pathfinder* today, but I ran out of juice. Just another 22 kilometers to go!

An unremarkable drive. Navigation wasn't a problem. As Lighthouse receded into the distance, the rim of Hamelin crater came into view.

I left Acidalia Planitia behind a long time ago. I'm well into Ares Vallis now. The desert plains are giving way to bumpier terrain, strewn with ejecta that never got buried by sand. It makes driving a chore; I have to pay more attention.

Up till now, I've been driving right over the rock-strewn landscape. But as I travel farther south, the rocks are getting bigger and more plentiful. I have to go around some of them or risk damage to my suspension. The good news is I don't have to do it for long. Once I get to *Pathfinder*, I can turn around and go the other way.

The weather's been very good. No discernible wind, no storms. I think I got lucky there. There's a good chance my rover tracks from the past few sols are intact. I should be able to get back to Lewis Valley just by following them.

After setting up the solar panels today, I went for a little walk. I never left sight of the rover; the last thing I want to do is get lost on foot. But I couldn't stomach crawling back into that cramped, smelly rat's nest. Not right away.

It's a strange feeling. Everywhere I go, I'm the first. Step outside the rover? First guy ever to be there! Climb a hill? First guy to climb that hill! Kick a rock? That rock hadn't moved in a million years!

I'm the first guy to drive long-distance on Mars. The first guy to spend more than thirty-one sols on Mars. The first guy to grow crops on Mars. First, first, first!

I wasn't expecting to be first at anything. I was the fifth crewman out of the MDV when we landed, making me the seventeenth person to set foot on Mars. The egress order had been determined years earlier. A month before launch, we all got tattoos of our "Mars numbers." Johanssen almost refused to get her "15" because she was afraid it would hurt. Here's a woman who had survived the centrifuge, the vomit comet, hard-landing drills and 10k runs. A woman who fixed a simulated MDV computer failure while being spun around upside-down. But she was afraid of a tattoo needle.

Man, I miss those guys.

Jesus Christ, I'd give anything for a five-minute conversation with anyone. Anyone, anywhere. About anything.

I'm the first person to be alone on an entire planet.

Okay, enough moping. I *am* having a conversation with someone: whoever reads this log. It's a bit one-sided but it'll have to do. I might die, but damn it, someone will know what I had to say.

And the whole point of this trip is to get a radio. I could be reconnected with mankind before I even die.

So here's another first: Tomorrow I'll be the first person to recover a Mars probe.

LOG ENTRY: SOL 82

Victory! I found it!

I knew I was in the right area when I spotted Twin Peaks in the distance. The two small hills are under a kilometer from the landing site. Even better, they were on the far side of the site. All I had to do was aim for them until I found the lander.

And there it was! Right where it was supposed to be! I excitedly stumbled out and rushed to the site.

Pathfinder's final stage of descent was a balloon-covered tetrahedron. The balloons absorbed the impact of landing. Once it came to rest, they deflated, and the tetrahedron unfolded to reveal the probe.

It's actually two separate components. The lander itself, and the Sojourner rover. The lander was immobile, while Sojourner wandered around and got a good look at the local rocks. I'm taking both back with me, but the important part is the lander. That's the part that can communicate with Earth.

I can't explain how happy I was to find it. It was a *lot* of work to get here, and I'd succeeded.

The lander was half-buried. With some quick and careful digging, I exposed the bulk of it, though the large tetrahedron and the deflated balloons still lurked below the surface.

After a quick search, I found Sojourner. The little fella was only two meters from the lander. I vaguely remember it was farther away when they last saw it. It probably entered a contingency mode and started circling the lander, trying to communicate.

I quickly deposited Sojourner in my rover. It's small, light, and easily fit in the airlock. The lander was a different story.

I had no hope of getting the whole thing back to the Hab. It was just too big, but I only needed the probe itself. It was time for me to put on my mechanical engineer hat.

The probe was on the central panel of the unfolded tetrahedron. The other three sides were each attached to the central panel with a metal hinge. As anyone at JPL will tell you, probes are delicate things. Weight is a serious concern, so they're not made to stand up to much punishment.

When I took a crowbar to the hinges, they popped right off!

Then things got difficult. When I tried to lift the central panel assembly, it didn't budge.

Just like the other three panels, the central panel had deflated balloons underneath it.

Over the decades, the balloons had ripped and filled with sand.

I could cut off the balloons, but I'd have to dig to get to them. It wouldn't be hard, it's just sand. But the other three panels were in the damn way.

I quickly realized I didn't give a crap about the condition of the other panels. I went back to my rover, cut some strips of Hab material, then braided them into a primitive but strong rope. I can't take credit for it being strong. Thank NASA for that. I just made it rope-shaped.

I tied one end to a panel and the other to the rover. The rover was made for traversing extremely rugged terrain, often at steep angles. It may not be fast, but it has great torque. I towed the panel away like a redneck removing a tree stump.

Now I had a place to dig. As I exposed each balloon, I cut it off. The whole task took an hour.

Then I hoisted the central panel assembly up and carried it confidently to the rover!

At least, that's what I wanted to do. The damn thing is still heavy as hell. I'm guessing it's 200 kilograms. Even in Mars's gravity that's a bit much. I could carry it around the Hab easily enough, but lifting it while wearing an awkward EVA suit? Out of the question.

So I dragged it to the rover.

Now for my next feat: getting it on the roof.

The roof was empty at the moment. Even with mostly full batteries, I had set up the solar cells when I stopped. Why not? Free energy.

I'd worked it out in advance. On the way here, two stacks of solar panels occupied the whole roof. On the way back, I'll use a single stack to make room for the probe. It's a little more dangerous; the stack might fall over. Also, the cells will be a pain in the ass to stack that high. But I'll get it done.

I can't just throw a rope over the rover and hoist *Pathfinder* up the side. I don't want to break it. I mean, it's already broken; they lost contact in 1997. But I don't want to break it *more*.

I came up with a solution, but I'd done enough physical labor for one day, and I was almost out of daylight.

Now I'm in the rover, looking at Sojourner. It seems all right. No physical damage on the outside. Doesn't look like anything got too baked by the sunlight. The dense layer of Mars crap all over it protected it from long-term solar damage.

You may think Sojourner isn't much use to me. It can't communicate with Earth. Why do I care about it?

Because it has a lot of moving parts.

If I establish a link with NASA, I can talk to them by holding a page of text up to the lander's camera. But how would they talk to me? The only moving parts on the lander are the high-gain antenna (which would have to stay pointed at Earth) and the camera boom. We'd have to come up with a system where NASA could talk by rotating the camera head. It would be painfully slow.

But Sojourner has six independent wheels that rotate reasonably fast. It'll be much easier to communicate with those. I could draw letters on the wheels. NASA could rotate them to spell things at me.

That all assumes I can get the lander's radio working at all.

Time to turn in. I've got a lot of backbreaking physical labor to do tomorrow. I'll need my rest.

LOG ENTRY: SOL 83

Oh God, I'm sore.

But it's the only way I could think of to get the lander safely onto the roof.

I built a ramp out of rocks and sand. Just like the ancient Egyptians did.

And if there's one thing Ares Vallis has, it's rocks!

First, I experimented to find out how steep the grade could be. I piled some rocks near the lander and dragged it up the pile and back down again. Then I made the pile steeper and made sure I could drag the lander up and down. I repeated this over and over until I found the best grade for my ramp: 30 degrees. Anything more was too risky. I might lose my grip and send the lander tumbling down the ramp.

The roof of the rover is over two meters from the ground. So I'd need a ramp almost four meters long. I got to work.

The first few rocks were easy. Then they started feeling heavier and heavier. Hard physical labor in a space suit is murder. Everything's more effort because you're lugging 20 kilograms of suit around with you, and your movement is limited. I was panting within twenty minutes.

So I cheated. I upped my O_2 mixture. It really helped a lot. Probably shouldn't make that a habit. Also, I didn't get hot. The suit leaks heat faster than my body could ever generate it. The heating system is what keeps the temperature bearable. My physical labor just meant the suit didn't have to heat itself as much.

After hours of grueling labor, I finally got the ramp made. Nothing more than a pile of rocks against the rover, but it reached the roof.

I stomped up and down the ramp first, to make sure it was stable, then I dragged the lander up. It worked like a charm!

I was all smiles as I lashed the lander in place. I made sure it was firmly secured, and even stacked the solar cells in a big single stack (why waste the ramp?).

But then it hit me. The ramp would collapse as I drove away, and the rocks might damage the wheels or undercarriage. I'd have to take the ramp apart to keep that from happening.

Ugh.

Tearing the ramp down was easier than putting it up. I didn't need to carefully put each rock in a stable place. I just dropped them wherever. It only took me an hour.

And now I'm done!

I'll start heading home tomorrow, with my new 200-kilogram broken radio.

CHAPTER 10

LOG ENTRY: SOL 90

Seven days since *Pathfinder*, and seven days closer to home.

As I'd hoped, my inbound tracks gave me a path back to Lewis Valley. Then it was four sols of easy driving. The hills to my left made it impossible to get lost, and the terrain was smooth.

But all good things come to an end. I'm back in Acidalia Planitia now. My outgoing tracks are long gone. It's been sixteen days since I was last here. Even timid weather would clear them out in that time.

On my way out, I should have made a pile of rocks every time I camped. The land is so flat they'd be visible for kilometers.

On second thought, thinking back to making that damn ramp . . . ugh.

So once again I am the desert wanderer, using Phobos to navigate and hoping I don't stray too far. All I need to do is get within 40 kilometers of the Hab and I'll pick up the beacon.

I'm feeling optimistic. For the first time, I think I might get off this planet alive. With that in mind, I'm taking soil and rock samples every time I do an EVA.

At first, I figured it was my duty. If I survive, geologists will love me for it. But then it started to get fun. Now, as I drive, I look forward to that simple act of bagging rocks.

It just feels nice to be an astronaut again. That's all it is. Not a reluctant farmer, not an electrical engineer, not a long-haul trucker. An astronaut. I'm doing what astronauts do. I missed it.

LOG ENTRY: SOL 92

I got two seconds of signal from the Hab beacon today, then lost it. But it's a good sign. I've been traveling vaguely north-northwest for two days. I must be a good hundred kilometers from the Hab; it's a miracle I got any signal at all. Must have been a moment of perfect weather conditions.

During the boring-ass days, I'm working my way through *The Six Million Dollar Man* from Commander Lewis's inexhaustible collection of seventies tripe.

I just watched an episode where Steve Austin fights a Russian Venus probe that landed on Earth by mistake. As an expert in interplanetary travel, I can tell you there are *no* scientific inaccuracies in the story. It's quite common for probes to land on the wrong planet. Also, the probe's large, flat-panel hull is ideal for the high-pressure Venusian atmosphere. And, as we all know, probes often refuse to obey directives, choosing instead to attack humans on sight.

So far, *Pathfinder* hasn't tried to kill me. But I'm keeping an eye on it.

LOG ENTRY: SOL 93

I found the Hab signal today. No more chance to get lost. According to the computer, I'm 24,718 meters away.

I'll be home tomorrow. Even if the rover has a catastrophic failure, I'll be fine. I can *walk* to the Hab from here.

I don't know if I've mentioned this before, but I am really fucking sick of being in this rover. I've spent so much time seated or lying down, my back is all screwed up. Of all my crewmates, the one I miss most right now is Beck. He'd fix my aching back.

Though he'd probably give me a bunch of shit about it. "Why didn't you do stretching exercises? Your body is important! Eat more fiber," or whatever.

At this point, I'd welcome a health lecture.

During training, we had to practice the dreaded "Missed Orbit" scenario. In the event of a second-stage failure during MAV ascent, we'd be in orbit, but too low to reach *Hermes*. We'd be skimming the upper atmosphere, so our orbit would rapidly decay. NASA would remotely operate *Hermes* and bring it in to pick us up. Then we'd get the hell out of there before *Hermes* caught too much drag.

To drill this, they made us stay in the MAV simulator for three miserable days. Six people in an ascent vehicle originally designed for a twenty-three-minute flight. It got a little cramped. And by "a little cramped" I mean "we wanted to kill each other."

I'd give anything to be in that cramped capsule with those guys again.

Man, I hope I get *Pathfinder* working again.

LOG ENTRY: SOL 94

Home sweet home!

Today I write from my gigantic, cavernous Hab!

The first thing I did when I got in was wave my arms wildly while running in circles. Felt great! I was in that damn rover for twenty-two sols and couldn't even walk without suiting up.

I'll need to endure twice that to get to Ares 4, but that's a problem for later.

After a few celebratory laps around the Hab, it was time to get to work.

First, I fired up the oxygenator and atmospheric regulator.

Checking the air levels, everything looked good. There was still CO_2, so the plants hadn't suffocated without me exhaling for them.

Naturally I did an exhaustive check on my crops, and they're all healthy.

I added my bags of shit to the manure pile. Lovely smell, I can tell you. But once I mixed some soil in, it died down to tolerable levels. I dumped my box o' pee into the water reclaimer.

I'd been gone over three weeks and had left the Hab very humid for the sake of the crops. That much water in the air can cause any amount of electrical problems, so I spent the next few hours doing full systems checks on everything.

Then I kind of lounged around for a while. I wanted to spend the rest of the day relaxing, but I had more to do.

After suiting up, I went out to the rover and dragged the solar cells off the roof. Over the next few hours, I put them back where they belonged, wiring them into the Hab's power grid.

Getting the lander off the roof was a hell of a lot easier than getting it up there. I detached a strut from the MAV platform and dragged it over to the rover. By leaning it against the hull and digging the other end into the ground for stability, I had a ramp.

I should have brought that strut with me to the *Pathfinder* site. Live and learn.

There's no way to get the lander in the airlock. It's just too big. I could probably dismantle it and bring it in a piece at a time, but there's a pretty compelling reason not to.

With no magnetic field, Mars has no defense against harsh solar radiation. If I were exposed to it, I'd get so much cancer, the cancer would have cancer. So the Hab canvas shields from electromagnetic waves. This means the Hab itself would block any transmissions if the lander were inside.

Speaking of cancer, it was time to get rid of the RTG.

It *pained* me to climb back into the rover, but it had to be done. If the RTG ever broke open, it would kill me to death.

NASA decided four kilometers was the safe distance, and I wasn't about to second-guess them. I drove back to where Commander Lewis had originally dumped it, ditched it in the same hole, and drove back to the Hab.

I'll start work on the lander tomorrow.

Now to enjoy a good, long sleep in an actual cot. With the comforting knowledge that when I wake, my morning piss will go into a toilet.

LOG ENTRY: SOL 95

Today was all about repairs!

The *Pathfinder* mission ended because the lander had an unknown critical failure. Once JPL lost contact with the lander, they had no idea what became of Sojourner. It might be in better shape. Maybe it just needs power. Power it couldn't get with its solar panels hopelessly caked with dust.

I set the little rover on my workbench and pried open a panel to peek inside. The battery was a lithium thionyl chloride nonrechargeable. I figured that out from some subtle clues: the shape of the connection points, the thickness of the insulation, and the fact that it had "LiSOCl2 NON-RCHRG" written on it.

I cleaned the solar panels thoroughly, then aimed a small, flexible lamp directly at them. The battery's long dead. But the panels might be okay, and Sojourner can operate directly off them. We'll see if anything happens.

Then it was time to take a look at Sojourner's daddy. I suited up and headed out.

On most landers, the weak point is the battery. It's the most delicate component, and when it dies, there's no way to recover.

Landers can't just shut down and wait when they have low batteries. Their electronics won't work unless they're at a minimum temperature. So they have heaters to keep the electronics warm. It's a problem that rarely comes up on Earth, but hey. Mars.

Over time, the solar panels get covered with dust. Then winter brings colder temperatures and less daylight. This all combines into a big "fuck you" from Mars to your lander. Eventually it's using more power to keep warm than it's getting from the meager daylight that makes it through the dust.

Once the battery runs down, the electronics get too cold to operate, and the whole system dies. The solar panels will recharge the battery somewhat, but there's nothing to tell the system to reboot. Anything that could make that decision would be electronics, which would not be working. Eventually, the now-unused battery will lose its ability to retain charge.

That's the usual cause of death. And I sure hope it's what killed *Pathfinder.*

I piled some leftover parts of the MDV into a makeshift table and ramp. Then I dragged the lander up to my new outdoor workbench. Working in an EVA suit is annoying enough. Bending over the whole time would have been torture.

I got my tool kit and started poking around. Opening the outer panel wasn't too hard and I identified the battery easily enough. JPL labels everything. It's a 40 amp-hour Ag-Zn battery with an optimal voltage of 1.5. Wow. They really made those things run on nothin' back then.

I detached the battery and headed back inside. I checked it with my electronics kit, and sure enough it's dead, dead, dead. I could shuffle across a carpet and hold more charge.

But I knew what the lander needed: 1.5 volts.

Compared to the makeshift crap I've been gluing together since Sol 6, this was a breeze. I have voltage controllers in my kit! It only took me fifteen minutes to put a controller on a reserve power line, then another hour to go outside and run the line to where the battery used to be.

Then there's the issue of heat. It's a good idea to keep electronics above −40°C. The temperature today is a brisk −63°C.

The battery was big and easy to identify, but I had no clue where the heaters were. Even if I knew, it'd be too risky to hook them directly to power. I could easily fry the whole system.

So instead, I went to good old "Spare Parts" Rover 1 and stole its environment heater. I've gutted that poor rover so much, it looks like I parked it in a bad part of town.

I lugged the heater to my outdoor "workbench," and hooked it to Hab power. Then I rested it in the lander where the battery used to be.

Now I wait. And hope.

LOG ENTRY: SOL 96

I was really hoping I'd wake up to a functional lander, but no such luck. Its high-gain antenna is right where I last saw it. Why does that matter? Well, I'll tell ya . . .

If the lander comes back to life (and that's a big if), it'll try to establish contact with Earth. Problem is nobody's listening. It's not like the *Pathfinder* team is hanging around JPL just in case their long-dead probe is repaired by a wayward astronaut.

The Deep Space Network and SETI are my best bets for picking up the signal. If either of them caught a blip from *Pathfinder*, they'd tell JPL.

JPL would quickly figure out what was going on, especially when they triangulated the signal to my landing site.

They'd tell the lander where Earth is, and it would angle the high-gain antenna appropriately. That there, the angling of the antenna, is how I'll know if it linked up.

So far, no action.

There's still hope. Any number of reasons could be delaying

things. The rover heater is designed to heat air at one atmosphere, and the thin Martian air severely hampers its ability to work. So the electronics might need more time to warm up.

Also, Earth is only visible during the day. I (hopefully) fixed the lander yesterday evening. It's morning now, so most of the intervening time has been night. No Earth.

Sojourner's showing no signs of life, either. It's been in the nice, warm environment of the Hab all night, with plenty of light on its sparkling clean solar cells. Maybe it's running an extended self-check, or staying still until it hears from the lander or something.

I'll just have to put it out of my mind for now.

```
Pathfinder LOG: SOL 0
BOOT SEQUENCE INITIATED
TIME 00:00:00
LOSS OF POWER DETECTED, TIME/DATE UNRELIABLE
LOADING OS . . .


VXWARE OPERATING SYSTEM (C) WIND RIVER SYSTEMS PERFORMING
    HARDWARE CHECK:
INT. TEMPERATURE: -34°C
EXT. TEMPERATURE: NONFUNCTIONAL
BATTERY: FULL
HIGAIN: OK
LOGAIN: OK
WIND SENSOR: NONFUNCTIONAL
METEOROLOGY: NONFUNCTIONAL
ASI: NONFUNCTIONAL
IMAGER: OK
ROVER RAMP: NONFUNCTIONAL
SOLAR A: NONFUNCTIONAL
SOLAR B: NONFUNCTIONAL
SOLAR C: NONFUNCTIONAL
HARDWARE CHECK COMPLETE
```

```
BROADCASTING STATUS
LISTENING FOR TELEMETRY SIGNAL . . .
LISTENING FOR TELEMETRY SIGNAL . . .
LISTENING FOR TELEMETRY SIGNAL
SIGNAL ACQUIRED . . .
```

CHAPTER 11

"SOMETHING'S COMING IN . . . yes . . . yes! It's *Pathfinder*!"

The crowded room burst into applause and cheers. Venkat slapped an unknown technician on the back while Bruce pumped his fist in the air.

The ad-hoc *Pathfinder* control center was an accomplishment in itself. Over the last twenty days, a team of JPL engineers had worked around the clock to piece together antiquated computers, repair broken components, network everything, and install hastily made software that allowed the old systems to interact with the modern Deep Space Network.

The room itself was formerly a conference room; JPL had no space ready for the sudden need. Already jam-packed with computers and equipment, the cramped space had turned positively claustrophobic with the many spectators now squeezing into it.

One Associated Press camera team pressed against the back wall, trying—and failing—to stay out of everyone's way while recording the auspicious moment. The rest of the media would have to satisfy themselves with the live AP feed, and await a press conference.

Venkat turned to Bruce. "God damn, Bruce. You really pulled a rabbit out of your hat this time! Good work!"

"I'm just the director," Bruce said modestly. "Thank the guys who got all this stuff working."

"Oh I will!" Venkat beamed. "But first I have to talk to my new best friend!"

Turning to the headsetted man at the communications console, Venkat asked, "What's your name, new best friend?"

"Tim," he said, not taking his eyes off the screen.

"What now?" Venkat asked.

"We sent the return telemetry automatically. It'll get there in just over eleven minutes. Once it does, *Pathfinder* will start high-gain transmissions. So it'll be twenty-two minutes till we hear from it again."

"Venkat's got a doctorate in physics, Tim," Bruce said. "You don't need to explain transmission time to him."

Tim shrugged. "You can never tell with managers."

"What was in the transmission we got?" Venkat asked.

"Just the bare bones. A hardware self-check. It's got a lot of 'nonfunctional' systems, 'cause they were on the panels Watney removed."

"What about the camera?"

"It says the imager's working. We'll have it take a panorama as soon as we can."

LOG ENTRY: SOL 97

It worked!

Holy shit, it worked!

I just suited up and checked the lander. The high-gain antenna is angled *directly* at Earth! *Pathfinder* has no way of knowing where it is, so it has no way of knowing where Earth is. The *only* way for it to find out is getting a signal.

They know I'm alive!

I don't even know what to say. This was an insane plan and some-how it worked! I'm going to be talking to someone again. I spent three months as the loneliest man in history and it's finally over.

Sure, I might not get rescued. But I won't be alone.

The whole time I was recovering *Pathfinder*, I imagined what this moment would be like. I figured I'd jump up and down a bit, cheer, maybe flip off the ground (because this whole damn planet is my enemy), but that's not what happened. When I got back to the Hab and took off the EVA suit, I sat down in the dirt and cried. Bawled like a little kid for several minutes. I finally settled down to mild sniffling and then felt a deep calm.

It was a good calm.

It occurs to me: Now that I might live, I have to be more careful about logging embarrassing moments. How do I delete log entries? There's no obvious way. . . . I'll get to it later. I've got more important things to do.

I've got people to talk to!

● ● ●

VENKAT GRINNED as he took the podium in the JPL press room.

"We received the high-gain response just over half an hour ago," he said to the assembled press. "We immediately directed *Pathfinder* to take a panoramic image. Hopefully, Watney has some kind of message for us. Questions?"

The sea of reporters raised their hands.

"Cathy, let's start with you," Venkat said, pointing to the CNN reporter.

"Thanks," she said. "Have you had any contact with the Sojourner rover?"

"Unfortunately, no," he replied. "The lander hasn't been able to connect to Sojourner, and we have no way to contact it directly."

"What might be wrong with Sojourner?"

"I can't even speculate," Venkat said. "After spending that long on Mars, *anything* could be wrong with it."

"Best guess?"

"Our best guess is he took it into the Hab. The lander's signal wouldn't be able to reach Sojourner through Hab canvas." Pointing to another reporter, he said, "You, there."

"Marty West, NBC News," Marty said. "How will you communicate with Watney once everything's up and running?"

"That'll be up to Watney," said Venkat. "All we have to work with is the camera. He can write notes and hold them up. But how we talk back is trickier."

"How so?" Marty asked.

"Because all we have is the camera platform. That's the only moving part. There are plenty of ways to get information across with just the platform's rotation, but no way to tell Watney about them. He'll have to come up with something and tell us. We'll follow his lead."

Pointing to the next reporter, he said, "Go ahead."

"Jill Holbrook, BBC. With a twenty-two-minute round-trip and nothing but a single rotating platform to talk with, it'll be a dreadfully slow conversation, won't it?"

"Yes it will," Venkat confirmed. "It's early morning in Acidalia Planitia right now, and just past three a.m. here in Pasadena. We'll be here all night, and that's just for a start. No more questions for now. The panorama is due back in a few minutes. We'll keep you posted."

Before anyone could ask a follow-up, Venkat strode out the side door and hurried down the hall to the makeshift *Pathfinder* control center. He pressed through the throng to the communications console.

"Anything, Tim?"

"Totally," he replied. "But we're staring at this black screen because it's way more interesting than pictures from Mars."

"You're a smart-ass, Tim," Venkat said.

"Noted."

Bruce pushed his way forward. "Still another few seconds on the clock," he said.

The time passed in silence.

"Getting something," Tim said. "Yup. It's the panoramic."

Sighs of relief and muted conversation replaced tense silence as the image began coming through. It filled out from left to right at a snail's pace due to the bandwidth limitations of the antique probe sending it.

"Martian surface . . . ," Venkat said as the lines slowly filled in. "More surface . . ."

"Edge of the Hab!" Bruce said, pointing to the screen.

"Hab," Venkat smiled. "More Hab now . . . more Hab . . . Is that a message? That's a message!"

As the image grew, it revealed a handwritten note, suspended at the camera's height by a thin metal rod.

"We got a note from Mark!" Venkat announced to the room.

Applause filled the room, then quickly died down. "What's it say?" someone asked.

Venkat leaned closer to the screen. "It says . . . 'I'll write questions here—Are you receiving?'"

"Okay . . . ?" said Bruce.

"That's what it says," Venkat shrugged.

"Another note," said Tim, pointing to the screen as more of the image came through.

Venkat leaned in again. "This one says 'Point here for yes.'"

He folded his arms. "All right. We have communication with Mark. Tim, point the camera at 'Yes.' Then, start taking pictures at ten-minute intervals until he puts another question up."

LOG ENTRY: SOL 97 (2)

"Yes!" They said, "Yes!"

I haven't been this excited about a "yes" since prom night!

Okay, calm down.

I have limited paper to work with. These cards were intended to label batches of samples. I have about fifty cards. I can use both sides, and if it comes down to it, I can re-use them by scratching out the old question.

The Sharpie I'm using will last much longer than the cards, so ink isn't a problem. But I have to do all my writing in the Hab. I don't know what kind of hallucinogenic crap that ink is made of, but I'm pretty sure it would boil off in Mars's atmosphere.

I'm using old parts of the antenna array to hold the cards up. There's a certain irony in that.

We'll need to talk faster than yes/no questions every half hour. The camera can rotate 360 degrees, and I have plenty of antenna parts. Time to make an alphabet. But I can't just use the letters A through Z. Twenty-six letters plus my question card would be twenty-seven cards around the lander. Each one would only get 13 degrees of arc. Even if JPL points the camera perfectly, there's a good chance I won't know which letter they meant.

So I'll have to use ASCII. That's how computers manage characters. Each character has a numerical code between 0 and 255. Values between 0 and 255 can be expressed as 2 hexadecimal digits. By giving me pairs of hex digits, they can send any character they like, including numbers, punctuation, etc.

How do I know which values go with which characters? Because Johanssen's laptop is a wealth of information. I knew she'd have an ASCII table in there somewhere. All computer geeks do.

So I'll make cards for 0 through 9, and A through F. That makes 16 cards to place around the camera, plus the question card. Seventeen cards means over 21 degrees each. Much easier to deal with.

Time to get to work!

Spell with ASCII. 0–F at 21-degree increments. Will watch camera starting 11:00 my time. When message done, return to this position. Wait 20 minutes after completion to take picture (so I can write and post reply). Repeat process at top of every hour.

S . . . T . . . A . . . T . . . U . . . S

No physical problems. All Hab components functional. Eating 3/4 rations. Successfully growing crops in Hab with cultivated soil. Note: Situation not Ares 3 crew's fault. Bad luck.

H . . . O . . . W . . . A . . . L . . . I . . . V . . . E

Impaled by antenna fragment. Knocked out by decompression. Landed facedown, blood sealed hole. Woke up after crew left. Biomonitor computer destroyed by puncture. Crew had reason to think me dead. Not their fault.

C . . . R . . . O . . . P . . . S . . . ?

Long story. Extreme botany. Have 126 m2 farmland growing potatoes. Will extend food supply, but not enough to last until Ares 4 landing. Modified rover for long-distance travel, plan to drive to Ares 4.

W . . . E . . . S . . . A . . . W . . . — . . . S . . . A . . . T . . . L . . . I . . . T . . . E

Government watching me with satellites? Need tinfoil hat! Also need faster way to communicate. Speak&Spell taking all damn day. Any ideas?

B . . . R . . . I . . . N . . . G . . . S . . . J . . . R . . . N . . . R . . . O . . . U . . . T

Sojourner rover brought out, placed 1 meter due north of lander. If you can contact it, I can draw hex numbers on the wheels and you can send me six bytes at a time.

S . . . J . . . R . . . N . . . R . . . N . . . O . . . T . . . R . . . S . . . P . . . N . . . D

Damn. Any other ideas? Need faster communication.

W . . . O . . . R . . . K . . . I . . . N . . . G . . . O . . . N . . . I . . . T

Earth is about to set. Resume 08:00 my time tomorrow morning. Tell family I'm fine. Give crew my best. Tell Commander Lewis disco sucks.

· · ·

VENKAT BLINKED his bleary eyes several times as he tried to organize the papers on his desk. His temporary desk at JPL was nothing more than a folding table set up in the back of a break room. People were in and out picking up snacks all day, but on the plus side the coffeepot was nearby.

"Excuse me," said a man approaching the table.

"Yes, they're out of Diet Coke," Venkat said without looking up. "I don't know when Site Services refills the fridge."

"I'm actually here to talk to you, Dr. Kapoor."

"Huh?" said Venkat, looking up. He shook his head. "Sorry, I was up all night." He gulped his coffee. "Who are you again?"

"Jack Trevor," said the thin, pale man before Venkat. "I work in software engineering."

"What can I do for you?"

"We have an idea for communication."

"I'm all ears."

"We've been looking through the old *Pathfinder* software. We got duplicate computers up and running for testing. Same computers they used to find a problem that almost killed the original mission. Real interesting story, actually; turns out there was a priority inversion in Sojourner's thread management and—"

"Focus, Jack," interrupted Venkat.

"Right. Well, the thing is, *Pathfinder* has an OS update process. So we can change the software to anything we want."

"How does this help us?"

"*Pathfinder* has two communications systems. One to talk to us, the other to talk to Sojourner. We can change the second system to broadcast on the Ares 3 rover frequency. And we can have it pretend to be the beacon signal from the Hab."

"You can get *Pathfinder* talking to Mark's rover?"

"It's the only option. The Hab's radio is dead, but the rover has communications equipment made for talking to the Hab and the other rover. Problem is, to implement a new comm system, both ends of it need to have the right software running. We can remotely update *Pathfinder*, but not the rover."

"So," Venkat said, "you can get *Pathfinder* to talk to the rover, but you can't get the rover to listen or talk back."

"Right. Ideally, we want our text to show up on the rover screen, and whatever Watney types to be sent back to us. That requires a change to the rover's software."

Venkat sighed. "What's the point of this discussion if we can't update the rover's software?"

Jack grinned as he continued. "*We* can't do the patch, but Watney can! We can just send the data, and have him enter the update into the rover himself."

"How much data are we talking about?"

"I have guys working on the rover software right now. The patch file will be twenty meg, minimum. We can send one byte to Watney every four seconds or so with the 'Speak&Spell.' It'd take three years of constant broadcasting to get that patch across. Obviously, that's no good."

"But you're talking to me, so you have a solution, right?" Venkat probed, resisting the urge to scream.

"Of course!" Jack beamed. "Software engineers are sneaky bastards when it comes to data management."

"Enlighten me," said Venkat.

"Here's the clever part," Jack said, conspiratorially. "The rover currently parses the signal into bytes, then identifies the specific sequence the Hab sends. That way, natural radio waves won't throw off the homing. If the bytes aren't right, the rover ignores them."

"Okay, so what?"

"It means there's a spot in the code base where it's got the parsed bytes. We can insert a tiny bit of code, just twenty instructions, to write the parsed bytes to a log file before checking their validity."

"This sounds promising . . . ," Venkat said.

"It is!" Jack said excitedly. "First, we update *Pathfinder* so it knows how to talk to the rover. Then, we tell Watney exactly how to hack the rover software to add those twenty instructions. Then we have *Pathfinder* broadcast new software to the rover. The rover logs the bytes to a file. Finally, Watney launches the file as an executable and the rover patches itself!"

Venkat furrowed his brow, taking in far more information than his sleep-deprived mind wanted to accept.

"Um," Jack said. "You're not cheering or dancing."

"So we just need to send Watney those twenty instructions?" Venkat asked.

"That, and how to edit the files. And where to insert the instructions in the files."

"Just like that?"

"Just like that!"

Venkat was silent for a moment. "Jack, I'm going to buy your whole team autographed *Star Trek* memorabilia."

"I prefer *Star Wars*," he said, turning to leave. "The original trilogy only, of course."

"Of course," Venkat said.

As Jack walked away, a woman approached Venkat's table.

"Yes?" Venkat said.

"I can't find any Diet Coke, are we out?"

"Yes," Venkat said. "I don't know when Site Services refills the fridge."

"Thanks," she said.

Just as he was about to get back to work, his mobile rang. He groaned loudly at the ceiling as he snatched the phone from his desk.

"Hello?" he said as cheerfully as he could.

"I need a picture of Watney."

"Hi, Annie. Nice to hear from you, too. How are things back in Houston?"

"Cut the shit, Venkat. I need a picture."

"It's not that simple," Venkat explained.

"You're talking to him with a fucking camera. How hard can it be?"

"We spell out our message, wait twenty minutes, and *then* take a picture. Watney's back in the Hab by then."

"So tell him to be around when you take the next picture," Annie demanded.

"We can only send one message per hour, and only when Acidalia Planitia is facing Earth," Venkat said. "We're not going to waste a message just to tell him to pose for a photo. Besides, he'll be in his EVA suit. You won't even be able to see his face."

"I need something, Venkat," Annie said. "You've been in contact for twenty-four hours and the media is going ape shit. They want an image for the story. It'll be on every news site in the world."

"You have the pictures of his notes. Make do with that."

"Not enough," Annie said. "The press is crawling down my throat for this. And up my ass. Both directions, Venkat! They're gonna meet in the middle!"

"It'll have to wait a few days. We're going to try and link *Pathfinder* to the rover computer—"

"A few days!?" Annie gasped. "This is all anyone cares about right now. In the world. This is the biggest story since Apollo 13. Give me a fucking picture!"

Venkat sighed. "I'll try to get it tomorrow."

"Great!" she said. "Looking forward to it."

LOG ENTRY: SOL 98

I have to be watching the camera when it spells things out. It's half a byte at a time. So I watch a pair of numbers, then look them up on an ASCII cheat sheet I made. That's one letter.

I don't want to forget any letters, so I scrape them into the dirt with a rod. The process of looking up a letter and scraping it in the dirt takes a couple of seconds. Sometimes when I look back at the camera, I've missed a number. I can usually guess it from context, but other times I just miss out.

Today, I got up hours earlier than I needed to. It was like Christmas morning! I could hardly wait for 08:00 to roll around. I had breakfast, did some unnecessary checks on Hab equipment, and read some Poirot. Finally the time came!

CNHAKRVR2TLK2PTHFDRPRP4LONGMSG

Yeah. Took me a minute. "Can hack rover to talk to *Pathfinder*. Prepare for long message."

That took some mental gymnastics to work out. But it was great news! If we could get that set up, we'd only be limited by transmission time! I set up a note that said, *Roger.*

Not sure what they meant by "long message," but I figured I better be ready. I went out fifteen minutes before the top of the hour and smoothed out a big area of dirt. I found the longest antenna rod I had, so I could reach into the smooth area without having to step on it.

Then I stood by. Waiting.

At exactly the top of the hour, the message came.

LNCHhexiditONRVRCMP,OPENFILE-/usr/lib/habcomm.so -SCROLLTILIDXONLFTIS:2AAE5,OVRWRT141BYTSWTHDATA WE'LLSNDNXTMSG,STANDINVIEW4NXTPIC20MINFTERTHS DONE

Jesus. Okay . . .

They want me to launch "hexedit" on the rover's computer, then open the file /usr/lib/habcomm.so, scroll until the index reading on the left of the screen is 2AAE5, then replace the bytes there with a 141-byte sequence NASA will send in the next message. Fair enough.

Also, for some reason, they want me to hang around for the next pic. Not sure why. You can't see any part of me when I'm in the suit. Even the faceplate would reflect too much light. Still, it's what they want.

I went back in and copied down the message for future reference. Then I wrote a short note and came back out. Usually I'd pin up the note and go back in. But this time I had to hang around for a photo op.

I gave the camera a thumbs-up to go along with my note, which said, *Ayyyyyy!*

Blame the seventies TV.

...

"I ASK for a picture, and I get the Fonz?" Annie asked, admonishing Venkat.

"You got your picture, quit bitching," he said, cradling the phone on his shoulder. He paid more attention to the schematics in front of him than the conversation.

"Ayyyyyy!" Annie mocked. "Why would he do that?"

"Have you *met* Mark Watney?"

"Fine, fine," Annie said. "But I want a pic of his face ASAP."

"Can't do that."

"Why not?"

"Because if he takes off his helmet, he'll die. Annie, I have to go, one of the JPL programmers is here and it's urgent. Bye!"

"But—" Annie said as he hung up.

Jack, in the doorway, said, "It's not urgent."

"Yeah, I know," Venkat said. "What can I do for you?"

"We were thinking," Jack began. "This rover hack might get kind of detailed. We may have to do a bunch of back-and-forth communication with Watney."

"That's fine," Venkat said. "Take your time, do it right."

"We could get things done faster with a shorter transmission time," Jack said.

Venkat gave him a puzzled look. "Do you have a plan for moving Earth and Mars closer together?"

"Earth doesn't have to be involved," Jack said. "*Hermes* is seventy-three million kilometers from Mars right now. Only four light-minutes away. Beth Johanssen is a great programmer. She could talk Mark through it."

"Out of the question," Venkat said.

"She's the mission sysop." Jack pressed on. "This is her exact area of expertise."

"Can't do it, Jack. The crew still doesn't know."

"What is with you? Why won't you just tell them?"

"Watney's not my only responsibility," Venkat said. "I've got five other astronauts in deep space who have to concentrate on their return trip. Nobody thinks about it, but statistically they're in more danger than Watney right now. He's on a planet. They're in space."

Jack shrugged. "Fine, we'll do it the slow way."

LOG ENTRY: SOL 98 (2)

Ever transcribed 141 random bytes, one-half of a byte at a time?

It's boring. And it's tricky when you don't have a pen.

Earlier, I had just written letters in the sand. But this time, I needed a way to get the numbers onto something portable. My first plan was: Use a laptop!

Each crewman had their own laptop. So I have six at my disposal. Rather, I *had* six. I now have five. I thought a laptop would be fine outside. It's just electronics, right? It'll keep warm enough to operate in the short term, and it doesn't need air for anything.

It died instantly. The screen went black before I was out of the airlock. Turns out the "L" in "LCD" stands for "Liquid." I guess it either froze or boiled off. Maybe I'll post a consumer review. "Brought product to surface of Mars. It stopped working. 0/10."

So I used a camera. I've got lots of them, specially made for working on Mars. I wrote the bytes in the sand as they came in, took a picture, then transcribed them in the Hab.

It's night now, so no more messages. Tomorrow, I'll enter this into the rover and the geeks at JPL can take it from there.

. . .

A NOTABLE smell hung in the air of the makeshift *Pathfinder* control room. The ventilation system was not designed for so many people, and everyone had been working every waking moment without much time for personal hygiene.

"Come on up here, Jack," said Venkat. "You get to be the most Timward today."

"Thanks," said Jack, taking Venkat's place next to Tim. "Heya, Tim!"

"Jack," said Tim.

"How long will the patch take?" Venkat asked.

"Should be pretty much instant," Jack answered. "Watney entered the hack earlier today, and we confirmed it worked. We updated *Pathfinder*'s OS without any problems. We sent the rover patch, which *Pathfinder* rebroadcast. Once Watney executes the patch and reboots the rover, we should get a connection."

"Jesus, what a complicated process," Venkat said.

"Try updating a Linux server sometime," Jack said.

After a moment of silence, Tim said, "You know he was telling a joke, right? That was supposed to be funny."

"Oh," said Venkat. "I'm a physics guy, not a computer guy."

"He's not funny to computer guys, either."

"You're a very unpleasant man, Tim," Jack said.

"System's online," said Tim.

"What?"

"It's online. FYI."

"Holy crap!" Jack said.

"It worked!" Venkat announced to the room.

...

[11:18] JPL: Mark, this is Venkat Kapoor. We've been watching you since Sol 49. The whole world's been rooting for you. Amazing job, getting Pathfinder. We're working on rescue plans. JPL is adjusting Ares 4's MDV to do a short overland flight. They'll pick you up, then take you with them to Schiaparelli. We're putting together a supply mission to keep you fed till Ares 4 arrives.

[11:29] WATNEY: Glad to hear it. Really looking forward to not dying. I want to make it clear it wasn't the crew's fault. Side question: What did they say when they found out I was alive? Also, "Hi, Mom!"

[11:41] JPL: Tell us about your "crops." We estimated your food packs would last until Sol 400 at 3/4 ration per meal. Will your crops affect that number? As to your question: We haven't told the crew you're alive yet. We wanted them to concentrate on their own mission.

[11:52] WATNEY: The crops are potatoes, grown from the ones we were supposed to prepare on Thanksgiving. They're doing great, but the available farmland isn't enough for sustainability. I'll run out of food around Sol 900. Also: Tell the crew I'm alive! What the fuck is wrong with you?

[12:04] JPL: We'll get botanists in to ask detailed questions and double-check your work. Your life is at stake, so we want to be sure. Sol 900 is great news. It'll give us a lot more time to get the supply mission together. Also, please watch your language. Everything you type is being broadcast live all over the world.

[12:15] WATNEY: Look! A pair of boobs! -> (.Y.)

"THANK YOU, Mr. President," Teddy said into the phone. "I appreciate the call, and I'll pass your congratulations on to the whole organization."

He terminated the call and put his phone on the corner of his desk, flush with the desktop's edges.

Mitch knocked on the open door to the office.

"This a good time?" Mitch asked.

"Come in, Mitch," Teddy said. "Have a seat."

"Thanks," Mitch said, sitting in a fine leather couch. He reached up to his earpiece and lowered the volume.

"How's Mission Control?" Teddy asked.

"Fantastic," Mitch said. "All's well with *Hermes*. And everyone's in great spirits thanks to what's going on at JPL. Today was a damn good day for a change!"

"Yes, it was," Teddy agreed. "Another step closer to getting Watney back alive."

"Yeah, about that," said Mitch. "You probably know why I'm here."

"I can take a guess," said Teddy. "You want to tell the crew Watney's alive."

"Yes," Mitch said.

"And you're bringing this up with me while Venkat is in Pasadena, so he can't argue the other side."

"I shouldn't have to clear this with you or Venkat or anyone else. I'm the flight director. It should have been my call from the beginning, but you two stepped in and overrode me. Ignoring all that, we agreed we'd tell them when there was hope. And now there's hope. We've got communication, we have a plan for rescue in the works, and his farm buys us enough time to get him supplies."

"Okay, tell them," Teddy said.

Mitch paused. "Just like that?"

"I knew you'd be here sooner or later, so I already thought it through and decided. Go ahead and tell them."

Mitch stood up. "All right. Thanks," he said as he left the office.

Teddy swiveled in his chair and looked out his windows to the night sky. He pondered the faint, red dot among the stars. "Hang in there, Watney," he said. "We're coming."

CHAPTER 12

WATNEY SLEPT peacefully in his bunk. He shifted slightly as some pleasant dream put a smile on his face. He'd done three EVAs the previous day, all filled with labor-intensive Hab maintenance. So he slept deeper and better than he had in a long time.

"Good morning, crew!" Lewis called out. "It's a brand-new day! Sol 6! Up and at 'em!"

Watney added his voice to a chorus of groans.

"Come on," Lewis prodded, "no bitching. You got forty minutes more sleep than you would've on Earth."

Martinez was first out of his bunk. An air force man, he could match Lewis's navy schedule with ease. "Morning, Commander," he said crisply.

Johanssen sat up, but made no further move toward the harsh world outside her blankets. A career software engineer, mornings were never her forte.

Vogel slowly lumbered from his bunk, checking his watch. He wordlessly pulled on his jumpsuit, smoothing out what wrinkles he could. He sighed inwardly at the grimy feeling of another day without a shower.

Watney turned away, hugging a pillow to his head. "Noisy people, go away," he mumbled.

"Beck!" Martinez called out, shaking the mission's doctor. "Rise and shine, bud!"

"Yeah, okay," Beck said blearily.

Johanssen fell out of her bunk, then remained on the floor.

Pulling the pillow from Watney's hands, Lewis said, "Let's move, Watney! Uncle Sam paid a hundred thousand dollars for every second we'll be here."

"Bad woman take pillow," Watney groaned, unwilling to open his eyes.

"Back on Earth, I've tipped two-hundred-pound men out of their bunks. Want to see what I can do in 0.4 g?"

"No, not really," Watney said, sitting up.

Having rousted the troops, Lewis sat at the comm station to check overnight messages from Houston.

Watney shuffled to the ration cupboard and grabbed a breakfast at random.

"Hand me an 'eggs,' will ya," Martinez said.

"You can tell the difference?" Watney said, passing Martinez a pack.

"Not really," Martinez said.

"Beck, what'll you have?" Watney continued.

"Don't care," Beck said. "Give me whatever."

Watney tossed a pack to him.

"Vogel, your usual sausages?"

"*Ja*, please," Vogel responded.

"You know you're a stereotype, right?"

"I am comfortable with that," Vogel replied, taking the proffered breakfast.

"Hey Sunshine," Watney called to Johanssen. "Eating breakfast today?"

"Mnrrn," Johanssen grunted.

"Pretty sure that's a no," Watney guessed.

The crew ate in silence. Johanssen eventually trudged to the ration cupboard and got a coffee packet. She clumsily added hot water, then sipped until wakefulness crept in.

"Mission updates from Houston," Lewis said. "Satellites show a storm coming, but we can do surface ops before it gets here. Vogel, Martinez, you'll be with me outside. Johanssen, you're stuck tracking weather reports. Watney, your soil experiments are bumped up to today. Beck, run the samples from yesterday's EVA through the spectrometer."

"Should you really go out with a storm on the way?" Beck asked.

"Houston authorized it," Lewis said.

"Seems needlessly dangerous."

"Coming to Mars was needlessly dangerous," Lewis said. "What's your point?"

Beck shrugged. "Just be careful."

...

THREE FIGURES looked eastward. Their bulky EVA suits rendered them nearly identical. Only the European Union flag on Vogel's shoulder distinguished him from Lewis and Martinez, who wore the Stars and Stripes.

The darkness to the east undulated and flickered in the rays of the rising sun.

"The storm," Vogel said in his accented English, "it is closer than Houston reported."

"We've got time," Lewis said. "Focus on the task at hand. This EVA's all about chemical analysis. Vogel, you're the chemist, so you're in charge of what we dig up."

"*Ja*," Vogel said. "Please dig thirty centimeters and get soil samples. At least one hundred grams each. Very important is thirty centimeters down."

"Will do," Lewis said. "Stay within a hundred meters of the Hab," she added.

"Mm," Vogel said.

"Yes, ma'am," said Martinez.

They split up. Greatly improved since the days of Apollo, Ares EVA suits allowed much more freedom of motion. Digging, bending over, and bagging samples were trivial tasks.

After a time, Lewis asked, "How many samples do you need?"

"Seven each, perhaps?"

"That's fine," Lewis confirmed. "I've got four so far."

"Five here," Martinez said. "Of course, we can't expect the navy to keep up with the air force, now can we?"

"So that's how you want to play it?" Lewis said.

"Just call 'em as I see 'em, Commander."

"Johanssen here." The sysop's voice came over the radio. "Houston's upgraded the storm to 'severe.' It's going to be here in fifteen minutes."

"Back to base," Lewis said.

■■■

THE HAB shook in the roaring wind as the astronauts huddled in the center. All six of them now wore their flight space suits, in case they had to scramble for an emergency takeoff in the MAV. Johanssen watched her laptop while the rest watched her.

"Sustained winds over one hundred kph now," she said. "Gusting to one twenty-five."

"Jesus, we're gonna end up in Oz," Watney said. "What's the abort wind speed?"

"Technically one fifty kph," Martinez said. "Any more than that and the MAV's in danger of tipping."

"Any predictions on the storm track?" Lewis asked.

"This is the edge of it," Johanssen said, staring at her screen. "It's gonna get worse before it gets better."

The Hab canvas rippled under the brutal assault as the internal supports bent and shivered with each gust. The cacophony grew louder by the minute.

"All right," Lewis said. "Prep for abort. We'll go to the MAV and hope for the best. If the wind gets too high, we'll launch."

Leaving the Hab in pairs, they grouped up outside Airlock 1. The driving wind and sand battered them, but they were able to stay on their feet.

"Visibility is almost zero," Lewis said. "If you get lost, home in on my suit's telemetry. The wind's gonna be rougher away from the Hab, so be ready."

Pressing through the gale, they stumbled toward the MAV, with Lewis and Beck in the lead and Watney and Johanssen bringing up the rear.

"Hey," Watney panted. "Maybe we could shore up the MAV. Make tipping less likely."

"How?" Lewis huffed.

"We could use cables from the solar farm as guylines." He wheezed for a few moments, then continued. "The rovers could be anchors. The trick would be getting the line around the—"

Flying wreckage slammed Watney, carrying him off into the wind.

"Watney!" Johanssen exclaimed.

"What happened?" Lewis said.

"Something hit him!" Johanssen reported.

"Watney, report," Lewis said.

No reply.

"Watney, report," Lewis repeated.

Again, she was met with silence.

"He's offline," Johanssen reported. "I don't know where he is!"

"Commander," Beck said, "before we lost telemetry, his decompression alarm went off!"

"Shit!" Lewis exclaimed. "Johanssen, where did you last see him?"

"He was right in front of me and then he was gone," she said. "He flew off due west."

"Okay," Lewis said. "Martinez, get to the MAV and prep for launch. Everyone else, home in on Johanssen."

"Dr. Beck," Vogel said as he stumbled through the storm, "how long can a person survive decompression?"

"Less than a minute," Beck said, emotion choking his voice.

"I can't see anything," Johanssen said as the crew crowded around her.

"Line up and walk west," Lewis commanded. "Small steps. He's probably prone; we don't want to step over him."

Staying in sight of one another, they trudged through the chaos.

Martinez fell into the MAV airlock and forced it closed against the wind. Once it pressurized, he quickly doffed his suit. Having climbed the ladder to the crew compartment, he slid into the pilot's couch and booted the system.

Grabbing the emergency launch checklist with one hand, he flicked switches rapidly with the other. One by one, the systems reported flight-ready status. As they came online, he noted one in particular.

"Commander," he radioed. "The MAV's got a seven-degree tilt. It'll tip at 12.3."

"Copy that," Lewis said.

"Johanssen," Beck said, looking at his arm computer, "Watney's bio-monitor sent something before going offline. My computer just says 'Bad Packet.'"

"I have it, too," Johanssen said. "It didn't finish transmitting. Some data's missing, and there's no checksum. Gimme a sec."

"Commander," Martinez said. "Message from Houston. We're officially scrubbed. The storm's definitely gonna be too rough."

"Copy," Lewis said.

"They sent that four and a half minutes ago," Martinez continued, "while looking at satellite data from nine minutes ago."

"Understood," Lewis said. "Continue prepping for launch."

"Copy," Martinez said.

"Beck," Johanssen said. "I have the raw packet. It's plaintext: BP 0, PR 0, TP 36.2. That's as far as it got."

"Copy," Beck said morosely. "Blood pressure zero, pulse rate zero, temperature normal."

The channel fell silent for some time. They continued pressing forward, shuffling through the sandstorm, hoping for a miracle.

"Temperature normal?" Lewis said, a hint of hope in her voice.

"It takes a while for the——" Beck stammered. "It takes a while to cool."

"Commander," Martinez said. "Tilting at 10.5 degrees now, with gusts pushing it to eleven."

"Copy," Lewis said. "Are you at pilot-release?"

"Affirmative," Martinez replied. "I can launch anytime."

"If it tips, can you launch before it falls completely over?"

"Uh," Martinez said, not expecting the question. "Yes, ma'am. I'd take manual control and go full throttle. Then I'd nose up and return to preprogrammed ascent."

"Copy that," Lewis said. "Everyone home in on Martinez's suit. That'll get you to the MAV airlock. Get in and prep for launch."

"What about you, Commander?" Beck asked.

"I'm searching a little more. Get moving. And Martinez, if you start to tip, launch."

"You really think I'll leave you behind?" Martinez said.

"I just ordered you to," Lewis replied. "You three, get to the ship."

They reluctantly obeyed Lewis's order and made their way toward the MAV. The punishing wind fought them every step of the way.

Unable to see the ground, Lewis shuffled forward. Remembering something, she reached to her back and got a pair of rock-drill bits. She had added the one-meter bits to her equipment that morning, anticipating geological sampling later in the day. Holding one in each hand, she dragged them along the ground as she walked.

After twenty meters, she turned around and walked the opposite direction. Walking a straight line proved to be impossible. Not only did she lack visual references, the endless wind pushed her off course. The sheer volume of attacking sand buried her feet with each step. Grunting, she pressed on.

Beck, Johanssen, and Vogel squeezed into the MAV airlock. Designed for two, it could be used by three in emergencies. As it equalized, Lewis's voice came over the radio.

"Johanssen," she said, "would the rover IR camera do any good?"

"Negative," Johanssen replied. "IR can't get through sand any better than visible light."

"What's she thinking?" Beck asked after removing his helmet. "She's a geologist. She knows IR can't get through a sandstorm."

"She is grasping," Vogel said, opening the inner door. "We must get to the couches. Please hurry."

"I don't feel good about this," Beck said.

"Neither do I, Doctor," said Vogel, climbing the ladder, "but the commander has given us orders. Insubordination will not help."

"Commander," Martinez radioed, "we're tilting 11.6 degrees. One good gust and we're tipping."

"What about the proximity radar?" Lewis said. "Could it detect Watney's suit?"

"No way," Martinez said. "It's made to see *Hermes* in orbit, not the metal in a single space suit."

"Give it a try," Lewis said.

"Commander," said Beck, putting on a headset as he slid into his acceleration couch, "I know you don't want to hear this, but Watn— . . . Mark's dead."

"Copy," Lewis said. "Martinez, try the radar."

"Roger," Martinez radioed.

He brought the radar online and waited for it to complete a self-check. Glaring at Beck, he said, "What's the matter with you?"

"My friend just died," Beck answered. "And I don't want my commander to die, too."

Martinez gave him a stern look. Turning his attention back to the radar, he radioed, "Negative contact on proximity radar."

"Nothing?" Lewis asked.

"It can barely see the Hab," he replied. "The sandstorm's fucking things up. Even if it wasn't, there's not enough metal in— Shit!"

"Strap in!" he yelled to the crew. "We're tipping!"

The MAV creaked as it tilted faster and faster.

"Thirteen degrees," Johanssen called out from her couch.

Buckling his restraints, Vogel said, "We are far past balance. We will not rock back."

"We can't leave her!" Beck yelled. "Let it tip, we'll fix it!"

"Thirty-two metric tons including fuel," Martinez said, his hands flying over the controls. "If it hits the ground, it'll do structural damage to the tanks, frame, and probably the second-stage engine. We'd never be able to fix it."

"You can't abandon her!" Beck said. "You can't."

"I've got one trick. If that doesn't work, I'm following her orders."

Bringing the orbital maneuvering system online, he fired a sustained burn from the nose cone array. The small thrusters fought against the lumbering mass of the slowly tilting spacecraft.

"You are firing the OMS?" Vogel asked.

"I don't know if it'll work. We're not tipping very fast," Martinez said. "I think it's slowing down . . ."

"The aerodynamic caps will have automatically ejected," Vogel said. "It will be a bumpy ascent with three holes in the side of the ship."

"Thanks for the tip," Martinez said, maintaining the burn and watching the tilt readout. "C'mon . . . "

"Still thirteen degrees," Johanssen reported.

"What's going on up there?" Lewis radioed. "You went quiet. Respond."

"Stand by," Martinez replied.

"Twelve point nine degrees," Johanssen said.

"It is working," Vogel said.

"For now," Martinez said. "I don't know if maneuvering fuel will last."

"Twelve point eight now," Johanssen supplied.

"OMS fuel at sixty percent," Beck said. "How much do you need to dock with *Hermes*?"

"Ten percent if I don't fuck anything up," Martinez said, adjusting the thrust angle.

"Twelve point six," Johanssen said. "We're tipping back."

"Or the wind died down a little," Beck postulated. "Fuel at forty-five percent."

"There is danger of damage to the vents," Vogel cautioned. "The OMS was not made for prolonged thrusts."

"I know," Martinez said. "I can dock without nose vents if I have to."

"Almost there . . . ," Johanssen said. "Okay we're under 12.3."

"OMS cutoff," Martinez announced, terminating the burn.

"Still tipping back," Johanssen said. "11.6 . . . 11.5 . . . holding at 11.5."

"OMS Fuel at twenty-two percent," Beck said.

"Yeah, I see that," Martinez replied. "It'll be enough."

"Commander," Beck radioed, "you need to get to the ship now."

"Agreed," Martinez radioed. "He's gone, ma'am. Watney's gone."

The four crewmates awaited their commander's response.

"Copy," she finally replied. "On my way."

They lay in silence, strapped to their couches and ready for launch. Beck looked at Watney's empty couch and saw Vogel doing the same. Martinez ran a self-check on the nose cone OMS thrusters. They were no longer safe for use. He noted the malfunction in his log.

The airlock cycled. After removing her suit, Lewis made her way to the flight cabin. She wordlessly strapped into her couch, her face a frozen mask. Only Martinez dared speak.

"Still at pilot-release," he said quietly. "Ready for launch."

Lewis closed her eyes and nodded.

"I'm sorry, Commander," Martinez said. "You need to verbally—"

"Launch," she said.

"Yes, ma'am," he replied, activating the sequence.

The retaining clamps ejected from the launch gantry, falling to the ground. Seconds later, preignition pyros fired, igniting the main engines, and the MAV lurched upward.

The ship slowly gained speed. As it did, wind shear blew it laterally off course. Sensing the problem, the ascent software angled the ship into the wind to counteract it.

As fuel was consumed, the ship got lighter, and the acceleration more pronounced. Rising at this exponential rate, the craft quickly reached maximum acceleration, a limit defined not by the ship's power, but by the delicate human bodies inside.

As the ship soared, the open OMS ports took their toll. The crew rocked in their couches as the craft shook violently. Martinez and the ascent software kept it trim, though it was a constant battle. The turbulence tapered off and eventually fell to nothing as the atmosphere became thinner and thinner.

Suddenly, all force stopped. The first stage had been completed. The crew experienced weightlessness for several seconds, then were pressed back into their couches as the next stage began. Outside, the now-empty first stage fell away, eventually to crash on some unknown area of the planet below.

The second stage pushed the ship ever higher, and into low orbit. Lasting less time than the massive first stage, and thrusting much more smoothly, it seemed almost like an afterthought.

Abruptly, the engine stopped, and an oppressive calm replaced the previous cacophony.

"Main engine shutdown," Martinez said. "Ascent time: eight minutes, fourteen seconds. On course for *Hermes* intercept."

Normally, an incident-free launch would be cause for celebration. This one earned only silence broken by Johanssen's gentle sobbing.

...

Four months later . . .

Beck tried not to think about the painful reason he was doing zero-g plant growth experiments. He noted the size and shape of the fern leaves, took photos, and made notes.

Having completed his science schedule for the day, he checked his watch. Perfect timing. The data dump would be completing soon. He floated past the reactor to the Semicone-A ladder.

Traveling feet-first along the ladder, he soon had to grip it in earnest as the centripetal force of the rotating ship took hold. By the time he reached Semicone-A he was at 0.4 g.

No mere luxury, the centripetal gravity of *Hermes* kept them fit. Without it, they would have spent their first week on Mars barely able to walk. Zero-g exercise regimens could keep the heart and bones healthy, but none had been devised that would give them full function from Sol 1.

Because the ship was already designed for it, they used the system on the return trip as well.

Johanssen sat at her station. Lewis sat in the adjacent seat while Vogel and Martinez hovered nearby. The data dump carried e-mails and videos from home. It was the high point of the day.

"Is it here yet?" Beck asked as he entered the bridge.

"Almost," Johanssen said. "Ninety-eight percent."

"You're looking cheerful, Martinez," Beck said.

"My son turned three yesterday." He beamed. "Should be some pics of the party. How about you?"

"Nothing special," Beck said. "Peer reviews of a paper I wrote a few years back."

"Complete," Johanssen said. "All the personal e-mails are dispatched to your laptops. Also there's a telemetry update for Vogel and a system update for me. Huh . . . there's a voice message addressed to the whole crew."

She looked over her shoulder to Lewis.

Lewis shrugged. "Play it."

Johanssen opened the message, then sat back.

"*Hermes*, this is Mitch Henderson," the message began.

"Henderson?" Martinez said, puzzled. "Talking directly to us without CAPCOM?"

Lewis held her hand up to signal for silence.

"I have some news," Mitch's voice continued. "There's no subtle way to put this: Mark Watney's still alive."

Johanssen gasped.

"Wha—" Beck stammered.

Vogel stood with his mouth agape as a shocked expression swept across his face.

Martinez looked to Lewis. She leaned forward and pinched her chin.

"I know that's a surprise," Mitch continued. "And I know you'll have a lot of questions. We're going to answer those questions. But for now I'll just give you the basics.

"He's alive and healthy. We found out two months ago and decided not to tell you; we even censored personal messages. I was *strongly* against all that. We're telling you now because we finally have communication with him and a viable rescue plan. It boils down to Ares 4 picking him up with a modified MDV.

"We'll get you a full write-up of what happened, but it's definitely not your fault. Mark stresses that every time it comes up. It was just bad luck.

"Take some time to absorb this. Your science schedules are cleared for tomorrow. Send all the questions you want and we'll answer them. Henderson out."

The message's end brought stunned silence to the bridge.

"He . . . He's alive?" Martinez said, then smiled.

Vogel nodded excitedly. "He lives."

Johanssen stared at her screen in wide-eyed disbelief.

"Holy shit," Beck laughed. "Holy shit! Commander! He's alive!"

"I left him behind," Lewis said quietly.

The celebrations ceased immediately as the crew saw their commander's expression.

"But," Beck began, "we all left togeth—"

"You followed orders," Lewis interrupted. "I left him behind. In a barren, unreachable, godforsaken wasteland."

Beck looked to Martinez pleadingly. Martinez opened his mouth, but could find no words to say.

Lewis trudged off the bridge.

CHAPTER 13

The employees of Deyo Plastics worked double shifts to finish the Hab canvas for Ares 3. There was talk of triple shifts, if NASA increased the order again. No one minded. The overtime pay was spectacular, and the funding was limitless.

Woven carbon thread ran slowly through the press, which sandwiched it between polymer sheets. The completed material was folded four times and glued together. The resulting thick sheet was then coated with soft resin and taken to the hot-room to set.

LOG ENTRY: SOL 114

Now that NASA can talk to me, they won't shut the hell up.

They want constant updates on every Hab system, and they've got a room full of people trying to micromanage my crops. It's *awesome* to have a bunch of dipshits on Earth telling me, a botanist, how to grow plants.

I mostly ignore them. I don't want to come off as arrogant here, but I'm the best botanist on the planet.

One big bonus: e-mail! Just like the days back on *Hermes*, I get data dumps. Of course, they relay e-mail from friends and family, but NASA also sends along choice messages from the public. I've gotten e-mail from rock stars, athletes, actors and actresses, and even the President.

One of them was from my alma mater, the University of Chicago. They say once you grow crops somewhere, you have officially "colonized" it. So technically, I colonized Mars.

In your *face*, Neil Armstrong!

But my favorite e-mail was the one from my mother. It's exactly what you'd expect. Thank God you're alive, stay strong, don't die, your father says hello, etc.

I read it fifty times in a row. Hey, don't get me wrong, I'm not a mama's boy or anything. I'm a full-grown man who only occasionally wears diapers (you have to in an EVA suit). It's totally manly and normal for me to cling to a letter from my mom. It's not like I'm some homesick kid at camp, right?

Admittedly, I have to schlep to the rover five times a day to check e-mail. They can get a message from Earth to Mars, but they can't get it another ten meters to the Hab. But hey, I can't bitch. My odds of living through this are way higher now.

Last I heard, they'd solved the weight problem on Ares 4's MDV. Once it lands here, they'll ditch the heat shield, all the life support stuff, and a bunch of empty fuel tanks. Then they can take the seven of us (Ares 4's crew plus me) all the way to Schiaparelli. They're already working on my duties for the surface ops. How cool is that?

In other news, I'm learning Morse code. Why? Because it's our backup communications system. NASA figured a decades-old probe isn't ideal as a sole means of communication.

If *Pathfinder* craps out, I'll spell messages with rocks, which NASA will see with satellites. They can't reply, but at least we'd have one-way communication. Why Morse code? Because making dots and dashes with rocks is a lot easier than making letters.

It's a shitty way to communicate. Hopefully it won't come up.

All chemical reactions complete, the sheet was sterilized and moved to a clean room. There, a worker cut a strip off the edge, divided it into squares, and put each through a series of rigorous tests.

Having passed inspection, the sheet was then cut to shape. The edges were folded over, sewn, and resealed with resin. A man with a clipboard made final inspections, independently verifying the measurements, then approved it for use.

<hr>

LOG ENTRY: SOL 115

The meddling botanists have grudgingly admitted I did a good job. They agree I'll have enough food to last till Sol 900. Bearing that in mind, NASA has fleshed out the mission details of the supply probe.

At first, they were working on a desperate plan to get a probe here before Sol 400. But I bought another five hundred sols of life with my potato farm, so they have more time to work on it.

They'll launch next year during the Hohmann Transfer Window, and it'll take almost nine months to get here. It should arrive around Sol 856. It'll have plenty of food, a spare oxygenator, water reclaimer, and comm system. Three comm systems, actually. I guess they aren't taking any chances, what with my habit of being nearby when radios break.

Got my first e-mail from *Hermes* today. NASA's been limiting direct contact. I guess they're afraid I'll say something like "You abandoned me on Mars, you assholes!" I know the crew was surprised to hear from the Ghost of Mars Missions Past, but c'mon! I wish NASA was less of a nanny sometimes. Anyway, they finally let one e-mail through from the Commander:

> Watney, obviously we're very happy to hear you
> survived. As the person responsible for your situation,
> I wish there was more I could do to directly help. But it
> looks like NASA has a good rescue plan. I'm sure you'll

continue to show your incredible resourcefulness and get
through this. Looking forward to buying you a beer back
on Earth.

   —Lewis

My reply:

   Commander, pure bad luck is responsible for my
situation, not you. You made the right call and saved
everyone else. I know it must have been a tough decision,
but any analysis of that day will show it was the right
one. Get everyone else home and I'll be happy.
   I will take you up on that beer, though.

   —Watney

   *The employees carefully folded the sheet and placed it in an argon-
filled airtight shipping container. The man with the clipboard placed a
sticker on the package. "Project Ares 3; Hab Canvas; Sheet AL102."*
   *The package was placed on a charter plane and flown to Edwards
Air Force Base in California. It flew abnormally high, at great cost of
fuel, to ensure a smoother flight.*
   *Upon arrival, the package was carefully transported by special con-
voy to Pasadena. Once there, it was moved to the JPL Spacecraft Assembly Facility. Over the next five weeks, engineers in white bodysuits
assembled Presupply 309. It contained AL102 as well as twelve other
Hab Canvas packages.*

LOG ENTRY: SOL 116

It's almost time for the second harvest.
   Ayup.
   I wish I had a straw hat and some suspenders.
   My reseed of the potatoes went well. I'm beginning to see that

crops on Mars are extremely prolific, thanks to the billions of dollars' worth of life support equipment around me. I now have four hundred healthy potato plants, each one making lots of calorie-filled taters for my dining enjoyment. In just ten days they'll be ripe!

And this time, I'm not replanting them as seed. This is my food supply. All natural, organic, Martian-grown potatoes. Don't hear that every day, do you?

You may be wondering how I'll store them. I can't just pile them up; most of them would go bad before I got around to eating them. So instead, I'll do something that wouldn't work at all on Earth: throw them outside.

Most of the water will be sucked out by the near-vacuum; what's left will freeze solid. Any bacteria planning to rot my taters will die screaming.

In other news, I got an e-mail from Venkat Kapoor:

> Mark, some answers to your earlier questions:
> No, we will not tell our Botany Team to "Go fuck themselves." I understand you've been on your own for a long time, but we're in the loop now, and it's best if you listen to what we have to say.
> The Cubs finished the season at the bottom of the NL Central.
> The data transfer rate just isn't good enough for the size of music files, even in compressed formats. So your request for "Anything, oh God, ANYTHING but Disco" is denied. Enjoy your boogie fever.
> Also, an uncomfortable side note . . . NASA is putting together a committee. They want to see if there were any avoidable mistakes that led you to being stranded. Just a heads-up. They may have questions for you later on.
> Keep us posted on your activities.
> —Kapoor

My reply:

> Venkat, tell the investigation committee they'll have to
> do their witch hunt without me. And when they inevitably
> blame Commander Lewis, be advised I'll publicly refute it.
> I'm sure the rest of the crew will do the same.
>
> Also, please tell them that each and every one of their
> mothers is a prostitute.
>
> —Watney
>
> PS: Their sisters, too.

The presupply probes for Ares 3 launched on fourteen consecutive days during the Hohmann Transfer Window. Presupply 309 was launched third. The 251-day trip to Mars was uneventful, needing only two minor course adjustments.

After several aerobraking maneuvers to slow down, it made its final descent toward Acidalia Planitia. First, it endured reentry via a heat shield. Later, it released a parachute and detached the now-expended shield.

Once its onboard radar detected it was thirty meters from the ground, it cut loose the parachute and inflated balloons all around its hull. It fell unceremoniously to the surface, bouncing and rolling, until it finally came to rest.

Deflating its balloons, the onboard computer reported the successful landing back to Earth.

Then it waited twenty-three months.

LOG ENTRY: SOL 117

The water reclaimer is acting up.

Six people will go through 18 liters of water per day. So it's made to process 20. But lately, it hasn't been keeping up. It's doing 10, tops.

Do I generate 10 liters of water per day? No, I'm not the urinating champion of all time. It's the crops. The humidity inside the Hab is a lot higher than it was designed for, so the water reclaimer is constantly filtering it out of the air.

I'm not worried about it. If need be, I can piss directly onto the plants. The plants will take their share of water and the rest will condense on the walls. I could make something to collect the condensation, I'm sure. Thing is, the water can't go anywhere. It's a closed system.

Okay, *technically* I'm lying. The plants aren't entirely water-neutral. They strip the hydrogen from some of it (releasing the oxygen) and use it to make the complex hydrocarbons that are the plant itself. But it's a very small loss and I made like 600 liters of water from MDV fuel. I could take *baths* and still have plenty left over.

NASA, however, is absolutely shitting itself. They see the water reclaimer as a critical survival element. There's no backup, and they think I'll die instantly without it. To them, equipment failure is terrifying. To me, it's "Tuesday."

So instead of preparing for my harvest, I have to make extra trips to and from the rover to answer their questions. Each new message instructs me to try some new solution and report the results back.

So far as we've worked out it's not the electronics, refrigeration system, instrumentation, or temperature. I'm sure it'll turn out to be a little hole somewhere, then NASA will have four hours of meetings before telling me to cover it with duct tape.

Lewis and Beck opened Presupply 309. Working as best they could in their bulky EVA suits, they removed the various portions of Hab canvas and laid them on the ground. Three entire presupply probes were dedicated to the Hab.

Following a procedure they had practiced hundreds of times, they

efficiently assembled the pieces. Special seal-strips between the patches
ensured airtight mating.

After erecting the main structure of the Hab, they assembled the
three airlocks. Sheet AL102 had a hole perfectly sized for Airlock
1. Beck stretched the sheet tight to the seal-strips on the airlock's
exterior.

Once all airlocks were in place, Lewis flooded the Hab with air and
AL102 felt pressure for the first time. Lewis and Beck waited an hour.
No pressure was lost; the setup had been perfect.

LOG ENTRY: SOL 118

My conversation with NASA about the water reclaimer was boring
and riddled with technical details. So I'll paraphrase it for you:

Me: "This is obviously a clog. How about I take it apart and
check the internal tubing?"

NASA: (after five hours of deliberation) "No. You'll fuck it up
and die."

So I took it apart.

Yeah, I know. NASA has a lot of ultra-smart people and I should
really do what they say. And I'm being too adversarial, considering
they spend all day working on how to save my life.

I just get sick of being told how to wipe my ass. Independence
was one of the qualities they looked for when choosing Ares astronauts. It's a thirteen-month mission, most of it spent many light-
minutes away from Earth. They wanted people who would act on
their own initiative.

If Commander Lewis were here, I'd do whatever she said, no
problem. But a committee of faceless bureaucrats back on Earth?
Sorry, I'm just having a tough time with it.

I was really careful. I labeled every piece as I dismantled it, and
laid everything out on a table. I have the schematics in the computer, so nothing was a surprise.

And just as I'd suspected, there was a clogged tube. The water reclaimer was designed to purify urine and strain humidity out of the air (you exhale almost as much water as you piss). I've mixed my water with soil, making it mineral water. The minerals built up in the water reclaimer.

I cleaned out the tubing and put it all back together. It completely solved the problem. I'll have to do it again someday, but not for a hundred sols or so. No big deal.

I told NASA what I did. Our (paraphrased) conversation was:

Me: "I took it apart, found the problem, and fixed it."

NASA: "Dick."

AL102 shuddered in the brutal storm. Withstanding forces far greater than it was designed for, it rippled violently against the airlock seal-strip. Other sections of canvas undulated along their seal-strips together, acting as a single sheet, but AL102 had no such luxury. The airlock barely moved, leaving AL102 to take the full force of the tempest.

The layers of plastic, constantly bending, heated the resin from pure friction. The new, more yielding environment allowed the carbon fibers to separate.

AL102 stretched.

Not much. Only four millimeters. But the carbon fibers, usually 500 microns apart, now had a gap eight times that width in their midst.

After the storm abated, the lone remaining astronaut performed a full inspection of the Hab. But he didn't notice anything amiss. The weak part of canvas was concealed by a seal-strip.

Designed for a mission of thirty-one sols, AL102 continued well past its planned expiration. Sol after sol went by, with the lone astronaut traveling in and out of the Hab almost daily. Airlock 1 was closest to the rover charging station, so the astronaut preferred it to the other two.

When pressurized, the airlock expanded slightly; when depressur-ized, it shrunk. Every time the astronaut used the airlock, the strain on AL102 relaxed, then tightened anew.

Pulling, stressing, weakening, stretching . . .

<u>LOG ENTRY: SOL 119</u>

I woke up last night to the Hab shaking.

The medium-grade sandstorm ended as suddenly as it began. It was only a category three storm with 50 kph winds. Nothing to worry about. Still, it's a bit disconcerting to hear howling winds when you're used to utter silence.

I'm worried about *Pathfinder*. If the sandstorm damaged it, I'll have lost my connection to NASA. Logically, I shouldn't worry. The thing's been on the surface for decades. A little gale won't do any harm.

When I head outside, I'll confirm *Pathfinder*'s still functional be-fore moving on to the sweaty, annoying work of the day.

Yes, with each sandstorm comes the inevitable Cleaning of the Solar Cells, a time-honored tradition among hearty Martians such as myself. It reminds me of growing up in Chicago and having to shovel snow. I'll give my dad credit; he never claimed it was to build character or teach me the value of hard work.

"Snowblowers are expensive," he used to say. "You're free."

Once, I tried to appeal to my mom. "Don't be such a wuss," she suggested.

In other news, it's seven sols till the harvest, and I still haven't prepared. For starters, I need to make a hoe. Also, I need to make an outdoor shed for the potatoes. I can't just pile them up outside. The next major storm would cause the Great Martian Potato Migration.

Anyway, all that will have to wait. I've got a full day today. After cleaning the solar cells, I have to check the whole solar array to make sure the storm didn't hurt it. Then I'll need to do the same for the rover.

I better get started.

· · ·

AIRLOCK 1 SLOWLY depressurized to 0.006 atmospheres. Watney, wearing an EVA suit, stood inside it waiting for the cycle to complete. He had done it literally hundreds of times. Any apprehension he may have had on Sol 1 was long gone. Now it was merely a boring chore before exiting to the surface.

As the depressurization continued, the Hab's atmosphere compressed the airlock, and AL102 stretched for the last time.

On Sol 119, the Hab breached.

The initial tear was less than one millimeter. The perpendicular carbon fibers should have prevented the rip from growing. But countless abuses had stretched the vertical fibers apart and weakened the horizontal ones beyond use.

The full force of the Hab's atmosphere rushed through the breach. Within a tenth of a second, the rip was a meter long, running parallel to the seal-strip. It propagated all the way around until it met its starting point. The airlock was no longer attached to the Hab.

The unopposed pressure launched the airlock like a cannonball as the Hab's atmosphere explosively escaped through the breach. Inside, the surprised Watney slammed against the airlock's back door with the force of the expulsion.

The airlock flew forty meters before hitting the ground. Watney, barely recovered from the earlier shock, now endured another as he hit the front door, face-first.

His faceplate took the brunt of the blow, the safety glass shattering into hundreds of small cubes. His head slammed against the inside of the helmet, knocking him senseless.

The airlock tumbled across the surface for a further fifteen meters. The heavy padding of Watney's suit saved him from many broken bones. He tried to make sense of the situation, but he was barely conscious.

Finally done tumbling, the airlock rested on its side amid a cloud of dust.

Watney, on his back, stared blankly upward through the hole in his shattered faceplate. A gash in his forehead trickled blood down his face.

Regaining some of his wits, he got his bearings. Turning his head to the side, he looked through the back door's window. The collapsed Hab rippled in the distance, a junkyard of debris strewn across the landscape in front of it.

Then, a hissing sound reached his ears. Listening carefully, he realized it was not coming from his suit. Somewhere in the phone booth–sized airlock, a small breach was letting air escape.

He listened intently to the hiss, then he touched his broken faceplate. Then he looked out the window again.

"You fucking kidding me?" he said.

CHAPTER 14

AUDIO LOG TRANSCRIPT: SOL 119

You know what!? Fuck this! Fuck this airlock, fuck that Hab, and fuck this whole planet!

Seriously, this is it! I've had it! I've got a few minutes before I run out of air and I'll be damned if I spend them playing Mars's little game. I'm so god damned sick of it I could puke!

All I have to do is sit here. The air will leak out and I'll die.

I'll be done. No more getting my hopes up, no more self-delusion, and no more problem-solving. I've fucking *had it!*

AUDIO LOG TRANSCRIPT: SOL 119 (2)

Sigh . . . okay. I've had my tantrum and now I have to figure out how to stay alive. Again. Okay, let's see what I can do here . . . .

I'm in the airlock. I can see the Hab out the window; it's a good 50 meters away. Normally, the airlock is *attached* to the Hab. So that's a problem.

The airlock's on its side, and I can hear a steady hiss. So either it's leaking or there are snakes in here. Either way, I'm in trouble.

Also, during the . . . whatever the fuck happened . . . I got bounced around like a pinball and smashed my faceplate. Air is notoriously uncooperative when it comes to giant, gaping holes in your EVA suit.

Looks like the Hab is completely deflated and collapsed. So even if I had a functional EVA suit to leave the airlock with, I wouldn't have anywhere to go. So that sucks.

I gotta think for a minute. And I have to get out of this EVA suit. It's bulky, and the airlock is cramped. Besides, it's not like it's doing me any good.

AUDIO LOG TRANSCRIPT: SOL 119 (3)

Things aren't as bad as they seem.

I'm still fucked, mind you. Just not as deeply.

Not sure what happened to the Hab, but the rover's probably fine. It's not ideal, but at least it's not a leaky phone booth.

I have a patch kit on my EVA suit, of course. The same kind that saved my life back on Sol 6. But don't get excited. It won't do the suit any good. The patch kit is a cone-shaped valve with super-sticky resin on the wide end. It's just too small to deal with a hole larger than eight centimeters. And really, if you have a nine-centimeter hole, you're going to be dead way before you could whip out the kit.

Still, it's an asset, and maybe I can use it to stop the airlock leak. And that's my top priority right now.

It's a small leak. With the faceplate gone, the EVA suit is effectively managing the whole airlock. It's been adding air to make up for the missing pressure. But it'll run out eventually.

I need to find the leak. I think it's near my feet, judging by the sound. Now that I'm out of the suit, I can turn around and get a look. . . .

I don't see anything. . . . I can hear it, but . . . it's down here somewhere, but I don't know where.

I can only think of one way to find it: Start a fire!

Yeah, I know. A lot of my ideas involve setting something on fire. And yes, deliberately starting a fire in a tiny, enclosed space is usually a terrible idea. But I need the smoke. Just a little wisp of it.

As usual, I'm working with stuff that was deliberately designed not to burn. But no amount of careful design by NASA can get around a determined arsonist with a tank of pure oxygen.

Unfortunately, the EVA suit is made entirely of nonflammable materials. So is the airlock. My clothes are fireproof as well, even the thread.

I was originally planning to check the solar array, doing repairs as needed after last night's storm. So I have my toolbox with me. But looking through it, I see it's all metal or nonflammable plastic.

I just realized I do have something flammable: my own hair. It'll have to do. There's a sharp knife in the tool kit. I'll shave some arm hairs off into a little pile.

Next step: oxygen. I don't have anything so refined as pure oxygen flow. All I can do is muck with the EVA suit controls to increase oxygen percentage in the whole airlock. I figure bumping it to 40 percent will do.

All I need now is a spark.

The EVA suit has electronics, but it runs on very low voltage. I don't think I could get an arc with it. Besides, I don't want to mess with the suit. I need it working to get from the airlock to the rover.

The airlock itself has electronics, but it ran on Hab power. I guess NASA never considered what would happen if it was launched fifty meters. Lazy bums.

Plastic might not burn, but anyone who's played with a balloon knows it's great at building up static charge. Once I do that, I should be able to make a spark just by touching a metal tool.

Fun fact: This is exactly how the Apollo 1 crew died. Wish me luck!

I'm in a box full of burning-hair smell. It's not a good smell.

On my first try, the fire lit, but the smoke just drifted randomly around. My own breathing was screwing it up. So I held my breath and tried again.

My second try, the EVA suit threw everything off. There's a gentle flow of air coming out of the faceplate as the suit constantly replaces the missing air. So I shut the suit down, held my breath, and tried again. I had to be quick; the pressure was dropping.

My third try, the quick arm movements I used to set the fire messed everything up. Just moving around makes enough turbulence to send the smoke everywhere.

The fourth time I kept the suit turned off, held my breath, and when the time came to light the fire, I did it very slowly. Then I watched as the little wisp of smoke drifted toward the floor of the airlock, disappearing through a hairline fracture.

I have you now, little leak!

I gasped for air and turned the EVA suit back on. The pressure had dropped to 0.9 atmospheres during my little experiment. But there was plenty of oxygen in the air for me and my hair-fire to breathe. The suit quickly got things back to normal.

Looking at the fracture, I see that it's pretty tiny. It would be a cinch to seal it with the suit's patch kit, but now that I think about it, that's a bad idea.

I'll need to do some kind of repair to the faceplate. I don't know how just yet, but the patch kit and its pressure-resistant resin are probably really important. And I can't do it bit by bit, either. Once I break the seal on the patch kit, the binary components of the resin mix and I have sixty seconds before it hardens. I can't just take a little to fix the airlock.

Given time, I might be able to come up with a plan for the faceplate. Then, I could take a few seconds during that plan to scrape resin over the airlock fracture. But I don't have time.

I'm down to 40 percent of my N_2 tank. I need to seal that fracture now, and I need to do it without using the patch kit.

First idea: Little Dutch Boy. I'm licking my palm and placing it over the crack.

Okay . . . I can't quite make a perfect seal, so there's airflow . . . getting colder now . . . getting pretty uncomfortable . . . Okay, fuck this.

On to idea number two. Tape!

I have duct tape in my toolbox. Let's slap some on and see if it slows the flow. I wonder how long it will last before the pressure rips it. Putting it on now.

There we go . . . still holding . . .

Lemme check the suit . . . . Readouts say the pressure is stable. Looks like the duct tape made a good seal.

Let's see if it holds. . . .

AUDIO LOG TRANSCRIPT: SOL 119 (5)

It's been fifteen minutes, and the tape is still holding. Looks like that problem is solved.

Sort of anticlimactic, really. I was already working out how to cover the breach with ice. I have two liters of water in the EVA suit's "hamster-feeder." I could have shut off the suit's heating systems and let the airlock cool to freezing. Then I'd . . . Well, whatever.

Coulda done it with ice. I'm just sayin'.

All right. On to my next problem: How do I fix the EVA suit? Duct tape might seal a hairline crack, but it can't hold an atmosphere of pressure against the size of my broken faceplate.

The patch kit is too small, but still useful. I can spread the resin around the edge of where the faceplate was, then stick something on to cover the hole. Problem is, what do I use to cover the hole? Something that can stand up to a lot of pressure.

Looking around, the only thing I see that can hold an atmosphere is the EVA suit itself. There's plenty of material to work with, and I can even cut it. Remember when I was cutting Hab canvas into strips? Those same shears are right here in my tool kit.

Cutting a chunk out of my EVA suit leaves it with another hole. But a hole I can control the shape and location of.

Yeah . . . I think I see a solution here. I'm going to cut off my arm!

Well, no. Not *my* arm. The EVA suit's arm. I'll cut right below the left elbow. Then I can cut along its length, turning it into a rectangle. It'll be big enough to seal the faceplate, and it'll be held in place by the resin.

Material designed to withstand atmospheric pressure? Check.

Resin designed to seal a breach against that pressure? Check.

And what about the gaping hole on the stumpy arm? Unlike my faceplate, the suit's material is flexible. I'll press it together and seal it with resin. I'll have to press my left arm against my side while I'm in the suit, but there'll be room.

I'll be spreading the resin pretty thin, but it's literally the strongest adhesive known to man. And it doesn't have to be a perfect seal. It just has to last long enough for me to get to safety.

And where will that "safety" be? Not a damn clue.

Anyway, one problem at a time. Right now I'm fixing the EVA suit.

AUDIO LOG TRANSCRIPT: SOL 119 (6)

Cutting the arm off the suit was easy; so was cutting along its length to make a rectangle. Those shears are strong as hell.

Cleaning the glass off the faceplate took longer than I'd expected. It's unlikely it would puncture EVA suit material, but I'm not taking any chances. Besides, I don't want glass in my face when I'm wearing it.

Then came the tricky part. Once I broke the seal on the patch kit, I had sixty seconds before the resin set. I scooped it off the patch kit with my fingers and quickly spread it around the rim of the faceplate. Then I took what was left and sealed the arm hole.

I pressed the rectangle of suit material onto the helmet with both hands while using my knee to keep pressure on the arm's seam.

I held on until I'd counted 120 seconds. Just to be sure.

It seemed to work well. The seal looked strong and the resin was rock-hard. I did, however, glue my hand to the helmet.

Stop laughing.

In retrospect, using my fingers to spread the resin wasn't the best plan. Fortunately, my left hand was still free. After some grunting and a lot of profanities, I was able to reach the toolbox. Once I got a screwdriver, I chiseled myself free (feeling really stupid the whole time). It was a delicate process because I didn't want to flay the skin off my fingers. I had to get the screwdriver between the helmet and the resin. I freed my hand and didn't draw blood, so I call that a win. Though I'll have hardened resin on my fingers for days, just like a kid who played with Krazy Glue.

Using the arm computer, I had the suit overpressurize to 1.2 atmospheres. The faceplate patch bowed outward but otherwise held firm. The arm filled in, threatening to tear the new seam, but stayed in one piece.

Then I watched the readouts to see how airtight things were.

Answer: Not very.

It absolutely *pissed* the air out. In five minutes it leaked so much it pressurized the whole airlock to 1.2 atmospheres.

The suit is designed for eight hours of use. That works out to 250 milliliters of liquid oxygen. Just to be safe, the suit has a full liter of O_2 capacity. But that's only half the story. The rest of the air is nitrogen. It's just there to add pressure. When the suit leaks, that's what it backfills with. The suit has two liters of liquid N_2 storage.

Let's call the volume of the airlock two cubic meters. The inflated EVA suit probably takes up half of it. So it took five minutes to add 0.2 atmospheres to 1 cubic meter. That's 285 grams of air (trust me on the math). The air in the tanks is around 1 gram per cubic centimeter, meaning I just lost 285 milliliters.

The three tanks combined had 3000 milliliters to start with. A lot of that was used to maintain pressure while the airlock was leaking. Also, my breathing turned some oxygen into carbon dioxide, which was captured by the suit's CO_2 filters.

Checking the readouts, I see that I have 410 milliliters of oxygen, 738 milliliters of nitrogen. Together, they make almost 1150 milliliters to work with. That, divided by 285 milliliters lost per minute . . .

Once I'm out of the airlock, this EVA suit will only last four minutes.

Fuck.

AUDIO LOG TRANSCRIPT: SOL 119 (7)

Okay, I've been thinking some more.

What good is going to the rover? I'd just be trapped there instead. The extra room would be nice, but I'd still die eventually. No water reclaimer, no oxygenator, no food. Take your pick; all of those problems are fatal.

I need to fix the Hab. I know what to do; we practiced it in training. But it'll take a long time. I'll have to scrounge around in the now-collapsed canvas to get the spare material for patching. Then I have to find the breach and seal-strip a patch in place.

But it'll take hours to repair, and my EVA suit is useless.

I'll need another suit. Martinez's used to be in the rover. I hauled it all the way to the *Pathfinder* site and back, just in case I needed a spare. But when I returned, I put it back in the Hab.

Damn it!

All right, so I'll need to get another suit before going to the rover. Which one? Johanssen's is too small for me (tiny little gal, our Johanssen). Lewis's is full of water. Actually, by now it's full of slowly sublimating ice. The mangled, glued-together suit I have with me is my original one. That leaves just Martinez, Vogel, and Beck's.

I left Martinez's near my bunk, in case I needed a suit in a hurry. Of course, after that sudden decompression, it could be anywhere. Still, it's a place to start.

Next problem: I'm like 50 meters from the Hab. Running in 0.4 g while wearing a bulky EVA suit isn't easy. At best, I can trundle 2 meters per second. That's a precious 25 seconds; almost an eighth of my four minutes. I've got to bring that down.

But how?

AUDIO LOG TRANSCRIPT: SOL 119 (8)

I'll roll the damn airlock.

It's basically a phone booth on its side. I did some experiments.

I figured if I want it to roll, I'll need to hit the wall as hard as possible. And I have to be in the air at the time. I can't press against some other part of the airlock. The forces would cancel each other out and it wouldn't move at all.

First I tried launching myself off one wall and slamming into the other. The airlock slid a little, but that's it.

Next, I tried doing a super-push-up to get airborne (0.4 g yay!) then kicking the wall with both feet. Again, it just slid.

The third time, I got it right. The trick was to plant both my feet on the ground, near the wall, then launch myself to the top of the opposite wall and hit with my back. When I tried that just now, it gave me enough force and leverage to tip the airlock and roll it one face toward the Hab.

The airlock is a meter wide, so . . . sigh . . . I have to do it like fifty more times.

I'm gonna have a hell of a backache after this.

I have a hell of a backache.

The subtle and refined "hurl my body at the wall" technique had some flaws. It worked only one out of every ten tries, and it hurt a lot. I had to take breaks, stretch out, and generally convince myself to body-slam the wall again and again.

It took all damn night, but I made it.

I'm ten meters from the Hab now. I can't get any closer, 'cause the debris from the decompression is all over the place. This isn't an "all-terrain" airlock. I can't roll over that shit.

It was morning when the Hab popped. Now it's morning again. I've been in this damn box for an entire day. But I'm leaving soon.

I'm in the EVA suit now, and ready to roll.

All right . . . Okay . . . Once more through the plan: Use the manual valves to equalize the airlock. Get out and hurry to the Hab. Wander around under the collapsed canvas. Find Martinez's suit (or Vogel's if I run into it first). Get to the rover. Then I'm safe.

If I run out of time before finding a suit, I'll just run to the rover. I'll be in trouble, but I'll have time to think and materials to work with.

Deep breath . . . here we go!

I'm alive! And I'm in the rover!

Things didn't go exactly as planned, but I'm not dead, so it's a win.

Equalizing the airlock went fine. I was out on the surface within thirty seconds. Skipping toward the Hab (the fastest way to move in this gravity), I passed through the field of debris. The rupture had really sent things flying, myself included.

It was hard to see; my faceplate was covered by the makeshift patch. Fortunately, my arm had a camera. NASA discovered that turning your whole EVA-suited body to look at something was a strenuous waste of time. So they mounted a small camera on the right arm. The feed is projected on the inner faceplate. This allows us to look at things just by pointing at them.

The faceplate patch wasn't exactly smooth or reflective, so I had to look at a rippled, messed-up version of the camera feed. Still, it was enough to see what was going on.

I beelined for where the airlock used to be. I knew there had to be a pretty big hole there, so I'd be able to get in. I found it easily. And boy is it a nasty rip! It's going to be a pain in the ass to fix it.

That's when the flaws in my plan started to reveal themselves. I only had one arm to work with. My left arm was pinned against my body, while the stumpy arm of the suit bounced freely. So as I moved around under the canvas, I had to use my one good arm to hold the canvas up. It slowed me down.

From what I could see, the interior of the Hab is chaos. Everything's moved. Entire tables and bunks are meters away from where they started. Lighter objects are wildly jumbled, many of them out on the surface. Everything's covered in soil and mangled potato plants.

Trudging onward, I got to where I'd left Martinez's suit. To my shock, it was still there!

"Yay!" I naively thought. "Problem solved."

Unfortunately, the suit was pinned under a table, which was held down by the collapsed canvas. If I'd had both arms, I could have pulled it free, but with only one, I just couldn't do it.

Running low on time, I detached the helmet. Setting it aside, I reached past the table to get Martinez's patch kit. I found it with the help of the arm-camera. I dropped it in the helmet and hauled ass out of there.

I barely made it to the rover in time. My ears were popping from pressure loss just as the rover's airlock filled with wonderful 1-atmosphere air.

Crawling in, I collapsed and panted for a moment.

So I'm back in the rover. Just like I was back on the Great *Path-finder* Recovery Expedition. Ugh. At least this time it smells a little better.

NASA's probably pretty worried about me by now. They probably saw the airlock move back to the Hab, so they know I'm alive, but they'll want status. And as it happens, it's the rover that communicates with *Pathfinder*.

I tried to send a message, but *Pathfinder* isn't responding. That's not a big surprise. It's powered directly from the Hab, and the Hab is offline. During my brief, panicked scramble outside, I saw that *Pathfinder* was right where I left it, and the debris didn't reach that far out. It should be fine, once I get it some power.

As for my current situation, the big gain is the helmet. They're interchangeable, so I can replace my broken-ass one with Martinez's. The stumpy arm is still an issue, but the faceplate was the main source of leaks. And with the fresh patch kit, I can seal the arm with more resin.

But that can wait. I've been awake for over twenty-four hours. I'm not in any immediate danger, so I'm going to sleep.

LOG ENTRY: SOL 121

Got a good night's sleep and made real progress today.

First thing I did was reseal the arm. Last time, I had to spread the resin pretty thin; I'd used most of it for the faceplate patch. But this time I had a whole patch kit just for the arm. I got a perfect seal.

I still only had a one-armed suit, but at least it didn't leak.

I'd lost most of my air yesterday, but I had a half hour of oxygen left. Like I said earlier, a human body doesn't need much oxygen. Maintaining pressure was the problem.

With that much time, I was able to take advantage of the rover's EVA tank-refill. Something I couldn't do with the leaky suit.

The tank-refill is an emergency measure. The expected use of the rover is to start with full EVA suits and come back with air to spare. It wasn't designed for long trips, or even overnighters. But, just in case of emergency, it has refill hoses mounted on the exterior. Inside space was limited already, and NASA concluded that most air-related emergencies would be outdoors.

But refilling is slow, slower than my suit was leaking. So it wasn't any use to me until I swapped helmets. Now, with a solid suit capable of holding pressure, refilling the tanks was a breeze.

After refilling, and making sure the suit was still not leaking, I had a few immediate tasks to take care of. Much as I trust my handiwork, I wanted a two-armed suit.

I ventured back into the Hab. This time, not being rushed, I was able to use a pole to leverage the table off Martinez's suit. Pulling it loose, I dragged it back to the rover.

After a thorough diagnostic to be sure, I finally had a fully functional EVA suit! It took me two trips to get it, but I got it.

Tomorrow, I'll fix the Hab.

LOG ENTRY: SOL 122

The first thing I did today was line up rocks near the rover to spell "A-okay." That should make NASA happy.

I went into the Hab again to assess damage. My priority will be to get the structure intact and holding pressure. From there, I can work on fixing stuff that broke.

The Hab is normally a dome, with flexible support poles maintaining the arch and rigid, folding floor material to keep its base flat. The internal pressure was a vital part of its support. Without it, the whole thing collapsed. I inspected the poles, and none of them had broken. They're just lying flat is all. I'll have to re-couple a few of them, but that'll be easy.

The hole where Airlock 1 used to be is huge, but surmountable.

I have seal-strips and spare canvas. It'll be a lot of work, but I can get the Hab together again. Once I do, I'll reestablish power and get *Pathfinder* back online. From there, NASA can tell me how to fix anything I can't figure out on my own.

I'm not worried about any of that. I have a much bigger problem.

The farm is dead.

With a complete loss of pressure, most of the water boiled off. Also, the temperature is well below freezing. Not even the bacteria in the soil can survive a catastrophe like that. Some of the crops were in pop-tents off the Hab. But they're dead, too. I had them connected directly to the Hab via hoses to maintain air supply and temperature. When the Hab blew, the pop-tents depressurized as well. Even if they hadn't, the freezing cold would have killed the crops.

Potatoes are now extinct on Mars.

So is the soil bacteria. I'll never grow another plant so long as I'm here.

We had it all planned out. My farm would give me food till Sol 900. A supply probe would get here on Sol 856; way before I ran out. With the farm dead, that plan is history.

The ration packs won't have been affected by the explosion. And the potatoes I've already grown may be dead, but they're still food. I was just about to harvest, so it was a good time for this to happen, I guess.

The rations will last me till Sol 400. I can't say for sure how long the potatoes will last, until I see how many I got. But I can estimate. I had 400 plants, probably averaging 5 potatoes each: 2000 taters. At 150 calories each, I'll need to eat 10 per sol to survive. That means they'll last me 200 sols. Grand total: I have enough food to last till Sol 600.

By Sol 856 I'll be long dead.

CHAPTER 15

[08:12] WATNEY: Test.

[08:25] JPL: Received! You gave us quite a scare there. Thanks for the "A-okay" message. Our analysis of satellite imagery shows a complete detachment of Airlock 1. Is that correct? What's your status?

[08:39] WATNEY: If by "detachment" you mean "shot me out like a cannon" then yeah. Minor cut on my forehead. Had some issues with my EVA suit (I'll explain later). I patched up the Hab and repressurized it (main air tanks were intact). I just got power back online. The farm is dead. I've recovered as many potatoes as I could and stored them outside. I count 1841. That will last me 184 days. Including the remaining mission rations, I'll start starving on Sol 584.

[08:52] JPL: Yeah, we figured. We're working on solutions to the food issue. What's the status of the Hab systems?

[09:05] WATNEY: Primary air and water tanks were unharmed. The rover, solar array, and Pathfinder were out of the blast range. I'll run diagnostics on the Hab's systems while I wait for your next reply. By the way, who am I talking to?

[09:18] JPL: Venkat Kapoor in Houston. Pasadena relays my messages. I'm going to handle all direct communication with you from now on. Check the oxygenator and water reclaimer first. They're the most important.

[09:31] WATNEY: Duh. Oxygenator functioning perfectly. Water reclaimer is completely offline. Best guess is water froze up inside and burst some tubing. I'm sure I can fix it. The Hab's main computer is also functioning without any problems. Any idea what caused the Hab to blow up?

[09:44] JPL: Best guess is fatigue on the canvas near Airlock 1. The pressurization cycle stressed it until it failed. From now on, alternate Airlock 2 and 3 for all EVAs. Also, we'll be getting you a checklist and procedures for a full canvas exam.

[09:57] WATNEY: Yay, I get to stare at a wall for several hours! Let me know if you come up with a way for me to not starve.

[10:11] JPL: Will do.

...

"IT's SOL 122," Bruce said. "We have until Sol 584 to get a probe to Mars. That's four hundred and sixty-two sols, which is four hundred and seventy-five days."

The assembled department heads of JPL furrowed their brows and rubbed their eyes.

He stood from his chair. "The positions of Earth and Mars aren't ideal. The trip will take four hundred and fourteen days. Mounting the probe to the booster and dealing with inspections will take thirteen days. That leaves us with just forty-eight days to make this probe."

Sounds of whispered exasperation filled the room. "Jesus," someone said.

"It's a whole new ball game," Bruce continued. "Our focus is food. Anything else is a luxury. We don't have time to make a powered-descent lander. It'll have to be a tumbler. So we can't put anything delicate inside. Say good-bye to all the other crap we'd planned to send."

"Where's the booster coming from?" asked Norm Toshi, who was in charge of the reentry process.

"The EagleEye 3 Saturn probe," Bruce said. "It was scheduled to launch next month. NASA put it on hold so we can have the booster."

"I bet the EagleEye team was pissed about that," Norm said.

"I'm sure they were," Bruce said. "But it's the only booster we have that's big enough. Which brings me to my next point: We only get one shot at this. If we fail, Mark Watney dies."

He looked around the room and let that sink in.

"We do have some things going for us," he finally said. "We have some of the parts built for the Ares 4 presupply missions. We can steal from them, and that'll save us some time. Also, we're sending food, which is pretty robust. Even if there's a reentry problem and the probe impacts at high velocity, food is still food.

"And we don't need a precision landing. Watney can travel hundreds of kilometers if necessary. We just need to land close enough for him to reach it. This ends up being a standard tumble-land presupply. All we have to do is make it quickly. So let's get to it."

...

[08:02] JPL: We've spun up a project to get you food. It's been in progress for a week or so. We can get it to you before you starve, but it'll be tight. It'll just be food and a radio. We can't send an oxygenator, water reclaimer, or any of that other stuff without powered descent.

[08:16] WATNEY: No complaints here! You get me the food, I'll be a happy camper. I've got all Hab systems up and running again. The water reclaimer is working fine now that I replaced the burst hoses. As for water supply, I have 620 liters remaining. I started with 900 liters (300 to start with, 600 more from reducing hydrazine). So I lost almost 300 liters to sublimation. Still, with the water reclaimer operational again, it's plenty.

[08:31] JPL: Good, keep us posted on any mechanical or electronic problems. By the way, the name of the probe we're sending is Iris. Named after the Greek goddess who traveled the heavens with the speed of wind. She's also the goddess of rainbows.

[08:47] WATNEY: Gay probe coming to save me. Got it.

...

RICH PURNELL sipped coffee in the silent building. He ran a final test on the software he'd written. It passed. With a relieved sigh, he sank back in his chair. Checking the clock on his computer, he shook his head. 3:42 a.m.

As an astrodynamicist, Rich rarely had to work late. His job was to find the exact orbits and course corrections needed for any given mission. Usually, it was one of the first parts of a project, all the other steps being based on the orbit.

But this time, things were reversed. Iris needed an orbital path, and nobody knew when it would launch.

Planets move as time goes by. A course calculated for a specific launch date will work only for that date. Even a single day's difference would result in missing Mars entirely.

So Rich had to calculate *many* courses. He had a range of twenty-five days during which Iris might launch. He calculated one course for each.

He began an e-mail to his boss.

Mike, he typed, *Attached are the courses for Iris, in 1-day increments. We should start peer review and vetting so they can be officially accepted. And you were right, I was here almost all night.*

It wasn't that bad. Nowhere near the pain of calculating orbits for Hermes. I know you get bored when I go into the math, so I'll summarize: The small, constant thrust of Hermes's ion drives is much harder to deal with than the large point-thrusts of presupply probes.

All 25 of the courses take 414 days, and vary only slightly in thrust duration and angle. The fuel requirement is nearly identical for the orbits and is well within the capacity of EagleEye's booster.

It's too bad. Earth and Mars are really badly positioned. Heck, it's almost easier to—

He stopped typing.

Furrowing his brow, he stared into the distance.

"Hmm," he said.

He grabbed his coffee cup and went to the break room for a refill.

...

TEDDY SCANNED the crowded conference room. It was rare to see such an assembly of NASA's most important people all in one place. He squared a small stack of notes he'd prepared and placed them neatly in front of him.

"I know you're all busy," Teddy said. "Thank you for making time for this meeting. I need status on Project Iris from all departments. Venkat, let's start with you."

"The mission team's ready," Venkat said, looking at spreadsheets on his laptop. "There was a minor turf war between the Ares 3 and

Ares 4 presupply control teams. The Ares 3 guys said they should run it, because while Watney's on Mars, Ares 3 is still in progress. The Ares 4 team points out it's their coopted probe in the first place. I ended up going with Ares 3."

"Did that upset Ares 4?" Teddy asked.

"Yes, but they'll get over it. They have thirteen other presupply missions coming up. They won't have time to be pissy."

"Mitch," Teddy said to the flight controller, "what about the launch?"

Mitch pulled the earpiece from his ear. "We've got a control room ready," he said. "I'll oversee the launch, then hand cruise and landing over to Venkat's guys."

"Media?" Teddy said, turning to Annie.

"I'm giving daily updates to the press," she said, leaning back in her chair. "Everyone knows Watney's fucked if this doesn't work. The public hasn't been this engaged in ship construction since Apollo 11. CNN's *The Watney Report* has been the number one show in its time slot for the past two weeks."

"The attention is good," Teddy said. "It'll help get us emergency funding from Congress." He looked up to a man standing near the entrance. "Maurice, thanks for flying out on short notice."

Maurice nodded.

Teddy gestured to him and addressed the room. "For those who don't know him, this is Maurice Stein from Cape Canaveral. He was the scheduled pad leader for EagleEye 3, so he inherited the role for Iris. Sorry for the bait and switch, Maurice."

"No problem," said Maurice. "Glad I can help out."

Teddy flipped the top page of his notes facedown beside the stack. "How's the booster?"

"It's all right for now," said Maurice. "But it's not ideal. Eagle-Eye 3 was set to launch. Boosters aren't designed to stand upright and bear the stress of gravity for long periods. We're adding external supports that we'll remove before launch. It's easier than disassembly. Also the fuel is corrosive to the internal tanks, so we had to drain it. In the meantime, we're performing inspections on all systems every three days."

"Good, thank you," Teddy said. He turned his attention to Bruce Ng, who stared back at him with heavy bloodshot eyes.

"Bruce, thank you for flying out, too. How's the weather in California these days?"

"I wouldn't know," Bruce said. "I rarely see the outdoors."

Subdued laughter filled the room for a few seconds.

Teddy flipped another page. "Time for the big question, Bruce. How's Iris coming along?"

"We're behind," Bruce said with a tired shake of his head. "We're going as fast as we can, but it's just not fast enough."

"I can find money for overtime," Teddy offered.

"We're already working around the clock."

"How far behind are we talking about?" Teddy asked.

Bruce rubbed his eyes and sighed. "We've been at it twenty-nine days; so we only have nineteen left. After that, the Pad needs thirteen days to mount it on the booster. We're at least two weeks behind."

"Is that as far behind as you're going to get?" Teddy asked, writing a note on his papers. "Or will you slip more?"

Bruce shrugged. "If we don't have any more problems, it'll be two weeks late. But we always have problems."

"Give me a number," Teddy said.

"Fifteen days," Bruce responded. "If we had another fifteen days, I'm sure we could get it done in time."

"All right," Teddy said, taking another note. "Let's create fifteen days."

Turning his attention to the Ares 3 flight surgeon, Teddy asked, "Dr. Keller, can we reduce Watney's food intake to make the rations last longer?"

"Sorry, but no," Keller said. "He's already at a minimal calorie count. In fact, considering the amount of physical labor he does, he's eating far less than he should. And it's only going to get worse. Soon his entire diet will be potatoes and vitamin supplements.

He's been saving protein-rich rations for later use, but he'll still be malnourished."

"Once he runs out of food, how long until he starves to death?" Teddy asked.

"Presuming an ample water supply, he might last three weeks. Shorter than a typical hunger strike, but remember he'll be malnourished and thin to begin with."

Venkat raised a hand and caught their attention. "Remember, Iris is a tumbler; he might have to drive a few days to get it. And I'm guessing it's hard to control a rover when you're literally starving to death."

"He's right," Dr. Keller confirmed. "Within four days of running out of food, he'll barely be able to stand up, let alone control a rover. Plus, his mental faculties will rapidly decline. He'd have a hard time even staying awake."

"So the landing date's firm," Teddy said. "Maurice, can you get Iris on the booster in less than thirteen days?"

Maurice leaned against the wall and pinched his chin. "Well . . . it only takes three days to actually mount it. The following ten are for testing and inspections."

"How much can you reduce those?"

"With enough overtime, I could get the mounting down to two days. That includes transport from Pasadena to Cape Canaveral. But the inspections can't be shortened. They're time-based. We do checks and rechecks with set intervals between them to see if something deforms or warps. If you shorten the intervals, you invalidate the inspections."

"How often do those inspections reveal a problem?" Teddy asked.

A silence fell over the room.

"Uh," Maurice stammered. "Are you suggesting we don't do the inspections?"

"No," said Teddy. "Right now I'm asking how often they reveal a problem."

"About one in twenty launches."

Teddy wrote that down. "And how often is the problem they find something that would have caused a mission failure?"

"I'm, uh, not sure. Maybe half the time?"

He wrote that down as well. "So if we skip inspections and testing, we have a one in forty chance of mission failure?" Teddy asked.

"That's two point five percent," Venkat said, stepping in. "Normally, that's grounds for a countdown halt. We can't take a chance like that."

" 'Normally' was a long time ago," Teddy said. "Ninety-seven point five percent is better than zero. Can anyone think of a safer way to get more time?"

He scanned the room. Blank faces stared back.

"All right, then," he said, circling something on his notes. "Speeding up the mounting process and skipping inspections buys us eleven days. If Bruce can pull a rabbit out of a hat and get done sooner, Maurice can do some inspections."

"What about the other four days?" Venkat asked.

"I'm sure Watney can stretch the food to last four extra days, malnutrition notwithstanding," Teddy said, looking to Dr. Keller.

"I—" Keller started. "I can't recommend—"

"Hang on," Teddy interrupted. He stood and straightened his blazer. "Everyone, I understand your positions. We have procedures. Skipping those procedures means risk. Risk means trouble for your department. But now isn't the time to cover our asses. We have to take risks or Mark Watney dies."

Turning to Keller, he said, "Make the food last another four days."

Keller nodded.

•••

"RICH," said Mike.

Rich Purnell concentrated on his computer screen. His cubicle was a landfill of printouts, charts, and reference books. Empty coffee cups rested on every surface; take-out packaging littered the ground.

"Rich," Mike said, more forcefully.

Rich looked up. "Yeah?"

"What the hell are you doing?"

"Just a little side project. Something I wanted to check up on."

"Well . . . that's fine, I guess," Mike said, "but you need to do your assigned work first. I asked for those satellite adjustments two weeks ago and you still haven't done them."

"I need some supercomputer time," Rich said.

"You need supercomputer time to calculate routine satellite adjustments?"

"No, it's for this other thing I'm working on," Rich said.

"Rich, seriously. You have to do your job."

Rich thought for a moment. "Would now be a good time for a vacation?" he asked.

Mike sighed. "You know what, Rich? I think now would be an *ideal* time for you to take a vacation."

"Great!" Rich smiled. "I'll start right now."

"Sure," Mike said. "Go on home. Get some rest."

"Oh, I'm not going home," said Rich, returning to his calculations.

Mike rubbed his eyes. "Okay, whatever. About those satellite orbits . . . ?"

"I'm on vacation," Rich said without looking up.

Mike shrugged and walked away.

· · ·

[08:01] WATNEY: How's my care package coming along?

[08:16] JPL: A little behind schedule, but we'll get it done. In the meantime, we want you to get back to work.

We're satisfied the Hab is in good condition. Maintenance
only takes you twelve hours per week. We're going to pack
the rest of your time with research and experiments.

[08:31] WATNEY: Great! I'm sick of sitting on my ass. I'm
going to be here for years. You may as well make use of
me.

[08:47] JPL: That's what we're thinking. We'll get you
a schedule as soon as the science team puts it together.
It'll be mostly EVAs, geological sampling, soil tests,
and weekly self-administered medical tests. Honestly,
this is the best "bonus Mars time" we've had since the
Opportunity lander.

[09:02] WATNEY: Opportunity never went back to Earth.

[09:17] JPL: Sorry. Bad analogy.

...

THE JPL Spacecraft Assembly Facility, known as the "clean room,"
was the little-known birthplace of the most famous spacecraft in
Mars exploration history. Mariner, Viking, Spirit, Opportunity, and
Curiosity, just to name a few, had all been born in this one room.

Today, the room was abuzz with activity as technicians sealed
Iris into the specially designed shipping container.

The off-duty techs watched the procedure from the observation
deck. They had rarely seen their homes in the last two months; a
makeshift bunk room had been set up in the cafeteria. Fully a third
of them would normally be asleep at this hour, but they did not
want to miss this moment.

The shift leader tightened the final bolt. As he retracted the
wrench, the engineers broke into applause. Many of them were in
tears.

After sixty-three days of grueling work, Iris was complete.

...

ANNIE TOOK the podium and adjusted the microphone. "The launch preparations are complete," she said. "Iris is ready to go. The scheduled launch is 9:14 a.m.

"Once launched, it will stay in orbit for at least three hours. During that time, Mission Control will gather exact telemetry in preparation for the trans-Mars injection burn. When that's complete, the mission will be handed off to the Ares 3 presupply team, who will monitor its progress over the following months. It will take four hundred and fourteen days to reach Mars."

"About the payload," a reporter asked, "I hear there's more than just food?"

"That's true." Annie smiled. "We allocated one hundred grams for luxury items. There are some handwritten letters from Mark's family, a note from the President, and a USB drive filled with music from all ages."

"Any disco?" someone asked.

"No disco," Annie said, as chuckles cascaded through the room.

CNN's Cathy Warner spoke up. "If this launch fails, is there any recourse for Watney?"

"There are risks to any launch," Annie said, sidestepping the question, "but we don't anticipate problems. The weather at the Cape is clear with warm temperatures. Conditions couldn't be better."

"Is there any spending limit to this rescue operation?" another reporter asked. "Some people are beginning to ask how much is too much."

"It's not about the bottom line," Annie said, prepared for the question. "It's about a human life in immediate danger. But if you want to look at it financially, consider the value of Mark Watney's extended mission. His prolonged mission and fight for survival are giving us more knowledge about Mars than the rest of the Ares program combined."

···

"Do you believe in God, Venkat?" Mitch asked.

"Sure, lots of 'em," Venkat said. "I'm Hindu."

"Ask 'em all for help with this launch."

"Will do."

Mitch stepped forward to his station in Mission Control. The room bustled with activity as the dozens of controllers each made final preparations for launch.

He put his headset on and glanced at the time readout on the giant center screen at the front of the room. He turned on his headset and said, "This is the flight director. Begin launch status check."

"Roger that, Houston" was the reply from the launch control director in Florida. "CLCDR checking all stations are manned and systems ready," he broadcast. "Give me a go/no-go for launch. Talker?"

"Go" was the response.

"Timer."

"Go," said another voice.

"QAM1."

"Go."

Resting his chin on his hands, Mitch stared at the center screen. It showed the pad video feed. The booster, amid cloudy water vapor from the cooling process, still had *EagleEye3* stenciled on the side.

"QAM2."

"Go."

"QAM3."

"Go."

Venkat leaned against the back wall. He was an administrator. His job was done. He could only watch and hope. His gaze was fixated on the far wall's displays. In his mind, he saw the numbers, the shift juggling, the outright lies and borderline crimes he'd committed to put this mission together. It would all be worthwhile, if it worked.

"FSC."

"Go."

"Prop One."

"Go."

Teddy sat in the VIP observation room behind Mission Control. His authority afforded him the very best seat: front-row center. His briefcase lay at his feet and he held a blue folder in his hands.

"Prop Two."

"Go."

"PTO."

"Go."

Annie Montrose paced in her private office next to the press room. Nine televisions mounted to the wall were each tuned to a different network; each network showed the launch pad. A glance at her computer showed foreign networks doing the same. The world was holding its breath.

"ACC."

"Go."

"LWO."

"Go."

Bruce Ng sat in the JPL cafeteria along with hundreds of engineers who had given everything they had to Iris. They watched the live feed on a projection screen. Some fidgeted, unable to find comfortable positions. Others held hands. It was 6:13 a.m. in Pasadena, yet every single employee was present.

"AFLC."

"Go."

"Guidance."

"Go."

Millions of kilometers away, the crew of *Hermes* listened as they crowded around Johanssen's station. The two-minute transmission time didn't matter. They had no way to help; there was no need to interact. Johanssen stared intently at her screen, although it displayed only the audio signal strength. Beck wrung his hands.

Vogel stood motionless, his eyes fixed on the floor. Martinez prayed silently at first, then saw no reason to hide it. Commander Lewis stood apart, her arms folded across her chest.

"PTC."

"Go."

"Launch Vehicle Director."

"Go."

"Houston, this is Launch Control, we are go for launch."

"Roger," Mitch said, checking the countdown. "This is Flight, we are go for launch on schedule."

"Roger that, Houston," Launch Control said. "Launch on schedule."

Once the clock reached −00:00:15, the television networks got what they were waiting for. The timer controller began the verbal countdown. "Fifteen," she said, "fourteen . . . thirteen . . . twelve . . . eleven . . ."

Thousands had gathered at Cape Canaveral, the largest crowd ever to watch an unmanned launch. They listened to the timer controller's voice as it echoed across the grandstands.

" . . . ten . . . nine . . . eight . . . seven . . ."

Rich Purnell, entrenched in his orbital calculations, had lost track of time. He didn't notice when his coworkers migrated to the large meeting room where a TV had been set up. In the back of his mind, he thought the office was unusually quiet, but he gave it no further thought.

" . . . six . . . five . . . four . . ."

"Ignition sequence start."

" . . . three . . . two . . . one . . ."

Clamps released, the booster rose amid a plume of smoke and fire, slowly at first, then racing ever faster. The assembled crowd cheered it on its way.

" . . . and liftoff of the Iris supply probe," the timer controller said.

As the booster soared, Mitch had no time to watch the spectacle on the main screen. "Trim?" he called out.

"Trim's good, Flight" was the immediate response.

"Course?" he asked.

"On course."

"Altitude one thousand meters," someone said.

"We've reached safe-abort," another person called out, indicating that the ship could crash harmlessly into the Atlantic Ocean if necessary.

"Altitude fifteen hundred meters."

"Pitch and roll maneuver commencing."

"Getting a little shimmy, Flight."

Mitch looked over to the ascent flight director. "Say again?"

"A slight shimmy. Onboard guidance is handling it."

"Keep an eye on it," Mitch said.

"Altitude twenty-five hundred meters."

"Pitch and roll complete, twenty-two seconds till staging."

...

WHEN DESIGNING Iris, JPL accounted for catastrophic landing failure. Rather than normal meal kits, most of the food was cubed protein bar material, which would still be edible even if Iris failed to deploy its tumble balloons and impacted at incredible speed.

Because Iris was an unmanned mission, there was no cap on acceleration. The contents of the probe endured forces no human could survive. But while NASA had tested the effects of extreme g-forces on protein cubes, they had not done so with a simultaneous lateral vibration. Had they been given more time, they would have.

The harmless shimmy, caused by a minor fuel mixture imbalance, rattled the payload. Iris, mounted firmly within the aeroshell atop the booster, held firm. The protein cubes inside Iris did not.

At the microscopic level, the protein cubes were solid food particles suspended in thick vegetable oil. The food particles compressed to less than half their original size, but the oil was barely affected at all. This changed the volume ratio of solid to liquid dramatically, which in turn made the aggregate act as a liquid. Known as "liquefaction," this process transformed the protein cubes from a steady solid into a flowing sludge.

Stored in a compartment that originally had no leftover space, the now-compressed sludge had room to slosh.

The shimmy also caused an imbalanced load, forcing the sludge toward the edge of its compartment. This shift in weight only aggravated the larger problem, and the shimmy grew stronger.

■ ■ ■

"Shimmy's getting violent," reported the ascent flight director.

"How violent?" Mitch said.

"More than we like," he said. "But the accelerometers caught it and calculated the new center of mass. The guidance computer is adjusting the engines' thrusts to counteract. We're still good."

"Keep me posted," Mitch said.

"Thirteen seconds till staging."

The unexpected weight shift had not spelled disaster. All systems were designed for worst-case scenarios; each did its job admirably. The ship continued toward orbit with only a minor course adjustment, implemented automatically by sophisticated software.

The first stage depleted its fuel, and the booster coasted for a fraction of a second as it jettisoned stage clamps via explosive bolts. The now-empty stage fell away from the craft as the second-stage engines prepared to ignite.

The brutal forces had disappeared. The protein sludge floated free in the container. Given two seconds, it would have re-expanded and solidified. But it was given only a quarter second.

As the second stage fired, the craft experienced a sudden jolt of immense force. No longer contending with the deadweight of the first stage, the acceleration was profound. The three hundred kilograms of sludge slammed into the back of its container. The point of impact was at the edge of Iris, nowhere near where the mass was expected to be.

Though Iris was held in place by five large bolts, the force was directed entirely to a single one. The bolt was designed to withstand immense forces; if necessary to carry the entire weight of the payload. But it was *not* designed to sustain a sudden impact from a loose three-hundred-kilogram mass.

The bolt sheared. The burden was then shifted to the remaining four bolts. The forceful impact having passed, their work was considerably easier than that of their fallen comrade.

Had the pad crew been given time to do normal inspections, they would have noticed the minor defect in one of the bolts. A defect that slightly weakened it, though it would not cause failure on a normal mission. Still, they would have swapped it out with a perfect replacement.

The off-center load presented unequal force to the four remaining bolts, the defective one bearing the brunt of it. Soon, it failed as well. From there, the other three failed in rapid succession.

Iris slipped from its supports in the aeroshell, slamming into the hull.

. . .

"WOAH!" exclaimed the ascent flight director. "Flight, we're getting a large precession!"

"What?" Mitch said as alerts beeped and lights flashed across all the consoles.

"Force on Iris is at seven g's," someone said.

"Intermittent signal loss," called another voice.

"Ascent, what's happening here?" Mitch demanded.

"All hell broke loose. It's spinning on the long axis with a seventeen-degree precession."

"How bad?"

"At least five rps, and falling off course."

"Can you get it to orbit?"

"I can't talk to it at all; signal failures left and right."

"Comm!" Mitch shot to the communications director.

"Workin' on it, Flight," was the response. "There's a problem with the onboard system."

"Getting some major g's inside, Flight."

"Ground telemetry shows it two hundred meters low of target path."

"We've lost readings on the probe, Flight."

"Entirely lost the probe?" he asked.

"Affirm, Flight. Intermittent signal from the ship, but no probe."

"Shit," Mitch said. "It shook loose in the aeroshell."

"It's dreideling, Flight."

"Can it limp to orbit?" Mitch said. "Even super-low EO? We might be able to—"

"Loss of signal, Flight."

"LOS here, too."

"Same here."

Other than the alarms, the room fell silent.

After a moment, Mitch said, "Reestablish?"

"No luck," said Comm.

"Ground?" Mitch asked.

"GC" was the reply. "Vehicle had already left visual range."

"SatCon?" Mitch asked.

"No satellite acquisition of signal."

Mitch looked forward to the main screen. It was black now, with large white letters reading "LOS."

"Flight," a voice said over the radio, "US destroyer *Stockton* reports debris falling from the sky. Source matches last known location of Iris."

Mitch put his head in his hands. "Roger," he said.

Then he uttered the words every flight director hopes never to say: "GC, Flight. Lock the doors."

It was the signal to start post-failure procedures.

From the VIP observation room, Teddy watched the despondent Mission Control Center. He took a deep breath, then let it out. He looked forlornly at the blue folder that contained his cheerful speech praising a perfect launch. He placed it in his briefcase and extracted the red folder, with the *other* speech in it.

...

VENKAT STARED out his office windows to the space center beyond. A space center that housed mankind's most advanced knowledge of rocketry yet had still failed to execute today's launch.

His mobile rang. His wife again. No doubt worried about him. He let it go to voice mail. He just couldn't face her. Or anyone.

A chime came from his computer. Glancing over, he saw an e-mail from JPL. A relayed message from *Pathfinder*:

[16:03] WATNEY: How'd the launch go?

CHAPTER 16

Martinez:

Dr. Shields says I need to write personal messages to each of the crew. She says it'll keep me tethered to humanity. I think it's bullshit. But hey, it's an order.

With you, I can be blunt:

If I die, I need you to check on my parents. They'll want to hear about our time on Mars firsthand. I'll need you to do that.

It won't be easy talking to a couple about their dead son. It's a lot to ask; that's why I'm asking you. I'd tell you you're my best friend and stuff, but it would be lame.

I'm not giving up. Just planning for every outcome. It's what I do.

• • •

GUO MING, director of the China National Space Administration, examined the daunting pile of paperwork at his desk. In the old days, when China wanted to launch a rocket, they just launched it. Now they were compelled by international agreements to warn other nations first.

It was a requirement, Guo Ming noted to himself, that did not apply to the United States. To be fair, the Americans publicly announced their launch schedules well in advance, so it amounted to the same thing.

He walked a fine line filling out the form: making the launch date and flight path clear, while doing everything possible to "conceal state secrets."

He snorted at the last requirement. "Ridiculous," he mumbled. The *Taiyang Shen* had no strategic or military value. It was an unmanned probe that would be in Earth orbit less than two days. After that, it would travel to a solar orbit between Mercury and Venus. It would be China's first heliology probe to orbit the sun.

Yet the State Council insisted all launches be shrouded in secrecy. Even launches with nothing to hide. This way, other nations could not infer from lack of openness which launches contained classified payloads.

A knock at the door interrupted his paperwork.

"Come," Guo Ming said, happy for the interruption.

"Good evening, sir," said Under Director Zhu Tao.

"Tao, welcome back."

"Thank you, sir. It's good to be back in Beijing."

"How were things at Jiuquan?" asked Guo Ming. "Not too cold, I hope? I'll never understand why our launch complex is in the middle of the Gobi Desert."

"It was cold, yet manageable," Zhu Tao said.

"And how are launch preparations coming along?"

"I am happy to report they are all on schedule."

"Excellent." Guo Ming smiled.

Zhu Tao sat quietly, staring at his boss.

Guo Ming looked expectantly back at him, but Zhu Tao neither stood to leave nor said anything further.

"Something else, Tao?" Guo Ming asked.

"Mmm," Zhu Tao said. "Of course, you've heard about the Iris probe?"

"Yes, I did," Guo frowned. "Terrible situation. That poor man's going to starve."

"Possibly," Zhu Tao said. "Possibly not."

Guo Ming leaned back in his chair. "What are you saying?"

"It's the *Taiyang Shen*'s booster, sir. Our engineers have run the numbers, and it has enough fuel for a Mars injection orbit. It could get there in four hundred and nineteen days."

"Are you kidding?"

"Have you ever known me to 'kid,' sir?"

Guo Ming stood and pinched his chin. Pacing, he said, "We can really send the *Taiyang Shen* to Mars?"

"No, sir," said Zhu Tao. "It's far too heavy. The massive heat shielding makes it the heaviest unmanned probe we've ever built. That's why the booster had to be so powerful. But a lighter payload could be sent all the way to Mars."

"How much mass could we send?" Guo Ming asked.

"Nine hundred and forty-one kilograms, sir."

"Hmm," Guo Ming said, "I bet NASA could work with that limitation. Why haven't they approached us?"

"Because they don't know," Zhu Tao said. "All our booster technology is classified information. The Ministry of State Security even spreads disinformation about our capabilities. This is for obvious reasons."

"So they don't *know* we can help them," Guo Ming said. "If we decide not to help, no one will know we could have."

"Correct, sir."

"For the sake of argument, let's say we decided to help. What then?"

"Time would be the enemy, sir," Zhu Tao answered. "Based on travel duration and the supplies their astronaut has remaining, any such probe would have to be launched within a month. Even then he would starve a little."

"That's right around when we planned to launch *Taiyang Shen*."

"Yes, sir. But it took them two months to build Iris, and it was so rushed it failed."

"That's their problem," Guo Ming said. "Our end would be providing the booster. We'd launch from Jiuquan; we can't ship an eight-hundred-ton rocket to Florida."

"Any agreement would hinge on the Americans reimbursing us for the booster," Zhu Tao said, "and the State Council would likely want political favors from the US government."

"Reimbursement would be pointless," Guo Ming said. "This was an expensive project, and the State Council grumbled about it all along. If they had a bulk payout for its value, they'd just keep it. We'd never get to build another one."

He clasped his hands behind his back. "And the American people may be sentimental, but their government is not. The US State Department won't trade anything major for one man's life."

"So it's hopeless?" asked Zhu Tao.

"Not hopeless," Guo Ming corrected. "Just hard. If this becomes a negotiation by diplomats, it will never be resolved. We need to keep this among scientists. Space agency to space agency. I'll get a translator and call NASA's administrator. We'll work out an agreement, then present it to our governments as a fait accompli."

"But what can they do for us?" Zhu Tao asked. "We'd be giving up a booster and effectively canceling *Taiyang Shen*."

Guo Ming smiled. "They'll give us something we can't get without them."

"And that is?"

"They'll put a Chinese astronaut on Mars."

Zhu Tao stood. "Of course." He smiled. "The Ares 5 crew hasn't even been selected yet. We'll insist on a crewman. One we get to pick and train. NASA and the US State Department would surely accept that. But will our State Council?"

Guo Ming smiled wryly. "Publicly rescue the Americans? Put a Chinese astronaut on Mars? Have the world see China as equal to the US in space? The State Council would sell their own *mothers* for that."

■ ■ ■

TEDDY LISTENED to the phone at his ear. The voice on the other end finished what it had to say, then fell silent as it awaited an answer.

He stared at nothing in particular as he processed what he'd just heard.

After a few seconds, he replied, "Yes."

■ ■ ■

Johanssen:
Your poster outsold the rest of ours combined. You're a hot chick who went to Mars. You're on dorm-room walls all over the world.

Looking like that, why are you such a nerd? And you are, you know. A serious nerd. I had to do some computer shit to get Pathfinder talking to the rover and oh my god. And I had NASA telling me what to do every step of the way.

You should try to be more cool. Wear dark glasses and a leather jacket. Carry a switchblade. Aspire to a level of coolness known only as . . . "Botanist Cool."

Did you know Commander Lewis had a chat with us men? If anyone hit on you, we'd be off the mission. I guess after a lifetime of commanding sailors, she's got an unfairly jaded view.

Anyway, the point is you're a nerd. Remind me to give you a wedgie next time I see you.

...

"OKAY, HERE we are again," said Bruce to the assembled heads of JPL. "You've all heard about the *Taiyang Shen,* so you know our friends in China have given us one more chance. But this time, it's going to be harder.

"*Taiyang Shen* will be ready to launch in twenty-eight days. If it launches on time, our payload will get to Mars on Sol 624, six weeks after Watney's expected to run out of food. NASA's already working on ways to stretch his supply.

"We made history when we finished Iris in sixty-three days. Now we have to do it in *twenty-eight*."

He looked across the table to the incredulous faces.

"Folks," he said, "this is going to be the most 'ghetto' space-craft ever built. There's only one way to finish that fast: no landing system."

"Sorry, what?" Jack Trevor stammered.

Bruce nodded. "You heard me. No landing system. We'll need guidance for in-flight course adjustments. But once it gets to Mars, it's going to crash."

"That's crazy!" Jack said. "It'll be going an *insane* velocity when it hits!"

"Yep," Bruce said. "With ideal atmospheric drag, it'll impact at three hundred meters per second."

"What good will a pulverized probe do Watney?" Jack asked.

"As long as the food doesn't burn up on the way in, Watney can eat it," Bruce said.

Turning to the whiteboard, he began drawing a basic organizational chart. "I want two teams," he began.

"Team One will make the outer shell, guidance system, and thrusters. All we need is for it to get to Mars. I want the safest possible system. Aerosol propellant would be best. High-gain radio so we can talk to it, and standard satellite navigational software.

"Team Two will deal with the payload. They need to find a way to contain the food during impact. If protein bars hit sand at three hundred meters per second, they'll make protein-scented sand. We need them *edible* after impact.

"We can weigh nine hundred and forty-one kilograms. At least three hundred of that needs to be food. Get crackin'."

. . .

"UH, DR. KAPOOR?" Rich said, peeking his head into Venkat's office. "Do you have a minute?"

Venkat gestured him in. "You are . . . ?"

"Rich, Rich Purnell," he said, shuffling into the office, his arms wrapped around a sheaf of disorganized papers. "From astrodynamics."

"Nice to meet you," Venkat said. "What can I do for you, Rich?"

"I came up with something a while ago. Spent a lot of time on it." He dumped the papers on Venkat's desk. "Lemme find the summary. . . ."

Venkat stared forlornly at his once-clean desk, now strewn with scores of printouts.

"Here we go!" Rich said triumphantly, grabbing a paper. Then his expression saddened. "No, this isn't it."

"Rich," Venkat said. "Maybe you should just tell me what this is about?"

Rich looked at the mess of papers and sighed. "But I had such a cool summary. . . ."

"A summary for what?"

"How to save Watney."

"That's already in progress," Venkat said. "It's a last-ditch effort, but—"

"The *Taiyang Shen*?" Rich snorted. "That won't work. You can't make a Mars probe in a month."

"We're sure as hell going to try," Venkat said, a note of annoyance in his voice.

"Oh, sorry, am I being difficult?" Rich asked. "I'm not good with people. Sometimes I'm difficult. I wish people would just tell me. Anyway, the *Taiyang Shen* is critical. In fact, my idea won't work without it. But a Mars probe? Pfft. C'mon."

"All right," Venkat said. "What's your idea?"

Rich snatched a paper from the desk. "Here it is!" He handed it to Venkat with a childlike smile.

Venkat took the summary and skimmed it. The more he read, the wider his eyes got. "Are you sure about this?"

"Absolutely!" Rich beamed.

"Have you told anyone else?"

"Who would I tell?"

"I don't know," Venkat said. "Friends?"

"I don't have any of those."

"Okay, keep it under your hat."

"I don't wear a hat."

"It's just an expression."

"Really?" Rich said. "It's a stupid expression."

"Rich, you're being difficult."

"Ah. Thanks."

● ● ●

Vogel:

Being your backup has backfired.

I guess NASA figured botany and chemistry are similar because they both end in "Y," One way or another, I ended up being your backup chemist.

Remember when they made you spend a day explaining your experiments to me? It was in the middle of intense mission prep. You may have forgotten.

You started my training by buying me a beer. For breakfast. Germans are awesome.

Anyway, now that I have time to kill, NASA gave me a pile of work. And all your chemistry crap is on the list. So now I have to do boring-ass experiments with test tubes and soil and pH levels and Zzzzzzzzzz . . . .

My life is now a desperate struggle for survival . . . with occasional titration.

Frankly, I suspect you're a super-villain. You're a chemist, you have a German accent, you had a base on Mars . . . what more can there be?

...

"WHAT THE fuck is 'Project Elrond'?" Annie asked.

"I had to make something up," Venkat said.

"So you came up with 'Elrond'?" Annie pressed.

"Because it's a secret meeting?" Mitch guessed. "The e-mail said I couldn't even tell my assistant."

"I'll explain everything once Teddy arrives." Venkat said.

"Why does 'Elrond' mean 'secret meeting'?" Annie asked.

"Are we going to make a momentous decision?" Bruge Ng asked.

"Exactly," Venkat said.

"How did you know that?" Annie asked, getting annoyed.

"Elrond," Bruce said. "The Council of Elrond. From *Lord of the Rings*. It's the meeting where they decide to destroy the One Ring."

"Jesus," Annie said. "*None* of you got laid in high school, did you?"

"Good morning," Teddy said as he walked into the conference room. Seating himself, he rested his hands on the table. "Anyone know what this meeting's about?" he asked.

"Wait," Mitch said, "*Teddy* doesn't even know?"

Venkat took a deep breath. "One of our astrodynamicists, Rich Purnell, has found a way to get *Hermes* back to Mars. The course he came up with would give *Hermes* a Mars flyby on Sol 549."

Silence.

"You shittin' us?" Annie demanded.

"Sol 549? How's that even possible?" asked Bruce. "Even Iris wouldn't have landed till Sol 588."

"Iris is a point-thrust craft," Venkat said. "*Hermes* has a constant-thrust ion engine. It's always accelerating. Also, *Hermes* has a *lot* of velocity right now. On their current Earth-intercept course, they have to decelerate for the next month just to slow down to Earth's speed."

Mitch rubbed the back of his head. "Wow . . . 549. That's thirty-five sols before Watney runs out of food. That would solve everything."

Teddy leaned forward. "Run us through it, Venkat. What would it entail?"

"Well," Venkat began, "if they did this 'Rich Purnell Maneuver,' they'd start accelerating right away, to preserve their velocity and gain even more. They wouldn't intercept Earth at all, but would come close enough to use a gravity assist to adjust course. Around that time, they'd pick up a resupply probe with provisions for the extended trip.

"After that, they'd be on an accelerating orbit toward Mars, arriving on Sol 549. Like I said, it's a Mary *flyby*. This isn't anything like a normal Ares mission. They'll be going too fast to fall into orbit. The rest of the maneuver takes them back to Earth. They'd be home two hundred and eleven days after the flyby."

"What good is a flyby?" Bruce asked. "They don't have any way to get Watney off the surface."

"Yeah . . . ," Venkat said. "Now for the unpleasant part: Watney would have to get to the Ares 4 MAV."

"Schiaparelli!?" Mitch gaped. "That's thirty-two hundred kilometers away!"

"Three thousand, two hundred, and thirty-five kilometers to be exact," Venkat said. "It's not out of the question. He drove to *Pathfinder*'s landing site and back. That's over fifteen hundred kilometers."

"That was over flat, desert terrain," Bruce chimed in, "but the trip to Schiaparelli—"

"Suffice it to say," Venkat interrupted, "it would be very difficult and dangerous. But we have a lot of clever scientists to help him trick out the rover. Also there would be MAV modifications."

"What's wrong with the MAV?" Mitch asked.

"It's designed to get to low Mars orbit," Venkat explained. "But *Hermes* would be on a flyby, so the MAV would have to escape Mars gravity entirely to intercept."

"How?" Mitch asked.

"It'd have to lose weight . . . a *lot* of weight. I can get rooms full of people working on these problems, if we decide to do this."

"Earlier," Teddy said, "you mentioned a supply probe for *Hermes*. We have that capability?"

"Yes, with the *Taiyang Shen*," Venkat said. "We'd shoot for a near-Earth rendezvous. It's a lot easier than getting a probe to Mars, that's for sure."

"I see," Teddy said. "So we have two options on the table: Send Watney enough food to last until Ares 4, or send *Hermes* back to get him right now. Both plans require the *Taiyang Shen*, so we can only do one."

"Yes," Venkat said. "We'll have to pick one."

They all took a moment to consider.

"What about the *Hermes* crew?" Annie asked, breaking the silence. "Would they have a problem with adding . . ." She did some quick math in her head. "Five hundred and thirty-three days to their mission?"

"They wouldn't hesitate," Mitch said. "Not for a second. That's why Venkat called this meeting." He glared at Venkat. "He wants us to decide instead."

"That's right," Venkat said.

"It should be Commander Lewis's call," Mitch said.

"Pointless to even ask her," Venkat said. "*We* need to make this decision; it's a matter of life and death."

"She's the mission commander," Mitch said. "Life-and-death decisions are her damn job."

"Easy, Mitch," Teddy said.

"Bullshit," Mitch said. "You guys have done end runs around the crew every time something goes wrong. You didn't tell them Watney was still alive; now you're not telling them there's a way to save him."

"We already have a way to keep him alive," Teddy said. "We're just discussing another one."

"The crash-lander?" Mitch said. "Does anyone think that'll work? Anyone?"

"All right, Mitch," Teddy said. "You've expressed your opinion, and we've heard it. Let's move on." He turned to Venkat. "Can *Hermes* function for five hundred and thirty-three days beyond the scheduled mission end?"

"It should," Venkat said. "The crew may have to fix things here and there, but they're well trained. Remember, *Hermes* was made to do all five Ares missions. It's only halfway through its designed life span."

"It's the most expensive thing ever built," Teddy said. "We can't make another one. If something went wrong, the crew would die, and the Ares Program with them."

"Losing the crew would be a disaster," Venkat said. "But we wouldn't lose *Hermes*. We can remotely operate it. So long as the reactor and ion engines continued to work, we could bring it back."

"Space travel is dangerous," Mitch said. "We can't make this a discussion about what's safest."

"I disagree," Teddy said. "This is *absolutely* a discussion about what's safest. And about how many lives are at stake. Both plans are risky, but resupplying Watney only risks one life while the Rich Purnell Maneuver risks six."

"Consider *degree* of risk, Teddy," Venkat said. "Mitch is right. The crash-lander is high-risk. It could miss Mars, it could reenter wrong and burn up, it could crash too hard and destroy the food . . . We estimate a thirty percent chance of success."

"A near-Earth rendezvous with *Hermes* is more doable?" Teddy asked.

"Much more doable," Venkat confirmed. "With sub-second transmission delays, we can control the probe directly from Earth rather than rely on automated systems. When the time comes to dock, Major Martinez can pilot it remotely from *Hermes* with no transmission delay at all. And *Hermes* has a human crew, able to overcome any hiccups that may happen. And we don't have to do a reentry; the supplies don't have to survive a three-hundred-meters-per-second impact."

"So," Bruce offered, "we can have a high chance of killing one person, or a low chance of killing six people. Jeez. How do we even make this decision?"

"We talk about it, then Teddy makes the decision," Venkat said. "Not sure what else we can do."

"We could let Lewis——" Mitch began.

"Yeah, other than that," Venkat interrupted.

"Question," Annie said. "What am I even here for? This seems like something for you nerds to discuss."

"You need to be in the loop," Venkat said. "We're not deciding right now. We'll need to quietly research the details internally. Something might leak, and you need to be ready to dance around questions."

"How long have we got to make a decision?" Teddy asked.

"The window for starting the maneuver ends in thirty-nine hours."

"All right," Teddy said. "Everyone, we discuss this only in person or on the phone; never e-mail. And don't talk to *anyone* about this, other than the people here. The last thing we need is public opinion pressing for a risky cowboy rescue that may be impossible."

...

Beck:

Hey, man. How ya been?

Now that I'm in a "dire situation," I don't have to follow social rules anymore. I can be honest with everyone.

Bearing that in mind, I have to say . . . dude . . . you need to tell Johanssen how you feel. If you don't, you'll regret it forever.

I won't lie: It could end badly. I have no idea what she thinks of you. Or of anything. She's weird.

But wait till the mission's over. You're on a ship with her for another two months. Also, if you guys got up to anything while the mission was in progress, Lewis would kill you.

...

VENKAT, MITCH, Annie, Bruce, and Teddy met for the second time in as many days. "Project Elrond" had taken on a dark connotation throughout the Space Center, veiled in secrecy. Many people knew the name, none knew its purpose.

Speculation ran rampant. Some thought it was a completely new program in the works. Others worried it might be a move to cancel Ares 4 and 5. Most thought it was Ares 6 in the works.

"It wasn't an easy decision," Teddy said to the assembled elite. "But I've decided to go with Iris 2. No Rich Purnell Maneuver."

Mitch slammed his fist on the table.

"We'll do all we can to make it work," Bruce said.

"If it's not too much to ask," Venkat began, "what made up your mind?"

Teddy sighed. "It's a matter of risk," he said. "Iris 2 only risks one life. Rich Purnell risks all six of them. I know Rich Purnell is more likely to work, but I don't think it's six times more likely."

"You coward," Mitch said.

"Mitch . . . ," Venkat said.

"You god damned coward," Mitch continued, ignoring Venkat. "You just want to cut your losses. You're on damage control. You don't give a shit about Watney's life."

"Of course I do," Teddy replied. "And I'm sick of your infantile attitude. You can throw all the tantrums you want, but the rest of us have to be adults. This isn't a TV show; the riskier solution isn't always the best."

"Space is dangerous," Mitch snapped. "It's what we do here. If you want to play it safe all the time, go join an insurance company. And by the way, it's not even your life you're risking. The crew can make up their own minds about it."

"No, they can't," Teddy fired back. "They're too emotionally involved. Clearly, so are you. I'm not gambling five additional lives to save one. Especially when we might save him without risking them at all."

"Bullshit!" Mitch shot back as he stood from his chair. "You're just *convincing* yourself the crash-lander will work so you don't have to take a risk. You're hanging him out to dry, you chickenshit son of a bitch!"

He stormed out of the room, slamming the door behind him.

After a few seconds, Venkat followed behind, saying, "I'll make sure he cools off."

Bruce slumped in his chair. "Sheesh," he said nervously. "We're scientists, for Christ's sake. What the hell!?"

Annie quietly gathered her things and placed them in her briefcase.

Teddy looked to her. "Sorry about that, Annie," he said. "What can I say? Sometimes men let testosterone take over—"

"I was hoping he'd kick your ass," she interrupted.

"What?"

"I know you care about the astronauts, but he's right. You *are* a fucking coward. If you had balls, we might be able to save Watney."

...

Lewis:

Hi, Commander.

Between training and our trip to Mars, I spent two years working with you. I think I know you pretty well. So I'm guessing you still blame yourself for my situation, despite my earlier e-mail asking you not to.

You were faced with an impossible scenario and made a tough decision. That's what commanders do. And your decision was right. If you'd waited any longer, the MAV would have tipped.

I'm sure you've run through all the possible outcomes in your head, so you know there's nothing you could have done differently (other than "be psychic").

You probably think losing a crewman is the worst thing that can happen. Not true. Losing the whole crew is worse. You kept that from happening.

But there's something more important we need to discuss: What is it with you and disco? I can understand the '70s TV because everyone loves hairy people with huge collars. But disco?

Disco!?

...

VOGEL CHECKED the position and orientation of *Hermes* against the projected path. It matched, as usual. In addition to being the mission's chemist, he was also an accomplished astrophysicist. Though his duties as navigator were laughably easy.

The computer knew the course. It knew when to angle the ship so the ion engines would be aimed correctly. And it knew the location of the ship at all times (easily calculated from the position of the sun and Earth, and knowing the exact time from an on-board atomic clock).

Barring a complete computer failure or other critical event, Vogel's vast knowledge of astrodynamics would never come into play.

After completing the check, he ran a diagnostic on the engines. They were functioning at peak. He did all this from his quarters. All onboard computers could control all ships' functions. Gone were the days of physically visiting the engines to check up on them.

Having completed his work for the day, he finally had time to read e-mail.

Sorting through the messages NASA deemed worthy to upload, he read the most interesting first and responded when necessary. His responses were cached and would be sent to Earth with Johanssen's next uplink.

A message from his wife caught his attention. Titled *"unsere kinder"* ("our children"), it contained nothing but an image attachment. He raised an eyebrow. Several things stood out at once. First, "kinder" should have been capitalized. Helena, a grammar school teacher in Bremen, was very unlikely to make that mistake. Also, to each other, they affectionately called their kids *die Affen*.

When he tried to open the image, his viewer reported that the file was unreadable.

He walked down the narrow hallway. The crew quarters stood against the outer hull of the constantly spinning ship to maximize simulated gravity. Johanssen's door was open, as usual.

"Johanssen. Good evening," Vogel said. The crew kept the same sleep schedule, and it was nearing bedtime.

"Oh, hello," Johanssen said, looking up from her computer.

"I have the computer problem," Vogel explained. "I wonder if you will help."

"Sure," she said.

"You are in the personal time," Vogel said. "Perhaps tomorrow when you are on the duty is better?"

"Now's fine," she said. "What's wrong?"

"It is a file. It is an image, but my computer cannot view."

"Where's the file?" she asked, typing on her keyboard.

"It is on my shared space. The name is 'kinder.jpg.'"

"Let's take a look," she said.

Her fingers flew over her keyboard as windows opened and closed on her screen. "Definitely a bad jpg header," she said. "Probably mangled in the download. Lemme look with a hex editor, see if we got anything at all. . . ."

After a few moments she said, "This isn't a jpeg. It's a plain ASCII text file. Looks like . . . well, I don't know what it is. Looks like a bunch of math formulae." She gestured to the screen. "Does any of this make sense to you?"

Vogel leaned in, looking at the text. *"Ja,"* he said. "It is a course maneuver for *Hermes*. It says the name is 'Rich Purnell Maneuver.'"

"What's that?" Johanssen asked.

"I have not heard of this maneuver." He looked at the tables. "It is complicated . . . very complicated. . . ."

He froze. "Sol 549!?" he exclaimed. *"Mein Gott!"*

. . .

THE *HERMES* crew enjoyed their scant personal time in an area called "the Rec." Consisting of a table and barely room to seat six, it ranked low in gravity priority. Its position amidships granted it a mere 0.2 g.

Still, it was enough to keep everyone in a seat as they pondered what Vogel told them.

" . . . and then mission would conclude with Earth intercept two hundred and eleven days later," he finished up.

"Thank you, Vogel," Lewis said. She'd heard the explanation earlier when Vogel came to her, but Johanssen, Martinez, and Beck were hearing it for the first time. She gave them a moment to digest.

"Would this really work?" Martinez asked.

"Ja." Vogel nodded. "I ran the numbers. They all check out. It is brilliant course. Amazing."

"How would he get off Mars?" Martinez asked.

Lewis leaned forward. "There was more in the message," she began. "We'd have to pick up a supply near Earth, and he'd have to get to Ares 4's MAV."

"Why all the cloak and dagger?" Beck asked.

"According to the message," Lewis explained, "NASA rejected the idea. They'd rather take a big risk on Watney than a small risk on all of us. Whoever snuck it into Vogel's e-mail obviously disagreed."

"So," Martinez said, "we're talking about going directly against NASA's decision?"

"Yes," Lewis confirmed, "that's exactly what we're talking about. If we go through with the maneuver, they'll have to send the supply ship or we'll die. We have the opportunity to force their hand."

"Are we going to do it?" Johanssen asked.

They all looked to Lewis.

"I won't lie," she said. "I'd sure as hell like to. But this isn't a normal decision. This is something NASA expressly rejected. We're talking about mutiny. And that's not a word I throw around lightly."

She stood and paced slowly around the table. "We'll only do it if we all agree. And before you answer, consider the consequences. If we mess up the supply rendezvous, we die. If we mess up the Earth gravity assist, we die.

"If we do everything perfectly, we add five hundred and thirty-three days to our mission. Five hundred and thirty-three days of unplanned space travel where anything could go wrong. Maintenance will be a hassle. Something might break that we can't fix. If it's life-critical, we die."

"Sign me up!" Martinez smiled.

"Easy, cowboy," Lewis said. "You and I are military. There's a good chance we'd be court-martialed when we got home. As for the rest of you, I guarantee they'll never send you up again."

Martinez leaned against the wall, arms folded with a half grin on his face. The rest silently considered what their commander had said.

"If we do this," Vogel said, "it would be over one thousand days of space. This is enough space for a life. I do not need to return."

"Sounds like Vogel's in," Martinez grinned. "Me, too, obviously."

"Let's do it," Beck said.

"If you think it'll work," Johanssen said to Lewis, "I trust you."

"Okay," Lewis said. "If we go for it, what's involved?"

Vogel shrugged. "I plot the course and execute it," he said. "What else?"

"Remote override," Johanssen said. "It's designed to get the ship back if we all die or something. They can take over *Hermes* from Mission Control."

"But we're right here," Lewis said. "We can undo whatever they try, right?"

"Not really," Johanssen said. "Remote override takes priority over any onboard controls. It assumes there's been a disaster and the ship's control panels can't be trusted."

"Can you disable it?" Lewis asked.

"Hmm . . ." Johanssen pondered. "*Hermes* has four redundant flight computers, each connected to three redundant comm systems. If any computer gets a signal from any comm system, Mission Control can take over. We can't shut down the comms; we'd lose telemetry and guidance. We can't shut down the computers; we need them to control the ship. I'll have to disable the remote override on each system . . . . It's part of the OS; I'll have to jump over the code. . . . Yes. I can do it."

"You're sure?" Lewis asked. "You can turn it off?"

"Shouldn't be hard," Johanssen said. "It's an emergency feature, not a security program. It isn't protected against malicious code."

"Malicious code?" Beck smiled. "So . . . you'll be a hacker?"

"Yeah." Johanssen smiled back. "I guess I will."

"All right," Lewis said. "Looks like we can do it. But I don't want peer pressure forcing anyone into it. We'll wait for twenty-four hours. During that time, anyone can change their mind. Just talk to me in private or send me an e-mail. I'll call it off and never tell anyone who it was."

Lewis stayed behind as the rest filed out. Watching them leave, she saw they were smiling. All four of them. For the first time since leaving Mars, they were back to their old selves. She knew right then no one's mind would change.

They were going back to Mars.

• • •

EVERYONE KNEW Brendan Hutch would be running missions soon.

He'd risen through NASA's ranks as fast as one could in the large, inertia-bound organization. He was known as a diligent worker, and his skill and leadership qualities were plain to all his subordinates.

Brendan was in charge of Mission Control from one a.m. to nine a.m. every night. Continued excellent performance in this role would certainly net him a promotion. It had already been announced he'd be backup flight controller for Ares 4, and he had a good shot at the top job for Ares 5.

"Flight, CAPCOM," a voice said through his headset.

"Go, CAPCOM," Brendan responded. Though they were in the same room, radio protocol was observed at all times.

"Unscheduled status update from *Hermes*."

With *Hermes* ninety light-seconds away, back-and-forth voice communication was impractical. Other than media relations, *Hermes* would communicate via text until they were much closer.

"Roger," Brendan said. "Read it out."

"I . . . I don't get it, Flight," came the confused reply. "No real status, just a single sentence."

"What's it say?"

"Message reads: 'Houston, be advised: Rich Purnell is a steely-eyed missile man.'"

"What?" Brendan asked. "Who the hell is Rich Purnell?"

"Flight, Telemetry," another voice said.

"Go, Telemetry," Brendan said.

"*Hermes* is off course."

"CAPCOM, advise *Hermes* they're drifting. Telemetry, get a correction vector ready—"

"Negative, Flight," Telemetry interrupted. "It's not drift. They adjusted course. Instrumentation uplink shows a deliberate 27.812-degree rotation."

"What the hell?" Brendan stammered. "CAPCOM, ask them what the hell."

"Roger, Flight . . . message sent. Minimum reply time three minutes, four seconds."

"Telemetry, any chance this is instrumentation failure?"

"Negative, Flight. We're tracking them with SatCon. Observed position is consistent with the course change."

"CAPCOM, read your logs and see what the previous shift did. See if a massive course change was ordered and somehow nobody told us."

"Roger, Flight."

"Guidance, Flight," Brendan said.

"Go, Flight," was the reply from the guidance controller.

"Work out how long they can stay on this course before it's irreversible. At what point will they no longer be able to intercept Earth?"

"Working on that now, Flight."

"And somebody find out who the hell Rich Purnell is!"

...

MITCH PLOPPED down on the couch in Teddy's office. He put his feet up on the coffee table and smiled at Teddy. "You wanted to see me?"

"Why'd you do it, Mitch?" Teddy demanded.

"Do what?"

"You know damn well what I'm talking about."

"Oh, you mean the *Hermes* mutiny?" Mitch said innocently. "You know, that'd make a good movie title. *The Hermes Mutiny*. Got a nice ring to it."

"We know you did it," Teddy said sternly. "We don't know how, but we know you sent them the maneuver."

"So you don't have any proof."

Teddy glared. "No. Not yet, but we're working on it."

"Really?" Mitch said. "Is that *really* the best use of our time? I mean, we have a near-Earth resupply to plan, not to mention figuring out how to get Watney to Schiaparelli. We've got a lot on our plates."

"You're damn right we have a lot on our plates!" Teddy fumed. "After your little stunt, we're committed to this thing."

"*Alleged* stunt," Mitch said, raising a finger. "I suppose Annie will tell the media we decided to try this risky maneuver? And she'll leave out the mutiny part?"

"Of course," Teddy said. "Otherwise we'd look like idiots."

"I guess everyone's off the hook then!" Mitch smiled. "Can't fire people for enacting NASA policy. Even Lewis is fine. What mutiny? And maybe Watney gets to live. Happy endings all around!"

"You may have killed the whole crew," Teddy countered. "Ever think of that?"

"*Whoever* gave them the maneuver," Mitch said, "only passed along information. Lewis made the decision to act on it. If she let emotion cloud her judgment, she'd be a shitty commander. And she's not a shitty commander."

"If I can ever prove it was you, I'll find a way to fire you for it," Teddy warned.

"Sure." Mitch shrugged. "But if I wasn't willing to take risks to save lives, I'd . . ." He thought for a moment. "Well, I guess I'd be you."

CHAPTER 17

LOG ENTRY: SOL 192

Holy shit!

They're coming back for me!

I don't even know how to react. I'm choked up!

And I've got a shitload of work to do before I catch that bus home.

They can't orbit. If I'm not in space when they pass by, all they can do is wave.

I have to get to Ares 4's MAV. Even NASA accepts that. And when the nannies at NASA recommend a 3200-kilometer overland drive, you know you're in trouble.

Schiaparelli, here I come!

Well . . . not right away. I still have to do the aforementioned shitload of work.

My trip to *Pathfinder* was a quick jaunt compared to the epic journey that's coming up. I got away with a lot of shortcuts because I only had to survive twenty-two sols. This time, things are different.

I averaged 80 kilometers per sol on my way to *Pathfinder*. If I do that well toward Schiaparelli, the trip'll take forty sols. Call it fifty to be safe.

But there's more to it than just travel. Once I get there, I'll need to set up camp and do a bunch of MAV modifications. NASA estimates they'll take thirty sols, forty-five to be safe. Between the trip and the MAV mods, that's ninety-five sols. Call it one hundred because ninety-five cries out to be approximated.

So I'll need to survive away from the Hab for a hundred sols.

"What about the MAV?" I hear you ask (in my fevered imagination). "Won't it have some supplies? Air and water at the very least?"

Nope. It's got dick-all.

It does have air tanks, but they're empty. An Ares mission needs lots of O_2, N_2, and water anyway. Why send more with the MAV? Easier to have the crew top off the MAV from the Hab. Fortunately for my crewmates, the mission plan had Martinez fill the MAV tanks on Sol 1.

The flyby is on Sol 549, so I'll need to leave by 449. That gives me 257 sols to get my ass in gear.

Seems like a long time, doesn't it?

In that time, I need to modify the rover to carry the "Big Three": the atmospheric regulator, the oxygenator, and the water reclaimer. All three need to be in the pressurized area, but the rover isn't big enough. All three need to be running at all times, but the rover's batteries can't handle that load for long.

The rover will also need to carry all my food, water, and solar cells, my extra battery, my tools, some spare parts, and *Pathfinder*. As my sole means of communication with NASA, *Pathfinder* gets to ride on the roof, Granny Clampett style.

I have a lot of problems to solve, but I have a lot of smart people to solve them. Pretty much the whole planet Earth.

NASA is still working on the details, but the idea is to use both rovers. One to drive around, the other to act as my cargo trailer.

I'll have to make structural changes to that trailer. And by "structural changes" I mean "cut a big hole in the hull." Then I can move the Big Three in and use Hab canvas to loosely cover the hole. It'll balloon out when I pressurize the rover, but it'll hold. How will

I cut a big chunk out of a rover's hull? I'll let my lovely assistant Venkat Kapoor explain further:

> [14:38] JPL: I'm sure you're wondering how to cut a hole in the rover.
>
> Our experiments show a rock sample drill can get through the hull. Wear and tear on the bit is minimal (rocks are harder than carbon composite). You can cut holes in a line, then chisel out the remaining chunks between them.
>
> I hope you like drilling. The drill bit is 1 cm wide, the holes will be 0.5 cm apart, and the length of the total cut is 11.4 m. That's 760 holes. And each one takes 160 seconds to drill.
>
> Problem: The drills weren't designed for construction projects. They were intended for quick rock samples. The batteries only last 240 seconds. You do have two drills, but you'd still only get 3 holes done before needing to recharge. And recharging takes 41 minutes.
>
> That's 173 hours of work, limited to 8 EVA hours per day. That's 21 days of drilling, and that's just too long. All our other ideas hinge on this cut working. If it doesn't, we need time to come up with new ones.
>
> So we want you to wire a drill directly to Hab power.
>
> The drill expects 28.8 V and pulls 9 amps. The only lines that can handle that are the rover recharge lines. They're 36 V, 10 amp max. Since you have two, we're comfortable with you modifying one.
>
> We'll send you instructions on how to step down the voltage and put a new breaker in the line, but I'm sure you already know how.

I'll be playing with high-voltage power tomorrow. Can't imagine anything going wrong with that!

I managed to not kill myself today, even though I was working with high voltage. Well, it's not as exciting as all that. I disconnected the line first.

As instructed, I turned a rover charging cable into a drill power source. Getting the voltage right was a simple matter of adding resistors, which my electronics kit has in abundance.

I had to make my own nine-amp breaker. I strung three three-amp breakers in parallel. There's no way for nine amps to get through that without tripping all three in rapid succession.

Then I had to rewire a drill. Pretty much the same thing I did with *Pathfinder*. Take out the battery and replace it with a power line from the Hab. But this time it was a lot easier.

Pathfinder was too big to fit through any of my airlocks, so I had to do all the rewiring outside. Ever done electronics while wearing a space suit? Pain in the ass. I even had to make a workbench out of MAV landing struts, remember?

Anyway, the drill fit in the airlock easily. It's only a meter tall, and shaped like a jackhammer. We did our rock sampling standing up, like Apollo astronauts.

Also, unlike my *Pathfinder* hatchet job, I had the full schematics of the drill. I removed the battery and attached a power line where it used to be. Then, taking the drill and its new cord outside, I connected it to the modified rover charger and fired it up.

Worked like a charm! The drill whirled away with happy abandon. Somehow, I had managed to do everything right the first try. Deep down, I thought I'd fry the drill for sure.

It wasn't even midday yet. I figured why not get a jump on drilling?

[10:07] WATNEY: Power line modifications complete. Hooked it up to a drill, and it works great. Plenty of daylight left. Send me a description of that hole you want me to cut.

[10:25] JPL: Glad to hear it. Starting on the cut sounds great. Just to be clear, these are modifications to Rover 1, which we've been calling "the trailer." Rover 2 (the one with your modifications for the trip to Pathfinder) should remain as is for now.

You'll be taking a chunk out of the roof, just in front of the airlock in the rear of the vehicle. The hole needs to be at least 2.5 m long and the full 2 m width of the pressure vessel.

Before any cuts, draw the shape on the trailer, and position the trailer where Pathfinder's camera can see it. We'll let you know if you got it right.

[10:43] WATNEY: Roger. Take a pic at 11:30, if you haven't heard from me by then.

The rovers are made to interlock so one can tow the other. That way you can rescue your crewmates if all hell breaks loose. For that same reason, rovers can share air via hoses you connect between them. That little feature will let me share atmosphere with the trailer on my long drive.

I'd stolen the trailer's battery long ago; it had no ability to move under its own power. So I hitched it up to my awesomely modified rover and towed it into place near *Pathfinder*.

Venkat told me to "draw" the shape I plan to cut, but he neglected to mention how. It's not like I have a Sharpie that can work out on the surface. So I vandalized Martinez's bed.

The cots are basically hammocks. Lightweight string woven loosely into something that's comfortable to sleep on. Every gram counts when making stuff to send to Mars.

I unraveled Martinez's bed and took the string outside, then taped it to the trailer hull along the path I planned to cut. Yes, of course duct tape works in a near-vacuum. Duct tape works anywhere. Duct tape is magic and should be worshiped.

I can see what NASA has in mind. The rear of the trailer has an airlock that we're not going to mess with. The cut is just ahead of it and will leave plenty of space for the Big Three to stand.

I have no idea how NASA plans to power the Big Three for twenty-four and a half hours a day and still have energy left to drive. I bet they don't know, either. But they're smart; they'll work something out.

> [11:49] JPL: What we can see of your planned cut looks good. We're assuming the other side is identical. You're cleared to start drilling.
>
> [12:07] WATNEY: That's what she said.
>
> [12:25] JPL: Seriously, Mark? Seriously?

First, I depressurized the trailer. Call me crazy, but I didn't want the drill explosively launched at my face.

Then I had to pick somewhere to start. I thought it'd be easiest to start on the side. I was wrong.

The roof would have been better. The side was a hassle because I had to hold the drill parallel to the ground. This isn't your dad's Black & Decker we're talking about. It's a meter long and only safe to hold by the handles.

Getting it to bite was nasty. I pressed it against the hull and turned it on, but it wandered all over the place. So I got my trusty hammer and screwdriver. With a few taps, I made a small chip in the carbon composite.

That gave the bit a place to seat, so I could keep drilling in one place. As NASA predicted, it took about two and a half minutes to get all the way through.

I followed the same procedure for the second hole and it went much smoother. After the third hole, the drill's overheat light came on.

The poor drill wasn't designed to operate constantly for so long.

Fortunately, it sensed the overheat and warned me. So I leaned it against the workbench for a few minutes, and it cooled down. One thing you can say about Mars: It's *really* cold. The thin atmosphere doesn't conduct heat very well, but it cools everything, eventually.

I had already removed the drill's cowling (the power cord needed a way in). A pleasant side effect is the drill cools even faster. Though I'll have to clean it thoroughly every few hours as dust accumulates.

By 17:00, when the sun began to set, I had drilled seventy-five holes. A good start, but there's still tons to do. Eventually (probably tomorrow) I'll have to start drilling holes that I can't reach from the ground. For that I'll need something to stand on.

I can't use my "workbench." It's got *Pathfinder* on it, and the last thing I'm going to do is mess with that. But I've got three more MAV landing struts. I'm sure I can make a ramp or something.

Anyway, that's all stuff for tomorrow. Tonight is about eating a *full* ration for dinner.

Awww yeah. That's right. I'm either getting rescued on Sol 549 or I'm dying. That means I have thirty-five sols of extra food. I can indulge once in a while.

LOG ENTRY: SOL 194

I average a hole every 3.5 minutes. That includes the occasional breather to let the drill cool off.

I learned this by spending all damn day drilling. After eight hours of dull, physically intense work, I had 137 holes to show for it.

It turned out to be easy to deal with places I couldn't reach. I didn't need to modify a landing strut after all. I just had to get something to stand on. I used a geological sample container (also known as "a box").

Before I was in contact with NASA, I would have worked more than eight hours. I can stay out for ten before even dipping into "emergency" air. But NASA's got a lot of nervous Nellies who don't want me out longer than spec.

With today's work, I'm about one-fourth of the way through the whole cut. At least, one-fourth of the way through the drilling. Then I'll have 759 little chunks to chisel out. And I'm not sure how well carbon composite is going to take to that. But NASA'll do it a thousand times back on Earth and tell me the best way to get it done.

Anyway, at this rate, it'll take four more sols of (boring-ass) work to finish the drilling.

I've actually exhausted Lewis's supply of shitty seventies TV. And I've read all of Johanssen's mystery books.

I've already rifled through other crewmates' stuff to find entertainment. But all of Vogel's stuff is in German, Beck brought nothing but medical journals, and Martinez didn't bring anything.

I got really bored, so I decided to pick a theme song!

Something appropriate. And naturally, it should be something from Lewis's godawful seventies collection. It wouldn't be right any other way.

There are plenty of great candidates: "Life on Mars?" by David Bowie, "Rocket Man" by Elton John, "Alone Again (Naturally)" by Gilbert O'Sullivan.

But I settled on "Stayin' Alive" by the Bee Gees.

LOG ENTRY: SOL 195

Another day, another bunch of holes: 145 this time (I'm getting better). I'm halfway done. This is getting really old.

But at least I have encouraging messages from Venkat to cheer me on!

> [17:12] WATNEY: 145 holes today. 357 total.
> [17:31] JPL: We thought you'd have more done by now.

Dick.

Anyway, I'm still bored at night. I guess that's a good thing. Nothing's wrong with the Hab. There's a plan to save me, and the physical labor is making me sleep wonderfully.

I miss tending the potatoes. The Hab isn't the same without them.

There's still soil everywhere. No point in lugging it back outside. Lacking anything better to do, I ran some tests on it. Amazingly, some of the bacteria survived. The population is strong and growing. That's pretty impressive, when you consider it was exposed to near-vacuum and subarctic temperatures for over twenty-four hours.

My guess is pockets of ice formed around some of the bacteria, leaving a bubble of survivable pressure inside, and the cold wasn't quite enough to kill them. With hundreds of millions of bacteria, it only takes one survivor to stave off extinction.

Life is amazingly tenacious. They don't want to die any more than I do.

LOG ENTRY: SOL 196

I fucked up.

I fucked up big-time. I made a mistake that might kill me.

I started my EVA around 08:45, same as always. I got my hammer and screwdriver and started chipping the trailer's hull. It's a pain in the ass to make a chip before each drilling, so I make all the day's chips in a single go.

After chipping out 150 divots (hey, I'm an optimist), I got to work.

It was the same as yesterday and the day before. Drill through, relocate. Drill through, relocate. Drill through a third time, then set the drill aside to cool. Repeat that process over and over till lunchtime.

At 12:00, I took a break. Back in the Hab, I enjoyed a nice lunch and played some chess against the computer (it kicked my ass). Then back out for the day's second EVA.

At 13:30 my ruination occurred, though I didn't realize it at the time.

The worst moments in life are heralded by small observations. The tiny lump on your side that wasn't there before. Coming home to your wife and seeing two wineglasses in the sink. Anytime you hear "We interrupt this program . . ."

For me, it was when the drill didn't start.

Only three minutes earlier, it was working fine. I had finished a hole and set the drill aside to cool. Same as always.

But when I tried to get back to work, it was dead. The power light wouldn't even come on.

I wasn't worried. If all else failed, I had another drill. It would take a few hours to wire it up, but that's hardly a concern.

The power light being off meant there was probably something wrong with the line. A quick glance at the airlock window showed the lights were on in the Hab. So there were no systemic power problems. I checked my new breakers, and sure enough, all three had tripped.

I guess the drill pulled a little too much amperage. No big deal. I reset the breakers and got back to work. The drill fired right up, and I was back to making holes.

Doesn't seem like a big deal, right? I certainly didn't think so at the time.

I finished my day at 17:00 after drilling 131 holes. Not as good as yesterday, but I lost some time to the drill malfunction.

I reported my progress.

[17:08] WATNEY: 131 holes today. 488 total. Minor drill issue; it tripped the breakers. There may be an intermittent short in the drill, probably in the attachment point of the power line. Might need to redo it.

Earth and Mars are just over eighteen light-minutes apart now. Usually, NASA responds within twenty-five minutes. Remember, I do all my communication from Rover 2, which relays everything through *Pathfinder*. I can't just lounge in the Hab awaiting a reply; I have to stay in the rover until they acknowledge the message.

> [17:38] WATNEY: Have received no reply. Last message sent 30 minutes ago. Please acknowledge.

I waited another thirty minutes. Still no reply. Fear started to take root.

Back when JPL's Nerd Brigade hacked the rover and *Pathfinder* to be a poor man's IM client, they sent me a cheat sheet for troubleshooting. I executed the first instruction:

> [18:09] WATNEY: system_command: STATUS
> [18:09] SYSTEM: Last message sent 00h31m ago. Last message received 26h17m ago. Last ping reply from probe received 04h24m ago. WARNING: 52 unanswered pings.

Pathfinder was no longer talking to the rover. It had stopped answering pings four hours and twenty-four minutes ago. Some quick math told me that was around 13:30 today.

The same time the drill died.

I tried not to panic. The troubleshooting sheet has a list of things to try if communication is lost. They are (in order):

1. Confirm power still flowing to *Pathfinder*.
2. Reboot rover.
3. Reboot *Pathfinder* by disconnecting/reconnecting power.
4. Install rover's comm software on the other rover's computer, try from there.
5. If both rovers fail, problem is likely with *Pathfinder*. Check connections very closely. Clean *Pathfinder* of Martian dust.

6. Spell message in Morse code with rocks, include things attempted. Problem may be recoverable with remote update of *Pathfinder*.

I only got as far as step 1. I checked *Pathfinder*'s connections and the negative lead was no longer attached.

I was elated! What a relief! With a smile on my face, I fetched my electronics kit and prepared to reattach the lead. I pulled it out of the probe to give it a good cleaning (as best I could with the gloves of my space suit) and noticed something strange. The insulation had melted.

I pondered this development. Melted insulation usually means a short. More current than the wire could handle had passed through. But the bare portion of the wire wasn't black or even singed, and the positive lead's insulation wasn't melted at all.

Then, one by one, the horrible realities of Mars came into play. The wire wouldn't be burned or singed. That's a result of oxidization. And there's no oxygen in the air. There likely was a short after all. But with the positive lead being unaffected, the power must have come from somewhere else. . . .

And the drill's breaker tripped around the same time. . . .

Oh . . . shit . . .

The internal electronics for *Pathfinder* included a ground lead to the hull. This way it could not build up a static charge in Martian weather conditions (no water and frequent sandblasting can make impressive static charge).

The hull sat on Panel A, one of four sides of the tetrahedron which brought *Pathfinder* to Mars. The other three sides are still in Ares Vallis where I left them.

Between Panel A and the workbench were the Mylar balloons *Pathfinder* had used to tumble-land. I had shredded many of them to transport it, but a lot of material remained—enough to reach around Panel A and be in contact with the hull. I should mention that Mylar is conductive.

At 13:30, I leaned the drill against the workbench. The drill's cowling was off to make room for the power line. The workbench is metal. If the drill leaned against the workbench just right, it could make a metal-to-metal connection.

And that's exactly what had happened.

Power traveled from the drill line's positive lead, through the workbench, through the Mylar, through *Pathfinder*'s hull, through a bunch of extremely sensitive and irreplaceable electronics, and out the negative lead of *Pathfinder*'s power line.

Pathfinder operates on 50 milliamps. It got *9000* milliamps, which plowed through the delicate electronics, frying everything along the way. The breakers tripped, but it was too late.

Pathfinder's dead. I've lost the ability to contact Earth.

I'm on my own.

CHAPTER 18

LOG ENTRY: SOL 197

Sigh . . .

Just once I'd like something to go as planned, ya know?

Mars keeps trying to kill me.

Well . . . Mars didn't electrocute *Pathfinder*. So I'll amend that:

Mars and my stupidity keep trying to kill me.

Okay, enough self-pity. I'm not doomed. Things will just be harder than planned. I have all I need to survive. And *Hermes* is still on the way.

I spelled out a Morse code message using rocks. "PF FRIED WITH 9 AMPS. DEAD FOREVER. PLAN UNCHANGED. WILL GET TO MAV."

If I can get to the Ares 4 MAV, I'll be set. But having lost contact with NASA, I have to design my own Great Martian Winnebago to get there.

For the time being, I've stopped all work on it. I don't want to continue without a plan. I'm sure NASA had all kinds of ideas, but now I have to come up with one on my own.

As I mentioned, the Big Three (atmospheric regulator, oxygenator, and water reclaimer) are critical components. I worked around them for my trip to *Pathfinder*. I used CO_2 filters to regulate the atmosphere, and brought enough oxygen and water for the whole trip. That won't work this time. I need the Big Three.

Problem is, they soak up a lot of power, and they have to run all day long. The rover batteries have 18 kilowatt-hours of juice. The oxygenator *alone* uses 44.1 kilowatt-hours per sol. See my problem?

You know what? "Kilowatt-hours per sol" is a pain in the ass to say. I'm gonna invent a new scientific unit name. One kilowatt-hour per sol is . . . it can be anything . . . um . . . I suck at this . . . I'll call it a "pirate-ninja."

All told, the Big Three need 69.2 pirate-ninjas, most of that going to the oxygenator and the atmospheric regulator. (The water reclaimer only needs 3.6 of that.)

There'll be cutbacks.

The easiest cutback is the water reclaimer. I have 620 liters of water (I had a lot more before the Hab blew up). I need only three liters of water per sol, so my supply will last 206 sols. There's only 100 sols after I leave and before I'm picked up (or die in the attempt).

Conclusion: I don't need the water reclaimer at all. I'll drink as needed and dump my waste outdoors. Yeah, that's right, Mars, I'm gonna piss and shit on you. That's what you get for trying to kill me all the time.

There. I saved myself 3.6 pirate-ninjas.

LOG ENTRY: SOL 198

I've had a breakthrough with the oxygenator!

I spent most of the day looking at the specs. It heats CO_2 to 900°C, then passes it over a zirconia electrolysis cell to yank the carbon atoms off. Heating the gas is what takes most of the energy. Why is that important? Because I'm just one guy and the oxygenator was made for six. One-sixth the quantity of CO_2 means one-sixth the energy to heat it.

The *spec* says it draws 44.1 pirate-ninjas, but all this time it's only been using 7.35 because of the reduced load. Now we're getting somewhere!

Then there's the matter of the atmospheric regulator. The regulator samples the air, figures out what's wrong with it, and corrects the problem. Too much CO_2? Take it out. Not enough O_2? Add some. Without it, the oxygenator is worthless. The CO_2 needs to be separated in order to be processed.

The regulator analyzes the air with spectroscopy, then separates the gasses by supercooling them. Different elements turn to liquid at different temperatures. On Earth, supercooling this much air would take ridiculous amounts of energy. But (as I'm acutely aware) this isn't Earth.

Here on Mars, supercooling is done by pumping air to a component outside the Hab. The air quickly cools to the outdoor temperature, which ranges from $-150°C$ to $0°C$. When it's warm, additional refrigeration is used, but cold days can turn air to liquid for free. The real energy cost comes from heating it back up. If it came back to the Hab unheated, I'd freeze to death.

"But wait!" You're thinking, "Mars's atmosphere isn't liquid. Why does the Hab's air condense?"

The Hab's atmosphere is over 100 times as dense, so it turns to liquid at much higher temperatures. The regulator gets the best of both worlds. Literally. Side note: Mars's atmosphere *does* condense at the poles. In fact, it solidifies into dry ice.

Problem: The regulator takes 21.5 pirate-ninjas. Even adding some of the Hab's power cells would barely power the regulator for a sol, let alone give me enough juice to drive.

More thinking is required.

LOG ENTRY: SOL 199

I've got it. I know how to power the oxygenator and atmospheric regulator.

The problem with small pressure vessels is CO_2 toxicity. You can have all the oxygen in the world, but once the CO_2 gets above 1 percent, you'll start to get drowsy. At 2 percent, it's like being drunk. At 5 percent, it's hard to stay conscious. Eight percent will eventually kill you. Staying alive isn't about oxygen, it's about getting rid of CO_2.

That means I need the regulator. But I don't need the oxygenator all the time. I just need to get CO_2 out of the air and back-fill with oxygen. I have 50 liters of liquid oxygen in two 25-liter tanks here in the Hab. That's 50,000 liters in gaseous form, enough to last 85 days. Not enough to see me through to rescue, but a hell of a lot.

The regulator can separate the CO_2 and store it in a tank, and it can add oxygen to my air from my oxygen tanks as needed. When I run low on oxygen, I can camp out for a day and use *all* my power to run the oxygenator on the stored CO_2. That way, the oxygenator's power consumption doesn't eat up my driving juice.

So I'll run the regulator all the time, but only run the oxygenator on days I dedicate to using it.

Now, on to the next problem. After the regulator freezes the CO_2 out, the oxygen and nitrogen are still gasses, but they're −75°C. If the regulator fed that back to my air without reheating it, I'd be a Popsicle within hours. Most of the regulator's power goes to heating the return air so that doesn't happen.

But I have a better way to heat it up. Something NASA wouldn't consider on their most homicidal day.

The RTG!

Yes, the RTG. You may remember it from my exciting trip to *Pathfinder*. A lovely lump of plutonium so radioactive it gives off 1500 watts of heat, which it uses to harvest 100 watts of electricity. So what happens to the other 1400 watts? It gets radiated out as heat.

On the trip to *Pathfinder*, I had to actually remove insulation from the rover to vent excess heat from the damn thing. I'll be taping that back in place because I'll need that heat to warm up the return air from the regulator.

I ran the numbers. The regulator uses 790 watts to constantly reheat air. The RTG's 1400 watts is more than equal to the task, as well as keeping the rover a reasonable temperature.

To test, I shut down the heaters in the regulator and noted its power consumption. After a few minutes, I turned them right back on again. Jesus Christ that return air was cold. But I got the data I wanted.

With heating, the regulator needs 21.5 pirate-ninjas. Without it . . . (drumroll) 1 pirate-ninja. That's right, almost *all* of the power was going to heat.

As with most of life's problems, this one can be solved by a box of *pure radiation*.

I spent the rest of the day double-checking my numbers and running more tests. It all checks out. I can do this.

<hr>

LOG ENTRY: SOL 200

I hauled rocks today.

I needed to know what kind of power efficiency the rover/trailer will get. On the way to *Pathfinder*, I got 80 kilometers from 18 kilowatt-hours. This time, the load will be a lot heavier. I'll be towing the trailer and all the other shit.

I backed the rover up to the trailer and attached the tow clamps. Easy enough.

The trailer has been depressurized for some time now (there's a couple of hundred little holes in it, after all), so I opened both airlock doors to have a straight shot at the interior. Then I threw a bunch of rocks in.

I had to guess at the weight. The heaviest thing I'll bring with me is the water. 620 kilograms' worth. My freeze-dried potatoes will add another 200 kilograms. I'll probably have more solar cells than before, and maybe a battery from the Hab. Plus the atmospheric regulator and oxygenator, of course. Rather than weigh all that shit, I took a guess and called it 1200 kilograms.

Half a cubic meter of basalt weighs about that much (more or less). After two hours of brutal labor, during which I whined a lot, I got it all loaded in.

Then, with both batteries fully charged, I drove circles around the Hab until I drained them both.

With a blistering top speed of 25 kph, it's not an action-packed thrill ride. But I was impressed it could maintain that speed with all the extra weight. The rover has spectacular torque.

But physical law is a pushy little shit, and it exacted revenge for the additional weight. I only got 57 kilometers before I was out of juice.

That was 57 kilometers on level ground, without having to power the regulator (which won't take much with the heater off). Call it 50 kilometers per day to be safe. At that rate it would take 64 days to get to Schiaparelli.

But that's just the travel time.

Every now and then, I'll need to break for a day and let the oxygenator use all the power. How often? After a bunch of math I worked out that my 18-pirate-ninja budget can power the oxygenator enough to make about 2.5 sols of O_2. I'd have to stop every two to three sols to reclaim oxygen. My sixty-four-sol trip would become ninety-two!

That's too long. I'll tear my own head off if I have to live in the rover that long.

Anyway, I'm exhausted from lifting rocks and whining about lifting rocks. I think I pulled something in my back. Gonna take it easy the rest of today.

Yeah, I definitely pulled something in my back. I woke up in agony.

So I took a break from rover planning. Instead, I spent the day taking drugs and playing with radiation.

First, I loaded up on Vicodin for my back. Hooray for Beck's medical supplies!

Then I drove out to the RTG. It was right where I left it, in a hole four kilometers away. Only an idiot would keep that thing near the Hab. So anyway, I brought it back to the Hab.

Either it'll kill me or it won't. A lot of work went into making sure it doesn't break. If I can't trust NASA, who can I trust? (For now I'll forget that NASA told us to bury it far away.)

I stored it on the roof of the rover for the trip back. That puppy really spews heat.

I have some flexible plastic tubing intended for minor water reclaimer repairs. After bringing the RTG into the Hab, I *very carefully* glued some tubing around the heat baffles. Using a funnel made from a piece of paper, I ran water through the tubing, letting it drain into a sample container.

Sure enough, the water heated up. That's not really a surprise, but it's nice to see thermodynamics being well behaved.

There's one tricky bit: The atmospheric regulator doesn't run constantly. The freeze-separation speed is driven by the weather outside. So the returning frigid air doesn't come as a steady flow. And the RTG generates a constant, predictable heat. It can't "ramp up" its output.

So I'll heat water with the RTG to create a heat reservoir, then I'll make the return air bubble through it. That way I don't have to worry about when the air comes in. And I won't have to deal with sudden temperature changes in the rover.

When the Vicodin wore off, my back hurt even more than before. I'm going to need to take it easy. I can't just pop pills forever.

So I'm taking a few days off from heavy labor. To that end, I made a little invention just for me. . . .

I took Johanssen's cot and cut out the hammock. Then I draped spare Hab canvas over the frame, making a pit inside the cot, with extra canvas around the edges. Once I weighed down the excess canvas with rocks, I had a water-tight bathtub!

It only took 100 liters to fill the shallow tub.

Then, I stole the pump from the water reclaimer. (I can go quite a while without the water reclaimer operating.) I hooked it up to my RTG water heater and put both the input and output lines into the tub.

Yes, I know this is ridiculous, but I hadn't had a bath since Earth, and my back hurts. Besides, I'm going to spend 100 sols with the RTG anyway. A few more won't hurt. That's my bullshit rationalization and I'm sticking with it.

It took two hours to heat the water to 37°C. Once it did, I shut off the pump and got in. Oh man! All I can say is "Ahhhhhh."

Why the *hell* didn't I think of this before?

LOG ENTRY: SOL 207

I spent the last week recovering from back problems. The pain wasn't bad, but there aren't any chiropractors on Mars, so I wasn't taking chances.

I took hot baths twice a day, lay in my bunk a lot, and watched shitty seventies TV. I've already seen Lewis's entire collection, but I didn't have much else to do. I was reduced to watching reruns.

I got a lot of thinking done.

I can make everything better by having more solar panels. The fourteen panels I took to *Pathfinder* provided the 18 kilowatt-hours that the batteries could store. When traveling, I stowed the panels on the roof. The trailer gives me room to store another seven (half of its roof will be missing because of the hole I'm cutting in it).

This trip's power needs will be driven by the oxygenator. It all comes down to how much power I can give that greedy little bastard in a single sol. I want to minimize how often I have days with no travel. The more juice I can give the oxygenator, the more oxygen it'll liberate, and the longer I can go between those "air sols."

Let's get greedy. Let's say I can find a home for fourteen more panels instead of seven. Not sure how to do that, but let's say I can. That would give me thirty-six pirate-ninjas to work with, which would net me five sols of oxygen per air sol. I'd only have to stop once per five sols. That's much more reasonable.

Plus, if I can arrange battery storage for the extra power, I could drive 100 kilometers per sol! Easier said than done, though. That extra 18 kilowatt-hours of storage will be tough. I'll have to take two of the Hab's 9-kilowatt-hour fuel cells and load them onto the rover or trailer. They aren't like the rover's batteries; they're not small or portable. They're light enough, but they're pretty big. I may have to attach them to the outside hull, and that would eat into my solar cell storage.

One hundred kilometers per sol is pretty optimistic. But let's say I could make 90 kilometers per sol, stopping every fifth sol to reclaim oxygen. I'd get there in forty-five sols. That would be sweet!

In other news, it occurred to me that NASA is probably shitting bricks. They're watching me with satellites and haven't seen me come out of the Hab for six days. With my back better, it was time to drop them a line.

I headed out for an EVA. This time, being very careful while lugging rocks around, I spelled out a Morse code message: "INJURED BACK. BETTER NOW. CONTINUING ROVER MODS."

That was enough physical labor for today. I don't want to overdo it.

Think I'll have a bath.

Today, it was time to experiment with the panels.

First, I put the Hab on low-power mode: no internal lights, all nonessential systems offline, all internal heating suspended. I'd be outside most of the day anyway.

Then I detached twenty-eight panels from the solar farm and dragged them to the rover. I spent four hours stacking them this way and that. The poor rover looked like the Beverly Hillbillies truck. Nothing I did worked.

The only way to get all twenty-eight on the roof was to make stacks so high they'd fall off the first time I turned. If I lashed them together, they'd fall off as a unit. If I found a way to attach them perfectly to the rover, the rover would tip. I didn't even bother to test. It was obvious by looking, and I didn't want to break anything.

I haven't removed the chunk of hull from the trailer yet. Half the holes are drilled, but I'm not committed to anything. If I left it in place, I could have four stacks of seven cells. That would work fine; it's just two rovers' worth of what I did for the trip to *Pathfinder*.

Problem is I need that opening. The regulator has to be in the pressurized area and it's too big to fit in the unmodified rover. Plus which, the oxygenator needs to be in a pressurized area while operating. I'll only need it every five sols, but what would I do on that sol? No, the hole has to be there.

As it is, I'll be able to stow twenty-one panels. I need homes for the other seven. There's only one place they can go: the sides of the rover and trailer.

One of my earlier modifications was "saddlebags" draped over the rover. One side held the extra battery (stolen from what is now the trailer), while the other side was full of rocks as counterweight.

I won't need the bags this time around. I can return the second battery to the trailer from whence it came. In fact, it'll save me the hassle of the mid-drive EVA I had to do every day to swap cables.

When the rovers are linked up, they share resources, including electricity.

I went ahead and reinstalled the trailer's battery. It took me two hours, but it's out of the way now. I removed the saddlebags and set them aside. They may be handy down the line. If I've learned one thing from my stay at Club Mars, it's that *everything* can be useful.

I had liberated the sides of the rover and the trailer. After staring at them for a while, I had my solution.

I'll make L-brackets that stick out from the undercarriages, with the hooks facing up. Two brackets per side to make a shelf. I can set panels on the shelves and lean them against the rover. Then I'll lash them to the hull with homemade rope.

There'll be four "shelves" total; two on the rover and two on the trailer. If the brackets stick out far enough to accommodate two panels, I could store eight additional panels that way. That would give me one more panel than I'd even planned for.

I'll make those brackets and install them tomorrow. I would have done it today, but it got dark and I got lazy.

LOG ENTRY: SOL 209

Cold night last night. The solar cells were still detached from the farm, so I had to leave the Hab in low-power mode. I did turn the heat back on (I'm not insane), but I set the internal temperature to 1°C to conserve power. Waking up to frigid weather felt surprisingly nostalgic. I grew up in Chicago, after all.

But nostalgia only lasts so long. I vowed to complete the brackets today, so I can return the panels to the farm. Then I can turn the damn heat back on.

I headed out to the MAV's landing strut array to scavenge metal for the shelves. Most of the MAV is made from composite, but the struts had to absorb the shock of landing. Metal was the way to go.

I brought a strut into the Hab to save myself the hassle of working in an EVA suit. It was a triangular lattice of metal strips held together with bolts. I disassembled it.

Shaping the brackets involved a hammer and . . . well, that's it, actually. Making an L doesn't take a lot of precision.

I needed holes where the bolts would pass through. Fortunately, my *Pathfinder*-murdering drill made short work of that task.

I was worried it would be hard to attach the brackets to the rover's undercarriage, but it ended up being simple. The undercarriage comes right off. After some drilling and bolting, I got the brackets attached to it and then mounted it back on the rover. I repeated the process for the trailer. Important note—the undercarriage is not part of the pressure vessel. The holes I drilled won't let my air out.

I tested the brackets by hitting them with rocks. This kind of sophistication is what we interplanetary scientists are known for.

After convincing myself the brackets wouldn't break at the first sign of use, I tested the new arrangement. Two stacks of seven solar cells on the roof of the rover; another seven on the trailer, then two per shelf. They all fit.

After lashing the cells in place, I took a little drive. I did some basic acceleration and deceleration, turned in increasingly tight circles, and even did a power-stop. The cells didn't budge.

Twenty-eight solar cells, baby! And room for one extra!

After some well-earned fist-pumping, I unloaded the cells and dragged them back to the farm. No Chicago morning for me tomorrow.

LOG ENTRY: SOL 211

I am smiling a great smile. The smile of a man who fucked with his car and *didn't break it*.

I spent today removing unnecessary crap from the rover and

trailer. I was pretty damn aggressive about it, too. Space inside the pressure vessels is at a premium. The more crap I clear out of the rover, the more space there is for me. The more crap I clear out of the trailer, the more supplies I can store in it, and the less I have to store in the rover.

First off: Each vehicle had a bench for passengers. Bye!

Next: There's no reason for the trailer to have life support. The oxygen tanks, nitrogen tanks, CO_2 filter assembly . . . all unnecessary. It'll be sharing air with the rover (which has its own copy of each of those), and it'll be carrying the regulator and oxygenator. Between the Hab components and the rover, I'll have two redundant life support systems. That's plenty.

Then I yanked the driver's seat and control panel out of the trailer. The linkup with the rover is physical. The trailer doesn't do anything but get dragged along and fed air. It doesn't need controls or brains. However, I did salvage its computer. It's small and light, so I'll bring it with me. If something goes wrong with the rover's computer en route, I'll have a spare.

The trailer had tons more space now. It was time for experimentation.

The Hab has twelve 9-kilowatt-hour batteries. They're bulky and awkward. Over two meters tall, a half meter wide, and three-quarters of a meter thick. Making them bigger makes them take less mass per kilowatt hour of storage. Yeah, it's counterintuitive. But once NASA figured out they could increase volume to decrease mass, they were all over it. Mass is the expensive part about sending things to Mars.

I detached two of them. As long as I return them before the end of the day, things should be fine. The Hab mostly uses the batteries at night.

With both of the trailer's airlock doors open I was able to get the first battery in. After playing real-life Tetris for a while I found a way to get the first battery out of the way enough to let the second battery in. Together, they eat up the whole front half of the trailer. If I hadn't cleared the useless shit out earlier today, I'd never have gotten them both in.

The trailer's battery is in the undercarriage, but the main power line runs through the pressure vessel, so I was able to wire the Hab batteries directly in (no small feat in the damn EVA suit).

A system check from the rover showed I had done the wiring correctly.

This may all seem minor, but it's awesome. It means I can have twenty-nine solar cells and 36 kilowatt-hours of storage. I'll be able to do my 100 kilometers per day after all.

Four days out of five, anyway.

According to my calendar, the *Hermes* resupply probe is being launched from China in two days (if there were no delays). If that screws up, the whole crew will be in deep shit. I'm more nervous about that than anything else.

I've been in mortal danger for months; I'm kind of used to it now. But I'm nervous again. Dying would suck, but my crewmates dying would be way worse. And I won't find out how the launch went till I get to Schiaparelli.

Good luck, guys.

CHAPTER 19

"HEY, MELISSA . . . ," said Robert. "Am I getting through? Can you see me?"

"Loud and clear, babe," said Commander Lewis. "The video link is solid."

"They say I have five minutes," Robert said.

"Better than nothing," Lewis said. Floating in her quarters, she gently touched the bulkhead to stop drifting. "It's nice to see you in real-time for a change."

"Yeah." Robert smiled. "I can hardly notice the delay. I gotta say, I wish you were coming home."

Lewis sighed. "Me, too, babe."

"Don't get me wrong," Robert quickly added. "I understand why you're doing all this. Still, from a selfish point of view, I miss my wife. Hey, are you floating?"

"Huh?" Lewis said. "Oh, yeah. The ship isn't spinning right now. No centripetal gravity."

"Why not?"

"Because we're docking with the *Taiyang Shen* in a few days. We can't spin while we dock with things."

"I see," said Robert. "So how are things up on the ship? Anyone giving you shit?"

"No." Lewis shook her head. "They're a good crew; I'm lucky to have them."

"Oh hey!" Robert said. "I found a great addition to our collection!"

"Oh? What'd you get?"

"An original-production eight-track of *Abba's Greatest Hits*. Still in the original packaging."

Lewis widened her eyes. "Seriously? A 1976 or one of the reprints?"

"1976 all the way."

"Wow! Good find!"

"I know, right!?"

...

WITH A final shudder, the jetliner came to a stop at the gate.

"Oh gods," said Venkat, massaging his neck. "That was the longest flight I've ever been on."

"Mm," said Teddy, rubbing his eyes.

"At least we don't have to go to Jiuquan till tomorrow," Venkat moaned. "Fourteen and a half hours of flying is enough for one day."

"Don't get too comfortable," Teddy said. "We still have to go through customs, and we'll probably have to fill out a bunch of forms because we're U.S. government officials. . . . It's gonna be hours before we sleep."

"Craaaap."

Gathering their carry-on luggage, they trudged off the plane with the rest of the weary travelers.

Beijing Capital International Airport's Terminal 3 echoed with the cacophony common to huge air terminals. Venkat and Teddy moved toward the long immigration line as the Chinese citizens from their flight split off to go to a simpler point-of-entry process.

As Venkat took his place in line, Teddy filed in behind him and scanned the terminal for a convenience store. Any form of caffeine would be welcome.

"Excuse me, gentlemen," came a voice from beside them.

They turned to see a young Chinese man wearing jeans and a polo shirt. "My name is Su Bin Bao," he said in perfect English. "I am an employee of the China National Space Administration. I will be your guide and translator during your stay in the People's Republic of China."

"Nice to meet you, Mr. Su," Teddy said. "I'm Teddy Sanders, and this is Dr. Venkat Kapoor."

"We need sleep," Venkat said immediately. "Just as soon as we get through customs, please get us to our hotel."

"I can do better than that, Dr. Kapoor." Su smiled. "You are official guests of the People's Republic of China. You have been preauthorized to bypass customs. I can take you to your hotel immediately."

"I love you," Venkat said.

"Tell the People's Republic of China we said thanks," Teddy added.

"I'll pass that along." Su Bin smiled.

. . .

"HELENA, MY LOVE," Vogel said to his wife. "*I trust you are well?*"

"*Yes,*" she said. "*I'm fine. But I do miss you.*"

"*Sorry.*"

"*Can't be helped.*" She shrugged.

"*How are our monkeys?*"

"*The children are fine.*" She smiled. "*Eliza has a crush on a new boy in her class, and Victor has been named goalkeeper for his high school's team.*"

"Excellent!" Vogel said. *"I hear you are at Mission Control. Was NASA unable to pipe the signal to Bremen?"*

"They could have," she said. *"But it was easier for them to bring me to Houston. A free vacation to the United States. Who am I to turn that down?"*

"Well played. And how is my mother?"

"As well as can be expected," Helena said. *"She has her good days and bad days. She did not recognize me on my last visit. In a way, it's a blessing. She doesn't have to worry about you like I do."*

"She hasn't worsened?" he asked.

"No, she's about the same as when you left. The doctors are sure she'll still be here when you return."

"Good," he said. *"I was worried I'd seen her for the last time."*

"Alex," Helena said, *"will you be safe?"*

"As safe as we can be," he said. *"The ship is in perfect condition, and after receiving the Taiyang Shen, we will have all the supplies we need for the remainder of the journey."*

"Be careful."

"I will, my love," Vogel promised.

...

"WELCOME TO JIUQUAN," Guo Ming said. *"I hope your flight was smooth?"*

Su Bin translated Guo Ming's words as Teddy took the second-best seat in the observation room. He looked through the glass to Jiuquan's Mission Control Center. It was remarkably similar to Houston's, though Teddy couldn't read any of the Chinese text on the big screens.

"Yes, thank you," Teddy said. "The hospitality of your people has been wonderful. The private jet you arranged to bring us here was a nice touch."

"*My people have enjoyed working with your advance team,*" Guo Ming said. "*The last month has been very interesting. Attaching an American probe to a Chinese booster. I believe this is the first time it's ever been done.*"

"It just goes to show," Teddy said. "Love of science is universal across all cultures."

Guo Ming nodded. "*My people have especially commented on the work ethic of your man, Mitch Henderson. He is very dedicated.*"

"He's a pain in the ass," Teddy said.

Su Bin paused before translating but pressed on.

Guo Ming laughed. "*You can say that,*" he said. "*I cannot.*"

...

"So explain it again," Beck's sister Amy said. "Why do you have to do an EVA?"

"I probably don't," Beck explained. "I just need to be ready to."

"Why?"

"In case the probe can't dock with us. If something goes wrong, it'll be my job to go out and grab it."

"Can't you just move *Hermes* to dock with it?"

"No way," Beck said. "*Hermes* is *huge*. It's not made for fine maneuvering control."

"Why does it have to be you?"

"'Cause I'm the EVA specialist."

"But I thought you were the doctor."

"I am," Beck said. "Everyone has multiple roles. I'm the doctor, the biologist, and the EVA specialist. Commander Lewis is our geologist. Johanssen is the sysop and reactor tech. And so on."

"How about that good-looking guy . . . Martinez?" Amy asked. "What does he do?"

"He pilots the MDV and MAV," Beck said. "He's also married with a kid, you lecherous homewrecker."

"Ah well. How about Watney? What did he do?"

"He's our botanist and engineer. And don't talk about him in the past tense."

"Engineer? Like Scotty?"

"Kind of," Beck said. "He fixes stuff."

"I bet that's coming in handy now."

"Yeah, no shit."

...

THE CHINESE had arranged a small conference room for the Americans to work in. The cramped conditions were luxurious by Jiuquan standards. Venkat was working on budget spreadsheets when Mitch came in, so he was glad for the interruption.

"They're a weird bunch, these Chinese nerds," Mitch said, collapsing into a chair. "But they make a good booster."

"Good," Venkat said. "How's the linkage between the booster and our probe?"

"It all checks out," Mitch said. "JPL followed the specs perfectly. It fits like a glove."

"Any concerns or reservations?" Venkat asked.

"Yeah. I'm concerned about what I ate last night. I think it had an eyeball in it."

"I'm sure there wasn't an eyeball."

"The engineers here made it for me special," Mitch said.

"There may have been an eyeball," Venkat said. "They hate you."

"Why?"

"'Cause you're a dick, Mitch," Venkat said. "A total dick. To everyone."

"Fair enough. So long as the probe gets to *Hermes*, they can burn me in effigy for all I care."

. . .

"WAVE TO DADDY!" Marissa said, waving David's hand at the camera. "Wave to Daddy!"

"He's too young to know what's going on," Martinez said.

"Just think of the playground cred he'll have later in life," she said. " 'My dad went to Mars. What's your dad do?' "

"Yes, I'm pretty awesome," he agreed.

Marissa continued to wave David's hand at the camera. David was more interested in his other hand, which was actively engaged in picking his nose.

"So," Martinez said, "you're pissed."

"You can tell?" Marissa asked. "I tried to hide it."

"We've been together since we were fifteen. I know when you're pissed."

"You volunteered to extend the mission five hundred and thirty-three days," she said, "asshole."

"Yeah," Martinez said. "I figured that'd be the reason."

"Your son will be in kindergarten when you get back. He won't have any memories of you."

"I know," Martinez said.

"I have to wait another five hundred and thirty-three days to get laid!"

"So do I," he said defensively.

"I have to worry about you that whole time," she added.

"Yeah," he said. "Sorry."

She took a deep breath. "We'll get past it."

"We'll get past it," he agreed.

···

"WELCOME TO CNN's *Mark Watney Report*. Today, we have the director of Mars operations, Venkat Kapoor. He's speaking to us live via satellite from China. Dr. Kapoor, thank you for joining us."

"Happy to do it," Venkat said.

"So, Dr. Kapoor, tell us about the *Taiyang Shen*. Why go to China to launch a probe? Why not launch it from the US?"

"*Hermes* isn't going to orbit Earth," Venkat said. "It's just passing by on its way to Mars. And its velocity is *huge*. We need a booster capable of not only escaping Earth's gravity but matching *Hermes*'s current velocity. Only the *Taiyang Shen* has enough power to do that."

"Tell us about the probe itself."

"It was a rush job," Venkat said. "JPL only had thirty days to put it together. They had to be as safe and efficient as they could. It's basically a shell full of food and other supplies. It has a standard satellite thruster package for maneuvering, but that's it."

"And that's enough to fly to *Hermes*?"

"The *Taiyang Shen* will send it to *Hermes*. The thrusters are for fine control and docking. And JPL didn't have time to make a guidance system. So it'll be remote-controlled by a human pilot."

"Who will be controlling it?" Cathy asked.

"The Ares 3 pilot, Major Rick Martinez. As the probe approaches *Hermes*, he'll take over and guide it to the docking port."

"And what if there's a problem?"

"*Hermes* will have their EVA specialist, Dr. Chris Beck, suited up and ready the whole time. If necessary, he will literally grab the probe with his hands and drag it to the docking port."

"Sounds kind of unscientific." Cathy laughed.

"You want unscientific?" Venkat smiled. "If the probe can't attach to the docking port for some reason, Beck will open the probe and carry its contents to the airlock."

"Like bringing in the groceries?" Cathy asked.

"Exactly like that," Venkat said. "And we estimate it would take four trips back and forth. But that's all an edge case. We don't anticipate any problems with the docking process."

"Sounds like you're covering all your bases." Cathy smiled.

"We have to," Venkat said. "If they don't get those supplies . . . Well, they need those supplies."

"Thanks for taking the time to answer our questions," Cathy said.

"Always a pleasure, Cathy."

. . .

JOHANSSEN'S FATHER fidgeted in the chair, unsure what to say. After a moment, he pulled a handkerchief from his pocket and mopped sweat from his balding head.

"What if the probe doesn't get to you?" he asked.

"Try not to think about that," Johanssen said.

"Your mother is so worried she couldn't even come."

"I'm sorry," Johanssen mumbled, looking down.

"She can't eat, she can't sleep, she feels sick all the time. I'm not much better. How can they make you do this?"

"They're not 'making' me do it, Dad. I volunteered."

"Why would you do that to your mother?" he demanded.

"Sorry," Johanssen mumbled. "Watney's my crewmate. I can't just let him die."

He sighed. "I wish we'd raised you to be more selfish."

She chuckled quietly.

"How did I end up in this situation? I'm the district sales manager of a napkin factory. Why is my daughter in space?"

Johanssen shrugged.

"You were always scientifically minded," he said. "It was great!

Straight-A student. Hanging around nerdy guys too scared to try anything. No wild side at all. You were every father's dream daughter."

"Thanks, Dad, I—"

"But then you got on a giant bomb that blasted you to Mars. And I mean that literally."

"Technically," she corrected, "the booster only took me into orbit. It was the nuclear-powered ion engine that took me to Mars."

"Oh, much better!"

"Dad, I'll be all right. Tell Mom I'll be all right."

"What good will that do?" he said. "She's going to be tied up in knots until you're back home."

"I know," Johanssen mumbled. "But . . ."

"What? But what?"

"I won't die. I really won't. Even if everything goes wrong."

"What do you mean?"

Johanssen furrowed her brow. "Just tell Mom I won't die."

"How? I don't understand."

"I don't want to get into the how," Johanssen said.

"Look," he said, leaning toward the camera, "I've always respected your privacy and independence. I never tried to pry into your life, never tried to control you. I've been really good about that, right?"

"Yeah."

"So in exchange for a lifetime of staying out of your business, let me nose in just this once. What are you not telling me?"

She fell silent for several seconds. Finally, she said, "They have a plan."

"Who?"

"They always have a plan," she said. "They work out everything in advance."

"What plan?"

"They picked me to survive. I'm youngest. I have the skills necessary to get home alive. And I'm the smallest and need the least food."

"What happens if the probe fails, Beth?" her father asked.

"Everyone would die but me," she said. "They'd all take pills and die. They'll do it right away so they don't use up any food. Commander Lewis picked me to be the survivor. She told me about it yesterday. I don't think NASA knows about it."

"And the supplies would last until you got back to Earth?"

"No," she said. "We have enough food left to feed six people for a month. If I was the only one, it would last six months. With a reduced diet I could stretch it to nine. But it'll be seventeen months before I get back."

"So how would you survive?"

"The supplies wouldn't be the only source of food," she said.

He widened his eyes. "Oh . . . oh my god . . ."

"Just tell Mom the supplies would last, okay?"

...

AMERICAN AND Chinese engineers cheered together at Jiuquan Mission Control.

The main screen showed *Taiyang Shen*'s contrail wafting in the chilly Gobi sky. The ship, no longer visible to the naked eye, pressed onward toward orbit. Its deafening roar dwindled to a distant rumbling thunder.

"Perfect launch," Venkat exclaimed.

"Of course," said Zhu Tao.

"You guys really came through for us," Venkat said. "And we're grateful!"

"Naturally."

"And hey, you guys get a seat on Ares 5. Everyone wins."

"Mmm."

Venkat looked at Zhu Tao sideways. "You don't seem too happy."

"I spent four years working on *Taiyang Shen*," he said. "So did countless other researchers, scientists, and engineers. Everyone poured their souls into construction while I waged a constant political battle to maintain funding.

"In the end, we built a beautiful probe. The largest, sturdiest unmanned probe in history. And now it's sitting in a warehouse. It'll never fly. The State Council won't fund another booster like that."

He turned to Venkat. "It could have been a lasting legacy of scientific research. Now it's a delivery run. We'll get a Chinese astronaut on Mars, but what science will he bring back that some other astronaut couldn't have? This operation is a net loss for mankind's knowledge."

"Well," Venkat said cautiously, "it's a net gain for Mark Watney."

"Mmm," Zhu Tao said.

...

"DISTANCE 61 meters, velocity 2.3 meters per second," Johanssen said.

"No problem," Martinez said, his eyes glued to his screens. One showed the camera feed from Docking Port A, the other a constant feed of the probe's telemetry.

Lewis floated behind Johanssen's and Martinez's stations.

Beck's voice came over the radio. "Visual contact." He stood in Airlock 3 (via magnetic boots), fully suited up with the outer door open. The bulky SAFER unit on his back would allow him free motion in space should the need arise. An attached tether led to a spool on the wall.

"Vogel," Lewis said into her headset. "You in position?"

Vogel stood in the still-pressurized Airlock 2, suited up save his helmet. "*Ja*, in position and ready," he replied. He was the emergency EVA if Beck needed rescue.

"All right, Martinez," Lewis said. "Bring it in."

"Aye, Commander."

"Distance 43 meters, velocity 2.3 meters per second," Johanssen called out.

"All stats nominal," Martinez reported.

"Slight rotation in the probe," Johanssen said. "Relative rotational velocity is 0.05 revolutions per second."

"Anything under 0.3 is fine," Martinez said. "The capture system can deal with it."

"Probe is well within manual recovery range," Beck reported.

"Copy," Lewis said.

"Distance 22 meters, velocity 2.3 meters per second," Johanssen said. "Angle is good."

"Slowing her down a little," Martinez said, sending instructions to the probe.

"Velocity 1.8 . . . 1.3 . . . ," Johanssen reported. "0.9 . . . stable at 0.9 meters per second."

"Range?" Martinez asked.

"Twelve meters," Johanssen replied. "Velocity steady at 0.9 meters per second."

"Angle?"

"Angle is good."

"Then we're in line for auto-capture," Martinez said. "Come to Papa."

The probe drifted gently to the docking port. Its capture boom, a long metal triangle, entered the port's funnel, scraping slightly along the edge. Once it reached the port's retractor mechanism, the automated system clamped on to the boom and pulled it in, aligning and orienting the probe automatically. After several loud clanks echoed through the ship, the computer reported success.

"Docking complete," Martinez said.

"Seal is tight," Johanssen said.

"Beck," Lewis said, "your services won't be needed."

"Roger that, Commander," Beck said. "Closing airlock."

"Vogel, return to interior," she ordered.

"Copy, Commander," he said.

"Airlock pressure to one hundred percent," Beck reported. "Re-entering ship. . . . I'm back in."

"Also inside," Vogel said.

Lewis pressed a button on her headset. "Houst— er . . . Jiuquan, probe docking complete. No complications."

Mitch's voice came over the comm. "Glad to hear it, *Hermes*. Report status of all supplies once you get them aboard and inspected."

"Roger, Jiuquan," Lewis said.

Taking off her headset, she turned to Martinez and Johanssen. "Unload the probe and stow the supplies. I'm going to help Beck and Vogel de-suit."

Martinez and Johanssen floated down the hall toward Docking Port A.

"So," he said, "who would you have eaten first?"

She glared at him.

"'Cause I think I'd be tastiest," he continued, flexing his arm. "Look at that. Good solid muscle there."

"You're not funny."

"I'm free-range, you know. Corn-fed."

She shook her head and accelerated down the hall.

"Come on! I thought you liked Mexican!"

"Not listening," she called back.

CHAPTER 20

<u>LOG ENTRY: SOL 376</u>

I'm finally done with the rover modifications!

The tricky part was figuring out how to maintain life support. Everything else was just work. A *lot* of work.

I haven't been good at keeping the log up to date, so here's a recap:

First I had to finish drilling holes with the *Pathfinder*-murderin' drill. Then I chiseled out a billion little chunks between the holes. Okay, it was 759 but it felt like a billion.

Then I had one big hole in the trailer. I filed down the edges to keep them from being too sharp.

Remember the pop-tents? I cut the bottom out of one and the remaining canvas was the right size and shape. I used seal-strips to attach it to the inside of the trailer. After pressurizing and sealing up leaks as I found them, I had a nice big balloon bulging out of the trailer. The pressurized area is easily big enough to fit the oxygenator and atmospheric regulator.

One hitch: I need to put the AREC outside. The imaginatively named "atmospheric regulator external component" is how the regulator freeze-separates air. Why sink a bunch of energy into freezing stuff when you have incredibly cold temperatures right outside?

The regulator pumps air to the AREC to let Mars freeze it. It does this along a tube that runs through a valve in the Hab's wall. The return air comes back through another tube just like it.

Getting the tubing through the balloon canvas wasn't too hard. I have several spare valve patches. Basically they're ten-by-ten-centimeter patches of Hab canvas with a valve in the middle. Why do I have these? Consider what would happen on a normal mission if the regulator valve broke. They'd have to scrub the whole mission. Easier to send spares.

The AREC is fairly small. I made a shelf for it just under the solar panel shelves. Now everything's ready for when I eventually move the regulator and AREC over.

There's still a lot to do.

I'm not in any hurry; I've been taking it slow. One four-hour EVA per day spent on work, the rest of the time to relax in the Hab. Plus, I'll take a day off every now and then, especially if my back hurts. I can't afford to injure myself now.

I'll try to be better about this log. Now that I might actually get rescued, people will probably read it. I'll be more diligent and log every day.

LOG ENTRY: SOL 380

I finished the heat reservoir.

Remember my experiments with the RTG and having a hot bath? Same principle, but I came up with an improvement: submerge the RTG. No heat will be wasted that way.

I started with a large rigid sample container (or "plastic box" to people who don't work at NASA). I ran a tube through the open top and down the inside wall. Then I coiled it in the bottom to make a spiral. I glued it in place like that and sealed the end. Using my smallest drill bit, I put dozens of little holes in the coil. The idea is for the freezing return air from the regulator to pass through the water as a bunch of little bubbles. The increased surface area will get the heat into the air better.

Then I got a medium flexible sample container ("Ziploc bag") and tried to seal the RTG in it. But the RTG has an irregular shape, and I couldn't get all the air out of the bag. I can't allow any air in there. Instead of heat going to the water, some would get stored in the air, which could superheat and melt the bag.

I tried a bunch of times, but there was always an air pocket I couldn't get out. I was getting pretty frustrated until I remembered I have an airlock.

Suiting up, I went to Airlock 2 and depressurized to a full vacuum. I plopped the RTG in the bag and closed it. Perfect vacuum seal.

Next came some testing. I put the bagged RTG at the bottom of the container and filled it with water. It holds twenty liters, and the RTG quickly heated it. It was gaining a degree per minute. I let it go until it was a good 40°C. Then I hooked up the regulator's return air line to my contraption and watched the results.

It worked great! The air bubbled through, just like I'd hoped. Even better, the bubbles agitated the water, which distributed the heat evenly.

I let it run for an hour, and the Hab started to get cold. The RTG's heat can't keep up with the total loss from the Hab's impressive surface area. Not a problem. I've already established it's plenty to keep the rover warm.

I reattached the return air line to the regulator and things got back to normal.

LOG ENTRY: SOL 381

I've been thinking about laws on Mars.

Yeah, I know, it's a stupid thing to think about, but I have a lot of free time.

There's an international treaty saying no country can lay claim to anything that's not on Earth. And by another treaty, if you're not in any country's territory, maritime law applies.

So Mars is "international waters."

NASA is an American nonmilitary organization, and it owns the Hab. So while I'm in the Hab, American law applies. As soon as I step outside, I'm in international waters. Then when I get in the rover, I'm back to American law.

Here's the cool part: I will eventually go to Schiaparelli and commandeer the Ares 4 lander. Nobody explicitly gave me permission to do this, and they can't until I'm aboard Ares 4 and operating the comm system. After I board Ares 4, before talking to NASA, I will take control of a craft in international waters without permission.

That makes me a pirate!

A space pirate!

LOG ENTRY: SOL 383

You may be wondering what else I do with my free time. I spend a lot of it sitting around on my lazy ass watching TV. But so do you, so don't judge.

Also, I plan my trip.

Pathfinder was a cake run. Flat, level ground all the way. The only problem was navigating. But the trip to Schiaparelli will mean going over massive elevation changes.

I have a rough satellite map of the whole planet. It doesn't have much detail, but I'm lucky to have it at all. NASA didn't expect me to wander 3200 kilometers from the Hab.

Acidalia Planitia (where I am) has a relatively low elevation. So does Schiaparelli. But between them it goes up and down by 10 kilometers. There's going to be a lot of dangerous driving.

Things will be smooth while I'm in Acidalia, but that's only the first 650 kilometers. After that comes the crater-riddled terrain of Arabia Terra.

I do have one thing going for me. And I swear it's a gift from God. For some geological reason, there's a valley called Mawrth Vallis that's *perfectly* placed.

Millions of years ago it was a river. Now it's a valley that juts into the brutal terrain of Arabia, almost directly toward Schiaparelli. It's much gentler terrain than the rest of Arabia Terra, and the far end looks like a smooth ascent out of the valley.

Between Acidalia and Mawrth Vallis I'll get 1350 kilometers of relatively easy terrain.

The other 1850 kilometers . . . well, that won't be so nice. Especially when I have to descend into Schiaparelli itself. Ugh.

Anyway. Mawrth Vallis. Awesome.

LOG ENTRY: SOL 385

The worst part of the *Pathfinder* trip was being trapped in the rover. I had to live in a cramped environment that was full of junk and reeked of body odor. Same as my college days.

Rim shot!

Seriously though, it sucked. It was twenty-two sols of abject misery.

I plan to leave for Schiaparelli 100 sols before my rescue (or death), and I swear to God I'll rip my own face off if I have to live in the rover for that long.

I need a place to stay where I can stand up and take a few steps without hitting things. And no, being outside in a goddamn EVA suit doesn't count. I need personal space, not 50 kilograms of clothing.

So today, I started making a tent. Somewhere I can relax while the batteries recharge; somewhere I can lie down comfortably while sleeping.

I recently sacrificed one of my two pop-tents to be the trailer balloon, but the other is in perfect shape. Even better, it has an attachment for the rover's airlock. Before I made it a potato farm, its original purpose was to be a lifeboat for the rover.

I could attach the pop-tent to either vehicle's airlock. I'm going with the rover instead of the trailer. The rover has the computer and controls. If I need to know the status of anything (like life support or how well the battery is charging), I'll need access. This way, I'll be able to walk right in. No EVA.

Also, while traveling, I'll keep the tent folded up in the rover. In an emergency, I can get to it fast.

The pop-tent is the basis of my "bedroom," but not the whole thing. The tent's not very big; not much more space than the rover. But it has the airlock attachment so it's a great place to start. My plan is to double the floor area and double the height. That'll give me a nice big space to relax in.

For the floor, I'll use the original flooring material from the two pop-tents. If I didn't, my bedroom would become a big hamster ball because Hab canvas is flexible. When you fill it with pressure, it wants to become a sphere. That's not a useful shape.

To combat this, the Hab and pop-tents have special flooring material. It unfolds as a bunch of little segments that won't open beyond 180 degrees, so it remains flat.

The pop-tent base is a hexagon. I have another base left over from what is now the trailer balloon. When I'm done, the bedroom will be two adjacent hexes with walls around them and a crude ceiling.

It's gonna take a lot of glue to make this happen.

LOG ENTRY: SOL 387

The pop-tent is 1.2 meters tall. It's not made for comfort. It's made for astronauts to cower in while their crewmates rescue them. I want two meters. I want to be able to stand! I don't think that's too much to ask.

On paper, it's not hard to do. I just need to cut canvas pieces to the right shapes, seal them together, then seal them to the existing canvas and flooring.

But that's a lot of canvas. I started this mission with six square meters and I've used up most of that. Mostly on sealing the breach from when the Hab blew up.

God damn Airlock 1.

Anyway, my bedroom will take 30 square meters of the stuff. Way the hell more than I have left. Fortunately, I have an alternate supply of Hab canvas: the Hab.

Problem is (follow me closely here, the science is pretty complicated), if I cut a hole in the Hab, the air won't stay inside anymore.

I'll have to depressurize the Hab, cut chunks out, and put it back together (smaller). I spent today figuring out the exact sizes and shapes of canvas I'll need. I need to not fuck this up, so I triple-checked everything. I even made a model out of paper.

The Hab is a dome. If I take canvas from near the floor, I can pull the remaining canvas down and reseal it. The Hab will become a lopsided dome, but that shouldn't matter. As long as it holds pressure. I only need it to last another sixty-two sols.

I drew the shapes on the wall with a Sharpie. Then I spent a long time re-measuring them and making sure, over and over, that they were right.

That was all I did today. Might not seem like much, but the math and design work took all day. Now it's time for dinner.

I've been eating potatoes for weeks. Theoretically, with my three-quarter ration plan, I should still be eating food packs. But three-quarter ration is hard to maintain, so now I'm eating potatoes.

I have enough to last till launch, so I won't starve. But I'm pretty damn sick of potatoes. Also, they have a lot of fiber, so . . . let's just say it's good I'm the only guy on this planet.

I saved five meal packs for special occasions. I wrote their names on each one. I get to eat "Departure" the day I leave for Schiaparelli. I'll eat "Halfway" when I reach the 1600-kilometer mark, and "Arrival" when I get there.

The fourth one is "Survived Something That Should Have Killed Me" because some fucking thing will happen, I just know it. I don't know what it'll be, but it'll happen. The rover will break down, or I'll come down with fatal hemorrhoids, or I'll run into hostile Martians, or some shit. When I do (if I live), I get to eat that meal pack.

The fifth one is reserved for the day I launch. It's labeled "Last Meal."

Maybe that's not such a good name.

LOG ENTRY: SOL 388

I started the day with a potato. I washed it down with some Martian coffee. That's my name for "hot water with a caffeine pill dissolved in it." I ran out of real coffee months ago.

My first order of business was a careful inventory of the Hab. I needed to root out anything that would have a problem with losing atmospheric pressure. Of course, everything in the Hab had a crash course in depressurization a few months back. But this time would be controlled, and I might as well do it right.

The main thing is the water. I lost 300 liters to sublimation when the Hab blew up. This time, that won't happen. I drained the water reclaimer and sealed all the tanks.

The rest was just collecting knickknacks and dumping them in Airlock 3. Anything I could think of that doesn't do well in a near-vacuum. All the pens, vitamin bottles (probably not necessary but I'm not taking chances), medical supplies, etc.

Then I did a controlled shutdown of the Hab. The critical components are designed to survive a vacuum. Hab depress is one of the many scenarios NASA accounted for. One system at a time, I cleanly shut them all down, ending with the main computer itself.

I suited up and depressurized the Hab. Last time, the canvas collapsed and made a mess of everything. That's not supposed to happen. The dome of the Hab is mostly supported by air pressure, but there are flexible reinforcing poles across the inside to hold up the canvas. It's how the Hab was assembled in the first place.

I watched as the canvas gently settled onto the poles. To confirm the depressurization, I opened both doors of Airlock 2. I left Airlock 3 alone. It maintained pressure for its cargo of random crap.

Then I cut shit up!

I'm not a materials engineer; my design for the bedroom isn't elegant. It's just a six-meter perimeter and a ceiling. No, it won't have right angles and corners (pressure vessels don't like those). It'll balloon out to a more round shape.

Anyway, it means I only needed to cut two big-ass strips of canvas. One for the walls and one for the ceiling.

After mangling the Hab, I pulled the remaining canvas down to the flooring and resealed it. Ever set up a camping tent? From the inside? While wearing a suit of armor? It was a pain in the ass.

I repressurized to one-twentieth of an atmosphere to see if it could hold pressure.

Ha ha ha! Of course it couldn't! Leaks galore. Time to find them.

On Earth, tiny particles get attached to water or wear down to nothing. On Mars, they just hang around. The top layer of sand is like talcum powder. I went outside with a bag and scraped along the surface. I got some normal sand, but plenty of powder, too.

I had the Hab maintain the one-twentieth atmosphere, backfilling as air leaked out. Then I "puffed" the bag to get the smallest particles to float around. They were quickly drawn to where the leaks were. As I found each leak, I spot-sealed it with resin.

It took hours, but I finally got a good seal. I'll tell ya, the Hab looks pretty "ghetto" now. One whole side of it is lower than the rest. I'll have to hunch down when I'm over there.

I pressurized to a full atmosphere and waited an hour. No leaks.

It's been a long, physically taxing day. I'm totally exhausted but

I can't sleep. Every sound scares the shit out of me. Is that the Hab popping? No? Okay. . . . What was that!? Oh, nothing? Okay. . . .

It's a terrible thing to have my life depend on my half-assed handiwork.

Time to get a sleeping pill from the medical supplies.

LOG ENTRY: SOL 389

What the hell is in those sleeping pills!? It's the middle of the day.

After two cups of Martian coffee, I woke up a little. I won't be taking another one of those pills. It's not like I have to go to work in the morning.

Anyway, as you can tell from how not dead I am, the Hab stayed sealed overnight. The seal is solid. Ugly as hell, but solid.

Today's task was the bedroom.

Assembling the bedroom was way easier than resealing the Hab. Because this time, I didn't have to wear an EVA suit. I made the whole thing inside the Hab. Why not? It's just canvas. I can roll it up and take it out an airlock when I'm done.

First, I did some surgery on the remaining pop-tent. I needed to keep the rover–airlock connector and surrounding canvas. The rest of the canvas had to go. Why hack off most of the canvas only to replace it with more canvas? Seams.

NASA is good at making things. I am not. The dangerous part of this structure won't be the canvas. It'll be the seams. And I get less total seam length by not trying to use the existing pop-tent canvas.

After hacking away most of the remaining tent, I seal-stripped the two pop-tent floors together. Then I sealed the new canvas pieces into place.

It was so much easier without the EVA suit on. So much easier!

Then I had to test it. Again, I did it in the Hab. I brought an EVA suit into the tent with me and closed the mini-airlock door. Then I fired up the EVA suit, leaving the helmet off. I told it to bump the pressure up to 1.2 atm.

It took a little while to bring it up to par, and I had to disable some alarms on the suit. ("Hey, I'm pretty sure the helmet's not on!"). It depleted most of the N_2 tank but was finally able to bring up the pressure.

Then I sat around and waited. I breathed; the suit regulated the air. All was well. I watched the suit readouts carefully to see if it had to replace any "lost" air. After an hour with no noticeable change, I declared the first test a success.

I rolled up the whole thing (wadded up, really) and took it out to the rover.

You know, I suit up a lot these days. I bet that's another record I hold. A typical Martian astronaut does, what, forty EVAs? I've done several hundred.

Once I brought the bedroom to the rover, I attached it to the airlock from the inside. Then I pulled the release to let it loose. I was still wearing my EVA suit, because I'm not an idiot.

The bedroom fired out and filled in three seconds. The open airlock hatchway led directly to it, and it appeared to be holding pressure.

Just like before, I let it sit for an hour. And just like before, it worked great. Unlike the Hab canvas resealing, I got this one right on the first try. Mostly because I didn't have to do it with a damn EVA suit on.

Originally, I planned to let my bedroom sit overnight and check on it in the morning. But I ran into a problem: I can't get out if I do that. The rover has only one airlock, and the bedroom was attached to it. There was no way for me to get out without detaching the bedroom, and no way to attach and pressurize the bedroom without being inside the rover.

It's a little scary. The first time I test the thing overnight will be with me in it. But that'll be later. I've done enough today.

I have to face facts. I'm done prepping the rover. I don't "feel" like I'm done. But it's ready to go:

Food: 1692 potatoes. Vitamin pills.

Water: 620 liters.

Shelter: Rover, trailer, bedroom.

Air: Rover and trailer combined storage: 14 liters liquid O_2, 14 liters liquid N_2.

Life Support: Oxygenator and atmospheric regulator. 418 hours of use-and-discard CO_2 filters for emergencies.

Power: 36 kilowatt-hours of storage. Carrying capacity for 29 solar cells.

Heat: 1400-watt RTG. Homemade reservoir to heat regulator's return air. Electric heater in rover as a backup.

Disco: Lifetime supply.

I'm leaving here on Sol 449. That gives me fifty-nine sols to test everything and fix whatever isn't working right. Then decide what's coming with me and what's staying behind. And plot a route to Schiaparelli using a grainy satellite map. And rack my brains trying to think of anything important I forgot.

Since Sol 6 all I've wanted to do was get the hell out of here. Now the prospect of leaving the Hab behind scares the shit out of me. I need some encouragement. I need to ask myself, "What would an Apollo astronaut do?"

He'd drink three whiskey sours, drive his Corvette to the launchpad, then fly to the moon in a command module smaller than my Rover. Man those guys were cool.

CHAPTER 21

LOG ENTRY: SOL 431

I'm working out how to pack. It's harder than it sounds.

I have two pressure vessels: the rover and the trailer. They're connected by hoses, but they're also not stupid. If one loses pressure, the other will instantly seal off the shared lines.

There's a grim logic to this: If the rover breaches, I'm dead. No point in planning around that. But if the trailer breaches, I'll be fine. That means I should put everything important in the rover.

Everything that goes in the trailer has to be comfortable in near-vacuum and freezing temperatures. Not that I anticipate that, but you know. Plan for the worst.

The saddlebags I made for the *Pathfinder* trip will come in handy for food storage. I can't just store potatoes in the rover or trailer. They'd rot in the warm, pressurized environment. I'll keep some in the rover for easy access, but the rest will be outside in the giant freezer that is this planet. The trailer will be packed pretty tight. It'll have two bulky Hab batteries, the atmospheric regulator, the oxygenator, and my homemade heat reservoir. It would be more convenient to have the reservoir in the rover, but it has to be near the regulator's return air feed.

The rover will be pretty packed, too. When I'm driving, I'll keep the bedroom folded up near the airlock, ready for emergency egress. Also, I'll have the two functional EVA suits in there with me and anything that might be needed for emergency repairs: tool kits, spare parts, my nearly depleted supply of sealant, the other rover's main computer (just in case!), and all 620 glorious liters of water.

And a plastic box to serve as a toilet. One with a good lid.

...

"How's Watney doing?" Venkat asked.

Mindy looked up from her computer with a start. "Dr. Kapoor?"

"I hear you caught a pic of him during an EVA?"

"Uh, yeah," Mindy said, typing on her keyboard. "I noticed things would always change around 9 a.m. local time. People usually keep the same patterns, so I figured he likes to start work around then. I did some minor realignment to get seventeen pics between 9 and 9:10. He showed up in one of them."

"Good thinking. Can I see the pic?"

"Sure." She brought up the image on her screen.

Venkat peered at the blurry image. "Is this as good as it gets?"

"Well, it is a photo taken from orbit," Mindy said. "The NSA enhanced the image with the best software they have."

"Wait, what?" Venkat stammered. "The NSA?"

"Yeah, they called and offered to help out. Same software they use for enhancing spy satellite imagery."

Venkat shrugged. "It's amazing how much red tape gets cut when everyone's rooting for one man to survive." He pointed to the screen. "What's Watney doing here?"

"I think he's loading something into the rover."

"When was the last time he worked on the trailer?" Venkat asked.

"Not for a while. Why doesn't he write us notes more often?"

Venkat shrugged. "He's busy. He works most of the daylight hours, and arranging rocks to spell a message takes time and energy."

"So . . . ," Mindy said. "Why'd you come here in person? We could have done all this over e-mail."

"Actually, I came to talk to you," he said. "There's going to be a change in your responsibilities. From now on, instead of managing the satellites around Mars, your sole responsibility is watching Mark Watney."

"What?" Mindy said. "What about course corrections and alignment?"

"We'll assign that to other people," Venkat said. "From now on, your only focus is examining imagery of Ares 3."

"That's a demotion," Mindy said. "I'm an orbital engineer, and you're turning me into a glorified Peeping Tom."

"It's short-term," Venkat said. "And we'll make it up to you. Thing is, you've been doing it for months, and you're an expert at identifying elements of Ares 3 from satellite pics. We don't have anyone else who can do that."

"Why is this suddenly so important?"

"He's running out of time," Venkat said. "We don't know how far along he is on the rover modifications. But we do know he's only got sixteen sols to get them done. We need to know exactly what he's doing. I've got media outlets and senators asking for his status all the time. The President even called me a couple of times."

"But seeing his status doesn't help," Mindy said. "It's not like we can do anything about it if he falls behind. This is a pointless task."

"How long have you worked for the government?" Venkat sighed.

LOG ENTRY: SOL 434

The time has come to test this baby out.

This presents a problem. Unlike on my *Pathfinder* trip, I have to take vital life support elements out of the Hab if I'm going to do a real dry run. When you take the atmospheric regulator and oxygenator out of the Hab, you're left with . . . a tent. A big round tent that can't support life.

It's not as risky as it seems. As always, the dangerous part about life support is managing carbon dioxide. When the air gets to 1 percent CO_2, you start getting symptoms of poisoning. So I need to keep the Hab's mix below that.

The Hab's internal volume is about 120,000 liters. Breathing normally, it would take me over two days to bring the CO_2 level up to 1 percent (and I wouldn't even put a dent in the O_2 level). So it's safe to move the regulator and oxygenator over for a while.

Both are way too big to fit through the trailer airlock. Lucky for me, they came to Mars with "some assembly required." They were too big to send whole, so they're easy to dismantle.

Over several trips, I moved all of their chunks to the trailer. I brought each chunk in through the airlock, one at a time. It was a pain in the ass reassembling them inside, let me tell you. There's barely enough room for all the shit the trailer's got to hold. There wasn't much left for our intrepid hero.

Then I got the AREC. It sat outside the Hab like an AC unit might on Earth. In a way, that's what it is. I hauled it over to the trailer and lashed it to the shelf I'd made for it. Then I hooked it up to the feed lines that led through the "balloon" to the inside of the trailer's pressure vessel.

The regulator needs to send air to the AREC, then the return air needs to bubble through the heat reservoir. The regulator also needs a pressure tank to contain the CO_2 it pulls from the air.

When gutting the trailer to make room, I left one tank in place for this. It's supposed to hold oxygen, but a tank's a tank. Thank God all the air lines and valves are standardized across the mission. That's no mistake. It was a deliberate decision to make field repairs easier.

Once I had the AREC in place, I hooked the oxygenator and regulator into the trailer's power and watched them power up. I ran both through full diagnostics to confirm they were working correctly. Then I shut down the oxygenator. Remember, I'll only use it one sol out of every five.

I moved to the rover, which meant I had to do an annoying tenmeter EVA. From there, I monitored the life support situation. It's worth noting that I can't monitor the actual support equipment from the rover (it's all in the trailer), but the rover can tell me all about the air. Oxygen, CO_2, temperature, humidity, etc. Everything seemed okay.

After getting back into the EVA suit, I released a canister of CO_2 into the rover's air. I watched the rover computer have a shit fit when it saw the CO_2 spike to lethal levels. Then, over time, the levels dropped to normal. The regulator was doing its job. Good boy!

I left the equipment running when I returned to the Hab. It'll be on its own all night and I'll check it in the morning. It's not a true test, because I'm not there to breathe up the oxygen and make CO_2, but one step at a time.

LOG ENTRY: SOL 435

Last night was weird. I knew *logically* that nothing bad would happen in just one night, but it was a little unnerving to know I had no life support other than heaters. My life depended on some math I'd done earlier. If I dropped a sign or added two numbers wrong, I might never wake up.

But I did wake up, and the main computer showed the slight rise in CO_2 I had predicted. Looks like I'll live another sol.

Live Another Sol would be an awesome name for a James Bond movie.

I checked up on the rover. Everything was fine. If I don't drive it, a single charge of the batteries could keep the regulator going for over a month (with the heater off). It's a pretty good safety margin to have. If all hell breaks loose on my trip, I'll have time to fix things. I'll be limited by oxygen consumption rather than CO_2 removal, and I have plenty of oxygen.

I decided it was a good time to test the bedroom.

I got in the rover and attached the bedroom to the outer airlock door from the inside. Like I mentioned before, this is the only way to do it. Then I turned it loose on an unsuspecting Mars.

As intended, the pressure from the rover blasted the canvas outward and inflated it. After that, chaos. The sudden pressure popped the bedroom like a balloon. It quickly deflated, leaving both itself and the rover devoid of air. I was wearing my EVA suit at the time; I'm not a fucking idiot. So I get to . . .

Live Another Sol! (Starring Mark Watney as . . . probably Q. I'm no James Bond.)

I dragged the popped bedroom into the Hab and gave it a good going-over. It failed at the seam where the wall met the ceiling. Makes sense. It's a right angle in a pressure vessel. Physics hates that sort of thing.

First, I patched it up, then I cut strips of spare canvas to place over the seam. Now it has double-thickness and double sealing resin all around. Maybe that'll be enough. At this point, I'm kind of guessing. My amazing botany skills aren't much use for this.

I'll test it again tomorrow.

LOG ENTRY: SOL 436

I'm out of caffeine pills. No more Martian coffee for me.

So it took a little longer for me to wake up this morning, and I quickly developed a splitting headache. One nice thing about living in a multibillion-dollar mansion on Mars: access to pure oxygen. For some reason, a high concentration of O_2 will kill most headaches. Don't know why. Don't care. The important thing is I don't have to suffer.

I tested out the bedroom again. I suited up in the rover and released the bedroom, same as last time. But this time it held. That's great, but having seen the fragile nature of my handiwork, I wanted a good long test of the pressure seal.

After a few minutes standing around in my EVA suit, I decided to make better use of my time. I may not be able to leave the rover/bedroom universe while the bedroom is attached to the airlock, but I can stay in the rover and close the door.

Once I did that, I took off the uncomfortable EVA suit. The bedroom was on the other side of the airlock door, still fully pressurized. So I'm still running my test, but I don't have to wear the EVA suit.

I arbitrarily picked eight hours for the test duration, so I was trapped in the rover until then.

I spent my time planning the trip. There wasn't much to add to what I already knew. I'll beeline out of Acidalia Planitia to Mawrth Vallis, then follow the valley until it ends. It'll take me on a zigzag route which will dump me in to Arabia Terra. After that, things get rough.

Unlike Acidalia Planitia, Arabia Terra is riddled with craters. And each crater represents two brutal elevation changes. First down, then up. I did my best to find the shortest path around them. I'm sure I'll have to adjust the course when I'm actually driving it. No plan survives first contact with the enemy.

...

MITCH TOOK his seat in the conference room. The usual gang was present: Teddy, Venkat, Mitch, and Annie. But this time there was also Mindy Park, as well as a man Mitch had never seen before.

"What's up, Venk?" Mitch asked. "Why the sudden meeting?"

"We've got some developments," Venkat said. "Mindy, why don't you bring them up to date?"

"Uh, yeah," Mindy said. "Looks like Watney finished the balloon addition to the trailer. It mostly uses the design we sent him."

"Any idea how stable it is?" Teddy asked.

"Pretty stable," she said. "It's been inflated for several days with no problems. Also, he built some kind of . . . room."

"Room?" Teddy asked.

"It's made of Hab canvas, I think," Mindy explained. "It attaches to the rover's airlock. I think he cut a section out of the Hab to make it. I don't know what it's for."

Teddy turned to Venkat. "Why would he do that?"

"We think it's a workshop," Venkat said. "There'll be a lot of work to do on the MAV once he gets to Schiaparelli. It'll be easier without an EVA suit. He probably plans to do as much as he can in that room."

"Clever," Teddy said.

"Watney's a clever guy," Mitch said. "How about getting life support in there?"

"I think he's done it," Mindy said. "He moved the AREC."

"Sorry," Annie interrupted. "What's an AREC?"

"It's the external component of the atmospheric regulator," Mindy said. "It sits outside the Hab, so I saw when it disappeared. He probably mounted it on the rover. There's no other reason to move it, so I'm guessing he's got life support online."

"Awesome," Mitch said. "Things are coming together."

"Don't celebrate yet, Mitch," Venkat said. He gestured to the newcomer. "This is Randall Carter, one of our Martian meteorologists. Randall, tell them what you told me."

Randall nodded. "Thank you, Dr. Kapoor." He turned his laptop around to show a map of Mars. "Over the past few weeks, a dust storm has been developing in Arabia Terra. Not a big deal in terms of magnitude. It won't hinder his driving at all."

"So what's the problem?" Annie asked.

"It's a low-velocity dust storm," Randall explained. "Slow winds, but fast enough to pick up very small particles on the surface and whip them into thick clouds. There are five or six of them every year. The thing is, they last for months, they cover huge sections of the planet, and they make the atmosphere thick with dust."

"I still don't see the problem," Annie said.

"Light," Randall said. "The total sunlight reaching the surface is very low in the area of the storm. Right now, it's twenty percent of normal. And Watney's rover is powered by solar panels."

"Shit," Mitch said, rubbing his eyes. "And we can't warn him."

"So he gets less power," Annie said. "Can't he just recharge longer?"

"The current plan already has him recharging all day long," Venkat explained. "With twenty percent of normal daylight, it'll take five times as long to get the same energy. It'll turn his forty five-sol trip into two hundred and twenty-five sols. He'll miss the *Hermes* flyby."

"Can't *Hermes* wait for him?" Annie asked.

"It's a flyby," Venkat said. "*Hermes* isn't going into Martian orbit. If they did, they wouldn't be able to get back. They need their velocity for the return trajectory."

After a few moments of silence, Teddy said, "We'll just have to hope he finds a way through. We can track his progress and—"

"No, we can't," Mindy interrupted.

"We can't?" Teddy said.

She shook her head. "The satellites won't be able to see through the dust. Once he enters the affected area, we won't see anything until he comes out the other side."

"Well . . . ," Teddy said. "Shit."

LOG ENTRY: SOL 439

Before I risk my life with this contraption, I need to test it.

And not the little tests I've been doing so far. Sure, I've tested power generation, life support, the trailer bubble, and the bedroom. But I need to test all aspects of it working together.

I'm going to load it up for the long trip and drive in circles. I won't ever be more than 500 meters from the Hab, so I'll be fine if shit breaks.

I dedicated today to loading up the rover and trailer for the test. I want the weight to match what it'll be on the real trip. Plus if cargo is going to shift around or break things, I want to know about it now.

I made one concession to common sense: I left most of my water supply in the Hab. I loaded twenty liters; enough for the test but no more. There are a lot of ways I could lose pressure in this mechanical abomination I've created, and I don't want all my water to boil off if that happens.

On the real trip, I'm going to have 620 liters of water. I made up the weight difference by loading 600 kilograms of rocks in with my other supplies.

Back on Earth, universities and governments are willing to pay millions to get their hands on Mars rocks. I'm using them as ballast.

I'm doing one more little test tonight. I made sure the batteries were good and full, then disconnected the rover and trailer from Hab power. I'll be sleeping in the Hab, but I left the rover's life support on. It'll maintain the air overnight, and tomorrow I'll see how much power it ate up. I've watched the power consumption while it's attached to the Hab, and there weren't any surprises. But this'll be the true proof. I call it the "plugs-out test."

Maybe that's not the best name.

■ ■ ■

THE CREW of *Hermes* gathered in the Rec.

"Let's get through status quickly," Lewis said. "We're all behind in our science assignments. Vogel, you first."

"I repaired the bad cable on VASIMR 4," Vogel reported. "It

was our last thick-gauge cable. If another such problem occurs, we will have to braid lower-gauge lines to carry the current. Also, the power output from the reactor is declining."

"Johanssen," Lewis said, "what's the deal with the reactor?"

"I had to dial it back," Johanssen said. "It's the cooling vanes. They aren't radiating heat as well as they used to. They're tarnishing."

"How can that happen?" Lewis asked. "They're outside the craft. There's nothing for them to react with."

"I think they picked up dust or small air leaks from *Hermes* itself. One way or another, they're definitely tarnishing. The tarnish is clogging the micro-lattice, and that reduces the surface area. Less surface area means less heat dissipation. So I limited the reactor enough that we weren't getting positive heat."

"Any chance of repairing the cooling vanes?"

"It's on the microscopic scale," Johanssen said. "We'd need a lab. Usually they replace the vanes after each mission."

"Will we be able to maintain engine power for the rest of the mission?"

"Yes, if the rate of tarnishing doesn't increase."

"All right, keep an eye on it. Beck, how's life support?"

"Limping," Beck said. "We've been in space way longer than it was designed to handle. There are a bunch of filters that would normally be replaced each mission. I found a way to clean them with a chemical bath I made in the lab, but it eats away at the filters themselves. We're okay right now, but who knows what'll break next?"

"We knew this would happen," Lewis said. "The design of *Hermes* assumed it would get an overhaul after each mission, but we've extended Ares 3 from 396 days to 898. Things are going to break. We've got all of NASA to help when that happens. We just need to stay on top of maintenance. Martinez, what's the deal with your bunk room?"

Martinez furrowed his brow. "It's still trying to cook me. The climate control just isn't keeping up. I think it's the tubing in the walls that brings the coolant. I can't get at it because it's built into the hull. We can use the room for storage of non-temperature-sensitive cargo, but that's about it."

"So did you move into Mark's room?"

"It's right next to mine," he said. "It has the same problem."

"Where have you been sleeping?"

"In Airlock 2. It's the only place I can be without people tripping over me."

"No good," Lewis said, shaking her head. "If one seal breaks, you die."

"I can't think of anywhere else to sleep," he said. "The ship is pretty cramped, and if I sleep in a hallway I'll be in people's way."

"Okay, from now on, sleep in Beck's room. Beck can sleep with Johanssen."

Johanssen blushed and looked down awkwardly.

"So . . . ," Beck said, "you know about that?"

"You thought I didn't?" Lewis said. "It's a small ship."

"You're not mad?"

"If it were a normal mission, I would be," Lewis said. "But we're way off-script now. Just keep it from interfering with your duties, and I'm happy."

"Million-mile-high club," Martinez said. "Nice!"

Johanssen blushed deeper and buried her face in her hands.

LOG ENTRY: SOL 444

I'm getting pretty good at this. Maybe when all this is over I could be a product tester for Mars rovers.

Things went well. I spent five sols driving in circles; I averaged 93 kilometers per sol. That's a little better than I'd expected. The terrain here is flat and smooth, so it's pretty much a best-case scenario. Once I'm going up hills and around boulders, it won't be nearly that good.

The bedroom is awesome. Large, spacious, and comfortable. On the first night, I ran into a little problem with the temperature. It was fucking cold. The rover and trailer regulate their own temperatures just fine, but things weren't hot enough in the bedroom.

Story of my life.

The rover has an electric heater that pushes air with a small fan. I don't use the heater itself for anything because the RTG provides all the heat I need, so I liberated the fan and wired it into a power line near the airlock. Once it had power, all I had to do was point it at the bedroom.

It's a low-tech solution, but it worked. There's plenty of heat, thanks to the RTG. I just needed to get it evenly spread out. For once, entropy was on my side.

I've discovered that raw potatoes are disgusting. When I'm in the Hab, I cook my taters using a small microwave. I don't have anything like that in the rover. I could easily bring the Hab's microwave into the rover and wire it in, but the energy required to cook ten potatoes a day would actually cut into my driving distance.

I fell into a routine pretty quickly. In fact, it was hauntingly familiar. I did it for twenty-two miserable sols on the *Pathfinder* trip. But this time, I had the bedroom and that makes all the difference. Instead of being cooped up in the rover, I have my own little Hab.

After waking up, I have a potato for breakfast. Then, I deflate the bedroom from the inside. It's kind of tricky, but I worked out how.

First, I put on an EVA suit. Then I close the inner airlock door, leaving the outer door (which the bedroom is attached to) open. This isolates the bedroom, with me in it, from the rest of the rover. Then I tell the airlock to depressurize. It thinks it's just pumping the air out of a small area, but it's actually deflating the whole bedroom.

Once the pressure is gone, I pull the canvas in and fold it. Then I detach it from the outer hatch and close the outer door. This is the most cramped part. I have to share the airlock with the entire folded-up bedroom while it repressurizes. Once I have pressure again, I open the inner door and more or less fall into the rover. Then I stow the bedroom and go back to the airlock for a normal egress to Mars.

It's a complicated process, but it detaches the bedroom without having to depressurize the rover cabin. Remember, the rover has all my stuff that doesn't play well with vacuum.

The next step is to gather up the solar cells I laid out the day before and stow them on the rover and trailer. Then I do a quick check on the trailer. I go in through its airlock and basically take a quick look at all the equipment. I don't even take off my EVA suit. I just want to make sure nothing's obviously wrong.

Then, back to the rover. Once inside, I take off the EVA suit and start driving. I drive for almost four hours, and then I'm out of power.

Once I park, it's back into the EVA suit for me, and out to Mars again. I lay the solar panels out and get the batteries charging.

Then I set up the bedroom. Pretty much the reverse of the sequence I use to stow it. Ultimately, it's the airlock that inflates it. In a way, the bedroom is just an extension of the airlock.

Even though it's possible, I don't rapid-inflate the bedroom. I did that to test it because I wanted to find where it'll leak. But it's not a good idea. Rapid inflation puts a lot of shock and pressure on it. It would eventually rupture. I didn't enjoy that time the Hab launched me like a cannonball. I'm not eager to repeat it.

Once the bedroom is set up again, I can take off my EVA suit and relax. I mostly watch crappy seventies TV. I'm indistinguishable from an unemployed guy for most of the day.

I followed that process for four sols, and then it was time for an "Air Day."

An Air Day turns out to be pretty much the same as any other day, but without the four-hour drive. Once I set up the solar panels, I fired up the oxygenator and let it work through the backlog of CO_2 that the regulator had stored up.

It converted all the CO_2 to oxygen and used up the day's power generation to do it.

The test was a success. I'll be ready on time.

LOG ENTRY: SOL 449

Today's the big day. I'm leaving for Schiaparelli.

The rover and trailer are all packed. They've been mostly packed since the test run. But now I even have the water aboard.

Over the last few days, I cooked all the potatoes with the Hab's microwave. It took quite a while, because the microwave can only hold four at a time. After cooking, I put them back out on the surface to freeze. Once frozen, I put them back in the rover's saddle-bags. This may seem like a waste of time, but it's critical. Instead of eating raw potatoes during my trip, I'll be eating (cold) precooked potatoes. First off, they'll taste a lot better. But more important, they'll be cooked. When you cook food, the proteins break down, and the food becomes easier to digest. I'll get more calories out of it, and I need every calorie I can get my hands on.

I spent the last several days running full diagnostics on everything. The regulator, oxygenator, RTG, AREC, batteries, rover life support (in case I need a backup), solar cells, rover computer, airlocks, and everything else with a moving part or electronic component. I even checked each of the motors. Eight in all, one for each wheel, four on the rover, four on the trailer. The trailer's motors won't be powered, but it's nice to have backups.

It's all good to go. No problems that I can see.

The Hab is a shell of its former self. I've robbed it of all critical components and a big chunk of its canvas. I've looted that poor Hab for everything it could give me, and in return it's kept me alive for a year and a half. It's like the Giving Tree.

I performed the final shutdown today. The heaters, lighting, main computer, etc. All the components I didn't steal for the trip to Schiaparelli.

I could have left them on. It's not like anyone would care. But the original procedure for Sol 31 (which was supposed to be the last day of the surface mission) was to completely shut down the Hab and deflate it, because NASA didn't want a big tent full of combustible oxygen next to the MAV when it launched.

I guess I did the shutdown as an homage to the mission Ares 3 could have been. A small piece of the Sol 31 I never got to have.

Once I'd shut everything down, the interior of the Hab was eerily silent. I'd spent 449 sols listening to its heaters, vents, and fans. But now it was dead quiet. It was a creepy kind of quiet that's hard to describe. I've been away from the noises of the Hab before, but always in a rover or an EVA suit, both of which have noisy machinery of their own.

But now there was nothing. I never realized how utterly silent Mars is. It's a desert world with practically no atmosphere to convey sound. I could hear my own heartbeat.

Anyway, enough waxing philosophical.

I'm in the rover right now. (That should be obvious, with the Hab main computer offline forever.) I've got two full batteries, all systems are go, and I've got forty-five sols of driving ahead of me.

Schiaparelli or bust!

CHAPTER 22

LOG ENTRY: SOL 458

Mawrth Vallis! I'm finally here!

Actually, it's not an impressive accomplishment. I've only been traveling ten sols. But it's a good psychological milestone.

So far, the rover and my ghetto life support are working admirably. At least, as well as can be expected for equipment being used ten times longer than intended.

Today is my second Air Day (the first was five sols ago). When I put this scheme together, I figured Air Days would be godawful boring. But now I look forward to them. They're my days off.

On a normal day, I get up, fold up the bedroom, stack the solar cells, drive four hours, set up the solar cells, unfurl the bedroom, check all my equipment (especially the rover chassis and wheels), then make a Morse code status report for NASA, if I can find enough nearby rocks.

On an Air Day, I wake up and turn on the oxygenator. The solar panels are already out from the day before. Everything's ready to go. Then I chill out in the bedroom or rover. I have the whole day to myself. The bedroom gives me enough space that I don't feel cooped up, and the computer has plenty of shitty TV reruns for me to enjoy.

Technically, I entered Mawrth Vallis yesterday. But I only knew that by looking at a map. The entrance to the valley is wide enough that I couldn't see the canyon walls in either direction.

But now I'm definitely in a canyon. And the bottom is nice and flat. Exactly what I was hoping for. It's amazing; this valley wasn't made by a river slowly carving it away. It was made by a mega-flood in a single day. It would have been a hell of a thing to see.

Weird thought: I'm not in Acidalia Planitia anymore. I spent 457 sols there, almost a year and a half, and I'll never go back. I wonder if I'll be nostalgic about that later in life.

If there is a "later in life," I'll be happy to endure a little nostalgia. But for now, I just want to go home.

•••

"Welcome back to CNN's *Mark Watney Report*," Cathy said to the camera. "We're speaking with our frequent guest, Dr. Venkat Kapoor. Dr. Kapoor, I guess what people want to know is, is Mark Watney doomed?"

"We hope not," Venkat responded, "but he's got a real challenge ahead of him."

"According to your latest satellite data, the dust storm in Arabia Terra isn't abating at all, and will block eighty percent of the sunlight?"

"That's correct."

"And Watney's only source of energy is his solar panels, correct?"

"Yes, that's right."

"Can his makeshift rover operate at twenty percent power?"

"We haven't found any way to make that happen, no. His life support alone takes more energy than that."

"How long until he enters the storm?"

"He's just entered Mawrth Vallis now. At his current rate of travel, he'll be at the edge of the storm on Sol 471. That's twelve days from now."

"Surely he'll see something is wrong," Cathy said. "With such low visibility, it won't take long for him to realize his solar cells will have a problem. Couldn't he just turn around at that point?"

"Unfortunately, everything's working against him," Venkat said. "The edge of the storm isn't a magic line. It's just an area where the dust gets a little more dense. It'll keep getting more and more dense as he travels onward. It'll be really subtle; every day will be slightly darker than the last. Too subtle to notice."

Venkat sighed. "He'll go hundreds of kilometers, wondering why his solar panel efficiency is going down, before he notices any visibility problems. And the storm is moving west as he moves east. He'll be too deep in to get out."

"Are we just watching a tragedy play out?" Cathy asked.

"There's always hope," Venkat said. "Maybe he'll figure it out faster than we think and turn around in time. Maybe the storm will dissipate unexpectedly. Maybe he'll find a way to keep his life support going on less energy than we thought was possible. Mark Watney is now an expert at surviving on Mars. If anyone can do it, it's him."

"Twelve days," Cathy said to the camera. "All of Earth is watching but powerless to help."

LOG ENTRY: SOL 462

Another uneventful sol. Tomorrow is an Air Day, so this is kind of my Friday night.

I'm about halfway through Mawrth Vallis now. Just as I'd hoped, the going has been easy. No major elevation changes. Hardly any obstacles. Just smooth sand with rocks smaller than half a meter.

You may be wondering how I navigate. When I went to *Path-*

finder, I watched Phobos transit the sky to figure out the east-west axis. But *Pathfinder* was an easy trip compared to this, and I had plenty of landmarks to navigate by.

I can't get away with that this time. My "map" (such as it is) consists of satellite images far too low-resolution to be of any use. I can only see major landmarks, like craters 50 kilometers across. They just never expected me to be out this far. The only reason I had high-res images of the *Pathfinder* region is because they were included for landing purposes; in case Martinez had to land way long of our target.

So this time around, I needed a reliable way to fix my position on Mars.

Latitude and longitude. That's the key. The first is easy. Ancient sailors on Earth figured that one out right away. Earth's 23.5-degree axis points at Polaris. Mars has a tilt of just over 25 degrees, so it's pointed at Deneb.

Making a sextant isn't hard. All you need is a tube to look through, a string, a weight, and something with degree markings. I made mine in under an hour.

So I go out every night with a homemade sextant and sight Deneb. It's kind of silly if you think about it. I'm in my space suit on Mars and I'm navigating with sixteenth-century tools. But hey, they work.

Longitude is a different matter. On Earth, the earliest way to work out longitude required them to know the exact time, then compare it to the sun's position in the sky. The hard part for them back then was inventing a clock that would work on a boat (pendulums don't work on boats). All the top scientific minds of the age worked on the problem.

Fortunately, I have accurate clocks. There are four computers in my immediate line of sight right now. And I have Phobos.

Because Phobos is ridiculously close to Mars, it orbits the planet in less than one Martian day. It travels west to east (unlike the sun and Deimos) and sets every eleven hours. And naturally, it moves in a very predictable pattern.

I spend thirteen hours every sol just sitting around while the solar panels charge the batteries. Phobos is guaranteed to set at least once during that time. I note the time when it does. Then I plug it into a nasty formula I worked out and I know my longitude.

So working out longitude requires Phobos to set, and working out latitude requires it to be night so I can sight Deneb. It's not a very fast system. But I only need it once a day. I work out my location when I'm parked, and account for it in the next day's travel. It's kind of a successive approximation thing. So far, I think it's been working. But who knows? I can see it now: me holding a map, scratching my head, trying to figure out how I ended up on Venus.

■ ■ ■

MINDY PARK zoomed in on the latest satellite photo with practiced ease. Watney's encampment was visible in the center, the solar cells laid out in a circular pattern as was his habit.

The workshop was inflated. Checking the time stamp on the image, she saw it was from noon local time. She quickly found the status report; Watney always placed it close to the rover when rocks were in abundance, usually to the north.

To save time, Mindy had taught herself Morse code, so she wouldn't have to look each letter up every morning. She opened an e-mail and addressed it to the ever-growing list of people who wanted Watney's daily status message.

"ON TRACK FOR SOL 494 ARRIVAL."

She frowned and added "Note: five sols until dust storm entry."

Mawrth Vallis was fun while it lasted. I'm in Arabia Terra now.

I just entered the edge of it, if my latitude and longitude calculations are correct. But even without the math, it's pretty obvious the terrain is changing.

For the last two sols, I've spent almost all my time on an incline, working my way up the back wall of Mawrth Vallis. It was a gentle rise, but a constant one. I'm at a much higher altitude now. Acidalia Planitia (where the lonely Hab is hanging out) is 3000 meters below elevation zero, and Arabia Terra is 500 meters below. So I've gone up two and a half kilometers.

Want to know what elevation zero means? On Earth, it's sea level. Obviously, that won't work on Mars. So lab-coated geeks got together and decided Mars's elevation zero is wherever the air pressure is 610.5 pascals. That's about 500 meters up from where I am right now.

Now things get tricky. Back in Acidalia Planitia, if I got off course, I could just point in the right direction based on new data. Later, in Mawrth Vallis, it was impossible to screw up. I just had to follow the canyon.

Now I'm in a rougher neighborhood. The kind of neighborhood where you keep your rover doors locked and never come to a complete stop at intersections. Well, not really, but it's bad to get off course here.

Arabia Terra has large, brutal craters that I have to drive around. If I navigate poorly, I'll end up at the edge of one. I can't just drive down one side and up the other. Rising in elevation costs a ton of energy. On flat ground, I can make 90 kilometers per day. On a steep slope, I'd be lucky to get 40 kilometers. Plus, driving on a slope is dangerous. One mistake and I could roll the rover. I don't even want to think about that.

Yes, I'll eventually have to drive down into Schiaparelli. No way around that. I'll have to be really careful.

Anyway, if I end up at the edge of a crater, I'll have to backtrack to somewhere useful. And it's a damn maze of craters out here. I'll have to be on my guard, observant at all times. I'll need to navigate with landmarks as well as latitude and longitude.

My first challenge is to pass between the craters Rutherford and Trouvelot. It shouldn't be too hard. They're 100 kilometers apart. Even I can't fuck that up, right?

Right?

LOG ENTRY: SOL 468

I managed to thread the needle between Rutherford and Trouvelot nicely. Admittedly, the needle was 100 kilometers wide, but hey.

I'm now enjoying my fourth Air Day of the trip. I've been on the road for twenty sols. So far, I'm right on schedule. According to my maps, I've traveled 1440 kilometers. Not quite halfway there, but almost.

I've been gathering soil and rock samples from each place I camp. I did the same thing on my way to *Pathfinder*. But this time, I know NASA's watching me. So I'm labeling each sample by the current sol. They'll know my location a hell of a lot more accurately than I do. They can correlate the samples with their locations later.

It might be a wasted effort. The MAV isn't going to have much weight allowance when I launch. To intercept *Hermes*, it'll have to reach escape velocity, but it was only designed to get to orbit. The only way to get it going fast enough is to lose a lot of weight.

At least that jury-rigging will be NASA's job to work out, not mine. Once I get to the MAV, I'll be back in contact with them and they can tell me what modifications to make.

They'll probably say, "Thanks for gathering samples. But leave them behind. And one of your arms, too. Whichever one you like least." But on the off chance I can bring the samples, I'm gathering them.

The next few days' travel should be easy. The next major obstacle is Marth Crater. It's right in my straight-line path toward Schiaparelli. It'll cost me a hundred kilometers or so to go around, but it can't be helped. I'll try to aim for the southern edge. The closer I get to the rim the less time I'll waste going around it.

...

"DID YOU read today's updates?" Lewis asked, pulling her meal from the microwave.

"Yeah," Martinez said, sipping his drink.

She sat across the Rec table from him and carefully opened the steaming package. She decided to let it cool a bit before eating. "Mark entered the dust storm yesterday."

"Yeah, I saw that," he said.

"We need to face the possibility that he won't make it to Schiaparelli," Lewis said. "If that happens, we need to keep morale up. We still have a long way to go before we get home."

"He was dead before," Martinez said. "It was rough on morale, but we soldiered on. Besides, he won't die."

"It's pretty bleak, Rick," Lewis said. "He's already fifty kilometers into the storm, and he'll go another ninety kilometers per sol. He'll get in too deep to recover soon."

Martinez shook his head. "He'll pull through, Commander. Have faith."

She smiled forlornly. "Rick, you know I'm not religious."

"I know," he said. "I'm not talking about faith in God, I'm talking about faith in Mark Watney. Look at all the shit Mars has thrown at him, and he's still alive. He'll survive this. I don't know how, but he will. He's a clever son of a bitch."

Lewis took a bite of her food. "I hope you're right."

"Want to bet a hundred bucks?" Martinez said with a smile.

"Of course not," Lewis said.

"Damn right," he smiled.

"I'd never bet on a crewmate dying," Lewis said. "But that doesn't mean I think he'll—"

"Blah blah blah," Martinez interrupted. "Deep down, you think he'll make it."

LOG ENTRY: SOL 473

My fifth Air Day, and things are going well. I should be skimming south of Marth Crater tomorrow. It'll get easier after that.

I'm in the middle of a bunch of craters that form a triangle. I'm calling it the Watney Triangle because after what I've been through, stuff on Mars should be named after me.

Trouvelot, Becquerel, and Marth form the points of the triangle, with five other major craters along the sides. Normally this wouldn't be a problem at all, but with my extremely rough navigation, I could easily end up at the lip of one of them and have to backtrack.

After Marth, I'll be out of the Watney Triangle (yeah, I'm liking that name more and more). Then I can beeline toward Schiaparelli with impunity. There'll still be plenty of craters in the way, but they're comparatively small, and going around them won't cost much time.

Progress has been great. Arabia Terra is certainly rockier than Acidalia Planitia, but nowhere near as bad as I'd feared. I've been able to drive over most of the rocks, and around the ones that are too big. I have 1435 kilometers left to go.

I did some research on Schiaparelli and found some good news. The best way in is right in my direct-line path. I won't have to drive the perimeter at all. And the way in is easy to find, even when you suck at navigating. The northwest rim has a smaller crater on it, and that's the landmark I'll be looking for. To the southwest of that little crater is a gentle slope into Schiaparelli Basin.

The little crater doesn't have a name. At least, not on the maps I have. So I dub it "Entrance Crater." Because I can.

In other news, my equipment is starting to show signs of age. Not surprising, considering it's way the hell past its expiration date. For the past two sols, the batteries have taken longer to recharge. The solar cells just aren't producing as much wattage as before. It's not a big deal, I just need to charge a little longer.

LOG ENTRY: SOL 474

Well, I fucked it up.

It was bound to happen eventually. I navigated badly and ended up at the ridge of Marth Crater. Because it's 100 kilometers wide, I can't see the whole thing, so I don't know where on the circle I am.

The ridge runs perpendicular to the direction I was going. So I have no clue which way I should go. And I don't want to take the long way around if I can avoid it. Originally I wanted to go around to the south, but north is just as likely to be the best path now that I'm off course.

I'll have to wait for another Phobos transit to get my longitude, and I'll need to wait for nightfall to sight Deneb for my latitude. So I'm done driving for the day. Luckily I'd made 70 kilometers out of the 90 kilometers I usually do, so it's not too much wasted progress.

Marth isn't too steep. I could probably just drive down one side and up the other. It's big enough that I'd end up camping inside it one night. But I don't want to take unnecessary risks. Slopes are bad and should be avoided. I gave myself plenty of buffer time, so I'm going to play it safe.

I'm ending today's drive early and setting up for recharge. Probably a good idea anyway with the solar cells acting up; it'll give them more time to work. They underperformed again last night. I checked all the connections and made sure there wasn't any dust on them, but they still just aren't 100 percent.

I'm in trouble.

I watched two Phobos transits yesterday and sighted Deneb last night. I worked out my location as accurately as I could, and it wasn't what I wanted to see. As far as I can tell, I hit Marth Crater dead-on.

Craaaaap.

I can go north or south. One of them will probably be better than the other, because it'll be a shorter path around the crater.

I figured I should put at least a little effort into figuring out which direction was best, so I took a little walk this morning. It was over a kilometer to the peak of the rim. That's the sort of walk people do on Earth without thinking twice, but in an EVA suit it's an ordeal.

I can't wait till I have grandchildren. "When I was younger, I had to walk to the rim of a crater. Uphill! In an EVA suit! On Mars, ya little shit! Ya hear me? Mars!"

Anyway, I got up to the rim, and damn, it's a beautiful sight. From my high vantage point, I got a stunning panorama. I figured I might be able to see the far side of Marth Crater, and maybe work out the best way around.

But I couldn't see the far side. There was a haze in the air. It's not uncommon; Mars has weather and wind and dust, after all. But it seemed hazier than it should. I'm accustomed to the wide-open expanses of Acidalia Planitia, my former prairie home.

Then it got weirder. I turned around and looked back toward the rover and trailer. Everything was where I'd left it (very few car thieves on Mars). But the view seemed a lot clearer.

I looked east across Marth again. Then west to the horizon. Then east, then west. Each turn required me to rotate my whole body, EVA suits being what they are.

Yesterday, I passed a crater. It's about 50 kilometers west of here. It's just visible on the horizon. But looking east, I can't see anywhere near that far. Marth Crater is 110 kilometers wide. With a visibility of 50 kilometers, I should at least be able to see a distinct curvature of the rim. But I can't.

At first, I didn't know what to make of it. But the lack of symmetry bothered me. And I've learned to be suspicious of everything. That's when a bunch of stuff started to dawn on me:

1. The only explanation for asymmetrical visibility is a dust storm.
2. Dust storms reduce the effectiveness of solar cells.
3. My solar cells have been slowly losing effectiveness for several sols.

From this, I concluded the following:

1. I've been in a dust storm for several sols.
2. Shit.

Not only am I in a dust storm, but it gets thicker as I approach Schiaparelli. A few hours ago, I was worried because I had to go around Marth Crater. Now I'm going to have to go around something a lot bigger.

And I have to hustle. Dust storms move. Sitting still means I'll likely get overwhelmed. But which way do I go? It's no longer an issue of trying to be efficient. If I go the wrong way this time, I'll eat dust and die.

I don't have satellite imagery. I have no way of knowing the size or shape of the storm, or its heading. Man, I'd give anything for a five-minute conversation with NASA. Now that I think of it, NASA must be shitting bricks watching this play out.

I'm on the clock. I have to figure out *how* to figure out what I need to know about the storm. And I have to do it now.

And right this second nothing comes to mind.

• • •

MINDY TRUDGED to her computer. Today's shift began at 2:10 p.m. Her schedule matched Watney's every day. She slept when he slept. Watney simply slept at night on Mars, while Mindy had to drift forty minutes forward every day, taping aluminum foil to her windows to get any sleep at all.

She brought up the most recent satellite images. She cocked an eyebrow. He had not broken camp yet. Usually he drove in the early morning, as soon as it was light enough to navigate. Then he capitalized on the midday sun to maximize recharging.

But today, he had not moved, and it was well past morning.

She checked around the rovers and the bedroom for a message. She found it in the usual place (north of the campsite). As she read the Morse code, her eyes widened.

"DUST STORM. MAKING PLAN."

Fumbling with her cell phone, she dialed Venkat's personal number.

CHAPTER 23

LOG ENTRY: SOL 476

I think I can work this out.

I'm on the very edge of a storm. I don't know its size or heading. But it's moving, and that's something I can take advantage of. I don't have to wander around exploring it. It'll come to me.

The storm is just dust in the air; it's not dangerous to the rovers. I can think of it as "percent power loss." I checked yesterday's power generation, and it was 97 percent of optimal. So right now, it's a 3 percent storm.

I need to make progress and I need to regenerate oxygen. Those are my two main goals. I use 20 percent of my overall power to reclaim oxygen (when I stop for Air Days). If I end up in an 81 percent part of the storm, I'll be in real trouble. I'll run out of oxygen even if I dedicate all available power to producing it. That's the fatal scenario. But really, it's fatal much earlier than that. I need power to move or I'll be stranded until the storm passes or dissipates. That could be months.

The more power I generate, the more I'll have for movement. With clear skies, I dedicate 80 percent of my total power toward movement. I get 90 kilometers per sol this way. So right now, at 3 percent loss, I'm getting 2.7 kilometers less than I should.

It's okay to lose some driving distance per sol. I have plenty of time, but I can't let myself get too deep in the storm or I'll never be able to get out.

At the very least, I need to travel faster than the storm. If I can go faster, I can maneuver around it without being enveloped. So I need to find out how fast it's moving.

I can do that by sitting here for a sol. I can compare tomorrow's wattage to today's. All I have to do is make sure to compare at the same times of day. Then I'll know how fast the storm is moving, at least in terms of percent power loss.

But I need to know the shape of the storm, too.

Dust storms are big. They can be thousands of kilometers across. So when I work my way around it, I'll need to know which way to go. I'll want to move perpendicular to the storm's movement, and in whatever direction has less storm.

So here's my plan:

Right now, I can go 86 kilometers (because I couldn't get a full battery yesterday). Tomorrow, I'm going to leave a solar cell here and drive 40 kilometers due south. Then I'll drop off another solar cell and drive another 40 kilometers due south. That'll give me three points of reference across 80 kilometers.

The next day, I'll go back to collect the cells and get the data. By comparing the wattage at the same time of day in those three locations, I'll learn the shape of the storm. If the storm is thicker to the south, I'll go north to get around it. If it's thicker north, I'll go south.

I'm hoping to go south. Schiaparelli is southeast of me. Going north would add a lot of time to my total trip.

There's one *slight* problem with my plan: I don't have any way to "record" the wattage from an abandoned solar cell. I can easily track and log wattage with the rover computer, but I need something I can drop off and leave behind. I can't just take readings as I drive along. I need readings at the same time in different places.

So I'm going to spend today working on some mad science. I

have to make something that can log wattage. Something I can leave behind with a single solar cell.

Since I'm stuck here for the day anyway, I'll leave the solar cells out. I may as well get a full battery out of it.

It took all day yesterday and today, but I think I'm ready to measure this storm.

I needed a way to log the time of day and the wattage of each solar cell. One of the cells would be with me, but the other two would be dropped off and left far away. And the solution was the extra EVA suit I brought along.

EVA suits have cameras recording everything they see. There's one on the right arm (or the left if the astronaut is left-handed) and another above the faceplate. A time stamp is burned into the lower left corner of the image, just like on the shaky home videos Dad used to take.

My electronics kit has several power meters. So I figured, why make my own logging system? I can just film the power meter all day long.

So that's what I set up. When I packed for this road trip, I made sure to bring all my kits and tools. Just in case I had to repair the rover en route.

First, I harvested the cameras from my spare EVA suit. I had to be careful; I didn't want to ruin the suit. It's my only spare. I extracted the cameras and the lines leading to their memory chips.

I put a power meter into a small sample container, then glued a camera to the underside of the lid. When I sealed up the container, the camera was properly recording the readout of the power meter.

For testing, I used rover power. How will my logger get power once I abandon it on the surface? It'll be attached to a two-square-meter solar cell! That'll provide plenty of power. And I put a small rechargeable battery in the container to tide it over during nighttime (again, harvested from the spare EVA suit).

The next problem was heat, or the lack thereof. As soon as I take this thing out of the rover, it'll start cooling down mighty fast. If it gets too cold, the electronics will stop working.

So I needed a heat source. And my electronics kit provided the answer: resistors. Lots and lots of them. Resistors heat up. It's what they do. The camera and the power meter only need a tiny fraction of what a solar cell can make. So the rest of the energy goes through resistors.

I made and tested two "power loggers" and confirmed that the images were being properly recorded.

Then I had an EVA. I detached two of my solar cells and hooked them up to the power loggers. I let them log happily for an hour, then brought them back in to check the results. They worked great.

It's getting toward nightfall now. Tomorrow morning, I'll leave one power logger behind and head south.

While I was working, I left the oxygenator going (why not?). So I'm all stocked up on O_2 and good to go.

The solar cell efficiency for today was 92.5 percent. Compared to yesterday's 97 percent. This proves the storm is moving east to west, because the denser part of the storm was to the east yesterday.

So right now, the sunlight in this area is dropping by 4.5 percent per sol. If I were to stay here another sixteen sols, it would get dark enough to kill me.

Just as well I'm not going to stay here.

LOG ENTRY: SOL 478

Everything went as planned today. No hiccups. I can't tell if I'm driving deeper into the storm or out of it. It's hard to tell if the ambient light is less or more than it was yesterday. The human brain works hard to abstract that out.

I left a power logger behind when I started out. Then, after 40 kilometers' travel due south, I had a quick EVA to set up another. Now I've gone the full 80 kilometers, set up my solar cells for charging, and I'm logging the wattage.

Tomorrow, I'll have to reverse course and pick up the power loggers. It may be dangerous; I'll be driving right back into a known storm area. But the risk is worth the gain.

Also, have I mentioned I'm sick of potatoes? Because, by God, I am sick of potatoes. If I ever return to Earth, I'm going to buy a nice little home in Western Australia. Because Western Australia is on the opposite side of Earth from Idaho.

I bring it up because I dined on a meal pack today. I had saved five packs for special occasions. I ate the first of them twenty-nine sols ago when I left for Schiaparelli, but I totally forgot to eat the second when I reached the halfway point a few sols ago. So I'm enjoying my belated halfway feast.

It's probably more accurate to eat it today anyway. Who knows how long it'll take me to go around this storm? And if I end up stuck in the storm and doomed to die, I'm totally eating the other earmarked meals.

LOG ENTRY: SOL 479

Have you ever taken the wrong freeway entrance? You just need to drive to the next exit to turn around, but you hate every inch of travel because you're going away from your goal.

I felt like that all day. I'm now back where I started yesterday morning. Yuk.

Along the way, I picked up the power logger I'd left behind at the halfway point. Just now I brought in the one I'd left here yesterday.

Both loggers worked the way I'd hoped. I downloaded each of their video recordings to a laptop and advanced them to noon. Finally I had solar efficiency readings from three locations along an 80-kilometer line, all from the same time of day.

As of noon yesterday, the northernmost logger showed 12.3 percent efficiency loss, the middle one had a 9.5 percent loss, and the rover recorded a 6.4 percent loss at its southernmost location. It paints a pretty clear picture: The storm's north of me. And I already worked out it's traveling west.

So I should be able to avoid it by heading south a ways, letting it pass me to the north, then heading east again.

Finally, some good news! Southeast is what I wanted. I won't lose much time.

Sigh . . . I have to drive the same god damned path a third time tomorrow.

LOG ENTRY: SOL 480

I think I'm getting ahead of the storm.

Having traveled along Mars Highway 1 all day, I'm back at my campsite from yesterday. Tomorrow, I'll finally make real headway again. I was done driving and had the camp set up by noon. The efficiency loss here is 15.6 percent. Compared to the 17 percent loss at yesterday's camp, this means I can outrun the storm as long as I keep heading south.

Hopefully.

The storm is *probably* circular. They usually are. But I could just be driving into an alcove. If that's the case, I'm just fucking dead, okay? There's only so much I can do.

I'll know soon enough. If the storm is circular, I should get better and better efficiency every day until I'm back to 100 percent. Once I reach 100 percent, that means I'm completely south of the storm and I can start going east again. We'll see.

If there were no storm, I'd be going directly southeast toward my goal. As it is, going only south, I'm not nearly as fast. I'm traveling 90 kilometers per day as usual, but I only get 37 kilometers closer to Schiaparelli because Pythagoras is a dick. I don't know when I'll finally clear the storm and be able to beeline to Schiaparelli again. But one thing's for sure: My plan to arrive on Sol 494 is boned.

Sol 549. That's when they come for me. If I miss it, I'll spend the rest of my very short life here. And I still have the MAV to modify before then, too.

Sheesh.

LOG ENTRY: SOL 482

Air Day. A time for relaxation and speculation.

For relaxation, I read eighty pages of Agatha Christie's *Evil Under the Sun* courtesy of Johanssen's digital book collection. I think Linda Marshall is the murderer.

As for speculation, I speculated on when the hell I'll get past this storm.

I'm still going due south every day; and still dealing with efficiency loss (though I'm keeping ahead of it). Every day of this crap I'm only getting 37 kilometers closer to the MAV instead of 90. Pissing me off.

I considered skipping the Air Day. I could go another couple of days before I ran out of oxygen, and getting away from the storm is pretty important. But I decided against it. I'm far enough ahead of the storm that I can afford one day of no movement. And I don't know if a couple more days would help. Who knows how far south the storm goes?

Well, NASA probably knows. And the news stations back on Earth are probably showing it. And there's probably a website like www.watch-mark-watney-die.com. So there's like a hundred million people or so who know exactly how far south it goes.

But I'm not one of them.

LOG ENTRY: SOL 484

Finally!

I am FINALLY past the god damned storm. Today's power regen was 100 percent. No more dust in the air. With the storm moving perpendicular to my direction of travel, it means I'm south of the southernmost point of the cloud (presuming it's a circular storm. If it's not, then fuck).

Starting tomorrow, I can go directly toward Schiaparelli. Which is good, 'cause I lost a lot of time. I went 540 kilometers due south while avoiding that storm. I'm catastrophically off course.

Mind you, it hasn't been that bad. I'm well into Terra Meridiani now, and the driving is a little easier here than the rugged, ass-kicking terrain of Arabia Terra. Schiaparelli is almost due east, and if my sextant and Phobos calculations are correct, I've got another 1030 kilometers to get there.

Accounting for Air Days and presuming 90 kilometers of travel per sol, I should arrive on Sol 498. Not too bad, really. The Nearly-Mark-Killin' storm only ended up delaying me by four sols.

I'll still have forty-four sols to do whatever MAV modifications NASA has in mind.

LOG ENTRY: SOL 487

I have an interesting opportunity here. And by "opportunity" I mean *Opportunity*.

I got pushed so far off course, I'm actually not far from the Mars exploration rover *Opportunity*. It's about 300 kilometers away. I could get there in about four sols.

Damn it's tempting. If I could get *Opportunity*'s radio working, I'd be in touch with humanity again. NASA would continually tell me my exact position and best course, warn me if another storm was on its way, and generally be there watching over me.

But if I'm being honest, that's not the real reason I'm interested. I'm sick of being on my own, damn it! Once I got *Pathfinder* working, I got used to talking to Earth. All that went away because I leaned a drill against the wrong table, and now I'm alone again. I could end that in just four sols.

But it's an irrational, stupid thought. I'm only eleven sols away from the MAV. Why go out of my way to dig up another broken-ass rover to use as a makeshift radio when I'll have a brand-new, fully functional communications system within a couple of weeks?

So, while it's really tempting that I'm within striking range of another rover (man, we really littered this planet with them, didn't we?), it's not the smart move.

Besides, I've defiled enough future historical sites for now.

LOG ENTRY: SOL 492

I need to put some thought into the bedroom.

Right now, I can only have it set up when I'm inside the rover. It attaches to the airlock, so I can't get out if it's there. During my road trip that doesn't matter, because I have to furl it every day anyway. But once I get to the MAV, I won't have to drive around anymore. Each decompress/recompress of the bedroom stresses the seams (I learned that lesson the hard way when the Hab blew up), so it's best if I can find a way to leave it out.

Holy shit. I just realized I actually believe I'll get to the MAV. See what I did there? I casually talked about what I'll do after I get to the MAV. Like it was nothing. No big deal. I'm just going to pop over to Schiaparelli and hang with the MAV there.

Nice.

Anyway, I don't have another airlock. I've got one on the rover and one on the trailer and that's it. They're firmly fixed in place, so it's not like I can detach one and attach it to the bedroom.

But I can seal the bedroom entirely. I don't even have to do any hatchet jobs on it. The airlock attachment point has a flap I can unroll and seal the opening with. Remember, I stole the airlock attachment from a pop-tent, which is an emergency feature for pressure loss while in the rover. It'd be pretty useless if it couldn't seal itself off.

Unfortunately, as an emergency device, it was never intended to be reusable. The idea was that people seal themselves in the pop-tent, then the rest of the crew drives to wherever they are in the other rover and rescues them. The crew of the good rover detaches the pop-tent from the breached rover and reattaches it to theirs. Then they cut through the seal from their side to recover their crewmates.

To make sure this would always be an option, mission rules dictated no more than three people could be in a rover at once, and both rovers had to be fully functional or we couldn't use either.

So here's my brilliant plan: I won't use the bedroom as a bedroom anymore once I get to the MAV. I'll use it to house the oxygenator and atmospheric regulator. Then I'll use the trailer as my bedroom. Neat, eh?

The trailer has tons of space. I put a shitload of work into making that happen. The balloon gives plenty of headroom. Not a lot of floor space, but still lots of vertical area.

Also, the bedroom has several valve apertures in its canvas. I have the Hab's design to thank for that. The canvas I stole from it has valve apertures (triple-redundant ones, actually). NASA wanted to make sure the Hab could be refilled from the outside if necessary.

In the end, I'll have the bedroom sealed with the oxygenator and atmospheric regulator inside. It'll be attached to the trailer via hoses to share the same atmosphere, and I'll run a power line through one of the hoses. The rover will serve as storage (because I won't need to get to the driving controls anymore), and the trailer will be completely empty. Then I'll have a permanent bedroom. I'll even be able to use it as a workshop for whatever MAV modifications I need to do on parts that can fit through the trailer's airlock.

Of course, if the atmospheric regulator or oxygenator have problems, I'll need to cut into the bedroom to get to them. But I've been here 492 sols and they've worked fine the whole time, so I'll take that risk.

LOG ENTRY: SOL 497

I'll be at the entrance to Schiaparelli tomorrow!

Presuming nothing goes wrong, that is. But hey, everything else has gone smoothly this mission, right? (That was sarcasm.)

Today's an Air Day, and for once, I don't want it. I'm so close to Schiaparelli, I can taste it. I guess it would taste like sand, mostly, but that's not the point.

Of course, that won't be the end of the trip. It'll take another three sols to get from the entrance to the MAV, but hot damn! I'm almost there!

I think I can even see the rim of Schiaparelli. It's way the hell off in the distance and it might just be my imagination. It's 62 kilometers away, so if I'm seeing it, I'm only just barely seeing it.

Tomorrow, once I get to Entrance Crater, I'll turn south and enter the Schiaparelli Basin via the "Entrance Ramp." I did some back-of-the-napkin math, and the slope should be pretty safe. The elevation change from the rim to the basin is 1.5 kilometers, and the ramp is at least 45 kilometers long. That makes for a two-degree grade. No problem.

Tomorrow night, I'll sink to an all-new low!

Lemme rephrase that. . . .

Tomorrow night, I'll be at rock bottom!

No, that doesn't sound good either. . . .

Tomorrow night, I'll be in Giovanni Schiaparelli's favorite hole!

Okay, I admit I'm just playing around now.

FOR MILLIONS of years, the rim of the crater had been under constant attack from wind. It eroded the rocky crest the way a river cuts through a mountain range. After eons, it finally breached the edge.

The high-pressure zone created by the wind now had an avenue to drain. The breach widened more and more with each passing millennium. As it widened, dust and sand particles carried along with the attack settled in the basin below.

Eventually, a balance point was reached. The sand had piled up high enough to be flush with the land outside the crater. It no longer built upward but outward. The slope lengthened until a new balance point was reached, one defined by the complex interactions of countless tiny particles and their ability to maintain an angled shape. Entrance Ramp had been born.

The weather brought dunes and desert terrain. Nearby crater impacts brought rocks and boulders. The shape became uneven.

Gravity did its work. The ramp compressed over time. But it did not compress evenly. Differing densities shrunk at different rates. Some areas became hard as rock while others remained as soft as talc.

While providing a small *average* slope into the crater, the ramp itself was rugged and bitterly uneven.

On reaching Entrance Crater, the lone inhabitant of Mars turned his vehicle toward the Schiaparelli Basin. The difficult terrain of the ramp was unexpected, but it looked no worse than other terrain he routinely navigated.

He went around the smaller dunes and carefully crested the larger ones. He took care with every turn, every rise or fall in elevation, and every boulder in his path. He thought through every course and considered all alternatives.

But it wasn't enough.

The rover, while descending down a seemingly ordinary slope, drove off an invisible ridge. The dense, hard soil suddenly gave way to soft powder. With the entire surface covered by at least five centimeters of dust, there were no visual hints to the sudden change.

The rover's left front wheel sank. The sudden tilt brought the right rear wheel completely off the ground. This in turn put more weight on the left rear wheel, which slipped from its precarious purchase into the powder as well.

Before the traveler could react, the rover rolled onto its side. As it did, the solar cells neatly stacked on the roof flew off and scattered like a dropped deck of cards.

The trailer, attached to the rover with a tow clamp, was dragged along. The torsion on the clamp snapped the strong composite like a brittle twig. The hoses connecting the two vehicles also snapped. The trailer plunged headlong into the soft soil and flipped over on to its balloon-roof, shuddering to an abrupt halt.

The rover was not so lucky. It continued tumbling down the hill, bouncing the traveler around like clothes in a dryer. After twenty meters, the soft powder gave way to more solid sand and the rover shuddered to a halt.

It had come to rest on its side. The valves leading to the now-missing hoses had detected the sudden pressure drop and closed. The pressure seal was not breached.

The traveler was alive, for now.

CHAPTER 24

THE DEPARTMENT heads stared at the satellite image on the projection screen.

"Jesus," Mitch said. "What the hell happened?"

"The rover's on its side," Mindy said, pointing to the screen. "The trailer's upside down. Those rectangles scattered around are solar cells."

Venkat put a hand on his chin. "Do we have any information on the state of the rover pressure vessel?"

"Nothing obvious," Mindy said.

"Any signs of Watney doing something after the accident? An EVA maybe?"

"No EVA," Mindy said. "The weather's clear. If he'd come out, there'd be visible footsteps."

"Is this the entire crash site?" Bruce Ng asked.

"I think so," Mindy said. "Up toward the top of the photo, which is north, there are ordinary wheel tracks. Right here," she pointed to a large disturbance in the soil, "is where I think things went wrong. Judging by where that ditch is, I'd say the rover rolled and slid from there. You can see the trench it left behind. The trailer flipped forward onto its roof."

"I'm not saying everything's okay," Bruce said, "but I don't think it's as bad as it looks."

"Go on," Venkat said.

"The rover's designed to handle a roll," Bruce explained. "And if there'd been pressure loss, there'd be a starburst pattern in the sand. I don't see anything like that."

"Watney may still be hurt inside," Mitch said. "He could have banged his head or broken an arm or something."

"Sure," Bruce said. "I'm just saying the rover is probably okay."

"When was this taken?"

Mindy checked her watch. "We got it seventeen minutes ago. We'll get another pic in nine minutes when MGS4's orbit brings it into view."

"First thing he'll do is an EVA to assess damage," Venkat said. "Mindy, keep us posted on any changes."

LOG ENTRY: SOL 498

Hmm.

Yeah.

Things didn't go well on the descent into Schiaparelli Basin. To give you some indication of how unwell they went, I'm reaching up to the computer to type this. Because it's still mounted near the control panel, and the rover is on its side.

I got bounced around a lot, but I'm a well-honed machine in times of crisis. As soon as the rover toppled, I curled into a ball and cowered. That's the kind of action hero I am.

It worked, too. 'Cause I'm not hurt.

The pressure vessel is intact, so that's a plus. The valves that lead to the trailer hoses are shut. Probably means the hoses disconnected. And that means the trailer junction snapped. Wonderful.

Looking around the interior here, I don't think anything is broken. The water tanks stayed sealed. There aren't any visible leaks in the air tanks. The bedroom came unfolded, and it's all over the place, but it's just canvas, so it can't have gotten too hurt.

The driving controls are okay, and the nav computer is telling me the rover is at an "unacceptably dangerous tilt." Thanks, Nav!

So I rolled. That's not the end of the world. I'm alive and the rover's fine. I'm more worried about the solar cells I probably rolled over. Also, since the trailer detached, there's a good chance it's fucked up, too. The balloon roof it has isn't exactly durable. If it popped, the shit inside will have been flung out in all directions and I'll have to go find it. That's my critical life support.

Speaking of life support, the rover switched over to the local tanks when the valves shut. Good boy, Rover! Here's a Scooby Snack.

I've got twenty liters of oxygen (enough to keep me breathing for forty days), but without the regulator (which is in the trailer) I'm back to chemical CO_2 absorption. I have 312 hours of filters left. Plus I have another 171 hours of EVA suit CO_2 filters as well. All told, that gives me 483 hours, which is close to twenty sols. So I have time to get things working again.

I'm really damn close to the MAV now. About 220 kilometers. I'm not going to let something like this stop me from getting there. And I don't need everything to work at top form anymore. I just need the rover to work for 220 more kilometers and the life support to work for fifty-one more sols. That's it.

Time to suit up and look for the trailer.

LOG ENTRY: SOL 498 (2)

I had an EVA and things aren't too bad. Mind you, they're not good.

I trashed three solar cells. They're under the rover and cracked all to hell. They might still be able to piss out a few watts, but I'm not holding out much hope. Luckily, I did come into this with one extra solar cell. I needed twenty-eight for my daily operations and I brought twenty-nine (fourteen on the rover's roof, seven on the trailer's roof, and eight on the makeshift shelves I installed on the sides of both vehicles).

I tried pushing the rover over, but I wasn't strong enough. I'll need to rig something to get a leverage advantage. Other than being on its side, I don't see any real problems.

Well, that's not true. The tow hook is ruined beyond repair. Half of it ripped clean off. Fortunately, the trailer also has a tow hook, so I have a spare.

The trailer's in a precarious situation. It's upside down and sitting on the inflated roof. I'm not sure which god smiled down on me and kept that balloon from popping, but I'm grateful. My first priority will be righting it. The longer it puts weight on that balloon, the larger the chances it'll pop.

While I was out, I collected the twenty-six solar cells that aren't under the rover and set them up to recharge my batteries. May as well, right?

So right now, I have a few problems to tackle: First, I need to right the trailer. Or at least get the weight off the balloon. Next, I need to right the rover. Finally, I need to replace the rover's tow hook with the one on the trailer.

Also, I should spell out a message for NASA. They're probably worried.

...

MINDY READ the Morse code aloud. "ROLLED. FIXING NOW."

"What? That's it?" Venkat said over the phone.

"That's all he said," she reported, cradling the phone as she typed out an e-mail to the list of interested parties.

"Just three words? Nothing about his physical health? His equipment? His supplies?"

"You got me," she said. "He left a detailed status report. I just decided to lie for no reason."

"Funny," Venkat said. "Be a smart-ass to a guy seven levels above you at your company. See how that works out."

"Oh no," Mindy said. "I might lose my job as an interplanetary voyeur? I guess I'd have to use my master's degree for something else."

"I remember when you were shy."

"I'm space paparazzi now. The attitude comes with the job."

"Yeah, yeah," Venkat said. "Just send the e-mail."

"Already sent."

LOG ENTRY: SOL 499

I had a busy day today, and I got a lot done.

I started out pretty sore. I had to sleep on the wall of the rover. The bedroom won't work when the airlock is facing up. I did get to use the bedroom, somewhat. I folded it up and used it as a bed.

Anyway, suffice it to say, the wall of the rover wasn't made for sleeping on. But after a morning potato and Vicodin, I was feeling much better.

At first I figured my top priority was the trailer. Then I changed my mind. After taking a good look at it, I decided I'd never be able to right it by myself. I'd need the rover.

So today was focused on getting the rover righted.

I brought all my tools along on this trip, figuring I'd need them for the MAV modifications. And along with them I brought cabling. Once I get set up at the MAV, my solar cells and batteries will be in a fixed position. I don't want to move the rover around every time I use a drill on the far side of the MAV. So I brought all the electrical cabling I could fit.

Good thing, too. Because it doubles as rope.

I dug up my longest cable. It's the same one I used to power the drill that destroyed *Pathfinder*. I call it my "lucky cable."

I plugged one end into the battery and the other into the infamous sample drill, then walked off with the drill to find solid ground. Once I found it, I kept going until I'd gone as far as the electrical line would reach. I drove a one-meter bit half a meter into a rock, unplugged the power line, and tied it around the base of the bit.

Then I went back to the rover and tied off the cord to the roof-rack bar on the high side. Now I had a long, taut line running perpendicular to the rover.

I walked to the middle of the cord and pulled it laterally. The leverage advantage on the rover was huge. I only hoped it wouldn't break the drill bit before it tipped the rover.

I backed away, pulling the line more and more. Something had to give, and it wasn't going to be me. I had Archimedes on my side. The rover finally tipped.

It fell onto its wheels, kicking up a large cloud of soft dust. It was a silent affair. I was far enough away that the thin atmosphere had no hope of carrying the sound to me.

I untied the power line, liberated the drill bit, and returned to the rover. I gave it a full system's check. That's a boring-as-hell task, but I had to do it.

Every system and subsystem was working correctly. JPL did a damn good job making these rovers. If I get back to Earth, I'm buying Bruce Ng a beer. Though I guess I should buy all the JPL guys a beer.

Beers for everyone if I get back to Earth.

Anyway, with the rover back on its wheels it was time to work on the trailer. Problem is, I ran out of daylight. Remember, I'm in a crater.

I had gotten part of the way down the Ramp when I rolled the rover. And the Ramp is up against the western edge of the crater. So the sun sets really early from my point of view. I'm in the shadow of the western wall. And that royally sucks.

Mars is not Earth. It doesn't have a thick atmosphere to bend light and carry particles that reflect light around corners. It's damn near a vacuum here. Once the sun isn't visible, I'm in the dark. Phobos gives me some moonlight, but not enough to work with. Deimos is a little piece of crap that's no good to anyone.

I hate to leave the trailer sitting on its balloon for another night, but there's not much else I can do. I figure it's survived a whole day like that. It's probably stable for now.

And hey, with the rover righted, I get to use the bedroom again! It's the simple things in life that matter.

LOG ENTRY: SOL 500

When I woke up this morning, the trailer hadn't popped yet. So that was a good start.

The trailer was a bigger challenge than the rover. I only had to tip the rover. I'd need to completely flip the trailer. That requires a lot more force than yesterday's little leverage trick.

The first step was to drive the rover to near the trailer. Then came the digging.

Oh God, the digging.

The trailer was upside down, with its nose pointed downhill. I decided the best way to right it was to take advantage of the slope and roll the trailer over its nose. Basically to make it do a somersault to land on its wheels.

I can make this happen by tying off the cable to the rear of the trailer and towing with the rover. But if I tried that without digging a hole first, the trailer would just slide along the ground. I needed it to tip up. I needed a hole for the nose to fall into.

So I dug a hole. A hole one meter across, three meters wide, and one meter deep. It took me four miserable hours of hard labor, but I got it done.

I hopped in the rover and drove it downhill, dragging the trailer with me. As I'd hoped, the trailer nosed into the hole and tipped up. From there, it fell onto its wheels with a huge plume of dust.

Then I sat for a moment, dumbstruck that my plan had actually worked.

And now I'm out of daylight again. I can't wait to get out of this damn shadow. All I need is one day of driving toward the MAV and I'll be away from the wall. But for now it's another early night.

I'll spend tonight without the trailer to manage my life support. It may be righted, but I have no idea if the shit inside still works. The rover still has ample supplies for me.

I'll spend the rest of the evening enjoying a potato. And by "enjoying" I mean "hating so much I want to kill people."

LOG ENTRY: SOL 501

I started the day with some nothin' tea. Nothin' tea is easy to make. First, get some hot water, then add nothin'. I experimented with potato skin tea a few weeks ago. The less said about that the better.

I ventured into the trailer today. Not an easy task. It's pretty cramped in there; I had to leave my EVA suit in the airlock.

The first thing I noticed was that it was really hot inside. It took me a few minutes to work out why.

The atmospheric regulator was still in perfect working order, but it had nothing to do. Without being connected to the rover, it no longer had my CO_2 production to deal with. The atmosphere in the trailer was perfect—why change anything?

With no regulation necessary, the air was not being pumped out to the AREC for freeze-separation. And thus it wasn't coming back in as a liquid in need of heating.

But remember, the RTG gives off heat all the time. You can't stop it. So the heat just built up. Eventually, things reached a balance point where the heat bled through the hull as fast as the RTG could add it. If you're curious, that balance point was a sweltering 41°C.

I did a full diagnostic on the regulator and the oxygenator, and I'm happy to report both are working perfectly.

The RTG's water tank was empty, which is no surprise. It has an open top, not intended to be turned upside down. The floor of the trailer has a lot of puddled water that took me quite a while to sop up with my jumpsuit. I topped the tank off with some more water from a sealed container that I'd stored in the trailer earlier. Remember, I need that water to have something for the returning air to bubble through. That's my heating system.

But all things considered, it was good news. The critical components are working fine, and both vehicles are back on their wheels.

The hoses that connected the rover and trailer were designed well, and released without breaking. I simply snapped them back into place and the vehicles were sharing life support again.

The one remaining thing to fix was the tow hook. It was absolutely ruined. It took the full force of the crash. But as I suspected, the trailer's tow hook was unscathed. So I transferred it to the rover and reconnected the two vehicles for travel.

All told, that little fender bender cost me four sols. But now I'm back in action!

Sort of.

What if I run into another powder pit? I got lucky this time. Next time I might not get off so easy. I need a way to know if the ground in front of me is safe. At least for the duration of my time on the Ramp. Once I'm in the Schiaparelli Basin proper, I can count on the normal sandy terrain I'm used to.

If I could have anything, it would be a radio to ask NASA the safe path down the Ramp. Well, if I could have *anything*, it would be for the green-skinned yet beautiful Queen of Mars to rescue me so she can learn more about this Earth thing called "lovemaking."

It's been a long time since I've seen a woman. Just sayin'.

Anyway, to ensure I don't crash again, I'll— Seriously . . . no women in like, years. I don't ask for much. Believe me, even back on Earth a botanist/mechanical engineer doesn't exactly have ladies lined up at the door. But still, c'mon.

Anyway. I'll drive slower. Like . . . a crawl. That should give me enough time to react if one wheel starts to sink. Also, the lower speed will give me more torque, making it less likely I'll lose traction.

Up till now I've been driving 25 kph, so I'm going to cut that to 5 kph. I'm still toward the top of the Ramp, but the whole thing is only 45 kilometers. I can take my time and get safely to the bottom in about eight hours.

I'll do it tomorrow. I'm already out of daylight again today. That's another bonus: Once I clear the ramp, I can start beelining toward the MAV, which will take me away from the crater wall. I'll be back to enjoying the entire day's sunlight instead of just half of it.

If I get back to Earth, I'll be famous, right? A fearless astronaut who beat all the odds, right? I bet women like that.

More motivation to stay alive.

...

"So, it looks like he's fixed everything," Mindy explained. "And his message today was 'ALL BETTER NOW,' so I guess he's got everything working."

She surveyed the smiling faces in the meeting room.

"Awesome," Mitch said.

"Great news." Bruce's voice came in through the speakerphone.

Venkat leaned forward to the phone. "How are the MAV modification plans coming, Bruce? Is JPL going to have that procedure soon?"

"We're working around the clock on it," Bruce said. "We're past most of the big hurdles. Working out the details now."

"Good, good," Venkat said. "Any surprises I should know about?"

"Um . . . ," Bruce said. "Yeah, a few. This might not be the best venue for it. I'll be back in Houston with the procedure in a day or two. We can go through it then."

"Ominous," Venkat said. "But okay, we'll pick it up later."

"Can I spread the word?" Annie asked. "It'd be nice to see something other than the rover crash site on the news tonight."

"Definitely," Venkat said. "It'll be nice to have some good news for a change. Mindy, how long until he gets to the MAV?"

"At his usual rate of 90 kilometers per sol," Mindy said, "he should get there on Sol 504. Sol 505 if he takes his time. He always drives in the early morning, finishing around noon." She checked an application on her laptop. "Noon on Sol 504 will be 11:41 a.m. this Wednesday here in Houston. Noon on Sol 505 will be 12:21 p.m. on Thursday."

"Mitch, who's handling Ares 4 MAV communications?"

"The Ares 3 Mission Control team," Mitch replied. "It'll be in Control Room 2."

"I assume you'll be there?"

"Bet your ass I'll be there."

"So will I."

LOG ENTRY: SOL 502

Every Thanksgiving, my family used to drive from Chicago to Sandusky, an eight-hour drive. It's where Mom's sister lived. Dad always drove, and he was the slowest, most cautious driver who ever took the wheel.

Seriously. He drove like he was taking a driver's test. Never exceeded the speed limit, always had his hands at ten and two, adjusted mirrors before each outing, you name it.

It was infuriating. We'd be on the freeway, cars blowing by left and right. Some of them would blare their horns because, honestly, driving the speed limit makes you a road hazard. I wanted to get out and push.

I felt that way all damn day today. Five kph is literally a walking pace. And I drove that speed for eight hours.

But the slow speed ensured that I wouldn't fall into any more powder pits along the way. And of course I didn't encounter any. I could have driven full speed and had no problems. But better safe than sorry.

The good news is I'm off the Ramp. I camped out as soon as the terrain flattened out. I've already overdone my driving time for the day. I could go further, I still have 15 percent battery power or so, but I want to get as much daylight on my solar cells as I can.

I'm in the Schiaparelli Basin at last! Far from the crater wall, too. I get a full day of sunlight every day from now on.

I decided it was time for a very special occasion. I ate the meal pack labeled "Survived Something That Should Have Killed Me." Oh my god, I forgot how good real food tastes.

With luck, I'll get to eat "Arrival" in a few sols.

LOG ENTRY: SOL 503

I didn't get as much recharge as I usually would yesterday. Because of my extended driving time, I only got up to 70 percent before night fell. So today's driving was abbreviated.

I got 63 kilometers before I had to camp out again. But I don't even mind. Because I'm only 148 kilometers from the MAV. That means I'll get there the sol after tomorrow.

Holy hell, I'm really going to make it!

LOG ENTRY: SOL 504

Holy shit, this is awesome! Holy shit! Holy shit!

Okay calm. Calm.

I made 90 kilometers today. By my estimate, I'm 50 kilometers from the MAV. I should get there sometime tomorrow. I'm excited about that, but here's what I'm really stoked about: I caught a blip from the MAV!

NASA has the MAV broadcasting the Ares 3 Hab homing signal. Why wouldn't they? It makes perfect sense. The MAV is a sleek, perfectly functional machine, ready to do what it's told. And they have it pretending to be the Ares 3 Hab, so my rover will see the signal and tell me where it is.

That is an *exceptionally* good idea! I won't have to wander around looking for the thing. I'm going straight to it.

I only caught a blip. I'll get more as I get closer. It's strange to think that a sand dune will stop me from hearing what the MAV has to say when it can talk to Earth no problem. The MAV has three redundant methods of communicating with Earth, but they're all extremely directed and are designed for line-of-sight communication. And there aren't any sand dunes between it and Earth when they talk.

Somehow they messed with things to make a radial signal, however weak it may be. And I heard it!

My message for the day was "GOT BEACON SIGNAL." If I'd had enough rocks, I would have added, "AWESOME IDEA!!!" But it's a really sandy area.

...

THE MAV waited in southwestern Schiaparelli. It stood an impressive twenty-seven meters tall, its conical body gleaming in the midday sun.

The rover crested a nearby dune with the trailer in tow. It slowed for a few moments, then continued toward the ship at top speed. It came to a stop twenty meters away.

There it remained for ten minutes while the astronaut inside suited up.

He stumbled excitedly out of the airlock, falling to the ground then scrambling to his feet. Beholding the MAV, he gestured to it with both arms, as if in disbelief.

He leaped into the air several times, arms held high with fists clenched. Then he knelt on one knee and fist-pumped repeatedly.

Running to the spacecraft, he hugged Landing Strut B. After a few moments, he broke off the embrace to perform another round of leaping celebrations.

Now fatigued, the astronaut stood with arms akimbo, looking up at the sleek lines of the engineering marvel before him.

Climbing the ladder on the landing stage, he reached the ascent stage and entered the airlock. He sealed the door behind him.

CHAPTER 25

LOG ENTRY: SOL 505

I finally made it! I'm at the MAV!

Well, right this second, I'm back in the rover. I did go into the MAV to do a systems check and boot-up. I had to keep my EVA suit on the whole time because there's no life support in there just yet.

It's going through a self-check right now, and I'm feeding it oxygen and nitrogen with hoses from the rover. This is all part of the MAV's design. It doesn't bring air along. Why would it? That's a needless weight when you'll have a Hab full of air right next door.

I'm guessing folks at NASA are popping champagne right now and sending me lots of messages. I'll read them in a bit. First things first: Get the MAV some life support. Then I'll be able to work inside comfortably.

And then I'll have a boring conversation with NASA. Well, the content may be interesting, but the fourteen-minute transmission time between here and Earth will be a bit dull.

• • •

[13:07] HOUSTON: Congratulations from all of us here at Mission Control! Well done! What's your status?

[13:21] MAV: Thanks! No health or physical problems. The rover and trailer are getting pretty worn out, but still functional. Oxygenator and regulator both working fine. I didn't bring the water reclaimer. Just brought the water. Plenty of potatoes left. I'm good to last till 549.

[13:36] HOUSTON: Glad to hear it. Hermes is still on track for a Sol 549 flyby. As you know, the MAV will need to lose some weight to make the intercept. We're going to get you those procedures within the day. How much water do you have? What did you do with urine?

[13:50] MAV: I have 550 liters of remaining water. I've been dumping urine outside along the way.

[14:05] HOUSTON: Preserve all water. Don't do any more urine dumps. Store it somewhere. Turn the rover's radio on and leave it on. We can contact it through the MAV.

...

BRUCE TRUDGED into Venkat's office and unceremoniously plopped down in a chair. He dropped his briefcase and let his arms hang limp.

"Have a good flight?" Venkat asked.

"I only have a passing memory of what sleep is," Bruce said.

"So is it ready?" Venkat asked.

"Yes, it's ready. But you're not going to like it."

"Go on."

Bruce steeled himself and stood, picking up his briefcase. He pulled a booklet from it. "Bear in mind, this is the end result of thousands of hours of work, testing, and lateral thinking by all the best guys at JPL."

"I'm sure it was hard to trim down a ship that's already designed to be as light as possible," Venkat said.

Bruce slid the booklet across the desk to Venkat. "The problem is the intercept velocity. The MAV is designed to get to low Mars orbit, which only requires 4.1 kps. But the *Hermes* flyby will be at 5.8 kps."

Venkat flipped through the pages. "Care to summarize?"

"First, we're going to add fuel. The MAV makes its own fuel from the Martian atmosphere, but it's limited by how much hydrogen it has. It brought enough to make 19,397 kilograms of fuel, as it was designed to do. If we can give it more hydrogen, it can make more."

"How much more?"

"For every kilogram of hydrogen, it can make thirteen kilograms of fuel. Watney has five hundred and fifty liters of water. We'll have him electrolyze it to get sixty kilograms of hydrogen." Bruce reached over the desk and flipped a few pages, pointing to a diagram. "The fuel plant can make seven hundred and eighty kilograms of fuel from that."

"If he electrolyzes his water, what'll he drink?"

"He only needs fifty liters for the time he has left. And a human body only borrows water. We'll have him electrolyze his urine, too. We need all the hydrogen we can get our hands on."

"I see. And what does seven hundred and eighty kilograms of fuel buy us?" Venkat asked.

"It buys us 300 kilograms of payload. It's all about fuel versus payload. The MAV's launch weight is over 12,600 kilograms. Even with the bonus fuel, we'll need to get that down to 7,300 kilograms. So the rest of this booklet is how to remove over 5,000 kilograms from the ship."

Venkat leaned back. "Walk me through it."

Bruce pulled another copy of the booklet from his briefcase. "There were some gimmes right off the bat. The design presumes five hundred kilograms of Martian soil and rock samples. Obviously we won't do that. Also, there's just one passenger instead of six.

That saves five hundred kilograms when you consider their weight plus their suits and gear. And we can lose the other five acceleration chairs. And of course, we'll remove all nonessential gear—the med kit, tool kit, internal harnessing, straps, and anything else that isn't nailed down. And some stuff that is.

"Next up," he continued, "We're ditching all life support. The tanks, pumps, heaters, air lines, CO_2 absorption system, even the insulation on the inner side of the hull. We don't need it. We'll have Watney wear his EVA suit for the whole trip."

"Won't that make it awkward for him to use the controls?" Venkat asked.

"He won't be using them," Bruce said. "Major Martinez will pilot the MAV remotely from *Hermes*. It's already designed for remote piloting. It was remotely landed, after all."

"What if something goes wrong?" Venkat asked.

"Martinez is the best trained pilot," Bruce said. "If there is an emergency, he's the guy you want controlling the ship."

"Hmm," Venkat said cautiously. "We've never had a manned ship controlled remotely before. But okay, go on."

"Since Watney won't be flying the ship," Bruce continued, "he won't need the controls. We'll ditch the control panels and all the power and data lines that lead to them."

"Wow," Venkat said. "We're really gutting this thing."

"I'm just getting started," Bruce said. "The power needs will be dramatically reduced now that life support is gone, so we'll dump three of the five batteries and the auxiliary power system. The orbital maneuvering system has three redundant thrusters. We'll get rid of those. Also, the secondary and tertiary comm systems can go."

"Wait, what?" Venkat said, shocked. "You're going to have a remote-controlled ascent with no backup comm systems?"

"No point," Bruce said. "If the comm system goes out during ascent, the time it takes to reacquire will be too long to do any good. The backups don't help us."

"This is getting really risky, Bruce."

Bruce sighed. "I know. There's just no other way. And I'm not even to the nasty stuff yet."

Venkat rubbed his forehead. "By all means, tell me the nasty stuff."

"We'll remove the nose airlock, the windows, and Hull Panel Nineteen."

Venkat blinked. "You're taking the front of the ship off?"

"Sure," Bruce said. "The nose airlock alone is four hundred kilograms. The windows are pretty damn heavy, too. And they're connected by Hull Panel Nineteen, so may as well take that, too."

"So he's going to launch with a big hole in the front of the ship?"

"We'll have him cover it with Hab canvas."

"Hab canvas? For a launch to orbit!?"

Bruce shrugged. "The hull's mostly there to keep the air in. Mars's atmosphere is so thin you don't need a lot of streamlining. By the time the ship's going fast enough for air resistance to matter, it'll be high enough that there's practically no air. We've run all the simulations. Should be good."

"You're sending him to space under a tarp."

"Pretty much, yeah."

"Like a hastily loaded pickup truck."

"Yeah. Can I go on?"

"Sure, can't wait."

"We'll also have him remove the back panel of the pressure vessel. It's the only other panel he can remove with the tools on hand. Also, we're getting rid of the auxiliary fuel pump. Sad to see it go, but it weighs too much for its usefulness. And we're nixing a Stage One engine."

"An engine?"

"Yeah. The Stage One booster works fine if one engine goes out. It'll save us a huge amount of weight. Only during the Stage One ascent, but still. Pretty good fuel savings."

Bruce fell silent.

"That it?" Venkat asked.

"Yeah."

Venkat sighed. "You've removed most of the safety backups. What's this do to the estimated odds of failure?"

"It's about four percent."

"Jesus Christ," Venkat said. "Normally we'd never even consider something that risky."

"It's all we've got, Venk," Bruce said. "We've tested it all out and run simulations galore. We should be okay if everything works the way it's supposed to."

"Yeah. Great," Venkat said.

...

[08:41] MAV: You fucking kidding me?

[09:55] HOUSTON: Admittedly, they are very invasive modifications, but they have to be done. The procedure doc we sent has instructions for carrying out each of these steps with tools you have on hand. Also, you'll need to start electrolyzing water to get the hydrogen for the fuel plant. We'll send you procedures for that shortly.

[09:09] MAV: You're sending me into space in a convertible.

[09:24] HOUSTON: There will be Hab canvas covering the holes. It will provide enough aerodynamics in Mars's atmosphere.

[09:38] MAV: So it's a ragtop. Much better.

On the way here, in my copious free time, I designed a "workshop." I figured I'd need space to work on stuff without having to wear an EVA suit. I devised a brilliant plan whereby the current bedroom would become the new home of the regulator and the oxygenator, and the now-empty trailer would become my workshop.

It's a stupid idea, and I'm not doing it.

All I need is a pressurized area that I can work in. I somehow convinced myself that the bedroom wasn't an option because it's a hassle to get stuff into it. But it won't be that bad.

It attaches to the rover airlock, so the getting stuff in is going to be annoying. Bring the stuff into the rover, attach the bedroom to the airlock from the inside, inflate it, bring the stuff into the bedroom. I'll also have to empty the bedroom of all tools and equipment to fold it up any time I need to do an EVA.

So yeah, it'll be annoying, but all it costs me is time. And I'm actually doing well on that front. I have forty-three more sols before *Hermes* flies by. And looking at the procedure NASA has in mind for the modifications, I can take advantage of the MAV itself as a workspace.

The lunatics at NASA have me doing all kinds of rape to the MAV, but I don't have to open the hull till the end. So the first thing I'll do is clear out a bunch of clutter, like chairs and control panels and the like. Once they're out, I'll have a lot of room in there to work.

But I didn't do anything to the soon-to-be-mutilated MAV today. Today was all about system checks. Now that I'm back in contact with NASA, I have to go back to being all "safety first." Strangely, NASA doesn't have total faith in my kludged-together rover or my method of piling everything into the trailer. They had me do a full systems check on every single component.

Everything's still working fine, though it's wearing down. The regulator and the oxygenator are at less-than-peak efficiency (to say the least), and the trailer leaks some air every day. Not enough to cause problems, but it's not a perfect seal. NASA's pretty uncomfortable with it, but we don't have any other options.

Then, they had me run a full diagnostic on the MAV. That's in much better shape. Everything's sleek and pristine and perfectly functional. I'd almost forgotten what new hardware even looks like.

Pity I'm going to tear it apart.

...

"YOU KILLED Watney," Lewis said.

"Yeah," Martinez said, scowling at his monitor. The words "Collision with Terrain" blinked accusingly.

"I pulled a nasty trick on him," Johanssen said. "I gave him a malfunctioning altitude readout and made Engine Three cut out too early. It's a deadly combination."

"Shouldn't have been a mission failure," Martinez said. "I should have noticed the readout was wrong. It was way off."

"Don't sweat it," Lewis said. "That's why we drill."

"Aye, Commander," Martinez said. He furrowed his brow and frowned at the screen.

Lewis waited for him to snap out of it. When he didn't, she put a hand on his shoulder.

"Don't beat yourself up," she said. "They only gave you two days of remote launch training. It was only supposed to happen if we aborted before landing; a cut-our-losses scenario where we'd launch the MAV to act as a satellite. It wasn't mission-critical so they didn't drill you too hard on it. Now that Mark's life depends on it, you've got three weeks to get it right, and I have no doubt you can do it."

"Aye, Commander," Martinez said, softening his scowl.

"Resetting the sim," Johanssen said. "Anything specific you want to try?"

"Surprise me," Martinez said.

Lewis left the control room and made her way to the reactor. As she climbed "up" the ladder to the center of the ship, the centripetal force on her diminished to zero. Vogel looked up from a computer console. "Commander?"

"How are the engines?" she asked, grabbing a wall-mounted handle to stay attached to the slowly turning room.

"All working within tolerance," Vogel said. "I am now doing a diagnostic on the reactor. I am thinking that Johanssen is busy with the launching training. So perhaps I do this diagnostic for her."

"Good idea," Lewis said. "And how's our course?"

"All is well," Vogel said. "No adjustments necessary. We are still on track to planned trajectory within four meters."

"Keep me posted if anything changes."

"*Ja*, Commander."

Floating to the other side of the core, Lewis took the other ladder out, again gaining gravity as she went "down." She made her way to the Airlock 2 ready room.

Beck held a coil of metal wire in one hand and a pair of work gloves in the other. "Heya, Commander. What's up?"

"I'd like to know your plan for recovering Mark."

"Easy enough if the intercept is good," Beck said. "I just finished attaching all the tethers we have into one long line. It's two hundred and fourteen meters long. I'll have the MMU pack on, so moving around will be easy. I can get going up to around ten meters per second safely. Any more, and I risk breaking the tether if I can't stop in time."

"Once you get to Mark, how fast a relative velocity can you handle?"

"I can grab the MAV easily at five meters per second. Ten meters per second is kind of like jumping onto a moving train. Anything more than that and I might miss."

"So, including the MMU safe speed, we need to get the ship within twenty meters per second of his velocity."

"And the intercept has to be within two hundred and fourteen meters," Beck said. "Pretty narrow margin of error."

"We've got a lot of leeway," Lewis said. "The launch will be fifty-two minutes before the intercept, and it takes twelve minutes. As soon as Mark's S2 engine cuts out, we'll know our intercept point and velocity. If we don't like it, we'll have forty minutes to correct. Our engine's two millimeters per second may not seem like much, but in forty minutes it can move us up to 5.7 kilometers."

"Good," Beck said. "And two hundred and fourteen meters isn't a hard limit, per se."

"Yes it is," Lewis said.

"Nah," Beck said. "I know I'm not supposed to go untethered, but without my leash I could get way out there—"

"Not an option." Lewis said.

"But we could double or even triple our safe intercept range—"

"We're done talking about this," Lewis said sharply.

"Aye, Commander."

LOG ENTRY: SOL 526

There aren't many people who can say they've vandalized a three-billion-dollar spacecraft, but I'm one of them.

I've been pulling critical hardware out of the MAV left and right. It's nice to know that my launch to orbit won't have any pesky backup systems weighing me down.

First thing I did was remove the small stuff. Then came the things I could disassemble, like the crew seats, several of the backup systems, and the control panels.

I'm not improvising anything. I'm following a script sent by NASA, which was set up to make things as easy as possible. Sometimes I miss the days when I made all the decisions myself. Then I shake it off and remember I'm infinitely better off with a bunch of geniuses deciding what I do than I am making shit up as I go along.

Periodically, I suit up, crawl into the airlock with as much junk as I can fit, and dump it outside. The area around the MAV looks like the set of *Sanford and Son*.

I learned about *Sanford and Son* from Lewis's collection. Seriously, that woman needs to see someone about her seventies problem.

LOG ENTRY: SOL 529

I'm turning water into rocket fuel.

It's easier than you'd think.

Separating hydrogen and oxygen only requires a couple of electrodes and some current. The problem is collecting the hydrogen. I don't have any equipment for pulling hydrogen out of the air. The atmospheric regulator doesn't even know how. The last time I had to get hydrogen out of the air (back when I turned the Hab into a bomb) I burned it to turn it into water. Obviously that would be counterproductive.

But NASA thought everything through and gave me a process. First, I disconnected the rover and trailer from each other. Then, while wearing my EVA suit, I depressurized the trailer and back-filled it with pure oxygen at one-fourth of an atmosphere. Then I opened a plastic box full of water and put a couple of electrodes in. That's why I needed the atmosphere. Without it, the water would just boil immediately and I'd be hanging around in a steamy atmosphere.

The electrolysis separated the hydrogen and oxygen from each other. Now the trailer was full of even more oxygen and also hydrogen. Pretty dangerous, actually.

Then I fired up the atmospheric regulator. I know I just said it doesn't recognize hydrogen, but it *does* know how to yank oxygen out of the air. I broke all the safeties and set it to pull 100 percent of the oxygen out. After it was done, all that was left in the trailer was hydrogen. That's why I started out with an atmosphere of pure oxygen, so the regulator could separate it later.

Then I cycled the rover's airlock with the inner door open. The airlock thought it was evacuating itself, but it was actually evacuating the whole trailer. The air was stored in the airlock's holding tank. And there you have it, a tank of pure hydrogen.

I carried the airlock's holding tank to the MAV and transferred the contents to the MAV's hydrogen tanks. I've said this many times before, but: Hurray for standardized valve systems!

Finally, I fired up the fuel plant, and it got to work making the additional fuel I'd need.

I'll need to go through this process several more times as the launch date approaches. I'm even going to electrolyze my urine. That'll make for a pleasant smell in the trailer.

If I survive this, I'll tell people I was pissing rocket fuel.

· · ·

[19:22] JOHANSSEN: Hello, Mark.

[19:23] MAV: Johanssen!? Holy crap! They finally letting you talk to me directly?

[19:24] JOHANSSEN: Yes, NASA gave the OK for direct communication an hour ago. We're only 35 light-seconds apart, so we can talk in near-real time. I just set up the system and I'm testing it out.

[19:24] MAV: What took them so long to let us talk?

[19:25] JOHANSSEN: The psych team was worried about personality conflicts.

[19:25] MAV: What? Just 'cause you guys abandoned me on a godforsaken planet with no chance of survival?

[19:26] JOHANSSEN: Funny. Don't make that kind of joke with Lewis.

[19:27] MAV: Roger. So uh . . . thanks for coming back to get me.

[19:27] JOHANSSEN: It's the least we could do. How is the MAV retrofit going?

[19:28] MAV: So far, so good. NASA put a lot of thought into the procedures. They work. That's not to say they're easy. I spent the last 3 days removing Hull Panel 19 and the front window. Even in Mars-g they're heavy motherfuckers.

[19:29] JOHANSSEN: When we pick you up, I will make wild, passionate love to you. Prepare your body.

[19:29] JOHANSSEN: I didn't type that! That was Martinez! I stepped away from the console for like 10 seconds!

[19:29] MAV: I've really missed you guys.

LOG ENTRY: SOL 543

I'm . . . done?

I think I'm done.

I did everything on the list. The MAV is ready to fly. And in six sols, that's just what it'll do. I hope.

It might not launch at all. I did remove an engine, after all. I could have fucked up all sorts of things during that process. And there's no way to test the ascent stage. Once you light it, it's lit.

Everything else, however, will go through tests from now until launch. Some done by me, some done remotely by NASA. They're not telling me the failure odds, but I'm guessing they're the highest in history. Yuri Gagarin had a much more reliable and safe ship than I do.

And Soviet ships were death traps.

. . .

"ALL RIGHT," Lewis said, "tomorrow's the big day."

The crew floated in the Rec. They had halted the rotation of the ship in preparation for the upcoming operation.

"I'm ready," Martinez said. "Johanssen threw everything she could at me. I got all scenarios to orbit."

"Everything other than catastrophic failures," Johanssen corrected.

"Well yeah," Martinez said. "Kind of pointless to simulate an ascent explosion. Nothing we can do."

"Vogel," Lewis said. "How's our course?"

"It is perfect," Vogel said. "We are within one meter of projected path and two centimeters per second of projected velocity."

"Good," she said. "Beck, how about you?"

"Everything's all set up, Commander," Beck said. "The tethers are linked and spooled in Airlock 2. My suit and MMU are prepped and ready."

"Okay, the battle plan is pretty obvious," Lewis said. She grabbed a handhold on the wall to halt a slow drift she had acquired. "Martinez will fly the MAV, Johanssen will sysop the ascent. Beck and Vogel, I want you in Airlock 2 with the outer door open before the MAV even launches. You'll have to wait fifty-two minutes, but I don't want to risk any technical glitches with the airlock or your suits. Once we reach intercept, it'll be Beck's job to get Watney."

"He might be in bad shape when I get him," Beck said. "The stripped-down MAV will get up to twelve g's during the launch. He could be unconscious and may even have internal bleeding."

"Just as well you're our doctor," Lewis said. "Vogel, if all goes according to plan, you're pulling Beck and Watney back aboard with the tether. If things go wrong, you're Beck's backup."

"Ja," Vogel said.

"I wish there was more we could do right now," Lewis said. "But all we have left is the wait. Your work schedules are cleared. All scientific experiments are suspended. Sleep if you can, run diagnostics on your equipment if you can't."

"We'll get him, Commander," Martinez said as the others floated out. "Twenty-four hours from now, Mark Watney will be right here in this room."

"Let's hope so, Major," Lewis said.

...

"FINAL CHECKS for this shift are complete," Mitch said into his headset. "Timekeeper."

"Go, Flight," said the timekeeper.

"Time until MAV launch?"

"Sixteen hours, nine minutes, forty seconds . . . mark."

"Copy that. All stations: Flight director shift change." He took his headset off and rubbed his eyes.

Brendan Hutch took the headset from him and put it on. "All stations, Flight director is now Brendan Hutch."

"Call me if anything happens," Mitch said. "If not, I'll see you tomorrow."

"Get some sleep, Boss," Brendan said.

Venkat watched from the observation booth. "Why ask the time-keeper?" he mumbled. "It's on the huge mission clock in the center screen."

"He's nervous," Annie said. "You don't often see it, but that's what Mitch Henderson looks like when he's nervous. He double- and triple-checks everything."

"Fair enough," Venkat said.

"They're camping out on the lawn, by the way," Annie said. "Reporters from all over the world. Our press rooms just don't have enough space."

"The media loves a drama." He sighed. "It'll be over tomorrow, one way or another."

"What's our role in all this?" Annie said. "If something goes wrong, what can Mission Control do?"

"Nothing," Venkat said. "Not a damned thing."

"Nothing?"

"It's all happening twelve light-minutes away. That means it takes twenty-four minutes for them to get the answer to any question they ask. The whole launch is twelve minutes long. They're on their own."

"So we're completely helpless?"

"Yes," Venkat said. "Sucks, doesn't it?"

LOG ENTRY: SOL 549

I'd be lying if I said I wasn't shitting myself. In four hours, I'm going to ride a giant explosion into orbit. This is something I've done a few times before, but never with a jury-rigged mess like this.

Right now, I'm sitting in the MAV. I'm suited up because there's a big hole in the front of the ship where the window and part of the hull used to be. I'm "awaiting launch instructions." Really, I'm just awaiting launch. I don't have any part in this. I'm just going to sit in the acceleration couch and hope for the best.

Last night, I ate my final meal pack. It's the first good meal I've had in weeks. I'm leaving forty-one potatoes behind. That's how close I came to starvation.

I carefully collected samples during my journey. But I can't bring any of them with me. So I put them in a container a few hundred meters from here. Maybe someday they'll send a probe to collect them. May as well make them easy to pick up.

This is it. There's nothing after this. There isn't even an abort procedure. Why make one? We can't delay the launch. *Hermes* can't stop and wait. No matter what, we're launching on schedule.

I face the very real possibility that I'll die today. Can't say I like it.

It wouldn't be so bad if the MAV blew up. I wouldn't know what hit me, but if I miss the intercept, I'll just float around in space until

I run out of air. I have a contingency plan for that. I'll drop the oxygen mixture to zero and breathe pure nitrogen until I suffocate. It wouldn't feel bad. The lungs don't have the ability to sense lack of oxygen. I'd just get tired, fall asleep, then die.

I still can't quite believe that this is really it. I'm really leaving. This frigid desert has been my home for a year and a half. I figured out how to survive, at least for a while, and I got used to how things worked. My terrifying struggle to stay alive became somehow routine. Get up in the morning, eat breakfast, tend my crops, fix broken stuff, eat lunch, answer e-mail, watch TV, eat dinner, go to bed. The life of a modern farmer.

Then I was a trucker, doing a long haul across the world. And finally, a construction worker, rebuilding a ship in ways no one ever considered before this. I've done a little of everything here, because I'm the only one around to do it.

That's all over now. I have no more jobs to do, and no more nature to defeat. I've had my last Martian potato. I've slept in the rover for the last time. I've left my last footprints in the dusty red sand. I'm leaving Mars today, one way or another.

About fucking time.

CHAPTER 26

THEY GATHERED.

Everywhere on Earth, they gathered.

In Trafalgar Square and Tiananmen Square and Times Square, they watched on giant screens. In offices, they huddled around computer monitors. In bars, they stared silently at the TV in the corner. In homes, they sat breathlessly on their couches, their eyes glued to the story playing out.

In Chicago, a middle-aged couple clutched each other's hands as they watched. The man held his wife gently as she rocked back and forth out of sheer terror. The NASA representative knew not to disturb them, but stood ready to answer any questions, should they ask.

"Fuel pressure green," Johanssen's voice said from a billion televisions. "Engine alignment perfect. Communications five by five. We are ready for preflight checklist, Commander."

"Copy." Lewis's voice. "CAPCOM."

"Go," Johanssen responded.

"Guidance."

"Go," Johanssen said again.

"Remote Command."

"Go," said Martinez.

"Pilot."

"Go," said Watney from the MAV.

A mild cheer coruscated through the crowds worldwide.

...

MITCH SAT at his station in Mission Control. The controllers monitored everything and were ready to help in any way they could, but the communication latency between *Hermes* and Earth rendered them powerless to do anything but watch.

"Telemetry," Lewis's voice said over the speakers.

"Go," Johanssen responded.

"Recovery," she continued.

"Go," said Beck from the airlock.

"Secondary Recovery."

"Go," said Vogel from beside Beck.

"Mission Control, this is *Hermes* Actual," Lewis reported. "We are go for launch and will proceed on schedule. We are T minus four minutes, ten seconds to launch . . . mark."

"Did you get that, Timekeeper?" Mitch said.

"Affirmative, Flight" was the response. "Our clocks are synched with theirs."

"Not that we can do anything," Mitch mumbled, "but at least we'll know what's supposedly happening."

...

"ABOUT FOUR minutes, Mark," Lewis said into her mic. "How you doing down there?"

"Eager to get up there, Commander," Watney responded.

"We're going to make that happen," Lewis said. "Remember,

you'll be pulling some pretty heavy g's. It's okay to pass out. You're in Martinez's hands."

"Tell that asshole no barrel rolls."

"Copy that, MAV," Lewis said.

"Four more minutes," Martinez said, cracking his knuckles. "You ready for some flying, Beth?"

"Yeah," Johanssen said. "It'll be strange to sysop a launch and stay in zero-g the whole time."

"I hadn't thought of it that way," Martinez said, "but yeah. I'm not going to be squashed against the back of my seat. Weird."

· · ·

BECK FLOATED in the airlock, tethered to a wall-mounted spool. Vogel stood beside him, his boots clamped to the floor. Both stared through the open outer door at the red planet below.

"Didn't think I'd be back here again," Beck said.

"Yes," Vogel said. "We are the first."

"First what?"

"We are the first to visit Mars twice."

"Oh yeah. Even Watney can't say that."

"He cannot."

They looked at Mars in silence for a while.

"Vogel," Beck said.

"Ja."

"If I can't reach Mark, I want you to release my tether."

"Dr. Beck," Vogel said, "the commander has said no to this."

"I know what the commander said, but if I need a few more meters, I want you to cut me loose. I have an MMU, I can get back without a tether."

"I will not do this, Dr. Beck."

"It's my own life at risk, and I say it's okay."

"You are not the commander."

Beck scowled at Vogel, but with their reflective visors down, the effect was lost.

"Fine," Beck said. "But I bet you'll change your mind if push comes to shove."

Vogel did not respond.

■ ■ ■

"T-minus ten," said Johanssen, "nine . . . eight . . ."

"Main engines start," said Martinez.

". . . seven . . . six . . . five . . . Mooring clamps released . . ."

"About five seconds, Watney," Lewis said to her headset. "Hang on."

"See you in a few, Commander," Watney radioed back.

". . . four . . . three . . . two . . ."

■ ■ ■

WATNEY LAY in the acceleration couch as the MAV rumbled in anticipation of liftoff.

"Hmm," he said to nobody. "I wonder how much longer—"

The MAV launched with incredible force. More than any manned ship had accelerated in the history of space travel. Watney was shoved back into his couch so hard he couldn't even grunt.

Having anticipated this, he had placed a folded up shirt behind his head in the helmet. As his head drove ever deeper into the makeshift cushion, the edges of his vision became blurry. He could neither breathe nor move.

Directly in his field of view, the Hab canvas patch flapped violently as the ship exponentially gained speed. Concentration became difficult, but something in the back of his mind told him that flapping was bad.

...

"VELOCITY SEVEN hundred and forty-one meters per second," Johanssen called out. "Altitude thirteen hundred and fifty meters."

"Copy," Martinez said.

"That's low," Lewis said. "Too low."

"I know," Martinez said. "It's sluggish; fighting me. What the fuck is going on?"

"Velocity eight hundred and fifty, altitude eighteen hundred and forty-three," Johanssen said.

"I'm not getting the power I need!" Martinez said.

"Engine power at a hundred percent," Johanssen said.

"I'm telling you it's sluggish," Martinez insisted.

"Watney," Lewis said to her headset. "Watney, do you read? Can you report?"

...

WATNEY HEARD Lewis's voice in the distance. Like someone talking to him through a long tunnel. He vaguely wondered what she wanted. His attention was briefly drawn to the fluttering canvas ahead of him. A rip had appeared and was rapidly widening.

But then he was distracted by a bolt in one of the bulkheads. It only had five sides. He wondered why NASA decided that bolt needed five sides instead of six. It would require a special wrench to tighten or loosen.

The canvas tore even further, the tattered material flapping wildly. Through the opening, Watney saw red sky stretching out infinitely ahead. "That's nice," he thought.

As the MAV flew higher, the atmosphere grew thinner. Soon, the canvas stopped fluttering and simply stretched toward Mark. The sky shifted from red to black.

"That's nice, too," Mark thought.

As consciousness slipped away, he wondered where he could get a cool five-sided bolt like that.

...

"I'M GETTING more response now," Martinez said.

"Back on track with full acceleration," Johanssen said. "Must have been drag. MAV's out of the atmosphere now."

"It was like flying a cow," Martinez grumbled, his hands racing over his controls.

"Can you get him up?" Lewis asked.

"He'll get to orbit," Johanssen said, "but the intercept course may be compromised."

"Get him up first," Lewis said. "Then we'll worry about intercept."

"Copy. Main engine cutoff in fifteen seconds."

"Totally smooth now," Martinez said. "It's not fighting me at all anymore."

"Well below target altitude," Johanssen said. "Velocity is good."

"How far below?" Lewis said.

"Can't say for sure," Johanssen said. "All I have is accelerometer data. We'll need radar pings at intervals to work out his true final orbit."

"Back to automatic guidance," Martinez said.

"Main shutdown in four," Johanssen said, ". . . three . . . two . . . one . . . Shutdown."

"Confirm shutdown," Martinez said.

"Watney, you there?" Lewis said. "Watney? Watney, do you read?"

"Probably passed out, Commander," Beck said over the radio. "He pulled twelve g's on the ascent. Give him a few minutes."

"Copy," Lewis said. "Johanssen, got his orbit yet?"

"I have interval pings. Working out our intercept range and velocity . . ."

Martinez and Lewis stared at Johanssen as she brought up the intercept calculation software. Normally, orbits would be worked out by Vogel, but he was otherwise engaged. Johanssen was his backup for orbital dynamics.

"Intercept velocity will be eleven meters per second . . . ," she began.

"I can make that work," Beck said over the radio.

"Distance at intercept will be—" Johanssen stopped and choked. Shakily, she continued. "We'll be sixty-eight kilometers apart." She buried her face in her hands.

"Did she say sixty-eight *kilometers*!?" Beck said. *"Kilometers!?"*

"God damn it," Martinez whispered.

"Keep it together," Lewis said. "Work the problem. Martinez, is there any juice in the MAV?"

"Negative, Commander," Martinez responded. "They ditched the OMS system to lighten the launch weight."

"Then we'll have to go to him. Johanssen, time to intercept?"

"Thirty-nine minutes, twelve seconds," Johanssen said, trying not to quaver.

"Vogel," Lewis continued, "how far can we deflect in thirty-nine minutes with the ion engines?"

"Perhaps five kilometers," he radioed.

"Not enough," Lewis said. "Martinez, what if we point our attitude thrusters all the same direction?"

"Depends on how much fuel we want to save for attitude adjustments on the trip home."

"How much do you need?"

"I could get by with maybe twenty percent of what's left."

"All right, if you used the other eighty percent—"

"Checking," Martinez said, running the numbers on his console. "We'd get a delta-v of thirty-one meters per second."

"Johanssen," Lewis said. "Math."

"In thirty-nine minutes we'd deflect . . . ," Johanssen quickly typed, "seventy-two kilometers!"

"There we go," Lewis said. "How much fuel—"

"Use seventy-five point five percent of remaining attitude adjust fuel," Johanssen said. "That'll bring the intercept range to zero."

"Do it," Lewis said.

"Aye, Commander," Martinez said.

"Hold on," Johanssen said. "That'll get the intercept *range* to zero, but the intercept *velocity* will be forty-two meters per second."

"Then we have thirty-nine minutes to figure out how to slow down," Lewis said. "Martinez, burn the jets."

"Aye," Martinez said.

...

"WHOA," Annie said to Venkat. "A lot of shit just happened really fast. Explain."

Venkat strained to hear the audio feed over the murmur of the VIPs in the observation booth. Through the glass, he saw Mitch throw his hands up in frustration.

"The launch missed badly," Venkat said, looking past Mitch to the screens beyond. "The intercept distance was going to be way too big. So they're using the attitude adjusters to close the gap."

"What do attitude adjusters usually do?"

"They rotate the ship. They're not made for thrusting it. *Hermes* doesn't have quick-reaction engines. Just the slow, steady ion engines."

"So . . . problem solved?" Annie said hopefully.

"No," Venkat said. "They'll get to him, but they'll be going forty-two meters per second when they get there."

"How fast is that?" Annie asked.

"About ninety miles per hour," Venkat said. "There's no hope of Beck grabbing Watney at that speed."

"Can they use the attitude adjusters to slow down?"

"They needed a lot of velocity to close the gap in time. They used all the fuel they could spare to get going fast enough. But now they don't have enough fuel to slow down." Venkat frowned.

"So what can they do?"

"I don't know," he said. "And even if I did, I couldn't tell them in time."

"Well fuck," Annie said.

"Yeah," Venkat agreed.

. . .

"Watney," Lewis said "Do you read? . . . Watney?" she repeated.

"Commander," Beck radioed. "He's wearing a surface EVA suit, right?"

"Yeah."

"It should have a bio-monitor," Beck said. "And it'll be broadcasting. It's not a strong signal; it's only designed to go a couple hundred meters to the rover or Hab. But maybe we can pick it up."

"Johanssen," Lewis said.

"On it," Johanssen said. "I have to look up the frequencies in the tech specs. Gimme a second."

"Martinez," Lewis continued. "Any idea how to slow down?"

He shook his head. "I got nothin', Commander. We're just going too damn fast."

"Vogel?"

"The ion drive is simply not strong enough," Vogel replied.

"There's got to be something," Lewis said. "Something we can do. Anything."

"Got his bio-monitor data," Johanssen said. "Pulse fifty-eight, blood pressure ninety-eight over sixty-one."

"That's not bad," Beck said. "Lower than I'd like, but he's been in Mars gravity for eighteen months, so it's expected."

"Time to intercept?" Lewis asked.

"Thirty-two minutes," Johanssen replied.

...

BLISSFUL unconsciousness became foggy awareness which transitioned into painful reality. Watney opened his eyes, then winced at the pain in his chest.

Little remained of the canvas. Tatters floated along the edge of the hole it once covered. This granted Watney an unobstructed view of Mars from orbit. The red planet's crater-pocked surface stretched out seemingly forever, its thin atmosphere a slight blur along the edge. Only eighteen people in history had personally seen this view.

"Fuck you," he said to the planet below.

Reaching toward the controls on his arm, he winced. Trying again, more slowly this time, he activated his radio. "MAV to *Hermes*."

"Watney!?" came the reply.

"Affirmative. That you, Commander?" Watney said.

"Affirmative. What's your status?"

"I'm on a ship with no control panel," he said. "That's as much as I can tell you."

"How do you feel?"

"My chest hurts. I think I broke a rib. How are you?"

"We're working on getting you," Lewis said. "There was a complication in the launch."

"Yeah," Watney said, looking out the hole in the ship. "The canvas didn't hold. I think it ripped early in the ascent."

"That's consistent with what we saw during the launch."

"How bad is it, Commander?" he asked.

"We were able to correct the intercept range with *Hermes*'s attitude thrusters. But there's a problem with the intercept velocity."

"How big a problem."

"Forty-two meters per second."

"Well shit."

...

"HEY, AT least he's okay for the moment," Martinez said.

"Beck," Lewis said, "I'm coming around to your way of thinking. How fast can you get going if you're untethered?"

"Sorry, Commander," Beck said. "I already ran the numbers. At best I could get twenty-five meters per second. Even if I could get to forty-two, I'd need *another* forty-two to match *Hermes* when I came back."

"Copy," Lewis said.

"Hey," Watney said over the radio, "I've got an idea."

"Of course you do," Lewis said. "What do you got?"

"I could find something sharp in here and poke a hole in the glove of my EVA suit. I could use the escaping air as a thruster and fly my way to you. The source of thrust would be on my arm, so I'd be able to direct it pretty easily."

"How does he come up with this shit?" Martinez interjected.

"Hmm," Lewis said. "Could you get forty-two meters per second that way?"

"No idea," Watney said.

"I can't see you having any control if you did that," Lewis said. "You'd be eyeballing the intercept and using a thrust vector you can barely control."

"I admit it's fatally dangerous," Watney said. "But consider this: I'd get to fly around like Iron Man."

"We'll keep working on ideas," Lewis said.

"Iron Man, Commander. *Iron Man.*"

"Stand by," Lewis said.

She furrowed her brow. "Hmm . . . Maybe it's not such a bad idea. . . ."

"You kidding, Commander?" Martinez said. "It's a terrible idea. He'd shoot off into space—"

"Not the whole idea, but part of it," she said. "Using atmosphere as thrust. Martinez, get Vogel's station up and running."

"Okay," Martinez said, typing at his keyboard. The screen changed to Vogel's workstation. Martinez quickly changed the language from German to English. "It's up. What do you need?"

"Vogel's got software for calculating course offsets caused by hull breaches, right?"

"Yeah," Martinez said. "It estimates course corrections needed in the event of—"

"Yeah, yeah," Lewis said. "Fire it up. I want to know what happens if we blow the VAL."

Johanssen and Martinez looked at each other.

"Um. Yes, Commander," Martinez said.

"The vehicular airlock?" Johanssen said. "You want to . . . open it?"

"Plenty of air in the ship," Lewis said. "It'd give us a good kick."

"Ye-es . . . ," Martinez said as he brought up the software. "And it might blow the nose of the ship off in the process."

"Also, all the air would leave," Johanssen felt compelled to add.

"We'll seal the bridge and reactor room. We can let everywhere else go vacuo, but we don't want explosive decompression in here or near the reactor."

Martinez entered the scenario into the software. "I think we'll just have the same problem as Watney, but on a larger scale. We can't direct that thrust."

"We don't have to," Lewis said. "The VAL is in the nose. Escaping air would make a thrust vector through our center of mass. We just need to point the ship directly away from where we want to go."

"Okay, I have the numbers," Martinez said. "A breach at the VAL, with the bridge and reactor room sealed off, would accelerate us twenty-nine meters per second."

"We'd have a relative velocity of thirteen meters per second afterward," Johanssen supplied.

"Beck," Lewis radioed. "Have you been hearing all this?"

"Affirmative, Commander," Beck said.

"Can you do thirteen meters per second?"

"It'll be risky," Beck replied. "Thirteen to match the MAV, then another thirteen to match *Hermes*. But it's a hell of a lot better than forty-two."

"Johanssen," Lewis said. "Time to intercept?"

"Eighteen minutes, Commander."

"What kind of jolt will we feel with that breach?" Lewis asked Martinez.

"The air will take four seconds to evacuate," he said. "We'll feel a little less than one g."

"Watney," she said to her headset, "we have a plan."

"Yay! A plan!" Watney replied.

...

"Houston," Lewis's voice rang through Mission Control. "Be advised we are going to deliberately breach the VAL to produce thrust."

"What?" Mitch said. "What!?"

"Oh . . . my god," Venkat said in the observation room.

"Fuck me raw," Annie said, getting up. "I better get to the press room. Any parting knowledge before I go?"

"They're going to breach the ship," Venkat said, still dumbfounded. "They're going to *deliberately* breach the ship. Oh my god . . ."

"Got it," Annie said, jogging to the door.

● ● ●

"How will we open the airlock doors?" Martinez asked. "There's no way to open them remotely, and if anyone's nearby when it blows—"

"Right," Lewis said. "We can open one door with the other shut, but how do we open the other?"

She thought for a moment. "Vogel," she radioed. "I need you to come back in and make a bomb."

"Um. Again, please, Commander?" Vogel replied.

"A bomb," Lewis confirmed. "You're a chemist. Can you make a bomb out of stuff on board?"

"*Ja*," Vogel said. "We have flammables and pure oxygen."

"Sounds good," Lewis said.

"It is of course dangerous to set off an explosive device on a spacecraft," Vogel pointed out.

"So make it small," Lewis said. "It just needs to poke a hole in the inner airlock door. Any hole will do. If it blows the door off, that's fine. If it doesn't, the air will get out slower, but for longer. The momentum change is the same, and we'll get the acceleration we need."

"Pressurizing Airlock 2," Vogel reported. "How will we activate this bomb?"

"Johanssen?" Lewis said.

"Uh . . . ," Johanssen said. She picked up her headset and quickly put it on. "Vogel, can you run wires into it?"

"*Ja*," Vogel said. "I will use threaded stopper with a small hole for the wires. It will have little effect on the seal."

"We could run the wire to Lighting Panel 41," Johanssen said. "It's next to the airlock, and I can turn it on and off from here."

"There's our remote trigger," Lewis said. "Johanssen, go set up the lighting panel. Vogel, get in here and make the bomb. Martinez, go close and seal the doors to the reactor room."

"Yes, Commander," Johanssen said, kicking off her seat toward the hallway.

"Commander," Martinez said, pausing at the exit, "you want me to bring back some space suits?"

"No point," Lewis said. "If the seal on the bridge doesn't hold, we'll get sucked out at close to the speed of sound. We'll be jelly with or without suits on."

"Hey, Martinez," said Beck over the radio. "Can you move my lab mice somewhere safe? They're in the bio lab. It's just one cage."

"Copy, Beck," said Martinez. "I'll move them to the reactor room."

"Are you back in yet, Vogel?" Lewis asked.

"I am just reentering now, Commander."

"Beck," Lewis said to her headset. "I'll need you back in, too. But don't take your suit off."

"Okay," Beck said. "Why?"

"We're going to have to literally blow up one of the doors," Lewis explained. "I'd rather we kill the inner one. I want the outer door unharmed, so we keep our smooth aerobraking shape."

"Makes sense," Beck responded as he floated back into the ship.

"One problem," Lewis said. "I want the outer door locked in the fully open position with the mechanical stopper in place to keep it from being trashed by the decompress."

"You have to have someone in the airlock to do that," Beck said. "And you can't open the inner door if the outer door is locked open."

"Right," Lewis said. "So I need you to come back inside, depressurize the VAL, and lock the outer door open. Then you'll need to crawl along the hull to get back to Airlock 2."

"Copy, Commander," Beck said. "There are latch points all over the hull. I'll move my tether along, mountain climber style."

"Get to it," Lewis said. "And Vogel, you're in a hurry. You have to make the bomb, set it up, get back to Airlock 2, suit up, depressurize it, and open the outer door, so Beck can get back in when he's done."

"He's taking his suit off right now and can't reply," Beck reported, "but he heard the order."

"Watney, how you doing?" Lewis's voice said in his ear.

"Fine so far, Commander," Watney replied. "You mentioned a plan?"

"Affirmative," she said. "We're going to vent atmosphere to get thrust."

"How?"

"We're going to blow a hole in the VAL."

"What!?" Watney said. "How!?"

"Vogel's making a bomb."

"I *knew* that guy was a mad scientist!" Watney said. "I think we should just go with my Iron Man idea."

"That's too risky, and you know it," she replied.

"Thing is," Watney said, "I'm selfish. I want the memorials back home to be just for me. I don't want the rest of you losers in them. I can't let you guys blow the VAL."

"Oh," Lewis said, "well if you won't let us then— Wait . . . wait a minute . . . . . I'm looking at my shoulder patch and it turns out I'm the commander. Sit tight. We're coming to get you."

"Smart-ass."

...

As a chemist, Vogel knew how to make a bomb. In fact, much of his training was to avoid making them by mistake.

The ship had few flammables aboard, due to the fatal danger of fire. But food, by its very nature, contained flammable hydrocarbons. Lacking time to sit down and do the math, he estimated.

Sugar has 4000 food-calories per kilogram. One food-calorie is 4184 Joules. Sugar in zero-g will float and the grains will separate, maximizing surface area. In a pure-oxygen environment, 16.7 million joules will be released for every kilogram of sugar used, releasing the explosive force of eight sticks of dynamite. Such is the nature of combustion in pure oxygen.

Vogel measured the sugar carefully. He poured it into the strongest container he could find, a thick glass beaker. The strength of the container was as important as the explosive. A weak container would simply cause a fireball without much concussive force. A strong container, however, would contain the pressure until it reached true destructive potential.

He quickly drilled a hole in the beaker's stopper, then stripped a section of wire. He ran the wire through the hole.

"*Sehr gefährlich,*" he mumbled as he poured liquid oxygen from the ship's supply into the container, then quickly screwed the stopper on. In just a few minutes, he had made a rudimentary pipe bomb.

"*Sehr, sehr, gefährlich.*"

He floated out of the lab and made his way toward the nose of the ship.

...

Johanssen worked on the lighting panel as Beck floated toward the VAL.

She grabbed his arm. "Be careful crawling along the hull."

He turned to face her. "Be careful setting up the bomb."

She kissed his faceplate then looked away, embarrassed. "That was stupid. Don't tell anyone I did that."

"Don't tell anyone I liked it." Beck smiled.

He entered the airlock and sealed the inner door. After depressurizing, he opened the outer door and locked it in place. Grabbing a handrail on the hull, he pulled himself out.

Johanssen watched until he was no longer in view, then returned to the lighting panel. She had deactivated it earlier from her workstation. After pulling a length of the cable out and stripping the ends, she fiddled with a roll of electrical tape until Vogel arrived.

He showed up just a minute later, carefully floating down the hall with the bomb held in both hands.

"I have used a single wire for igniting," he explained. "I did not want to risk two wires for a spark. It would be dangerous to us if we had static while setting up."

"How do we set it off?" Johanssen said.

"The wire must reach a high temperature. If you short power through it, that will be sufficient."

"I'll have to pin the breaker," Johanssen said, "but it'll work."

She twisted the lighting wires onto the bomb's and taped them off.

"Excuse me," Vogel said. "I have to return to Airlock 2 to let Dr. Beck back in."

"Mm," Johanssen said.

...

MARTINEZ FLOATED back into the bridge. "I had a few minutes, so I ran through the aerobrake lockdown checklist for the reactor room. Everything's ready for acceleration and the compartment's sealed off."

"Good thinking," Lewis said. "Prep the attitude correction."

"Roger, Commander," Martinez said, drifting to his station.

"The VAL's propped open," Beck's voice said over the comm. "Starting my traverse across the hull."

"Copy," Lewis said.

"This calculation is tricky," Martinez said. "I need to do everything backward. The VAL's in front, so the source of thrust will be exactly opposite to our engines. Our software wasn't expecting us to have an engine there. I just need to tell it we plan to thrust *toward* Mark."

"Take your time and get it right," Lewis said. "And don't execute till I give you the word. We're not spinning the ship around while Beck's out on the hull."

"Roger," he said. After a moment, he added "Okay, the adjustment's ready to execute."

"Stand by," Lewis said.

●●●

VOGEL, BACK in his suit, depressurized Airlock 2 and opened the outer door.

"'Bout time," Beck said, climbing in.

"Sorry for the delay," Vogel said. "I was required to make a bomb."

"This has been kind of a weird day," Beck said. "Commander, Vogel and I are in position."

"Copy" was Lewis's response. "Get up against the fore wall of the airlock. It's going to be about one g for four seconds. Make sure you're both tethered in."

"Copy," Beck said as he attached his tether. The two men pressed themselves against the wall.

"OKAY, MARTINEZ," Lewis said, "point us the right direction."

"Copy," said Martinez, executing the attitude adjustment.

Johanssen floated into the bridge as the adjustment was performed. The room rotated around her as she reached for a handhold. "The bomb's ready, and the breaker's jammed closed," she said. "I can set it off by remotely turning on Lighting Panel 41."

"Seal the bridge and get to your station," Lewis said.

"Copy," Johanssen said. Unstowing the emergency seal, she plugged the entrance to the bridge. With a few turns of the crank, the job was done. She returned to her station and ran a quick test. "Increasing bridge pressure to 1.03 atmospheres. . . . Pressure is steady. We have a good seal."

"Copy," Lewis said. "Time to intercept?"

"Twenty-eight seconds," Johanssen said.

"Wow," Martinez said. "We cut that pretty close."

"You ready, Johanssen?" Lewis asked.

"Yes," Johanssen said. "All I have to do is hit enter."

"Martinez, how's our angle?"

"Dead-on, Commander," Martinez reported.

"Strap in," Lewis said.

The three of them tightened the restraints of their chairs.

"Twenty seconds," Johanssen said.

...

TEDDY TOOK his seat in the VIP room. "What's the status?"

"Fifteen seconds till they blow the VAL," Venkat said. "Where have you been?"

"On the phone with the President," Teddy said. "Do you think this will work?"

"I have no idea," Venkat said. "I've never felt this helpless in my life."

"If it's any consolation," Teddy said, "pretty much everyone in the world feels the same way."

On the other side of the glass, Mitch paced to and fro.

...

". . . FIVE . . . four . . . three . . . ," Johanssen said.

"Brace for acceleration," Lewis said.

". . . two . . . one . . . ," Johanssen continued. "Activating Lighting Panel 41."

She pressed enter.

Inside Vogel's bomb, the full current of the ship's internal lighting system flowed through a thin, exposed wire. It quickly reached the ignition temperature of the sugar. What would have been a minor fizzle in Earth's atmosphere became an uncontrolled conflagration in the container's pure oxygen environment. In under one hundred milliseconds, the massive combustion pressure burst the container, and the resulting explosion ripped the airlock door to shreds.

The internal air of *Hermes* rushed through the open VAL, blasting *Hermes* in the other direction.

Vogel and Beck were pressed against the wall of Airlock 2. Lewis, Martinez, and Johanssen endured the acceleration in their seats. It was not a dangerous amount of force. In fact it was less than the force of Earth's surface gravity. But it was inconsistent and jerky.

After four seconds, the shaking died down and the ship returned to weightlessness.

"Reactor room still pressurized," Martinez reported.

"Bridge seal holding," Johanssen said. "Obviously."

"Damage?" Martinez said.

"Not sure yet," Johanssen said. "I have External Camera 4 pointed along the nose. I don't see any problems with the hull near the VAL."

"Worry about that later," Lewis said. "What's our relative velocity and distance to MAV?"

Johanssen typed quickly. "We'll get within twenty-two meters and we're at twelve meters per second. We actually got better than expected thrust."

"Watney," Lewis said, "it worked. Beck's on his way."

"Score!" Watney responded.

"Beck," Lewis said, "you're up. Twelve meters per second."

"Close enough!" Beck replied.

. . .

"I'M GOING to jump out," Beck said. "Should get me another two or three meters per second."

"Understood," Vogel said, loosely gripping Beck's tether. "Good luck, Dr. Beck."

Placing his feet on the back wall, Beck coiled and leaped out of the airlock.

Once free, he got his bearings. A quick look to his right showed him what he could not see from inside the airlock.

"I have visual!" Beck said. "I can see the MAV!"

The MAV barely resembled a spacecraft as Beck had come to know them. The once sleek lines were now a jagged mess of missing hull segments and empty anchor points where noncritical components used to be.

"Jesus, Mark, what did you *do* to that thing?"

"You should see what I did to the rover," Watney radioed back.

Beck thrust on an intercept course. He had practiced this many times. The presumption in those practice sessions was that he'd be rescuing a crewmate whose tether had broken, but the principle was the same.

"Johanssen," he said, "you got me on radar?"

"Affirmative," she replied.

"Call out my relative velocity to Mark every two seconds or so."

"Copy. Five point two meters per second."

"Hey Beck," Watney said, "the front's wide open. I'll get up there and be ready to grab at you."

"Negative," interrupted Lewis. "No untethered movement. Stay strapped to your chair until you're latched to Beck."

"Copy," Watney said.

"Three point one meters per second," Johanssen reported.

"Going to coast for a bit," Beck said. "Gotta catch up before I slow it down." He rotated himself in preparation for the next burn.

"Eleven meters to target," Johanssen said.

"Copy."

"Six meters," Johanssen said.

"Aaaaand counter-thrusting," Beck said, firing the MMU thrusters again. The MAV loomed before him. "Velocity?" he asked.

"One point one meters per second," Johanssen said.

"Good enough," he said, reaching for the ship. "I'm drifting toward it. I think I can get my hand on some of the torn canvas. . . ."

The tattered canvas beckoned as the only handhold on the otherwise smooth ship. Beck reached, extending as best he could, and managed to grab hold.

"Contact," Beck said. Strengthening his grip, he pulled his body forward and lashed out with his other hand to grab more canvas. "Firm contact!"

"Dr. Beck," Vogel said, "we have passed closest approach point and you are now getting further away. You have one hundred and sixty-nine meters of tether left. Enough for fourteen seconds."

"Copy," Beck said.

Pulling his head to the opening, he looked inside the compartment to see Watney strapped to his chair.

"Visual on Watney!" he reported.

"Visual on Beck!" Watney reported.

"How ya doin', man?" Beck said, pulling himself into the ship.

"I . . . I just . . ." Watney said. "Give me a minute. You're the first person I've seen in eighteen months."

"We don't have a minute," Beck said, kicking off the wall. "We've got eleven seconds before we run out of tether."

Beck's course took him to the chair, where he clumsily collided with Watney. The two gripped each other's arms to keep Beck from bouncing away. "Contact with Watney!" Beck said.

"Eight seconds, Dr. Beck," Vogel radioed.

"Copy," Beck said as he hastily latched the front of his suit to the front of Watney's with tether clips. "Connected," he said.

Watney released the straps on his chair. "Restraints off."

"We're outa here," Beck said, kicking off the chair toward the opening.

The two men floated across the MAV cabin to the opening. Beck reached out his arm and pushed off the edge as they passed through.

"We're out," Beck reported.

"Five seconds," Vogel said.

"Relative velocity to *Hermes*: twelve meters per second," Johanssen said.

"Thrusting," Beck said, activating his MMU.

The two accelerated toward *Hermes* for a few seconds. Then the MMU controls on Beck's heads-up display turned red.

"That's it for the fuel," Beck said. "Velocity?"

"Five meters per second," Johanssen replied.

"Stand by," Vogel said. Throughout the process, he had been feeding tether out of the airlock. Now he gripped the ever-shrinking remainder of the rope with both hands. He didn't clamp down on it; that would pull him out of the airlock. He simply closed his hands over the tether to create friction.

Hermes was now pulling Beck and Watney along, with Vogel's use of the tether acting as a shock absorber. If Vogel used too much force, the shock of it would pull the tether free from Beck's suit clips. If he used too little, the tether would run out before they matched speeds, then jerk to a hard stop at the end, which would also rip it out of Beck's suit clips.

Vogel managed to find the balance. After a few seconds of tense, gut-feel physics, he felt the force on the tether abate.

"Velocity zero!" Johanssen reported excitedly.

"Reel 'em in, Vogel," Lewis said.

"Copy," Vogel said. Hand over hand, he slowly pulled his crewmates toward the airlock. After a few seconds, he stopped actively pulling and simply took in the line as they coasted toward him.

They floated into the airlock, and Vogel grabbed them. Beck and Watney both reached for handholds on the wall as Vogel worked his way around them and closed the outer door.

"Aboard!" Beck said.

"Airlock 2 outer door closed," Vogel said.

"Yes!" Martinez yelled.

"Copy," Lewis said.

...

LEWIS'S VOICE echoed across the world: "Houston, this is *Hermes* Actual. Six crew safely aboard."

The control room exploded with applause. Leaping from their seats, controllers cheered, hugged, and cried. The same scene played out all over the world, in parks, bars, civic centers, living rooms, classrooms, and offices.

The couple in Chicago clutched each other in sheer relief, then pulled the NASA representative in for a group hug.

Mitch slowly pulled off his headset and turned to face the VIP room. Through the glass, he saw various well-suited men and women cheering wildly. He looked at Venkat and let out a heavy sigh of relief.

Venkat put his head in his hands and whispered, "Thank the gods."

Teddy pulled a blue folder from his briefcase and stood. "Annie will be wanting me in the press room."

"Guess you don't need the red folder today," Venkat said.

"Honestly, I didn't make one." As he walked out he added, "Good work, Venk. Now, get them home."

LOG ENTRY: MISSION DAY 687

That "687" caught me off guard for a minute. On *Hermes*, we track time by mission days. It may be Sol 549 down on Mars, but it's Mission Day 687 up here. And you know what? It doesn't matter what time it is on Mars because *I'm not there*!

Oh my god. I'm really not on Mars anymore. I can tell because there's no gravity and there are other humans around. I'm still adjusting.

If this were a movie, everyone would have been in the airlock, and there would have been high fives all around. But it didn't pan out that way.

I broke two ribs during the MAV ascent. They were sore the whole time, but they really started screaming when Vogel pulled us into the airlock by the tether. I didn't want to distract the people who were saving my life, so I muted my mic and screamed like a little girl.

It's true, you know. In space, no one can hear you scream like a little girl.

Once they got me into Airlock 2, they opened the inner door and I was finally aboard again. Hermes was still in vacuo, so we didn't have to cycle the airlock.

Beck told me to go limp and pushed me down the corridor toward his quarters (which serve as the ship's "sick bay" when needed).

Vogel went the other direction and closed the outer VAL door.

Once Beck and I got to his quarters, we waited for the ship to repressurize. *Hermes* had enough spare air to refill the ship two more times if needed. It'd be a pretty shitty long-range ship if it couldn't recover from a decompression.

After Johanssen gave us the all clear, Dr. Bossy-Beck made me wait while he first took off his suit, then took off mine. After he pulled my helmet off, he looked shocked. I thought maybe I had a major head wound or something, but it turns out it was the smell.

It's been a while since I washed . . . anything.

After that, it was X-rays and chest bandages while the rest of the crew checked the ship for damage.

Then came the (painful) high fives, followed by people staying as far away from my stench as possible. We had a few minutes of reunion before Beck shuttled everyone out. He gave me painkillers and told me to shower as soon as I could move my arms. So now I'm waiting for the drugs to kick in.

I think about the sheer number of people who pulled together just to save my sorry ass, and I can barely comprehend it. My crewmates sacrificed a year of their lives to come back for me. Countless people at NASA worked day and night to invent rover and MAV modifications. All of JPL busted their asses to make a probe that was destroyed on launch. Then, instead of giving up, they made *another* probe to resupply *Hermes*. The China National Space Administration abandoned a project they'd worked on for years just to provide a booster.

The cost for my survival must have been hundreds of millions of dollars. All to save one dorky botanist. Why bother?

Well, okay. I know the answer to that. Part of it might be what I represent: progress, science, and the interplanetary future we've dreamed of for centuries. But really, they did it because every human being has a basic instinct to help each other out. It might not seem that way sometimes, but it's true.

If a hiker gets lost in the mountains, people will coordinate a search. If a train crashes, people will line up to give blood. If an earthquake levels a city, people all over the world will send emergency supplies. This is so fundamentally human that it's found in every culture without exception. Yes, there are assholes who just don't care, but they're massively outnumbered by the people who do. And because of that, I had billions of people on my side.

Pretty cool, eh?

Anyway, my ribs hurt like hell, my vision is still blurry from acceleration sickness, I'm really hungry, it'll be another 211 days before I'm back on Earth, and, apparently, I smell like a skunk took a shit on some sweat socks.

This is the happiest day of my life.

THE MARTIAN

A Reader's Guide   373

A Conversation with Andy Weir   377

An Essay from Andy Weir:
How Science Made Me a Writer   383

EXTRA LIBRIS

ESSAYS,
READER'S GUIDES,
AND MORE

A Reader's Guide

A castaway story for the new millennium, *The Martian* presents a fresh take on the classic man-versus-nature battle for survival by setting it on the surface of Mars—a planet completely hostile to sustaining human life. Yet debut novelist and self-proclaimed space nerd Andy Weir manages to make every moment of astronaut Mark Watney's outer-space ordeal painstakingly realistic and believable.

After Mark Watney is injured, separated from his crew in a sandstorm, and left for dead alone on the red planet and cut off from any communication, his first priority is tending to his injury and making it through the first day—or sol. Soon he realizes he must do more than survive the day—he must plan long-term if he is to live for years until the next mission is due to arrive.

At its heart, *The Martian* is a tale of survival of the geekiest. Mark's scientific ingenuity, his radically inventive botanical solution to starvation, his ability to address seemingly insurmountable problems with rationality and practicality, his sanity-saving sense of humor, and his understated bravery become a moving testament to the human spirit. When the ground team at NASA and his crew discover he is alive, their commitment to rescuing one man against all odds likewise speaks to humanity's deeply rooted sense of connection.

Ultimately, *The Martian* transcends its undeniable nerdy thrills of how to survive on Mars to celebrate human resilience. We hope the following questions will make your reading group's experience truly out of this world.

QUESTIONS AND TOPICS FOR DISCUSSION

1. How did *The Martian* challenge your expectations of what the novel would be? What did you find most surprising about it?

2. What makes us root for a character to live in a survival story? In what ways do you identify with Mark? How does the author get you to care about Mark?

3. Do you believe the crew did the right thing in abandoning the search for Mark? Was there an alternative choice?

4. Did you find the science and technology behind Mark's problem solving accessible? How did that information add to the realism of the story?

5. What are some of the ways the author established his credibility with scientific detail? Which of Mark's solutions did you find most amazing, yet believable?

6. What is your visual picture of the surface of Mars, based on the descriptions in the book? Have you seen photographs of the planet?

7. Who knew potatoes, duct tape, and seventies' television reruns were the key to space survival? How does each of these items represent aspects of Mark's character that help him survive?

8. How is Mark's sense of humor as much a survival skill as his knowledge of botany? Do you have a favorite funny line of his?

9. To what extent does Mark's log serve as his companion? Do you think it's implicit in the narrative that maintaining a log keeps him sane?

10. The author provides almost no back story regarding Mark's life on Earth. Why do you think he made this choice? What do you imagine Mark's past life was like?

11. There's no mention of Mark having a romantic relationship on Earth. Do you think that makes it easier or harder to endure his isolation? How would the story be different if he were in love with someone back home?

12. Were there points in the novel when you became convinced Mark couldn't survive? What were they, and what made those situations seem so dire?

13. The first time the narrative switched from Mark's log entries to third-person authorial narrative back on Earth, were you surprised? How does alternating between Mark's point of view and the situation on Earth enhance the story?

14. Did you believe the commitment of those on

Earth to rescuing one astronaut? What convinced you most?

15. To what extent do you think guilt played a part in the crew's choice to go back to Mark? To what extent loyalty? How would you explain the difference?

16. How does the author handle the passage of time in the book? Did he transition smoothly from a day-to-day account to a span of one and a half years? How does he use the passage of time to build suspense?

17. Unlike other castaways, Mark can predict the approximate timing of his potential rescue. How does that knowledge help him? How could it work against him?

18. When Mark leaves the Hab and ventures out in the rover, did you feel a loss of security for him? In addition to time, the author uses distance to build suspense. Discuss how.

19. Where would you place *The Martian* in the canon of classic space exploration films such as *2001: A Space Odyssey, Apollo 13,* and *Gravity*? What does it have in common with these stories? How is it different?

20. A survival story has to resonate on a universal level to be effective, whether it's set on a desert island or another planet. How important are challenges in keeping life vital? To what extent are our everyday lives about problem solving and maintaining hope?

A Conversation with Andy Weir

Q. So it seems you're a bit of a science geek. You list space travel, orbital dynamics, relativistic physics, astronomy, and the history of manned spaceflight among your interests. How did you incorporate these passions into *The Martian*?

A. Those interests allowed me to come up with the story in the first place. I love reading up on current space research. At some point I came up with the idea of an astronaut stranded on Mars. The more I worked on it, the more I realized I had accidentally spent my life researching for this story. Early on I decided that I would be as scientifically accurate as possible. To a nerd like me, working out all the math and physics for Mark's problems and solutions was fun.

Q. Explain how the science in *The Martian* is true to life.

A. The basic structure of the Mars program in the book is very similar to a plan called Mars Direct (though I made changes here and there). It's the most likely way that we will have our first Mars mission in real life. All the facts about Mars are accurate, as well as the physics of space travel the story presents. I even calculated the various orbital paths involved in the story, which required me to write my own software to track constant-thrust trajectories.

Q. What inspired you to write *The Martian*?
A. I was thinking about how best to do a manned Mars mission (because that's the sort of dork I am). As the plan got more detailed, I started imagining what it would be like for the astronauts. Naturally, when designing a mission, you think up disaster scenarios and how likely the crew would be to survive. That's when I started to realize this had real story potential.

Q. Are you an advocate for a manned mission to Mars? Are you hopeful we'll actually make it out there sometime soon?
A. Of course I'm a huge fan of space travel, manned and unmanned. I would love to see people land on Mars in my lifetime. However, do I think it will actually happen? I'm not sure. Unlike the 1960s, we're not in a race with anyone to get there, so it's not a priority. Also, computer and robotics technologies are leaps and bounds better than they were during the days of Apollo. So logically you have to ask why we would risk human lives rather than just make better robots. Still, it would be awesome, and maybe that's reason enough.

Q. Do you have anything in common with your wisecracking hero Mark Watney?
A. I'm the same level of smart-ass that he is. It was a really easy book to write; I just had him say what I would say. However, he's smarter than I am and considerably more brave. I guess he's who I wish I were.

Q. In *The Martian*, **Watney has access to his crewmates' digital entertainment on Mars, including TV episodes of** *Three's Company*, **a variety of Beatles songs, and digital books including** *The Mysterious Affair at Styles*. **Any reason you chose to work those specific examples into the novel?**
A. It's a selection of things I loved when I was growing up.

Q. You're stranded on Mars and you can only take one book with you. What is it?
A. It's always hard to pick one "favorite book." Growing up, I loved early Robert Heinlein books most of all. So if I had to pick one, I'd go with *Tunnel in the Sky*. I do love a good survival story.

Q. How long do you think you'd last if you were left in Mark Watney's position?
A. Not long at all. I don't know how to grow crops or how to jury-rig the solutions he came up with. It's a lot easier to write about an ordeal than it is to experience it.

Q. You have the chance to meet any astronaut living or dead: Who is it and why?
A. John Young. He is the quintessential astronaut. Competent, fearless, highly intelligent, and seemingly immune to stress. When *Apollo 16* launched, his heart rate never got higher than 70. Most astronauts spike to at least 120 during launches.

Q. Watney seems to be able to maneuver his way around some pretty major problems with a little duct tape and ingenuity! So he's a bit like Mac-Gyver in that way. Did you watch the show as a kid? Any favorite episodes?
A. Indeed I did! I loved that show. My favorite episode was the one where engineering students had a barricade contest.

Q. *Star Wars* or *Star Trek*?
A. *Doctor Who.*

Q. Your idea of the perfect day . . .
A. Sleep in. Meet Buzz Aldrin for brunch. Head over to Jet Propulsion Lab and watch them control the Curiosity Mars rover. Dinner with the writing staff of *Doctor Who.*

Q. Your original, self-published version of *The Martian* became a phenomenon online. Were you expecting the overwhelmingly positive reception the book received?
A. I had no idea it was going to do so well. The story had been available for free on my website for months,

and I assumed anyone who wanted to read it had already read it. A few readers had requested I post a Kindle version because it's easier to download that way. So I went ahead and did it, setting the price to the minimum Amazon would allow. As it sold more and more copies I just watched in awe.

Q. Film rights to *The Martian* were sold to writer-producer Simon Kinberg (*Mr. & Mrs. Smith*, *Sherlock Holmes*, *X-Men: First Class*). What was your first reaction?

A. Of course I'm thrilled to have a movie in the works. The movie deal and print publishing deal came within a week of each other, so I was a little shell-shocked. In fact, it was such a sudden launch into the big leagues that I literally had a difficult time believing it. I actually worried it could all be an elaborate scam. So I guess that was my first reaction: "Is this really happening!?"

An Essay from Andy Weir:
How Science Made Me a Writer

I'm a nerd.

Okay, a lot of people say that these days. But I really am. I was hired as a computer programmer for a national laboratory at age fifteen. I have seen every existing episode of *Doctor Who* (classic and modern). I study orbital dynamics as a hobby. My idea of a good time is sitting down and drawing on that knowledge to imagine a space mission from beginning to end, getting right as many details as I can.

Pretty frickin' nerdy, right?

On top of that, as you might expect, I've also been a science-*fiction* fan ever since I was old enough to read, which was when I started plowing through my dad's nearly infinite collection of Heinlein, Clarke, Asimov, and all the other great authors of the genre.

One day, in between doing highly charismatic non-nerdy things, I started working up a manned Mars mission in my head. I even wrote my own software to calculate the orbital trajectory my imaginary crew would take to get from Earth to Mars. And not some boring Hohmann Transfer, either! I envisioned a constantly accelerating VASIMR-powered ship, which—ahem. Sorry, got carried away. Anyway, I had to account for failure scenarios on their surface mission. What if something went wrong? How could I design the mission so the crew would have contingency plans? What if they had multiple failures, one after another, that ruined those contingency plans?

While working that out, I started to realize their increasingly desperate solutions would make a pretty interesting story. That's when I came up with the idea for *The Martian*.

Oh, one more nerdy hobby I forgot to mention up top: I've also been a wannabe writer since I was a teenager. I wrote countless short stories and even penned two complete books before *The Martian*. My first book was so horrible I have deleted all copies of it. Thankfully, it was before the Internet so there are no lurking caches of it anywhere. I made up for that failure by writing a second book that was also crappy. This time I resolved to do better.

So I created an unlucky main character named Mark Watney and then spent 368 pages making his life a living hell. He's stranded on Mars, his crew has evacuated and thinks he's dead, and he has no way to contact Earth.

Even though my plan was to torture Mark, I knew from the very beginning that I didn't want my hero to suffer one unlikely, disastrous coincidence after the next. I decided that each problem Mark faced had to be a plausible consequence of his situation—or, better yet, an unintended consequence of his *solution* to a previous problem. He could suffer an equipment failure in machinery stretched beyond its intended use, but he couldn't be struck by lightning and then have a meteor crash on him.

I also really wanted Mark to be *fallible*. Yeah, okay, I made him smarter and more resourceful than you or I would be in that situation. But hey, it's only realistic to do that when your hero's an astronaut. Nevertheless, in a situation where even the smallest mistake can be catastrophic, and you're forced to make life-or-death decisions every day, even the brightest person is going to slip *sometimes* and invite disaster.

Was I worried about whether my scenario would give me enough plot to sustain a novel?

Did I wonder if being that realistic would make a boring story?

Hell yes.

But as I wrote, I bungled my way into a revelation: Science creates plot! As I worked out the intricacies of each problem and solution, little details I wouldn't have otherwise noticed became critical problems Mark had to solve. No need for meteor strikes—the surprises, catastrophes, and narrow escapes were coming fast and furious on their own.

And the deeper into the book I got, the more excited I became, because I found that I was arriving at that place writers dream of: I was coming up with plot twists that genuinely surprised *me*, yet felt totally organic to the situation I'd dreamed up. This allowed me to do what writers treasure more than anything else: catch the reader off-guard. There's nothing better than knowing you're going to outwit the reader. And the type of people who read sci-fi are very difficult to outwit.

I originally wrote *The Martian* as a free serial novel, posting one chapter at a time to my website. Thanks to my previous attempts at writing, I had a small but loyal following of readers who read each chapter as I finished it. This turned out to be an amazing process. I got tons of feedback as the story progressed, and I fine-tuned the novel as I went along.

Eventually, my website readers started bugging me to put the book up on Amazon so they could read it on their Kindles. So I formatted the book, slapped a public-domain photo of Mars on the cover, and tossed it up there. I priced it at 99 cents because Amazon wouldn't let me make it free permanently.

After that, things got a little crazy. Next thing I knew, it was one of Amazon's top five sci-fi bestsellers, and tens of thousands of people had downloaded it. Then a literary agent and publishers came knocking, and movie studios started bidding on the film rights. And ultimately, in one of the more surreal moments of my life, I found myself looking at my name on the *New York Times* bestseller list.

In those months since I first started putting chapters online, I've received fan e-mails from astronauts, people in Mission Control, nuclear submarine technicians, chemists, physicists, geologists, and folks in pretty much every other scientific discipline. All of them had nice things to say about the book's technical accuracy, though some of them also sent formal proofs detailing where I'd gone wrong. I corrected those problems (mostly) in the final edition that went to print.

Even more satisfying than those responses to the science, though, were all the readers who told me I'd succeeded in my *other* goal, the one that really made me tremble in fear as I was writing: People kept telling me how exciting and suspenseful and surprising the book was. My favorite fan mail is the kind that starts "Normally I don't read science-fiction, but . . ."

That response is pretty damn incredible, considering all I really did was write about how much I love science—albeit while tormenting my main character with the constant threat of death.

Eh. Mark's a smart guy. He can handle it.

A version of this essay was originally published on Salon.com.

For additional Extra Libris content from your other favorite authors and to enter great book giveaways, visit **ReadItForward.com/Extra-Libris.**

ESSAYS, READER'S GUIDES, AND MORE